Time and the Soldier

Books by David Dvorkin

Fiction

The Arm and Flanagan

Budspy

Business Secrets from the Stars

The Cavaradossi Killings

Central Heat

The Children of Shiny Mountain

Children of the Undead

Damon the Caiman

Dawn Crescent (with Daniel Dvorkin)

Earthmen and Other Aliens

The Green God

Pit Planet

The Prisoner of the Blood series

       Insatiable

       Unquenchable

Randolph Runner

The Seekers

Slit

Star Trek novels

       The Trellisane Confrontation

       Time Trap

       The Captains' Honor (with Daniel Dvorkin)

Time and the Soldier

Time for Sherlock Holmes

Ursus

Nonfiction

At Home with Solar Energy

The Dead Hand of Mrs. Stifle

Dust Net

Once a Jew, Always a Jew?

Self-Publishing Tools, Tips, and Techniques

The Surprising Benefits of Being Unemployed

When We Landed on the Moon: A Memoir

Time and the Soldier

David Dvorkin

Editing, print layout, e–book conversion,
and cover design by DLD Books
www.dldbooks.com
Editing and Self–Publishing Services

ISBN: 978-1-7345636-6-5

One

The center of the huge complex exploded at dawn on February 8, 1945. Two men had arrived in a wing of the complex seconds before. They were the only living beings there.

The explosives had been planted in the cafeteria, directly above the huge repository. The blast tore through the floor and into the repository, breaching the container shell and releasing the energy stored there. A wave of destruction rippled outwards through the building, setting off the explosives the team of saboteurs had placed earlier.

The two men had time to look around in confusion and to realize that they were in the wrong place, and then the destructive wave reached them. The smaller man was obliterated. The bigger man was obliterated from the waist down. His consciousness persisted for a moment more, and then he ceased to exist.

Secondary blasts followed. Smoke billowed out through empty window frames. The metal door of the main building began to melt within minutes. Great sections of the roof collapsed. Flames and embers shot high into the dry mountain air.

The fire raged on, consuming the building and the dead. It melted the equipment those people had put together and tested so painstakingly. It ate wood and flesh indiscriminately.

Twenty–four hours later, a man and a woman appeared in the smoking rubble.

They stared in bewilderment at the remnants of the machinery they remembered so well. In front of the shattered machinery lay the upper half of a man's body. He had been a large, blond man. His face was undamaged and unfamiliar.

The man who had just arrived brushed his shoe across the ashes beneath his feet, exposing part of a yellow circle.

"Why is it now?" he asked.

"Come on," the woman said.

They made their way through the ruins, moving clumsily in their heavy coats. The remaining heat kept them out of some areas. The charred floor sagged and creaked under them. Fifty feet away, what was left of a wall collapsed with a thud, sending up dust.

Hours passed. They found bodies, some burned to charcoal but some untouched by the fire. They were all dead—of slit throats or bullets in the forehead. They saw no sign of the two people they were looking for.

"He wouldn't be here," the woman said. "He left when we did. We know that."

"But what about her?" the man said in despair.

"I don't think she's here." She said that to encourage him, not because she believed it. "Come on."

It was noon now, but bitterly cold, and yet they were sweating inside their coats. For a moment, they stood looking up at the cracked face of the sandstone cliff. Then finally they turned and began to walk. Briefly, the woman stopped and turned around, thinking that she was being watched. But she saw nothing alive, and the two of them continued down the hillside and away.

Eight years earlier and two thousand miles away, a black-haired woman and her brown-haired daughter walked carefully along a country road in southern Michigan. The light was fading, catching the tops of the trees and the brilliant colors of autumn. The road in front of them was almost dark. They knew there were patches of ice on the road, but they couldn't see them.

Across the road, invisible in the darkness between the trees, a blond man watched them.

Absorbed in her thoughts, the younger woman drew further ahead of the older one. The watcher frowned. He had expected them to stay close together. This might be a complication.

The mother called out, "Dolores! *Espérame!*"

The girl stopped and turned around. "Sorry, Mama. I was thinking about that job."

"Good. You should be."

The girl laughed. She waited while her mother caught up with her.

Right next to each other, the watcher thought. That's good.

The headlights of a car swept across him. He threw his hand up to shade his face and stepped further back among the trees. He couldn't let anyone see him. He couldn't imagine what the boss would do if anything went wrong.

The car roared around a curve, coming from behind the

two women. It was upon them before they were aware of the car or the driver of them.

The watcher held his breath. Perfect.

Mother and daughter stood frozen in shock, caught in the lights, as the car rushed toward them.

The driver seemed to be just as frozen. At the last moment, the car swerved toward the middle of the road.

The watcher willed the car toward the mother and daughter. Hit them! Hit them!

The driver almost made it past the two. But the big rear right fender caught the mother on the hip and threw her against her daughter. They fell heavily to the ground and lay still.

The car skidded to a stop. The driver jumped from it and ran up to the two still figures. In the fading light, the watcher could tell that the driver was a well-dressed man. He couldn't see the man's face, but he read shock in the body language.

"Oh, God!" the driver said. "Oh, my God!"

He stood over the two bodies for a long time, hesitating. Then suddenly he turned and ran back to his car and sped off.

"About time," the watcher muttered.

All he had to do now was drag the girl's body into the woods, far enough from the road so that it wouldn't be found for a long time. Nature would do the rest.

He took out his pencil–sized flashlight, aimed the light at the ground, and walked quickly across the road. From close up, he could see that the mother was lying on her side. Her eyes were open and unmoving, and her skull was misshapen. Blood pooled under her.

He turned to the girl. Fortunately, she had landed on her back. He bent down and slid his hands under her back and into her armpits and started to pull her toward the edge of the road. She didn't weigh much. That was good. There didn't seem to be any blood under her, which was also good. Pretty thing, he thought, looking down at her face. Too bad.

She opened her eyes and looked up at him, confused. "Mama?"

"Shit!" He jumped back, letting her shoulders and head fall to the ground.

She struggled to sit up and managed at last. She held her arms wrapped tightly around herself. "Where's my mother? Who're you?"

"She's back there."

"Mama!" She was shouting, trying to get up, looking back at the still, dark figure in the road. "Mama!"

"Listen, Dolores. It's okay. My name's Hank. I'm going to take care of you. It'll be okay."

Except that it wouldn't be. This was a disaster. It wasn't supposed to happen like this at all, and the boss would be furious in that quiet, terrifying way of his.

The girl was dragging herself along the road, trying to crawl to her mother. She was whimpering. She kept one arm tightly against her middle.

Probably has internal injuries, Hank thought. She won't make it, anyway.

But he couldn't bet on that.

He sighed and shook his head. I hate shit like this, he thought. He turned the flashlight off and slid it into his pocket. He would do the rest by feel. He reached inside his shirt and drew the knife from the sheath strapped against his chest. He stepped over to the crying girl and slit her throat.

He waited till she had stopped moving and then, trying to avoid all the fresh blood, grasped the back of her shirt collar and dragged her into the woods, far enough that he was sure she wouldn't be found.

He told himself that the fresh blood was good. It would attract animals all the faster. The boss would never know the details.

I need a drink, he thought. Gotta get my car and go back to town and find a bar or something. No, gotta find one of those primitive telephones first, he corrected himself. Then the drink.

There were tough years ahead. There'd be more work like this. Eventually, in the future, there'd be a reward.

Two

Drifting curtains of rain hid the top of the hill, then exposed it. Frank focused intently on the hill's craggy top, oblivious to the rainwater dripping steadily from the back of his helmet onto the back of his neck. At first, he was sure that the shape at the top of the hill was a large rock, but every time he glimpsed it through the rain, it looked more like a man.

He whispered to the soldier lying in the mud beside him. "Which?"

"A man," Sammy said.

That was good enough for Frank. He might doubt his own eyes, but he would never doubt Sammy's. Sammy was ten years younger than Frank, and he had survived those eighteen years by hunting and trapping. His eyes were like an eagle's.

It could be a guard, which could mean a large camp somewhere at the base of the hill. Or it could be a sniper, put up there to cover the German retreat. They had made the Allies fight bitterly for every mile, ever since Sicily.

But whether it was a German camp or a German guard or sniper standing in the way, Frank was under orders to get his men to the top of that hill before nightfall.

"Could you get him from here?"

Sammy grinned. "Which eye you want me to put the bullet through?"

Frank trusted Sammy's marksmanship as much as he trusted his vision, but he couldn't risk alerting the Germans. Frank's lieutenant had stepped on a mine two weeks ago, the platoon was severely diminished in numbers, and the men were exhausted. The Germans were probably also exhausted, but Frank wouldn't risk his own men unnecessarily.

One man had to go ahead—across the open space and up the hillside, looking for German guards. If he found any, his men would hear the shooting. If he found none, he could climb the hill and silently eliminate the German soldier at the top.

Frank turned and looked his men over.

They stared back at him dully. Their uniforms were soaked by the rain and streaked with mud. They were all younger than Frank, but they had the faces of old men worn out by pain and labor.

The man Frank chose would probably die on this mission. German, Italian, American—Frank no longer cared. He had shortened too many men's lives already, Germans and Italians by shooting them, Americans by ordering them into deadly situations. It was enough.

He beckoned to a short, stocky man named Bellman. Bellman squelched through the mud to his side, trying to walk quietly but not succeeding. The sound made Frank's already taut nerves jangle. He took a moment to calm himself before muttering, "Sergeant, I'm going up the hill to take care of that guy. You're in charge. If I don't come back in half an hour, or if you hear shooting, get the men out of here and back to base."

Hughes nodded. "It would come back pretty quickly, I imagine. As for the German, given your academic grounding, I'm confident you could pick it up quickly. You were beginning graduate work in history at the time of Pearl Harbor, yes?"

"Yes." A lost world, Frank thought.

"And you never got anything less than an A as an undergraduate."

"If you already know the answers, why are you bothering with the questions?"

"All right," Hughes said. "I like directness. Lieutenant, Tempus is engaged in a project that could put an immediate end to this war and make sure that no other war will ever happen."

"A new weapon, you mean?"

"Not in the sense of a new kind of gun or airplane," Hughes said. "Anyway, innovations like that haven't stopped war yet. They've just changed its nature. No, we're working on something entirely different, something you would never guess at. In fact, I'd rather you didn't try to guess any further. Now, this project will involve sending a small team of people somewhere to eliminate certain enemies of our country. Our innovation lies in our ability to get you where you'll need to be in order to do that job."

"When you say eliminate, you mean kill, right?"

Hughes nodded. "Of course. Something you're particularly good at, as I said."

"With enemy soldiers, yes," Frank said. "But I have the feeling you're talking about civilians."

"If you could kill one mad civilian, one inherently evil man," Hughes said, "and by so doing stop all the other killing, all the young men of his country and ours slaughtering each other, wouldn't you do it?"

"Hitler," Frank said. "Yes, of course I would. Not that I'd have a chance of succeeding." Or of getting back alive if I did succeed, he thought. But it would be a price worth paying. "Killing Hitler wouldn't stop war forever. Maybe it wouldn't even stop this war."

Hughes smiled. "Let us worry about those details. We have experts who know about such matters and who will explain them to you in due time. You're in?"

Frank nodded. "I'm in."

He was in western Colorado a week later.

Three

Tommy was surprised at how beautiful the countryside was. He had expected something different. Men in berets sipping wine at sidewalk cafes. Beautiful women with long cigarette holders. Everything very picturesque.

Instead, this was farm country, rich and fertile. Once they had advanced beyond the coast, he found himself moving through rolling meadowlands covered with dark green grass and healthy young crops and forests and flowers. If you ignored the shattered farmhouses, the columns of smoke on the horizon, and the bodies beside the road, it was lovely. Tommy had the knack of ignoring such distractions.

Something he did not ignore, however, was the possibility that those dark woods on the right–hand side of the road or that high, thick hedge on the left could hide Germans. He kept his eyes moving from side to side and his finger on the trigger. The two men directly behind him, Slocum and Weinberg, did the same.

Tommy heard a whimpering, and a small white dog forced its way out of the hedge and limped toward them. Its tail wagged very slightly, tentatively.

Weinberg put his rifle to his shoulder quickly and fired. The dog was thrown backward. It died instantly, without so much as a yelp.

"Jesus, why'd you do that?" Slocum said.

"That was a Nazi dog," Weinberg said.

Tommy laughed. "Sounded to me like it had a French accent. That dog was an ally, Weinberg."

"Yeah, well, now it's just a dead dog."

"Dumb shit," Slocum said. "Looked like a nice dog."

"Forget the dog and stay alert," Tommy told them. "Keep your voices down, and don't fire without cause. There could be Germans all around us."

"If there are, we're dead men already," Weinberg pointed out.

Tommy sighed. "Let's just follow our orders, okay?"

They moved on, Tommy still in the lead.

They were part of a vast army. It was all around them, moving along the country roads, crashing across the meadows in tanks, roaring overhead. They could hear artillery fire in the distance ahead of them, bombers growling across the sky above, and now and again rifle shots.

Tommy felt lighter on his feet and more alive than he had ever felt as a civilian. Normandy in June was the beginning of the war for him, his first taste of the real thing, and he was already in love with it. This is the life, he thought. As long as you don't get shot.

Sunlight reflected off something in the woods ahead. Tommy dove into the minimal shelter of the hedge. Weinberg and Slocum did the same without hesitation. "What?" they said simultaneously.

for what we have in mind."

Engaged? Tommy thought. That German kid was engaged? Christ! Aloud, he said, "But I just got a Dear John letter from her yesterday, so that's not a problem anymore."

Hughes nodded. "That sounds okay for now. You others?"

Mallory said, "No wife, no fiancée, no girlfriend."

"Family?"

Mallory looked at the ground. "No. Not anymore."

Hughes turned to Tommy. "You?"

"I'm an orphan, and so were my parents." That would come as a surprise to his parents and brothers, he thought.

One of the remaining three men was married but separated, while the other two had girlfriends back home. Hughes looked unhappy with their answers. "Tell you what," he said, "I'm going to have to make a snap decision here."

Watching him, Tommy had the feeling that this man never made snap decisions.

"At this point," Hughes said, "we really only need one more man for our team." He pointed at Mallory and Tommy. "The choice will be between you two. The rest of you, thanks for volunteering. You can go back to your units now."

Tommy watched the three shuffle out. You can go back to the boredom now, he thought. Bye–bye.

Hughes pushed himself away from the desk and came to almost military style attention. "Names?" The voice had a snap to it.

Both men stiffened unconsciously in response.

"Jeffrey Mallory."

"Thomas Stillwell." Tommy hated the note of subservience he noticed in his own voice. It had been in Mallory's voice, too, though.

"All right. Get your stuff together and be back here in—" he checked his watch "—ten minutes. Mallory, go on. Stillwell, stay for a moment."

After Mallory had left, Hughes stepped in front of Tommy and stared at him for a moment. Tommy was startled to realize that their eyes were at the same level. Hughes said, "Stillwell, I like a man with a native quality of opportunism and the ability to think fast on his feet. That's why I decided to give you a chance at the remaining slot in spite of your lie about knowing German and being an orphan. Just don't lie to us again, or your father will receive a telegram about his son dying heroically during the invasion of Normandy."

Tommy might have tried bluster with another man, but he looked back at Hughes and decided against it. "Yes, sir," he said.

Hughes smiled and stepped back. "You'd better turn out to have a talent for German, Stillwell. And everything else we try to teach you." He waved his hand in dismissal.

When Tommy and Mallory returned with their packs, Hughes was waiting in the driver's seat of a Jeep with the engine running. He started moving as soon as they climbed in.

Four

The ad caught Ellen Maxwell's eye immediately. Relaxing with the newspaper and a Coke after another long day, she noticed a black–bordered box at the bottom of the first page. She read:

> *YOUNG WOMEN NEEDED*
> *TO SERVE THEIR COUNTRY!*
> *If you have both technical and secretarial skills, are physically fit, under 30 years of age, fearless, and an American citizen and patriot, then please contact us at the telephone number listed below to begin your involvement in our exciting project. You may become part of a small team of valiant Americans working to preserve our Nation.*

Ellen's first reaction was that this all seemed a bit silly and overblown. Her second reaction was that it was bound to be an improvement over the drudgery she endured every day.

The idea of being Rosie the Riveter had once seemed exciting, but it was an idea that suffered in the execution. The reality of hot, sweaty, mindlessly repetitive work in an armaments factory was not Ellen's idea of answering her country's call. On the posters and billboards, Rosie never sweated. Rosie was sexy. Ellen sweated all day long in an airless factory, and by quitting time, she felt exhausted and dirty and completely un–sexy.

For that matter, all the valiant, handsome young heroes she might have wanted to take to her bed were off fighting in Europe and the Pacific. The men who remained on the home front were the rejects, and not one of them was her type. They were all too old, too young, too weak, or—as in a couple of cases she knew—the most shameful kind of reject, conscientious objectors. All of them were attracted to her—some to her athletic body, some to the fragile beauty of her face. That made them all the more repellent to her.

Worst of all, she no longer felt that she was really contributing anything. Oh, sure, the bombs she was helping to manufacture were being dropped on the enemy. She had seen the newsreels, and she knew that American and British airmen were bombing Germany around the clock. Bit by bit, her bombs were reducing the Nazis' ability to make war. She could feel proud that she was indirectly saving Allied lives, because her bombs were destroying Nazi factories. Every bomb meant fewer bullets for German soldiers to fire at American and British and French and Russian boys.

All of which she told herself repeatedly, especially during the afternoon, after lunch, when her body was close to collapse but the assembly line kept on moving, when her hand could scarcely grip the screwdriver tightly enough, but the explosive trigger glared up at her from the bomb casing on the moving belt and demanded that she cover it with its protective shield. There were moments, during those endless afternoons, when part of her wanted to jam the point of the screwdriver into the trigger and set it off, set all the bombs on the line off, blow up the entire building and herself with it and her coworkers and the bosses and the whole world.

She read the advertisement and chose to believe it. She finished her Coke, dialed the number, and volunteered to help preserve the Nation.

She was told to appear for an interview in the morning.

When Ellen arrived for the interview, she found that the woman interviewing her seemed most interested in her shorthand and typing skills. Whatever it takes, Ellen told herself. Whatever it takes to escape from the factory and do something that counts.

"I must warn you right now," the woman said to Ellen, "that you will be tested rigorously in a number of skill areas, and also as to your physical strength and stamina and knowledge. Only a very small number of those we select through these interviews will make it to the end of the process."

"Is this something involving the government?" Ellen asked. "I want to be absolutely sure I'm working for the good guys, you know."

The woman across the desk, who had been grim faced and uncommunicative until then, smiled suddenly. "I think young women today watch too many motion pictures. It makes them think the country is full of Nazi spies and fifth columnists. Yes, dear, these are the good guys. It's not the government, it's a private company called Tempus, but they're working closely with the government. *Our* government. Now, given what you know, which is all I'm allowed to tell you, do you want to continue with the process?"

Ellen smiled back at her. "I do. And I want you to know that I'm a survivor. I expect to make it all the way through."

"We all do, dear."

Ellen and three others—all young, healthy women—were selected for the next stage. At the same office where Ellen had been interviewed, the woman who had conducted that interview handed out train tickets for Denver and told them they would be met at the station and driven to their final destination. The train was due to leave at noon the next day. "Any of you have any objections to that?" she asked the three young women. "Any problem being ready that soon?"

"No, ma'am," they all answered together.

No problem at all, Ellen thought. I don't have anyone to say goodbye to.

During the train trip, she struck up conversations with her fellow volunteers and found that none of them had had anyone to say goodbye to, either. The others found the parallel disturbing. It implied that they had let themselves in for something sinister and dangerous. To Ellen, though, it was an exciting discovery. She was sure now that she had done the right thing. This was an adventure, an exhilarating new stage in her life. The future stretched ahead of her, bright, exciting, filled with novelty and wonders.

It was early morning when they arrived in Denver. The other girls had spent the night sagging in their seats, trying to sleep, but Ellen had stayed alert. She had spent the night watching the lights of towns and cities pass by, and the ever longer stretches of darkness between them as the train moved steadily west. She had peopled the lighted places with heroes and villains and the dark places with dreams.

Breakfast had been simple and all too light—in Ellen's opinion, at least, although she noticed that her companions didn't finish what they were given. Outside, the landscape was disappointingly flat and barren. She had expected to see mountains by dawn, and she had always imagined Colorado to be covered with great pine forests.

Union Station in Denver seemed small to her. It was filled with civilians and men and women in uniform. She thought it would be interesting to explore the place, and then perhaps to explore the city lying outside its doors, but she was given no time. As they climbed from the train, the four young women were met by a civilian who identified himself as a representative of Tempus. He hustled them through the station in a tight group.

Outside the station, he led them to a small bus–like vehicle, painted olive green, parked at the curb. He motioned them to climb in.

"Say, Mister," Ellen said, "how about if we stop at that hotel across the street for a bite? I'm pretty hungry."

A couple of the other volunteers spoke up in support, although less boldly than Ellen.

He stepped forward to look more closely at Ellen. He was her height, making him short for a man, and he was quite a bit older than she was. Twenty years older, she guessed. Maybe more.

He looked her up and down, evaluatingly, but it was not a sexual evaluation, and there was nothing of invitation or suggestion in it.

"Call me Mr. Hughes," he said finally, "not Mister. We'll eat when we get to the site. It's only about five or six hours away, depending on traffic."

One of Ellen's companions said, "Five or six hours! I'm not going to make it that long, Mr. Hughes. I vote for eating now."

She was a tall girl, as blonde as Ellen, and even more athletic. Her name was Jeanne. Ellen didn't know her last name. Ellen had marked her earlier as one of the likely survivors, which made her a competitor.

Hughes stared up at Jeanne. "You're free to do anything you want to," he said pleasantly. "You all are. You can go across the street and spend all day eating, if you want to. And I'll give you your train tickets back home and say goodbye to you, because you will have said goodbye to me and Tempus and the program, and you will have proved that you're not the kind of women we want working for us."

"I had the impression you wanted strong women," Ellen said, "not spineless ones." Suddenly, she felt almost angry enough to quit and go back to imitating Rosie the Riveter.

"We want strong, capable, independent men and women who understand the importance of following orders," Hughes replied. "Make your choice immediately."

That put an end to the incipient revolt. They all climbed aboard, and the bus started off.

Hughes sat at the front, just behind the driver.

Ellen tried to content herself with what she could see of Denver through the bus windows.

The city itself struck her as small and uninteresting, just another collection of streets, buildings, and traffic. She didn't see any of the tall buildings she was used to in the East. She did,

towers.

When the plane had taxied to a stop and they emerged, Tommy was surprised by the chilliness of the air and the bite of the wind. He buttoned his Eisenhower jacket and shoved his hands deep into his pants pockets, cursing the inadequacy of his army cap.

Hughes came up from behind. "Here," he said, holding out a dark, bulky coat.

Gratefully, Tommy pulled it on over his uniform jacket. Hughes seemed to notice everything.

Hughes said to Mallory, "Do you need one, too?"

Mallory shook his head. "No problem."

"It's all civilian clothing here," Hughes told them. "When you get to the rooms we've assigned you, you'll find everything you need. You can put your uniforms away. If you make it through our selection process, you'll never have to take the uniforms out again."

"In that case," Tommy said. "I might as well just burn my uniform as soon as I've changed. Thank God and all his little angels for that."

Mallory looked at him scornfully. "Better hold onto it for a while, kid."

Tommy grinned at him. It always amused him when another man called him "kid" in an attempt to undermine his self-confidence.

Hughes watched the exchange and looked satisfied. He glanced at his watch. "Follow me. I have to get you checked in quickly before I head east to Denver."

Busy, busy, busy, Tommy thought. "Like some company in Denver?" he asked. "I've never been there."

"You'll have other things to occupy your time," Hughes said. Anger colored his tone. "Concentrate on your new job, Stillwell—making it through, so you don't have to go back to Normandy."

Don't fret yourself, Tommy thought. I'm just figuring out where the limits lie.

Now that they were on the ground, Tommy noticed the group of small buildings near the airstrip. But his attention was held by the broken red cliff and the huge building he had seen from the air. Hughes began walking up the gentle hill toward the building, and Tommy and Mallory followed him.

Eventually they reached a gravel path that skirted the lawn and led them between two of the building's annexes. They were long structures that seemed, from the outside, to follow the undulating surface of the ground. The number of floors varied, depending on the ground. There were windows, but only on their higher floors. On one upper floor, Tommy saw balconies.

From ground level, Tommy thought the annexes looked even more like the arms of an octopus than they had from the air. Despite the heavy coat Hughes had given him, Tommy shivered.

The path ended at the metal door Tommy had noticed from the air. Hughes spoke quietly into a grille beside the door, and the door swung open. He motioned the two soldiers in ahead of him. Mallory walked in without hesitation. Tommy took one last, quick look around, down at the lawn, up at the looming cliff face, then went in. Hughes followed him. The door closed behind them. Tommy heard a heavy, solid click.

Inside, the air was warmer. Tommy shrugged out of the coat and folded it over his arm.

The place was filled with life. A hallway stretched ahead of them, with doors on either side. People passed in and out of the doors and along the hallway. They were a diverse group, Tommy noticed—young and old, male and female. He heard accents of every kind and snatches of languages he could not identify.

As he and Mallory followed Hughes down the corridor, Tommy was struck by the respectful way everyone greeted Hughes and how careful the man was to return each greeting and to address each person by name.

Most of the doors they passed were open. The one Hughes stopped at was closed. SECURITY was painted on it. Hughes stood for a moment in front of it, and it opened inward. Again, Hughes motioned for Tommy and Mallory to precede him. This door, too, swung shut behind them without any of the three touching it.

They were in a bustling office. Men and women passed by constantly. Doors led off into other rooms, and there was a hum of conversation and a clattering of typewriters from every direction. The people in the office ignored Tommy and Mallory, but they didn't ignore Hughes. He earned the same respectful greeting from each one that Tommy had noticed before, and Hughes returned each greeting with the same punctiliousness.

"Wait here," Hughes said. He went to one of the desks lining one wall. The man sitting there stood up as Hughes approached. He towered over Hughes, but he bent forward so as to minimize the height difference. The two men spoke briefly and in voices too low for Tommy to hear their words. The man nodded and then followed Hughes back to the two soldiers. "Carver will take care of you," Hughes told them. "Follow his orders as you would mine." He left the office.

Following orders, Tommy thought. It's what infantrymen do best.

Carver led them into another room, and it was at this point that the strangeness and newness began to evaporate. Tommy was fingerprinted and photographed, weighed and measured, and it was just like being inducted into the Army all over again.

At the end of the process, Carver handed Tommy and Mallory small plastic cards with their pictures on them and pins attached to the back and told them to pin these badges to their shirts. Each badge bore a small white dot in the upper left-hand corner.

Carver wore a similar badge, but his had a red dot on it. He noticed Tommy looking at it. "Red means Tempus Security," Carver said. "White means probationary. We have six different colors for the six different divisions here. You'll learn them, if you become permanent. You see anyone without a badge, it means he's not authorized to be in here. If that happens, contact Security right away. We'll take care of it. Don't try to stop the guy yourself. We're trained, and we're tough."

Tommy laughed. "Yeah? So how many Nazis have *you* killed?"

Carver looked at him expressionlessly for a moment. "With bare hands, or with weapons?"

"Got it."

They walked down long hallways and up staircases, all of them crowded and buzzing with conversation. Tommy noticed that everyone wore a badge and that many of them were red. They're everywhere, he thought. It made him feel uneasy.

Tommy tried to guess where they were in the strangely

shaped, sprawling building. He tried to correlate their trip with the shape of the building, but he quickly lost track and became disoriented.

These guys must have a bundle, he thought. The building, the airplane, the numbers of people they were passing on their way, all implied a very large and very wealthy organization. Even if this doesn't turn out to be a great adventure, Tommy thought, Tempus looks like a good outfit to be part of. Much better than the U. S. Army.

His quarters consisted of a suite—bedroom, small study, bathroom, and a balcony looking out over the prairie.

Christ, he thought, I've never lived this well in my life.

He stepped onto the balcony. Instead of an horizon, he saw snowcapped mountains in the far distance with a bank of clouds above them, startlingly clear in the thin, dry, clear air. The walls to either side of the balcony extended so far that he could only see the view straight ahead, and nothing of the building to either side.

The closet and chest of drawers in his bedroom held more civilian clothing than he had ever owned before and it all fit him perfectly. He showered happily, washing off the grime of his hours of travel, and then began hunting through the new clothing to choose what he wanted to wear.

A telephone began to ring. He found it on a small table beside the bed. After a moment's hesitation, he picked it up. "Hello?"

"Mr. Stillwell, we'll be serving lunch in half an hour." It was a woman's voice. "Please get dressed right away. Then leave your room, turn right, follow the hallway to the stairs at the end, and go down one flight. You will see the door to the cafeteria ahead of you."

"Yeah, okay," Tommy said. He hung up and muttered to himself, "Turn right, stairs, one flight," while he began to pull on the outfit he had selected.

Suddenly, still wearing only underpants, he stopped. "Get dressed," the woman on the phone had said.

He looked around the room. "Like what you see, lady?" he called out.

He half expected the telephone to ring again, but there was no response. He shrugged and finished dressing. He told himself that this was still more privacy than he had had in the Army. Or at home before that, crammed with his family into a Chicago tenement.

Dressed in his new civilian slacks, shirt, and shoes, Tommy left the room. He noticed that the door had no lock and no keyhole.

The cafeteria was crowded when he got there. He saw men and women and could make out the now–familiar variety of languages through the general din. Adding to the noise was music playing in the background. Here, as in the outside world, Vera Lynn seemed to be popular. Tommy saw a sprinkling of uniforms, but most of the people were in civilian clothes. He did see one familiar face: Mallory, sitting alone at a small table.

Tommy found the trays and the beginning of the food line and went through the process of loading his tray. The food looked and smelled better than what the Army had been feeding him, and there was much more variety. The women behind the counter serving the food were friendly and eager to offer suggestions. This ain't the army, Mr. Jones, he told himself.

Everything looked too good to pass up. Tommy took as much as he could fit on his tray before giving up. Then he looked around the cafeteria for a place to sit. His first choice was next to the most attractive woman in the room. However, all the women he could see were surrounded by men.

There were a few empty seats at womanless tables. And then there was Mallory, still eating, and still seated alone. On a whim, Tommy strolled over to him. "Mind if I sit here?" he said.

Mallory looked up at him in surprise. "Shit, yeah, sit down. These people are treating me like I was a leper."

Tommy put his tray down and sat. "So screw 'em," he said. "How're your quarters, Mallory? Mine are great."

"Call me Jeff, okay?"

"Okay!" Tommy reached out his hand, and the two men shook hands across the table. "And call me Tommy."

They fell easily into conversation about their quarters, their new clothes, the food, the view from their balconies, and how different their current situation was from their recent past.

"It's great to have a real bed," Tommy said.

"And a shower," Mallory said.

"And no one shooting at you."

"Yeah. That's the best part of all."

This guy's okay, Tommy thought. Good to know that he came here to escape the excitement, not because he was looking for more.

As they were finishing their meal, a man approached their table. "Welcome to Tempus," he said. "I'm Frank Anderson. I'm in the same boat you guys are, except that I've been here a few months longer, and I've already been selected."

Tommy looked him up and down quickly. Anderson was tall, lean, and looked strong. He had an intelligent, serious face. "Tommy Stillwell," he said, standing up and shaking hands. Anderson had a powerful grip, which didn't surprise Tommy. It fit with the man's appearance.

Mallory stood up and leaned across the table to shake hands. "Jeff Mallory. So, listen, Frank, what have you been selected for? Tommy and I've been talking about it, and we realized that we really don't know why we're here."

"I'm not really sure myself. I just know that a couple of men who came here at the same time as I did were told they had washed out and were being sent back."

"Back where?" Mallory asked.

"The Army. The war."

"Crap," Mallory said.

"So while we wait," Tommy asked, "what's there to do around here all day?"

"Mostly I've been learning new ways to kill people. Studying, too."

"Studying what?" Tommy asked.

"Languages. German and Russian. Also German and Russian history. Great War era. World War One, I mean. I thought I knew that material pretty well, but I was wrong. When I first got here, I roamed around and tried to get to know the place. You should probably do that. Don't worry about going in the wrong places. There are signs and guards to make sure you don't go where you're not supposed to. Everywhere else is open. You can also go outside. There's not much to see outside, though, so that won't take you long to explore."

"Maybe we can go into town," Mallory said.

Frank laughed. "There isn't any town. This is the West. Wide open spaces—really wide, and really open."

"So what is the nearest town?" Tommy asked. "Make that city."

"Denver, I guess. But it's not much of a city. There's not much to do there."

stared into it but could see only darkness. It was easy to imagine that something was in there, some kind of troll watching him from its home inside the mountain.

He shivered. Even though the sun was higher than when he had arrived, and he could feel its light on his head almost as a physical pressure, the breeze was still cold enough to be unpleasant.

Well, he told himself, I've already scored whatever points I could by showing my adventurous side. Now I'll go back in and do a bit of exploring there. Assuming they'll let me back in.

He need not have worried. The metal door swung open as he approached and closed behind him when he was inside.

For the next few hours, Tommy wandered around the sprawling complex of interconnected buildings. He strolled down corridors, past unmarked doors that were all locked, and labeled doors that were usually open. He climbed and descended staircases. He came across a gymnasium and swimming pool, an indoor rifle range, what seemed to be classrooms, and a basement containing a furnace and some huge pieces of equipment whose purpose he could not guess. The busy polyglot crowds were ubiquitous. Earlier, he had estimated that the population of the building was in the hundreds. Now he suspected it might be over a thousand.

He also discovered that large sections of the building were off limits. The locked doors barring entry to these areas were sometimes flanked by heavily muscled armed men with Security badges. These guards wore civilian clothes much like Tommy's own, but their bearing was martial and they stood with legs apart and hands clasped behind their backs. As far as Tommy could see, their holsters, the leather belts to which the holsters were attached, and the pistol butts that protruded from the holsters were identical from one man to the next.

When Tommy found himself at the front door again, he stepped outside with a feeling of relief. He walked away from the building as he had the first time and looked down at the fence and the gate.

He was in time to see a vehicle driving in. He thought it looked like a miniaturized bus.

As soon as the bus had driven through the gate, a pair of guards swung the gate shut again and locked it. The bus drove the few hundred feet to the small parking lot and stopped. A figure climbed out. Tommy recognized it as Hughes. Other figures began to climb from the bus. One of them was another man, but the other four were women.

Tommy's interest quickened. He strolled down the hill and onto the parking lot. "Hello there, Mr. Hughes," he called out. "Welcome back to the site. Nice trip?"

Hughes looked him up and down with open annoyance. "Stillwell. Getting used to the place already, I see. That's good. Let me introduce you to some of your fellow volunteers."

Tommy's natural affinity was for blondes. He smiled politely at the two brunettes as Hughes spoke their names, then forgot both the women and their names. He paid much closer attention to the other two, both blondes, both very much to Tommy's taste. One was named Jeanne Evans. She was taller than Tommy, looked athletic and competent, and had a strong, interesting face. She and Tommy smiled at each other and shook hands, and Tommy felt something more than politeness pass between them.

Hughes introduced the fourth woman as Ellen Maxwell, and Tommy forgot about Jeanne Evans. Ellen was the same height as Tommy and lean and wiry in much the way he was.

Her face, though, was fine boned, giving her a delicate prettiness that bordered on beauty. Their hands lingered in each other's and they stared at each other for a long moment. Tommy held his breath without realizing it. Unnoticed by either of them, Jeanne moved away, looking resigned.

Ellen and Tommy became aware of the others watching them and broke the contact. Tommy realized that, while Ellen's three fellow volunteers looked interested in what had happened, Hughes was annoyed. Tommy also realized that he didn't care what Hughes thought. He sensed that what had just begun between him and Ellen Maxwell was more important than anything else in his life.

Then something else struck him. If Ellen was one of the people selected for whatever it was Tempus was planning, then Tommy had to stay in Hughes' good graces in order to stay at Tempus and thus with Ellen. He managed to paste on something approaching his usual breezy grin and said to the Tempus man, "Need help carrying things in, Mr. Hughes?"

Hughes stared at him for a moment and then nodded. "There's not much to carry, Stillwell, but you can help the driver with it while I take the new volunteers inside."

Tommy turned his attention to the small collection of bags and pretended to be unaware of Hughes and the four volunteers walking away toward the building. He was intensely aware of Ellen Maxwell all the time, though.

Six

T raining began the next day.

Tommy spent the morning in an elementary German class in which he was the only student. He concentrated intensely and was able to absorb and remember almost all of the material the teacher covered. Got to catch up with Mallory, he kept telling himself.

He was given a one-hour break for lunch. He saw Ellen at the cafeteria, eating with the three other female volunteers. All of the other seats at their table were occupied by attentive male Tempus personnel, so Tommy gave up and went off to eat by himself.

That afternoon, he was sent to another classroom where Mallory joined him for elementary Russian. Again, Tommy made rapid progress. He felt that he was remembering the two languages as much as learning them. His parents had spoken only English, but he had grown up surrounded by Germans, Russian, Poles, Latvians, and Lithuanians. Often, he had escaped to the polyglot households of his childhood friends. Disorganized and crowded though they were, they were nonetheless havens of calm and rationality compared to his own.

Mallory, though, seemed lost from the moment they were introduced to the Cyrillic alphabet.

Tommy wondered how Ellen was doing in her language classes. He also wondered why she wasn't in the same classes he was in.

The next day, though, the three men and four women were together as students in classes on the history and culture of Germany and Russia—Germany in the morning, Russia in the afternoon. Unlike what Frank had described, these lectures covered long periods in the histories of both countries.

"They're leaving out a lot," Frank said as they left the Russian history class that evening.

"Well, I didn't know any of that stuff," Tommy said. "It's kind of interesting."

"Yeah, interesting," Mallory said, "but there's so much of it. I hope they aren't going to test us."

Frank looked at him. "They've been testing me ever since I got here, one way or another."

"Shit," Mallory said.

Tommy glanced over his shoulder and saw Ellen Maxwell come out of the classroom with Jeanne Evans and turn the other way down the corridor. "Yeah, well, one thing at a time. Listen, I'll see you guys in the cafeteria in about half an hour, okay?" He turned and sprinted down the hallway.

The other two men watched him go. Mallory laughed and shook his head.

"Christ, she's beautiful," Frank said.

"The big blonde, you mean?" Mallory said. "Too tall for me. But you're tall, too, so it's okay."

"The other one," Frank said. "Ellen Maxwell." His voice caressed her name.

Tommy had caught up with the two women. Frank and Mallory saw Jeanne nod curtly and leave, and then Tommy and Ellen walked away together and turned a corner.

Mallory looked up at Frank. "Tough luck, pal."

Frank shrugged and forced a smile. "I'll live. Let's go get some dinner."

The pattern continued for the next few days. One day would be devoted to languages—German in the morning for Tommy, Russian in the afternoon for Tommy and Mallory. The following day would be history, with the three men and four women in the class together—again, German in the morning, Russian in the afternoon.

After a week of this, the language and history lessons were shortened in length and limited to the mornings. Afternoons were now devoted to physical training.

They started with conditioning work: calisthenics, running, climbing over, under, and through obstacles, all done in the building's gymnasium. After lunch, the women were given a rest and the men were put through two hours of exercises with dumbbells and barbells. The instructor for the weight exercises was a huge and powerful man. Tommy decided he had been recruited either from the Marine Corps or the prison guard roster at Alcatraz. The badge pinned to his t-shirt had a red dot. Tommy saw that and decided that it had been Alcatraz, after all, and maybe not from among the guards.

Again, Tommy did well, but Mallory had trouble. Frank, though, kept ahead of both of them. Tommy soon realized that

Frank wasn't really a fellow student in any of this, not the history classes or the exercise classes. He suspected that Frank was the instructor's assistant. Or maybe even, Tommy thought, an instructor himself. He guessed that Frank's role was to help evaluate the four of them.

At the end of the fourth week, Ellen told Tommy that two of the other women had been eliminated from the program. "They were pretty upset, poor girls. Now they've got to go back home to crummy jobs. They were both really hoping for something better."

"So now I guess it's between you and Jeanne Evans, assuming there's just one slot available."

"I guess so," Ellen said. "She's good, too. You should see her doing all the running and stuff. I'd choose her over me, if I were doing the choosing."

"I'd choose you over anybody," Tommy told her. "I already have."

Ellen laughed happily and kissed him. Tommy longed to go to either her room or his and do more than share a quick, furtive kiss. But after he had realized on his first day that those rooms were under constant observation, he didn't dare. There would be later opportunities for them. Assuming, he reminded himself, that both of them made it through the testing Frank had said was constantly underway.

"Say," he asked her, "how are you doing with the languages?"

"Oh, it's pretty simple stuff."

"Simple?" Tommy had feared that she might be having trouble. He was relieved to hear she wasn't, but a bit annoyed as well. "Gee, maybe you're not moving ahead as fast as we are." He held up the German textbook. "What chapter are you guys up to?"

Ellen took the book and flipped through it. "This looks interesting! We're not doing that, though." She handed the book back to him. "All we're doing is letters."

"Letters? A, B, C? The alphabet?"

"No. The kind of letters you write to people. Business letters, basically. And letters of introduction. Formal stuff. We're memorizing a few standard letter formats and using them over and over. We don't even really have to know what the German or Russian means, they say. I asked about that, and the teacher said we'd be told by someone else what to actually put in the letter. We just had to learn to write it out so that it looked nice."

"You mean type it, don't you?"

Ellen shook her head. "No, write it. I'd like to type it, that's for sure! My handwriting isn't too good in English, and in Russian it looks ridiculous."

He gripped her shoulders. "Work on it. Whatever they want you to do, whether it makes sense or not, be the best at it. I don't want to go back to Normandy now that I've met you, and I don't want you to go back home."

Ellen smiled at him. "Okay, Tommy. It's less boring than the munitions factory, that's for sure."

After they parted, Tommy strolled back toward his room, wondering how to kill the rest of the evening. The door to Mallory's room was open when he passed it, and he heard Frank's voice coming from inside. Tommy turned into the room. "Hi, guys."

Mallory was dressed in his Army fatigues, and he had his

David Dvorkin

duffel bag on his bed and was stuffing things into it carelessly. Frank was sitting in the room's single chair looking glum. He looked up and greeted Tommy.

"Hi, Tommy," Mallory said. "Guess I washed out. Oh, hell, I don't think I was cut out for this, anyway. It's better than having Germans shooting at you, but that's how it goes. I'll look you guys up when the war's over. Right?"

The three men exchanged home addresses and assured each other that they would stay in touch, and Frank and Tommy watched Mallory shoulder his duffel bag and trudge down the hallway toward the front door.

After he had gone, Tommy felt that he should have said more, should at least have said something like, "Keep your head down." I'll tell him that before it's too late, Tommy thought. He headed after Mallory, hoping to catch him before he either climbed into the bus for the trip to Denver or was flown out from the site's airfield.

But when he got outside, the bus was already pulling out of the parking lot. It sped away down the dirt road, leaving a cloud of dust behind it.

Tommy went back inside and back to his room. Damn, he thought. Damn. I really owed him a proper goodbye.

He stepped out on his balcony. He could see a cloud of dust moving across the prairie far away, and he thought it had a greenish tint to it. Maybe it was the bus. He wished he had binoculars so that he could tell for sure.

The cloud moved out of sight behind a small hill. Tommy waited for it to reappear on the far side of the hill, but it never did.

Then, faintly, he heard a sound he had heard often in

56

Normandy: the crackle of a number of rifles firing simultaneously.

Tommy gripped the balcony railing and leaned out over the edge, straining his eyes and his ears. For a long time, there was nothing. Then the bus appeared from behind the hill, heading back toward the Tempus building. It was moving fast, bouncing about, keeping ahead of the billowing dust.

Tommy's knees buckled. He sagged, barely holding himself up against balcony. "Oh, shit," he said. "Oh, Jeff, I'm sorry."

Now the training intensified.

Every day, the four remaining volunteers had total-immersion language training and grueling exercise sessions. The two men were told to spend an hour or two on the rifle range every day and were given as their goal a level of accuracy that Tommy considered absurd. He thought of Mallory, though, and disciplined himself sternly. His marksmanship improved steadily. In addition, Tommy was given training by Frank in one-to-one combat, armed and unarmed.

Ellen told Tommy that she and Jeanne were also being trained to fight.

"That's weird," he said. "Be careful. Don't get hurt."

She laughed. "I'm enjoying it."

One day, fed up with it all, so tired, so filled with aches, so covered with bruises that he no longer cared what had happened to Jeff Mallory, Tommy flopped to the ground in the middle of a session with Frank. "Enough," he said. "I'm not going to attack you again. I just don't give a shit anymore. I can't move."

Frank sat down beside him. He was breathing only slightly

more heavily than normal. "Okay. Time for a break."

Tommy forced himself to a sitting position and pulled his T-shirt away from his chest to let the air circulate over his skin. "I still don't even know why we're doing any of this stuff. No one has told me anything yet."

Frank hesitated for a moment, then said, "I suppose I can tell you what they told me at the beginning." He repeated what Hughes had said about the assassination of one man putting an instant end to the war.

"Yeah?" Tommy said. "So that's all this is? We're supposed to go inside Germany and kill Hitler? Hell, why bother? From what I could see, the Germans are finished anyway. With us from one side and the Russians from the other, it's just a matter of time."

"True. But a lot of good men will die in that time. Maybe we could stop it right away and save them."

"I guess," Tommy said unenthusiastically. "But what about the two girls? Ellen and Jeanne, I mean."

"Maybe they think a woman would have a better chance of getting close to Hitler than a man would."

"Maybe," Tommy said. He thought of Ellen being exposed to such danger. "Jesus. This is bad." Maybe Jeanne would be chosen instead of Ellen, he thought, so Ellen wouldn't have to go through that. But in that case, what would happen to Ellen? Not that you really know what happened to Mallory, he told himself. You're just guessing. "Frank, anyone ever say anything more about Jeff? I mean, how he's doing?"

"I asked Hughes about him the other day. He said he'd check into it."

"And?"

"Nothing yet."

Tommy stood up. "Let's go ask him."

Frank looked up at him and then slowly rose to his feet. "I don't think Hughes is the kind of guy you just walk in on for no reason."

Tommy grinned. "I'm demonstrating initiative and the ability to think on my feet."

They found Hughes in his office on the third floor. He was engrossed in a thick document and looked annoyed at the interruption. "Shouldn't you boys be busy?" He glanced at something on his desk. "I see you're scheduled for unarmed combat training at this time."

"We're taking a well–deserved break," Tommy said.

"We were thinking about Jeff Mallory," Frank said. "Wondering if you'd heard anything about him yet."

Hughes frowned. "Who?"

"Jeff Mallory," Tommy said. "Our buddy."

"Oh, yes, your fellow candidate. The one who didn't qualify. As a matter of fact, I did get a response to my inquiries." Hughes searched quickly through a pile of papers on his desk and then drew one out. He held it up facing them for long enough for them to see the eagle–and–shield logo of the Department of War. Then he scanned it quickly, reading parts of it aloud. "Response to your query of fourth instant, etc. Mallory, corporal. Hmm. Yes. Regret to inform you ..." He looked up at them, his face showing concern. "Yes, I remember now. I'm sorry, boys, but your friend didn't make it. He died in a German artillery bombardment the day after he got back to France. I'm very sorry. I didn't realize you had formed any kind of bond with him.

Perhaps this would be an appropriate time to point out to you both how inadvisable such bonds are in your circumstances."

"An artillery bombardment?" Tommy repeated. Where did the Army bury the pieces, you bastard? Near here, out in the desert? Aloud, he said, "Thank you, Mr. Hughes. We'll remember your advice. Come on, Frank." He turned and walked toward the door.

Frank followed him for a few paces, then turned back toward Hughes. "Pardon me, Mr. Hughes, but would it be possible for me to have that letter? I'd like it as a memento of my—of Mallory."

Hughes shook his head. "Of course not, Anderson. We need it for our files. I'm surprised at you. I think you should emulate Stillwell's attitude."

"Come along, Anderson," Tommy said from the door. "Let's get back to our training."

Frank followed him docilely, looking dazed. They were back in the gym before he spoke again. "An artillery bombardment! Jesus. If I hadn't tried so hard, maybe he'd have made the cut instead of me, and he'd still be here and alive."

"Yeah, and *you'd* be dead in a German artillery bombardment. Christ, Frank, wake up! Jeff was a nice enough guy, and I'm sorry for him, but now he's just another dead body."

Frank grimaced at that. "A hell of a way to look at it, Tommy."

"You saw a lot dead bodies at the front. Created a lot of them, too, right? There's stuff going on here that we're safer not asking about. Okay, let's forget about poor old Jeff for now and get to work at reducing the number of dead bodies at the front in the future."

"He was your *friend*, Tommy!"

Tommy shook his head. "He was a guy I thought was okay. You only have one friend, and that's yourself. I want to keep my friend alive and healthy."

"Ellen isn't your friend?"

Tommy looked uneasy. "That's different. I can't explain that, not even to myself. Hell, of course I want to keep Ellen alive and healthy. And I want to keep myself alive and healthy for her sake." He spoke those last words wonderingly, as if they were a new thought to him and he was surprised to hear them.

It also surprised him to realize that he didn't want Frank to get hurt either. Hughes was right: emotional bonds were dangerous.

That evening, Tommy told Ellen what Hughes had said to him and Frank. He also told her what he had heard on the day Mallory washed out of the program.

"I don't understand," she said. "You mean there was lightning in the distance, and it reminded you of rifle fire?"

"No, I mean there *was* rifle fire in the distance, not lightning. And not that far in the distance, either. I mean—" He paused and looked around. They were standing in the middle of the incongruously green lawn in front of the Tempus building, and no one else was in sight, but Tommy's fear of being observed and listened to by invisible spies had been growing ever since his visit to Hughes's office. He lowered his voice. "I mean that they took Mallory out into the desert and shot him. Buried him out there. They don't want any of us leaving this place alive unless we've been accepted into their team."

Ellen gasped. "But why? That doesn't make any sense at all!"

"Maybe it does make sense. I haven't told you about Frank's theory about our mission, have I? The assassination stuff?"

"No, you haven't, but Frank has."

Tommy was surprised. "I didn't realize you spend time talking to Frank when I'm not there."

"Sure. Occasionally." She smiled at his expression. "Don't be jealous, Tommy. Frank's a wonderful man, and I guess I'm honored that he thinks he's in love with me, but—"

"What?" Tommy's shout echoed off the building and the red cliff behind it. "He actually said that to you? God damn him!"

This time, Ellen laughed aloud. "No, he didn't say anything. He thinks he's keeping his feelings well hidden, but It's pretty easy to tell. I thought you knew all of this."

Tommy sighed, partly in relief, partly in frustration. "I guess I did. I mean, I could tell how he felt about you by the way he speaks about you. The way he says your name. I didn't think you knew, though."

"As I said, you don't have any reason to be jealous. I don't love Frank, I love you. I've told you that already, and I don't say 'I love you' casually. I hope you know that."

"I *do* know that. And I don't say it casually either," he lied. Before Ellen, he had said it casually and often.

"Okay," Ellen said, "so now that that's settled, what about Frank's theory about us going into Germany and assassinating Adolf? What does that have to do with Jeff and the sound you heard?"

"Frank knows about the assassination plan because Hughes

pretty much told him when he recruited him. Hughes must have known that Frank would tell the rest of us, since he didn't tell Frank to keep it to himself. So Tempus assumes that anyone who washes out, like Mallory, could be a source of information for Nazi spies. Tempus doesn't want the Nazis to know what we're planning, because then the Nazis would have traps prepared for us before we even got behind their lines."

"But from what I hear, lots of people have been trying to assassinate Hitler all through the war. Including Germans."

"Yeah, but this way, the Nazis would know exactly who we are and what we look like. Wouldn't that increase their chances of catching us? Probably the minute we show up in Berlin or wherever."

Ellen had grown pale. "I don't think I could kill anyone, Tommy. Not even Hitler."

"From what you've said about your training so far, honey, I don't think that's going to be your role. I think you're support. In fact, I'm probably just a backup man. Frank's probably the point man. He's the guy with the special talent for killing people. I know he's on the team. He was selected before I got here. I also know that Hughes told Mallory and me that there was one slot remaining to be filled, so that means I'm in. Now it's between you and Jeanne. Maybe they'll send both of you with us—two men, two women. We could pose as married couples. That'd be okay, huh?"

He grinned at Ellen, and she responded as always to his infectious good cheer with a grin of her own.

"And maybe that way Frank would get interested in Jeanne," Tommy continued thoughtfully. "She's more his type than you, anyway. I mean," he said quickly, "they're both tall, strong, and silent. They could have a whole bunch of tall, strong, silent kids. A tall, strong, silent family. Very quiet dinnertimes at the Anderson household."

Ellen laughed, but she said, "I don't think so. They seem to like each other okay, but there's no spark there."

"Like between us?"

"Yes."

They had not so much as touched hands during the entire conversation. Even before Hughes' warning about the danger of bonds between candidates for the team, they had both sensed that Tempus would disapprove of a romantic liaison between them, and that disapproval might mean that one or both of them would be dropped from consideration. And so they stood apart but yearning toward each other. Hughes might warn against a bond, but it was there, almost palpable in the evening air. What had passed between them at that first meeting had grown stronger with each word, each meeting of the eyes, each rare, furtive touch.

"Well," Ellen said, breaking the spell at last. "So. We'd better go in and go to bed. Another heavy day tomorrow." She turned toward the front door.

"Wait." Tommy stepped between her and the building. "Ellen, honey, you've got to survive. I'm sorry about Jeanne, but we've got our lives ahead of us, and I want us to spend them together. You've got to make it. If they are going to choose just one woman, then it's got to be you. For our sake."

Ellen said sadly, "Yes. That's right. For our sake."

Frank, though, was looking at Dolores Lujan, scarcely aware of what Hughes was saying.

Was this what Tommy was trying to describe to me? he wondered. How he felt when he first met Ellen? She looks a little bit like Ellen. The shape of her face, mainly. But there's so much more there. Oh, you're being ridiculous, he lectured himself. You know her name and what she looks like, and that's all. It's just chemistry, Frank, that's all. Grow up, boy.

Dolores was of average height and had light brown hair. She was slender and had the same lean intensity as Ellen, but where Ellen was beautiful, Dolores was pretty. The chemistry went much deeper than that, though, for Frank. It felt as though there were already a bond between them, soul to soul—an impression that Frank immediately told himself was absurd and baseless.

Dolores raised her eyes from the floor and her glance met Frank's. She looked frightened and looked away again.

She's scared of me! Frank thought, astonished.

He tried to concentrate on Hughes's lecture.

" ... against Hitler and Japan," Hughes was saying. "Some of us knew it was coming. All those people who were worried so much about German and Japanese imperialism were ignoring the greater threat, the one that existed before the Nazis and even before the First World War. It's the threat that will still exist after the Nazis and the present Japanese government are gone. That threat is Communism, Marxism. Those people predate the Soviet Union, but it's the Communists' control of the old Russian Empire that makes them so powerful and dangerous to the rest of the world.

"A small group of men with real foresight have concerned

themselves for a long time with the coming competition for world dominance between the United States and the Soviet Union. As you all know, President Roosevelt and Uncle Joe are making a great show of being friends and allies against the common enemy. Personally, I suspect it's not a show on FDR's part. I think he's really been taken in by Stalin. Time will tell. Anyway, Stalin knows that as soon as this war is over, the situation will return to what it was before the war: a battle between Communism and freedom for control of the world. FDR will be forced to wake up to reality then—unless it's too late, and the Soviets have won because we weren't paying attention.

"I don't think Churchill has been fooled. However, the British Empire is less important in the world every day, and I think that this war is draining them fast. I think that Churchill, after the war, will be entirely occupied with trying to hold his Empire together. So he'll be a minor player in the great battle for the survival of democracy. In effect, America will stand alone.

"Some of us, as I said, have seen this coming. The battle was underway long before Hitler, even before Mussolini. It began even before the Bolshevik Revolution of 1917, although that was the turning point, the crux in history, the point at which the battle became more than just a philosophical conflict. That was also the point at which we began to do our work. Are any of you familiar with the books of Herbert George Wells?"

Frank asked, "Isn't everyone?" Then he looked at his two teammates. "Guess not."

"I've read *The War of the Worlds*," Ellen said.

"Then only Mr. Stillwell is unfamiliar with Wells," Hughes said. "How unsurprising. For your benefit, Mr. Stillwell, H. G. Wells is an English writer, but very popular in this country, too.

Before the turn of the century, he published a novel called *The Time Machine*. It's the story of a man who invents a device for traveling through time."

He waited only a few seconds for them to absorb this concept. "I'll get back to Wells in a minute. At the end of the First World War, the group I mentioned decided to send a team into Russia to kill the leaders of the Bolshevik Revolution. With those leaders out of the way, we hoped, the Russians themselves would turn to America for help in setting up a new government.

"We trained our men and sent them in, and they were captured and killed. Only one man escaped. The damned Bolsheviks were already too well organized. What we should have done was send our teams in *before* the Bolsheviks took over Russia, before they had the power to protect themselves. It would have been even better if we could have sent someone into Germany during the first war, when Lenin was hiding there, and killed him then. All we really had to do back then was know the future, right?

"Well, what if, once we realized we'd missed our chance, we came up with some way of sending our men back in time to a point before we missed our chance?

"I see that I have your attention. I was the member of that team who survived. I wanted to go back and try again, but the people I was working for wouldn't let me. That was in 1922, when I was the same age Stillwell is now.

"The outfit I worked for was called the Subversion Monitoring Council. That was a nice, bland name, chosen so no Bolshevik spy would be likely to guess its real purpose. It drew its funds from some of the richest men in America—industrial tycoons, great inventors. We also had some friends inside the

Federal government who managed to slip a fair amount of public money our way—secretly, of course. When the Council realized that we would not succeed at assassinating the Soviet leadership, we changed direction.

"Our leaders were inspired by Wells' novel. They renamed the organization Tempus and started building up a team of top scientists. For twenty years, Tempus hired the best brains in the country and put them to work on our special project. We've even had to compete with our own government, which has been recruiting top people for weapons development, including one particular big, top-secret project for which they want the very best. We've been able to get some of those people ourselves, though, because we pay more. The goal of our research is the development of the ability to travel through time.

"We plan to send a team of assassins back to some point before 1917. That's you three. One point man, leader, top-notch killer: Anderson. One support man, backup, guard: Stillwell. One woman for general help, secretarial support, and social interface: Maxwell. You will kill Stalin and Lenin. Since we will have equipped you with everything we know about those men and their movements, you should have an easy time slipping through what security there was. That security was effective against me and my colleagues when we were over there, but it won't be against you. If that doesn't change our present-day world into something more to our liking, we'll send another team back and kill off Hitler at some point before he got into politics. If that still doesn't do the trick, then we'll send yet another team back, to some other point in history, with some other target. We'll just keep doing it until it works."

Tommy and Ellen were still staring at him with eyes and

mouths wide open, but Frank burst out laughing. "I loved that Wells book, Mr. Hughes. I read it when I was a boy, and everything else by Wells that I could find. Hell, I still keep my eye out for his new stuff. But it *is* just fiction. No one has ever traveled in time. No one ever will."

Hughes smiled nastily. "Stick to history and killing, Anderson. Don't make pronouncements about other people's specialties. Tempus has already succeeded. We have already sent people through time." He laughed at their expressions.

Tommy was the first of the three to speak. "Jesus, Hughes, you mean we can do it right now? Go back in time and kill off Hitler? Stop it all before it started?"

Hughes's smile faded. "Not exactly. Not quite yet. Miss Lujan will tell you more. She's from the technical side of the organization."

He stepped back, forcing Dolores Lujan into the center of the trio's attention. She still avoided their eyes, and she spoke in a voice that was too low for them to hear. They could tell only that her voice was trembling.

Tommy winked at Frank and said, "Could you speak up, please, ma'am? I think your voice is off somewhere traveling in time."

Dolores looked stricken.

Frank said, "Button it, Tommy. Miss Lujan, I apologize. We're all extremely interested in what you have to tell us."

She gave Frank a quick, grateful look and a smile and then looked at the floor again. Her voice was louder when she spoke again, although it still trembled.

"What we have managed to do so far," she said, "is to send a couple of volunteers forward in time over periods of a few days.

One week is the maximum we've tried. Even that takes a great deal of energy, so we haven't yet attempted longer time periods than that. So far, though, we can't reverse the process. I mean that we can't yet send anyone backward in time."

"Why not?" Frank asked.

"We're not sure."

Tommy said, "You mean, you don't know."

"I mean, we're not sure," Dolores said, annoyed. "We think we know, but we're not sure. When Tempus began working on time travel, the research was based on the idea that time is a river, a movement in a preferential direction in four-dimensional space."

"Oh, boy," Tommy muttered.

"However, that's misleading. Unlike a real river, nothing is actually moving. Nothing is flowing. It's a useful metaphor. I thought it would be easier for the four of you to think of it in such terms."

"What's the real way to think of it?" Frank asked.

"With mathematics."

"Tell us about the river," Tommy said.

Ellen laughed.

"What distinguishes a point along an actual river from a second point downstream from it? Physical distance, of course, but more important than that is energy. The downstream point has lower gravitational potential energy than the one upstream. Trying to wade or swim or canoe upstream is more difficult than heading downstream because in the first case you're trying to gain energy, whereas in the second you're simply letting the energy decrease."

"It's difficult to go upstream because the river keeps trying to kill you," Tommy said.

"A river does not have a mind," Dolores said. "Don't make the mistake of attributing intelligence to nature."

"Everything's trying to kill you," Tommy said. "Doesn't matter if it has a mind."

Dolores stared at him, but he had the odd feeling that she wasn't looking at him. "I'm aware that you see the world that way," she said at last. "However, please try to pay attention to what I'm telling you. The world isn't trying to kill you, but ignorance about the world might do just that.

"Events along the timestream are separated by the level of temporal energy. We have learned how to remove some of the energy from an object. That results in the object being displaced downstream to the point where its energy matches that of the surrounding timestream."

"So to send someone forward in time," Frank said, "you drain energy out of him."

Tommy said, "That's how I feel before my morning coffee." This time, Ellen didn't laugh. She didn't even seem to hear him. She was focused entirely on Frank and Dolores.

Dolores smiled approvingly at Frank. "Exactly!"

"What happens to that energy? Does it escape and heat everything up?"

"Good question."

Good boy, Tommy thought. Concentrate on teacher and forget all about Ellen.

"We're able to store the energy for a short while," Dolores said. "Then we let it drain away slowly. So far, the amount has been small, so it hasn't been a problem. I am a bit worried about what might happen when we send a number of objects some distance downstream, however. That's one reason for limiting ourselves to short time periods right now—to avoid problems with the amount of energy we have to store. A second reason is that, when our volunteers arrive, we can be there waiting for them to see if everything worked properly."

"What if you just put the energy back into them?" Tommy asked. "I mean, the energy you take out of them. Shouldn't that just shoot them back up the river, back to where they started? Seems to me that going back in time should be simple, now that you know how to control that time energy you're talking about."

Dolores stared at him in the strange way as before. After a moment, she said, "It should work that way, but it doesn't. We don't know why. I suspect that for some reason it takes far more energy to send someone upstream from Point B to Point A than it does to send them downstream from Point A to Point B. Since we can only store temporal energy and not generate it, we can't send anyone back, and we won't be able to until we learn how to generate that energy."

"Maybe the real problem is that you don't know what's going on. Maybe, before we let you guys experiment on us, we should talk to someone who really understands this stuff."

"There is no one who understands it better than Miss Lujan," Hughes said, showing more anger than Tommy had seen in him before. "She is the most important person on this project. Before she joined us, we were making little progress. She set us on the right path. Her time is too important for you to waste it."

An awkward silence settled over the room. Ellen finally broke it. "Were your volunteers all right when they arrived?"

"The younger, healthier ones were," Dolores said. "We experimented with five people. Three of them were in their twenties and healthy, and they suffered no side effects at all as far as we could tell. And it made no difference whether they went forward one day or one week. There were no ill effects in either case."

"What about the other two?" Tommy asked. "What about them?"

"One was a woman in her fifties. She's very healthy, very athletic, but the trip drained her strength so much that she hasn't fully recovered yet. It's been a couple of months. The fifth volunteer ... Well, he was a man in his mid–forties, very overweight, a heavy smoker. When he emerged, he was in the middle of a massive heart attack. We couldn't save him."

Hughes broke in. "That's one reason we were looking for young, healthy people when we set about recruiting you three."

"You already had three young, healthy volunteers," Ellen said. "Why did you need us?"

Hughes smiled at her. "Because they were all members of the scientific team. Much too valuable to send on the kind of mission we've been training you for. And none of them had the very special talents Anderson and Stillwell displayed at the front."

Tommy turned to Ellen. "In other words, we're good at killing, but we're not worth all that much otherwise." He turned back to Hughes. "Putting all your eggs in one basket, aren't you, Mr. Hughes? Us, I mean."

"Whether or not we have other baskets is not your concern, Stillwell."

Tommy shrugged, dismissing the matter in his usual easygoing way. "Miss Lujan," he said, "this time trip must be one hell of a ride. What's it like?"

"Like nothing much," Dolores told him. "The four survivors said they experienced some strange visual sensations, almost like hallucinations, but it's nothing they're able to describe very well."

"Not like in Wells' novel, then?" Frank asked, feeling disappointed. "In the book, the guy sees the world changing all around him, just like in real life, but speeded up tremendously as he goes forward. Trees growing and dying, buildings coming and going like dreams, the earth seeming to melt and flow."

Dolores smiled at him very directly, not looking away this time. "I liked that part of the book, too."

"You like Wells?"

"Love him. My father used to read his books to me."

"You had a much more enlightened father than I did."

Hughes interrupted. "Let's drop this personal chit-chat, shall we? Lujan, get on with your lecture, please. Anderson, listen more and talk less."

"Yes, Mr. Hughes," Dolores said. "We're still trying to find out how to send people backward in time. We have a few ideas, and one of them involves the three of you."

Tommy broke in. "Maybe there isn't any way. Maybe you'll never find out how to do it because it isn't possible. Maybe it's time to give the project up."

Hughes answered him. "You may be right, of course, Stillwell. But we don't think so. Moreover, if it *is* possible, then we *have* to be the first ones to find out how to do it. What if the Communists have a research project just like this one? What if they beat us to the development of backwards time travel? What if they've already beaten us?"

"No," Frank said. "If they had, they'd have used it already, and the past would be different. We'd all be speaking Russian and living under a worldwide Communist state. Since we aren't doing either, therefore they haven't yet developed the ability to travel backward in time."

Hughes nodded. "Good point. But they still may be well on their way to the secret, and we have to beat them to it."

"No," Frank said again. "See, if they *ever* beat us to it in the future, *then* they'll travel back into the past and change things, and again we'd be living in a worldwide Communist state and speaking Russian. Since we aren't, they won't. *Quod erat demonstrandum.*"

Hughes looked annoyed. "Sounds like shaky logic to hang the future of the world on, Anderson."

Frank ignored him. "Come to think of it," he said, "by the same argument, *we'll* never develop backward time travel, either. Because if we ever did, *we'd* go back and change the past, and the present would be different than it is. Since it isn't different, therefore we never will be able to travel backward."

Tommy burst into laughter and clapped loudly. "Frank, you just proved that Tempus has no reason to exist! Now we can all go home."

"It's too late for any of you to drop out now," Hughes said quietly.

He had their full attention again. He smiled at them. "Anderson, you've proved nothing with your logic–chopping except how complex the whole situation is and how difficult it is for human minds to comprehend the ramifications of time travel. Tempus is not prepared to entrust the security of this nation and the survival of freedom to questionable reasoning like yours. The project continues full bore. Because of this problem with reverse travel, we have recently had to change our immediate goal. But this means only a temporary delay. Lujan, continue."

"Since we can't send you backward as a team," Dolores said, "we've decided to send you forward instead. Individually.

"Just consider. If we've been able to do so much already with time travel, what will the scientists of the future be able to do? Tempus thinks that they'll know how to go backward in time as well as forward. But even if that discovery is made somewhere in the future, Tempus has no way of knowing when it will be. Fifty years? One hundred? Even more? So we're trying to stack the deck in our favor by sending you to different destinations.

"Tommy, we're sending you ahead fifty years, to 1995. Ellen, you're going one hundred years, to 2045. And Frank," she met his gaze again, "you're headed for 2095."

Hughes took up the thread. "Miss Lujan should have mentioned that we'll add six months to the trip for each of you, so that you'll arrive in August instead of February. This area is occasionally snowbound in winter. Not this year, but this is unusual. Since we can't predict the weather fifty years ahead, let alone one hundred and fifty, we won't take any chances. When you arrive, your mission will be to use your training and background as best you can in order to fit into the world you find waiting for you, to infiltrate whatever time–travel research project or industrial operation already exists there, and then to use the available time–travel equipment to bring the secret of reverse time travel back here with you."

"Why don't we bring it back to before this time?" Tommy asked. "Then we'll already have it, and we won't need to jump forward at all."

"Because we think you can't live through the same time twice. We think that if you try, the timestream will destroy you."

"You cannot step into the same river twice," Frank said, "for fresh waters are ever flowing in upon you."

"That's beautiful," Ellen said. "Did you just make that up?"

Frank laughed. "Nah. Heraclitus beat me to it. An ancient Greek."

"I'm always so amazed by all that stuff you know."

"Jesus Christ!" Tommy said. "This is totally loony!"

"It is," Frank agreed. "Hughes, the future world Wells' time traveler found almost killed him."

"Wells is a socialist," Hughes said, "which is to say, virtually a Communist. His whole point in that novel was to attack England's social policies and capitalism, not to seriously explore possible futures."

"It seems *impossible* to me," Ellen said. "Oh, not traveling forward in time. I'll take your word that you've already done it. But just think about the mission you're assigning to us! Even here and now, you've locked this place up so tightly that no Communist or Nazi spy has a chance of getting in—and they're people who know this world we all live in. But you want us to be *more* successful spies than they are, in a world that will be completely foreign to us. It's an impossible task."

Hughes nodded. "I'm afraid you're probably right. That is, if in the future time travel is as closely guarded a secret as it is here, at Tempus. But if it's more commonplace, it may be only loosely guarded, if at all. That's really what we're counting on. That and your desire to get back home again."

"Bastard," Tommy whispered.

Hughes looked at him and smiled. "Thank you, Stillwell. I pride myself on it. Now, when any one of you returns to this time and place with the secret, or the formula, or the device, or whatever form it takes, we will immediately use it to bring the other two back home. Thus, you will be working on behalf of your two friends as well as on your own behalf. And then, finally, we will be in a position to do what we wanted to do in the first place—send the three of you back, as a team, to the early part of this century to carry out the assassinations we have been training you for."

"When?" Frank asked. "I mean, when do we go into the future?"

"We're sticking to our original date. We set a date for the completion of your training based on the assumption that we would have solved our problem by then and would know how to send you backward. As it is, the only difference is that we'll be sending you forward instead of back."

"But what *is* that date?" Frank insisted.

"February 8."

"Oh, God, that's next Thursday!" Ellen said.

"Yes," Hughes said. "Some time in the afternoon, we expect. Our technical people would like to have the morning for final checks of all the equipment. After all, who can say what would happen if there were a malfunction while you were in the middle of being sent forward in time?"

"Pleasant thought," Tommy said. "Say, you know, we could be too late already. Like you said, maybe the commies are already on their way into the future before us. Maybe the Krauts, too. What do you think, Frank?"

"Possible, I guess. And the Japanese and the Italians. And

"Yes, I can see that," Charlie said. "We've sure been pressing on with it here. We've got really solid cooperation going with both Hoover's men and Donovan's, as you instructed."

"Without either one knowing about the other, of course?"

"Oh, of course, Mr. Hughes. Our problem remains in the White House, though."

"Understood." The White House had been the problem all along.

The heads of the FBI and the OSS had been responsive to offers of help from the Subversion Monitoring Council because they knew of the Council's competence and connections. Hoover had been more enthusiastic than Donovan. Hoover had always shared the Council's belief that Communism, not Nazism, was the important enemy. Hughes had long had doubts about the reliability of Donovan and his people. Nonetheless, the chance to gain access to the OSS's resources and funds had been too good to pass up.

Approaches to the White House, though, whether direct or through the FBI or the OSS, had been rebuffed. Hughes had always hated Roosevelt, and he couldn't see that the addition of Harry Truman to the team had changed things for the better. We have to get rid of both of them, Hughes thought. We need someone more cooperative in there.

He wished he could afford to spend more time in Washington, at the center of the action. He felt too far away from that center, too physically distant, but he could not afford to leave Tempus for long without his guiding hand. He wished he could create a duplicate of himself. He had often thought about that, and it had occasionally led him to wonder if the

Council should have concentrated on the stranger byways of biology and medicine instead of those of physics.

At least he had been able to keep the Subversion Monitoring Council itself going. He had had to fight to do so. After Tempus had had its early success, the other councilors had talked about disbanding the Council and concentrating all their resources entirely on time travel. With Tempus now facing a brick wall, the wisdom of Hughes' insistence on continuing with the Council's work as an entirely separate undertaking should be apparent to all of them.

"What's the progress abroad?" he asked.

"Okay in Britain," Charlie said. "Churchill's always agreed with us, so he's ordered his intelligence people to give us all the cooperation they can afford to. But of course they've been strapped by the war. Once the war's over, I predict that Britain will be one of our strongholds. Especially after the upcoming election, which I predict Churchill's party will win."

"Good, very good." Hughes had long had a soft spot for Churchill. What a pity the man couldn't come over to America and run for the presidency on the Republican ticket. He'd have a good chance of beating Roosevelt. No one else seemed able to.

"What I'm still hoping," Charlie said, "is that a good part of the present German government can survive the military defeat. They'll have to get rid of Adolf, or send him to jail, or hang him, or shoot him, but the rest of those guys share a lot of our views. If they could stay in power, I think we'd have a very, very strong presence in Germany. Same goes for the rest of Central Europe. The only problem will be getting the Soviets to let go of the territories they're taking from the Germans."

"Good analysis, Charlie," Hughes said. "The Council shares

your views."

The conversation continued for an hour on a much more detailed level. Charlie gave way to a series of other Council employees, each contributing to the mental picture Hughes liked to maintain of the Council's work. The details were interesting, but it was the overall picture that absorbed him. That picture was one of an organization constantly growing in resources and influence.

The Council had reached the point where it was no longer merely finding governmental officials who shared some of its views. Now the Council was being asked to help shape foreign and domestic policy. Occasionally it was even asked to lend personnel to certain government agencies in order to take over minor tasks. Soon, he hoped, sympathetic governments would be delegating the actual execution of policy to the Subversion Monitoring Council.

He had no doubt that the Council would rise as a power in the world in its own right, just as Hughes had risen from employee to Council member to most powerful man on the Council.

"Tempus has tried to guess what kind of situation you'll each find in the future," Dolores told the three. "But it's just guesswork. Will you find peace, prosperity, and superscience? Or a collapsed civilization and barbarism? Maybe a combination—advanced on the surface, but governed behind the scenes by dangerous, evil men who see everything and brutalize everyone, like the big brother of your nightmares."

"My big brother was always kind to me," Ellen said sadly.

Dolores smiled at her. "Bad analogy. Sorry. But they may

know you're coming. They may be waiting for you. You'll have to be careful. You'll have to be on your guard."

Frank noticed for the first time that Tommy and Ellen were holding hands, and both looked worried. They would never have displayed their affection in front of Hughes, let alone their fears for each other, but they seemed unafraid of doing so in front of Dolores. He wondered what Dolores's hand would feel like.

"You'll have to blend in," Dolores said. "but that may not be easy. Imagine if a man from one hundred years ago were transported to contemporary America. Imagine him trying to deal with the image of Rosie the Riveter, or even with real contemporary American women. Imagine him coping with the modern Negro. Or with the traffic and crime in any of our great cities. Then there's technology—cars, airplanes, radio, the telephone. His chances of survival would be low. You might find yourselves faced with a world at least as confusing and dangerous as that man would."

"But there'll still be people and their relationships," Frank pointed out. "Certain things are constant. Always have been, always will be. We can count on that, anyway."

"Time changes relationships too, Mr. Anderson. Any grownup should know that. One thing we hope will be a constant is Tempus itself. Tempus will try to maintain an organizational shell with offices in major cities. Find the nearest one as soon as you arrive.

"We're dropping your language and history lessons. We want you to concentrate on your physical training and conditioning between now and Thursday. Whatever kind of future you encounter, you're bound to have a better chance of survival the healthier and stronger you are and the better your self–defense skills are. Exercise and rest. That's your assignment from now on." She managed to meet their eyes and smile at them, and then she headed for the door.

Tommy leaned over toward Frank and whispered, "On your feet, soldier. You may never see her again."

Frank gave him a startled look, astonished that his feelings had been that obvious. Then he pushed himself away from his desk and followed Dolores.

Ellen watched him go. She smiled at Tommy. "Well done, Tommy!"

"The boy just needed a bit of a push."

Frank caught up with Dolores in the hallway. "I have a couple of questions," he said.

She frowned and looked nervous again, as if she feared being alone with him. "Mr. Anderson, I have a lot of work to do in preparation for Thursday."

"Well, that's obviously very important," Frank said. "I think it's also very important that you call me Frank, considering what you're going to be doing to me in a few days."

"Frank. All right. But I really am busy."

"Before you go, tell me about those hallucinations your time travelers saw. Were there common elements between what the different people saw?"

She looked surprised. "That's an odd question. Why should there be common elements?"

"No reason, but if there were, then maybe we're dealing with something real, not just with hallucinations."

Dolores thought for a moment, then said, "From what I remember, there was a feeling of being in a vast space, a place where anything could happen. I remember that one of them said he felt like he was standing in the middle of a giant crossroads, with infinitely many roads heading off in all directions. Does that tell you anything?"

Frank had hardly been listening to her words. He had been staring at her, at her eyes, at her hair, at her mouth as she spoke, feeling ever more entranced by her and physically drawn to her, but at the same time feeling ever more strongly that they had met before. "Dolores, listen. I don't know where a guy is supposed to take a girl on a date around here. There's nothing except the prairie, and Tempus sure doesn't provide much in the way of entertainment. The best I can do is ask you to go to the cafeteria with me for dinner this evening. How about that?"

He had expected her to be amused, but instead she displayed the same fear as before. "You're a very nice man, Frank. But we have to just remain friends, and that's all, okay?" She turned from him and walked quickly away down the hallway.

Frank watched her go. Her back was stiff, wary, defensive. Repelled, he thought. Jesus!

So he was to go off into the unknown future with no one waiting behind for him, just as he had gone off to the war in Europe a few years earlier with no one waiting behind for him. It was to be the pattern of his life, he feared—now or in some future century.

Nine

Tommy threw himself into the intensified physical training. It helped keep his mind off the coming separation from Ellen. Ellen tried to follow his example. The result was that they both ended their days too physically exhausted to think of anything but sleep.

When they could, they talked. That seemed more important now than sex. They told each other about their lives. They both wanted to know as much as they could, to fill their minds and memories with each other as a talisman against the coming separation.

"I miss them both so much," Ellen said. "And I'm still so angry at both of them."

She would never forget the way her sister looked when she found her. "Why did she have to kill herself? Why didn't she come to me? I could have helped her. After that, my brother was the only one I had left. I needed him. When my sister died, he was already in the Pacific."

He had signed up the day after Pearl Harbor. Ellen had pleaded with him not to. "We need you," she had said. "Louise needs you. Something's wrong with her. I don't know what it is, but she needs both of us."

"My country needs me," he had said. "I want to go over there and kill some Japs."

"Instead, they killed him," she said bitterly. "The War Department sent me some kind of medal, and that's all I have left of him."

"He was doing his duty," Tommy said. He felt uncomfortable talking about duty. His duty had always been to survive. Now it included keeping Ellen alive, too. He couldn't really understand what her brother had been thinking, or how the man could have sacrificed his life and the happiness of those who loved him. For Ellen's sake, Tommy tried to say the conventional things he heard others say. "Sometimes, duty makes people do things they don't want to do. Your brother felt that he had to serve his country. I served with a lot of men like that. They were good men."

"Were? Are they all dead?"

"A lot of them, yeah." He tried to change the subject. "You said your parents drank too much to be real parents. My pop, his idea of being a father was either ignoring me or beating me. I spent most of my time staying out of his way or trying not to set him off."

"What about your mother?"

"She was too scared of him to do anything for me. I used to wish I wasn't the youngest. I wanted a kid brother or sister."

"That's sweet. You mean, someone you could protect?"

"No! Someone weaker he would hit instead of me!"

"At least my parents didn't hit us. I think they loved us. It's just that they were both so unhappy all the time, it was like they couldn't fit us into their world. Their unhappiness took up all the space they had. I want to do it right. I want to have kids and be a real mother to them." She kissed Tommy suddenly. "I want you to be their father. I know you'll be a wonderful father."

"Maybe," Tommy said uncomfortably. "Or maybe I'd just be like my old man. Maybe it would be better if I never had kids. Maybe I'll be another ice man."

"Ice man?"

"That was my secret name for my pop. My old man almost never drank. I used to wish he was a drunk. I used to think he'd be safer to be around if he was passed out than the way he was. That cold look of his. There was nothing behind it. Ice man." In France, sometimes Tommy would imagine that his father was on the other side, wearing a German uniform. It was easy to imagine.

"I've tried to understand why they drank so much," Ellen said. "Daddy was gone a lot. He was a salesman. He traveled all over the Upper Midwest. They argued all the time. Anything would set them off. I remember one time my mother couldn't find a ring that belonged to my grandmother. Daddy's mother, I mean. Daddy said it belonged to him, and he could do anything he wanted to with it. She screamed at him. I think ... I think maybe he had a second family. I overheard my mother saying something about another wife and another child."

"Cripes," Tommy said, "that's terrible. That must have made you feel—" He caught himself. Abandoned, he had almost said. "Like his love was divided."

"Maybe it was. You know, that really didn't bother me. I used to pretend that I had a half-sister named Linda, and some day we'd meet and be best friends. Later on, I used to imagine that maybe she could be the one family member who'd stay with me, who wouldn't die and leave me." She shrugged. "Just a fantasy. After my parents died, I knew I'd never find out the truth. If I do still have some family out there, I'll never know about it."

"You wanted to hold onto your family, and I wanted to get away from mine. Strange, isn't it?"

Ellen put her hand on his arm. "We'll make a new family that you'll never want to leave."

Frank tried to throw himself into the training, too, but he missed the mental stimulation of the classroom. And no matter how he drove himself physically, how drained of energy he was by bedtime, he could not avoid thinking about Thursday morning. Not only would he be parting from Tommy and Ellen, who had become his only real friends. Not only would he be leaving Dolores Lujan and any chance, no matter how small, of establishing a relationship with her. He would also be leaving his own time, his own century, with no guarantee of ever returning to it.

Despite what they had been told about Tempus' partially successful experiments, Frank wondered if any of them would even live to see the future. He wondered whether they had been told the truth. Tempus had tested the time–travel equipment over a period of days. What would happen when the trips were over periods of decades?

We're too valuable for them to simply throw our lives away, he thought, trying to reassure himself. Not after all the money they've spent on our training so far.

But he thought of Lyman Hughes, of that impenetrable mask of a face, and he felt worried all over again.

During those days, Frank saw Dolores occasionally. It was always in passing, in the hallway or the cafeteria. Her behavior toward him was stiff and formal. When she could, she avoided meeting his eyes and tried to pretend that she hadn't seen him.

At dinnertime on Wednesday evening, February 7, Frank sat at a table with Tommy and Ellen. No one else seemed interested in joining them. The Tempus personnel who had been friendly toward them during previous weeks now avoided them. In a sea of people, they were as isolated as three sailors stranded on a rock in the ocean.

"It's like we're already time travelers," Ellen remarked. "Or ghosts. Yes, it's like we're ghosts. We can see them and hear them, but they're unaware of us."

"*Trying* to be unaware of us," Tommy said.

Ellen nodded. "Because we're ghosts, and they're scared of us for some reason. I don't know why that is, though."

Tommy laughed. "Because ghosts are scary."

"No," Frank said, "it's because ghosts come from the other side. They can infect you with death just by their presence, if you get too close to them." As he spoke, he was staring at Dolores Lujan, who was seated across the room at a table all of whose other occupants were men. Dolores seemed fascinated by the conversation of her companions, who were vying with each other for her attention.

Ellen reached across the table and squeezed Frank's hand briefly. "*I'd* choose you over any of those guys, Frank."

Frank smiled at her. "I guess a ghost shouldn't fall in love, huh?"

"Only with another ghost," Tommy said, putting his arm around Ellen's shoulder.

"She's coming this way," Ellen said. "Maybe your luck's changed."

Dolores stopped at their table. "Are the three of you finished eating?" she asked. She looked down at the table and not at them. "I wanted to show you the equipment ahead of time, so you'll be prepared tomorrow and we won't have to waste time then."

Frank answered for the three of them. "Sure, we're finished. Lead the way."

"Hey, wait, I'm not finished," Tommy said.

"Yes, you are," Frank told him. "You're putting on some weight, Tommy boy. I noticed it when I threw you this afternoon."

"Well, gee, okay, Pop," Tommy said. "Father Frank says go on a diet, huh?"

Frank nodded. "Yep. Father Frank says take some of that lard off or you'll land in 1985 instead of 1995."

Dolores looked unsettled by their banter. "If you're ready," she said, "please follow me." She turned away and headed for the nearest exit.

As they followed her, Tommy said in a low tone to Frank, "Next time, Pop, fall in love with a woman with a sense of humor."

"Next time will be a hundred and fifty years from now."

"Women will be the same."

Dolores led them through the building to an area they had never been allowed to enter before. They came to a set of double metal doors guarded by two typically large Tempus Security men with grim faces. Their grimness gave way to obsequiousness when Dolores appeared, and one of the men unlocked the double doors and pulled on one of the handles. The door swung open slowly, out toward them. The security man stood by the door as the four of them passed through. The door clanged shut behind them, and they heard a bolt sliding into place.

"I guess it'd be a problem for anyone in here if there was a fire," Tommy said.

Dolores looked at him in surprise. "Why, yes, I suppose it would be. But there won't be a fire, so don't worry about it. Come along."

"Yes, teacher," Tommy said.

Dolores ignored him and headed off down yet another hallway. The three followed her, Frank in the lead, staring intently at her back, and Tommy and Ellen in the rear, holding hands. Tommy's usual lightheartedness had vanished. He gripped Ellen's hand tightly as they walked. After a few minutes, he put his arm around her shoulder and pulled her against him, holding her as close as he could. Dolores looked back from time to time, as if she didn't trust them to follow.

Finally Dolores unlocked an unmarked, heavy wooden door and ushered them into a room. She shut and locked the door behind them.

The room was immense and filled with huge, bulky equipment. Heavy electric cables hung in loops from the high ceiling. The smell of hot insulation and metal filled the air. Thick rubber tubing was bolted to the ceiling and walls. The air was chilly, and a cold breeze blew constantly.

The strangeness of the place brought a trace of Tommy's good humor back. "Gee, you guys hired Thomas Edison, didn't you?"

"We probably would have, if he were still alive," Dolores said. "Come over here."

She led them to a point roughly in the middle of the room. Here the floor was clear of equipment. Three circles had been painted on the floor in yellow paint. One circle had a red dot in the center of it, the one beside it had a green dot, and the third circle had a brown dot. Dolores said, "Tommy, you're the red. Ellen, you're the green. And Mr. Ander—Frank, you're the brown. Look." She pointed up.

They craned their necks and looked up at the ceiling above them. Three giant contraptions of glass and metal dangled there, one directly above each of the circles. A long, thick glass tube pointed directly down at each dot.

"Doesn't look like what Wells described at all," Frank said.

"Of course not," Dolores said, surprised. "Why should it? That was fiction. This is the real thing. Tomorrow afternoon, you'll step into those circles and we'll send you forward."

Tommy was still staring at the glass and metal device depending from the ceiling. He looked down, stepped into the yellow circle with the red dot, and looked up again. "Jesus," he said. "It's all real, isn't it?"

"Oh, yes," Dolores said. "It's real, and it works. Tomorrow afternoon, you'll be off."

Ellen had joined Tommy in his circle, and the two of them stood silently, with their arms about each other.

"Ellen," Dolores said sharply, "remember that you're in the circle with the green dot. Don't get them mixed up. Everything depends on it."

"Leave them alone," Frank said quietly to her. "They've got other things to think about."

He looked at them, lost in his own thoughts, unaware that Dolores was watching him or that her face was filled with anger.

Hughes had wanted to watch the three of them being sent forward. His desire was not based on sentiment. If something went wrong, which he thought more likely than not, he wanted to see the problem with his own eyes as it happened. For post-mortem analysis of the mishap, he would of course depend on the excellent technical people employed by Tempus, Dolores Lujan chief among them. Nonetheless, atavistically, or perhaps superstitiously, despite the advanced science surrounding him, he wanted to observe it himself.

But Yalta worried him. He was sure that Roosevelt would give away too much. Perhaps Hughes could do something through his contacts in Washington. This was not a matter to be left to subordinates.

So here he was, being driven to Denver in the middle of the night, trying to read papers by flashlight. The road was rough and winding, rising and falling. Bouncing around in the back seat, Hughes struggled to stay awake and to read.

Late though it was, and despite the altitude of the road, the air inside the car was hot and stuffy. Hughes rolled the window down. The breeze was cool, but a layer of dust soon covered the back seat. Over the roaring of the car's laboring engine, he could occasionally catch the sound of a river far below.

It was too distracting. He closed the window again.

His attention drifted. He gave up on the papers and turned the flashlight off. Perhaps he'd be able to read them on the plane that would take him to Washington.

He'd always hated not being in control. He hated it now. He

wished he were driving, even while he admitted to himself that if he were behind the wheel, he would not be able to stay awake, and the car would go off the road and down into the river. He trusted his driver just as much as he trusted the people in charge of the time travel project. He trusted his people because he knew everything about them. Betrayal lurked in the gaps of his knowledge of others, and he had made sure there were no gaps. If a gap could not be eliminated, then the person was.

His thoughts mingled with stray memories that drifted into dreams. He started awake, fought against fatigue, and then began to drift again.

He remembered reports he had received eight years earlier from the construction crew building the Tempus site on what was then a barren hillside. Among the inevitable injuries and deaths, there had been one case that had worried the crew chief. A worker had stepped in front of a truck and had been hit and killed. The crew chief had written to Hughes that such carelessness was completely out of character for the victim. Hughes had shrugged it off at the time, but now that almost forgotten injury report returned to nag at him.

The summary for that day had also mentioned that one of the workers had reported seeing two unidentified people at the construction site. The worker had insisted that they were dressed in ordinary clothing, not work clothes, and he had been adamant that one of the two was a woman. The crew boss had added a note that he considered the worker unreliable. Hughes had thought little of it. There were no towns nearby—the Tempus site had been chosen partly with that in mind—and hence no fear of inquisitive locals. In any case, the guards and the fence had been put in place before the construction work had begun, so he didn't see how locals could have gained access without being seen and stopped.

But now, just like the report of that man's death, the brief description of one of the two supposed interlopers began to nag at him. The worker who had claimed to see them had had just a brief glimpse, but he had given his supervisor a description of the woman's face. It was annoyingly sketchy, but there was something about it that rang a bell. Hughes felt it should mean something to him.

His inability to focus his thoughts properly infuriated him. At last, he gave up. He realized it would be best to use this opportunity to get a short nap. He'd be in the air in a few hours, and then, his mind refreshed by sleep and coffee, he'd have time to concentrate on this.

On that last night, Tommy and Ellen spent their first night together.

Ellen had argued against taking the chance. Tempus in general, and Hughes in particular, were so odd, so unpredictable, that she feared their reaction. "They'll know I'm here," she said, not even bothering to whisper. They took it for granted that Tempus Security was watching and listening to them all the time, anywhere inside the building, including their bedrooms. "They may get angry and do something to us."

She did not put into words her feelings about the prospect of being watched and overheard while making love. She had almost become used to the thought of being watched while she dressed, undressed, and bathed. It still made her skin crawl when she allowed herself to dwell on it, so she tried not to. But this—this was an even more terrible invasion, a desecration of what should be sacred.

"It may be our last chance ever," Tommy said, and that decided her.

Later, as they were sliding into his bed together, Tommy said loudly, his words aimed more at the invisible listeners than at Ellen, "By now, they need us more than we need them. Anyway, they've got less than twenty-four hours to put up with us. Then we'll be out of their hair."

They made love frantically and clumsily the first time. By the second time, they were already more familiar with each other's bodies and rhythms, and they moved more slowly and deliberately, more involved with and focused on each other's needs and satisfaction. The third time was the slowest, lasted the longest, and was the most filled with love and the promise of future harmony and happiness despite the machinery that was being made ready for the next afternoon.

After that, Tommy drifted into sleep. He lay curled on his side facing Ellen, his forehead pressed into her shoulder, his arm across her stomach, a slight smile on his face. Ellen watched him for a while, smiling in response. Then she reached up behind her and pressed the wall button to turn off the room's overhead light.

She wondered if Tempus Security could see them still, in the dark. She realized that she had forgotten all about the surveillance as soon as she and Tommy had begun to make love. She stuck her tongue out in the darkness.

But she could not as easily defy the future. She lay awake worrying for perhaps another hour before finally drifting off.

Not far away, Frank lay awake. He turned from side to side, onto his back, onto his stomach, but could find no position that was comfortable enough to make him stop thinking and fall asleep. Every now and then he held his arm up and looked at his watch, glowing in the dark. Each time, he was surprised at how little time had passed since he had last checked.

Seconds feel like hours when you're alone in the universe, he told himself.

It had been obvious to him that Tommy and Ellen would spend the night together. He tried hard to feel happy for them. Mostly, though, he could not avoid feeling sorry for himself and envious of Tommy. He wondered what it would be like to have Ellen beside him. He wondered what it would be like to have Dolores Lujan there.

He had only made love to a woman once. It had been a brief, fumbling encounter during his last leave, three years earlier. He was sure that every other man of his age had had many sexual encounters. Depending on what happened tomorrow afternoon, he might never have a second.

With such thoughts, Frank tortured himself into the night. The last time he checked his watch, it was almost 1:00 a.m. Some time after that, he fell into a restless sleep.

He dreamed of war. He dreamed he was back in North Africa, squirming desperately into the sand as an artillery battle roared about him. A shell landed somewhere nearby. The explosion pounded at him and made his ears ring. He awoke with his heart racing and sweat covering his face.

He forced himself to breathe deeply and regularly, trying to achieve calm. He thought of Dolores and fell asleep again and dreamed of her.

It seemed only moments later that someone was shaking him awake. The overhead light was on.

Frank squinted his eyes against the light and saw Dolores Lujan bending over him. For a second or two, he confused the reality with the dream of her that he had just been enjoying.

But the real Dolores was pale and trembling. "Wake up, wake up!" she was saying. "Please, wake up!"

"Okay, okay." Frank sat up in bed, rubbing his eyes with the heels of his hands. "Oh, Jesus," he muttered. "Morning already? Why're you here?" He checked his watch. "It's only 4:00 a.m.! What's happened?"

"Something terrible," Dolores said. She looked over her shoulder quickly, making sure she had closed the door behind her. "Security just told me that Soviet agents have penetrated the project. They're planning to kill everyone and blow the place up. We don't know where they are, only that they're inside. I just tried to leave the building, but the main door wouldn't open. Then some armed men showed up and tried to grab me."

"Jesus!" Frank was fully awake. Unaware of his nakedness, he jumped from bed and grabbed Dolores's shoulders. "Are you okay?"

"Yes, I'm fine. I got away in time. Please get dressed."

"What? Oh, yeah." He turned away from her and began pulling on his clothes from the day before. "The men you ran into were strangers? They weren't from Security?"

"No, they weren't from Security. I tried a couple of the side doors, but they were also locked, and my keys don't work anymore."

Frank paused in the process of tightening his belt. "What side doors?"

"You don't know about them. I tried to get hold of Security again, but they didn't answer the phone. That's never supposed to happen. I tried to go back over to their main office, but I saw other armed men along the way, also not Security. They didn't try to stop me, but I think they're taking over the building quietly, and then they'll start to do whatever it is they're here to do."

"Kill us all off and destroy the place?"

"Yes."

"Okay, I'll go get Tommy, and we'll find some weapons. This is what we're both trained for."

"Don't be an idiot! You're not well trained enough to fight off an army. No one is. You *are* very valuable to Tempus, though, all three of you. I've got a better idea than fighting. As you said, let's get Tommy. Ellen, too. Then I'll explain."

Frank followed her from the room, admiring the speed with which she had recovered from her earlier fright and taken command.

She seemed nervous again as they were walking the short distance to Tommy's room, but they passed no one. When they reached Tommy's room, Dolores put her hand on the door handle. Frank put his hand on her shoulder and said, "Wait." He knocked. When there was no response, he knocked again.

They heard the sound of a quick, low conversation from inside. Then Tommy's voice: "Who is it?"

"Frank. There's a problem. Dolores Lujan's with me."

There was another muffled conversation. At the bottom of the door, a strip of light showed. Tommy said, "Come on in."

Inside, they found Tommy sitting up in bed, naked above the waist, covered by the bedclothes below. Beside him, Ellen lay with the covers clutched up beneath her chin.

Sexual jealousy warred in Frank with guilt at disturbing Tommy and Ellen. By a slender margin, guilt won. "I'm really sorry, both of you, but we're all in danger. Dolores, tell them what you told me."

Dolores was staring in horror at Tommy and Ellen. She shook her head. "It's all wrong," she muttered. "I don't understand this."

"Jesus, does that matter now?" Frank said. "Come on, Dolores!"

She looked at him. "What? Oh." She shut her eyes for a moment, and when she opened them, she was cool and detached again. Quickly and calmly, she repeated what she had told Frank earlier.

Tommy reacted as Frank had earlier. "We've got to arm ourselves," he said. "Frank and me. We'll take care of them."

"Out of the question," Dolores said. "There are too many of them, and you're too valuable to Tempus now." The muscles in her jaw bunched. "Think of Ellen too," she added, her voice harsh.

"So what are we supposed to do?" Ellen asked her.

Dolores stared at her for a moment, as though she had never seen her clearly before. Then she said, "The important thing now is to get the three of you out of here safely."

"But you just said there's no way out," Tommy said.

Ellen sat up and put her arm around Tommy's back. The covers slid down to her waist, but she seemed unaware that she was exposing herself. "There's still one way out."

"What?" Tommy said. "What're you talking about?"

"The future," Ellen told him. "That's the only direction we

can go in. They can't stop us." She looked at Dolores. "That's what you mean, isn't it?"

"Yes, that's what I mean," Dolores said. "The longer we wait, the greater the chance that the Soviet agents will destroy the equipment. So we have to send the three of you into the future right now. It's what we were planning anyway. We're just a few hours ahead of schedule."

Ellen said, "But I thought the equipment wasn't ready yet."

"It's ready. It's been ready for a while. The techs were testing each component and circuit, and they were going to spend a few more hours doing that, but it's probably okay as it is."

"*Probably* okay?" Tommy said.

Frank said, "We're not in a position to be picky. Let's get moving."

Tommy pushed the covers away and slid out of bed. "I guess so."

Dolores spun on her heel and stood with her back to Tommy and Ellen. Frank glanced at Dolores and then back at Tommy, who was grinning. Frank turned around and stood with his back to the two of them. Let Tommy ascribe it to prudishness on his part, he thought. The less Frank saw of Ellen in the nude, the easier it would be on him. He wished he could shut his ears to the sound of rustling clothing behind him.

"Say," Tommy said, "I just thought of something. When we get the secret of backwards time travel, up there in the future, then we can return to yesterday or the day before, or maybe even a few months ago, and nip this Soviet invasion in the bud. We'll let Tempus Security know about the penetration of Tempus long before it happens. What do you say?"

"Great idea, Tommy," Frank said. "You're a genius."

Tommy chuckled. "I'm good at what I do. Right, Ellen?"

Dolores said sharply, "Are you two ready? We have to get moving."

"We're ready," Ellen said. "Tommy, button yourself."

Dolores led them through empty corridors along the same route they had traversed the day before.

Frank kept looking around for armed Soviet agents, but he saw no one at all. The feeling of tension began to fade. He wondered if Dolores had been imagining everything. They had only her word for it that the danger existed, that there was a Soviet team moving about within the building, threatening their lives. Perhaps she had dreamed the whole thing. Perhaps she was crazy.

Frank's doubts vanished when they reached the great metal double doors. The doors were open, hanging askew from broken hinges, their inner surfaces blackened. The two Security guards lay on their backs in the corridor, unmoving, eyes and mouths open. Blood covered their chests and pooled beneath them.

Frank knelt by each man in turn, checking for a pulse. Both were dead but still warm.

"Oh, my God," Dolores whispered, "they got here ahead of us!"

Ellen tore her eyes from the two dead men. "And they're in there with the equipment!"

"Uh uh," Tommy said. "They *were* in there. The door's been blown open from the other side. They may already have destroyed everything."

"Let's hope they didn't know what they were looking for," Dolores said. "Come on." She stepped over the corpses and passed through the doorway.

Tommy followed her immediately. He still held Ellen's hand, and he pulled her along. Frank paused for a moment. He could have been back in North Africa after all, as in his dream. Always more corpses, he thought.

Now, from far away, they could hear men shouting and banging noises. They crept along the wall and looked around constantly as they went, but they didn't encounter anyone.

The door to the room containing the time–travel machinery was locked, as it had been the day before. Dolores unlocked the door quickly, motioned them all in ahead of her, and closed and locked the door behind her. In a low voice, she said, "They'll get here eventually. We have to hurry."

"What do you want us to do?" Frank asked her. In spite of the imminent danger, he found himself as fascinated as he had been the day before with the masses of equipment and cabling jamming the cavernous room. He shivered in the room's cold air, realizing for the first time how heavily he was sweating from tension.

"I want you to do exactly what I showed you yesterday," Dolores said. "You remember which circle is yours, I hope."

Frank walked over to the middle of the room, where the three circles were painted on the floor. He stared at his, the one with the brown dot at its center. He looked up at the weird machine dangling above the circle. Deep within the device, something glowed red, like the filament within a vacuum tube. Or like an eye. He took a deep breath and stepped into the circle.

He turned around to see Dolores, Tommy, and Ellen

watching him. "Fire at will," he said.

Dolores gestured. "Tommy, Ellen, go on."

Tommy and Ellen embraced each other fiercely and kissed. They clung to each other as though unable to move away.

Something thumped against the door to the room.

"My God!" Dolores said. "Hurry!"

Tommy and Ellen jumped for their circles.

Dolores bent over a piece of equipment nearby. "Just a second," she said. "That's all it takes. It's already warmed up. Hold on!"

Frank looked up. Within the device above him, the red glow grew brighter. The color shifted toward white.

Something thumped against the door again, and this time Frank heard the wood crack. He glanced over at Tommy and Ellen. They were standing so close to him that he could have reached out and touched them. Their faces were white and strained, and they were staring at Dolores, not even watching each other. Frank looked at Dolores again. He heard a loud crack from the door and men yelling.

Dolores was working steadily on the equipment before her. She glanced over her shoulder at the door and then looked at Frank.

They stared into each other's eyes. Frank had time to wonder what the exchanged look meant to Dolores before she and the room faded away and he found himself locked eternally for an infinitesimal moment in the crossroads of time.

Ten

Delia Garrison was born in Houston in 1963 in a house owned by two women named Harriet and Rosa. Her parents often talked about Harriet and Rosa and their animals and plants. "You'd have loved it there," they told her. "You'd have loved them. And they'd have loved you."

Her parents once told her that the year she was born was the year everything changed. Later, she decided that that wasn't true. For her, everything changed in 1971, just before her eighth birthday.

Once, she asked her parents about her name. "Why did you name me Delia?"

Her mother said, "We named you after a friend. She was a woman who saved my life."

"Can we go visit her?"

Her father said, "I'm sorry, honey. We don't even know where she is right now."

A lot of her parents' friends seemed to come and go quickly. The person she was named after was just another one of them, vague and unreal. Even her name sometimes seemed vague and unreal to her. Until she was eight years old, no one but her parents called her Delia. Before that, the family moved frequently and changed their names with each move. Her earliest memories were of rootlessness, of constant movement, of the awkwardness of making new friends in a new place and then of the pain of having to leave friends and place behind suddenly, without warning.

Almost as soon as she could talk, she began to ask why. Why leave this place where she was starting to feel happy, where she was trying to make friends? Why did they have to move suddenly, in the middle of the night?

Years later, she could still remember crying and her mother touching her cheek and bending over and kissing her forehead.

"I'm sorry, darling," her mother said. The lamp on Delia's chest of drawers behind her shone through her blonde hair and gleamed on the silver ones. "I know how hard it is, but we have to leave. It's not safe here any more."

It's not safe here any more. In later years, when she thought of her parents, she would hear that phrase in her mind.

Delia's father entered the room. He glanced over his shoulder. Delia didn't understand what was happening, but she sensed the urgent need to go. Even so, he too took the time to comfort her. Surrounded by their love and protection, Delia became calmer. She knew she could do her part.

There would be another long drive in their car, her parents switching off so that they didn't have to stop anywhere for the night. It would end at a strange house filled with strange people whom her parents seemed to know. There would be a new identity to learn, a new town, a new school, new friends.

Eventually, they would leave that place, too.

She fell into the habit of not making new friends. Her parents were the only constant in her life. They surrounded her with love just as they filled the house with music. It wasn't the protest songs or pounding rock favored by the people who constantly came to see her parents. It was softer, older music that her mother played constantly on their small, portable record player. The records were scratchy and worn, but her mother didn't seem to mind. She'd listen to the songs with a soft smile on her face and a distant look in her eyes. When a friend laughed at the music and told her she was listening to mere sentimental music from the wrong war, her mother said that the old songs were the best, and her father said, "All wars are the same war."

Wherever they were, their house was a meeting place. Some of her parents' friends ignored her or treated her half as a child, half as a pet. Most, though, spoke to her as though she were a fellow adult. Her parents had always spoken to her that way, and Delia expected that from adults. The grownups on the outside, as she thought of it, tended not to do that, and they also tended to react with alarm or even fear when she talked intelligently to them and as though she was their social equal. That was one of the main reasons she preferred to talk to the adults inside her house.

Her parents often speculated about where Delia's high intelligence and love of science came from. "Not from my side," her mother said. "And not from mine," her father said, and they both laughed.

They encouraged her to pursue her interests. They hoped that constant reading would keep her occupied, keep her from longing for friends, and keep her safely inside.

She did inherit some of her father's love of history. She liked to listen to him talk about it. She liked the way his face softened when he told her about ancient times and places, how the lines of worry and tension smoothed out, how he seemed to go halfway into the world he was telling her about, as though he wished he were there instead of here. She loved that look on his face, but at the same time, she would hold his hand tightly as he spoke, to keep him with her.

"Human events are like a great river," he told her. "It's enormous and irresistible, and along much of its course, no one can change its flow. But here and there, it's possible for the right man to change it. It's very difficult. And dangerous." The worried frown came back.

Delia had been thinking a lot about danger. She asked, "Could I have a doggie?"

"A dog? Honey, I don't think a dog would be happy with us."

"A big doggie. He could bark. He could keep us safe."

He knelt down and hugged her. "Oh, honey. I'm sorry. It's just not practical. We don't have the room for a big dog."

"How about a little doggie?"

He laughed. "A little dog wouldn't be able to keep us safe, would he? We'd have to protect him!"

She imagined a dog who belonged just to her and loved her and slept next to her bed and protected her. She imagined it licking her face. She imagined petting it. She never mentioned a dog to her parents again.

Inside their house, there was a sense of purpose in the air, of dedication. They were all working toward something important. Delia didn't understand it, but she sensed it. She felt caught up in it and wanted to be part of it. They let her help with making signs. There were always people in the house making signs.

When she was five, her parents let her carry a small sign in a parade. She was surrounded by excited, yelling people. There were signs and colorful clothing. Everyone was charmed by her.

Before long, she became tired. She stumbled a couple of times and whimpered.

Her mother said, "Jerry!" That was the name her father was using.

Delia's father laughed and picked her up.

"My sign!" Delia said.

"I'll hold it," her father said. "See?" He held her in one arm and he held her sign high with the other hand.

"Okay, Daddy." She put her arms around his neck and her head on his shoulder and began to fall asleep. She felt her mother's hand stroking her hair, and then she drifted away, let herself be carried away.

As she grew, Delia marched regularly with her parents. She understood more clearly what they were marching for. She knew about the war they hated, about the evil they said America was doing in a small country far away.

The moves and changes of identity came more often. She was almost eight when they moved to Oregon. Her parents put her in a small alternative school run by a couple they knew. Many of the other students were the children of faculty members at the nearby university, and for the first time, Delia thought she might be able to find some friends among them.

The school was five blocks away from home, in a quiet,

hilly, semi–rural neighborhood. In this peaceful town, her parents were finally willing to let her walk to and from school by herself. She took her time going both ways—time to look at the trees and greenery and the amusing squirrels and to listen to the birds.

She liked going this way because of a huge German Shepherd who lived in one of the yards. The other kids were terrified of him. When they passed by and he dashed toward the chain link fence, they'd run screaming, sure that the dog intended to jump the fence and attack them. The very first time, Delia had stopped at the fence, entranced, and the big dog had put his forepaws on the top of the fence and stood there, his eyes at the same level as hers, staring intently at her, and wagging his tail madly.

From then on, every time she passed the yard and the dog was there, he'd run up to the fence and she would pet him and let him lick her face, which he did enthusiastically. Sometimes, she'd save part of her school lunch as a present for the dog. She loved how neat and polite he was about taking it from her. She'd hold the food out and he would take it delicately from her fingers with his teeth, being careful not to nip her.

She had no idea what the dog's name was. Nor had she ever seen his owners. So she made up a name: Rufus. She liked to imagine that Rufus had a secret underground tunnel that led from his house to hers. She pretended that he was on guard in her house, carefully keeping himself hidden from her and her parents, but always ready to spring to the attack if anyone threatened them.

Rufus wasn't in his yard today. She stood at the fence for a while, hoping he'd appear. Eventually, she realized he wasn't going to.

She had brought a slice of chicken breast with her, wrapped in a napkin. She unwrapped the chicken and pushed it through the fence. It would make a nice surprise for Rufus when he was let out. She was sure he'd know who had left it for him.

"'Bye, Rufus," she said softly. Dogs had very good hearing. She had read about that. Maybe he'd be able to hear her. "See you tomorrow."

Her birthday was a month away. Her parents had promised her a party. She would be able to invite some of the children from school. She thought about which ones she should invite. By the time she reached home, she had settled on three names, the children she was beginning to feel most comfortable with. They would become her first real friends in this new place.

Delia smiled and walked faster. All of this had made her start to feel comfortable and at home here. She wanted to tell her parents about it. She knew they'd be happy for her.

She went around to the back of the small house as she usually did. There was a herb garden on one side of the door. That was her mother's latest enthusiasm. On the other side, there was a wild stand of greenery and wood and wires that had once been a grape arbor that had been untended for years. Delia had adopted it as her place—a shady retreat where she could read in peace and quiet and nibble on grapes from the surviving vines.

The back door was always unlocked during the daytime. She opened it and walked into the kitchen. "Mom? Dad? I'm home."

The house was surprisingly silent. The hum of conversation and the laughter of her parents' friends was so common that normally she didn't even notice it. Now she noticed its absence.

Two men entered the kitchen through the archway leading into the dining room. Both were tall, broad across the shoulders, clean shaven, and wearing suits. One was very blond, and the other was very dark. Delia's father was tall and broad across the shoulders, and she had once seen him almost kill a man who had threatened her mother, so the men's height and strength didn't seem remarkable to her. The suits, though, were something she had never seen among the adult men her parents associated with. Also, her father and all of their male friends had beards. Most of them also had long hair, unlike these two, whose haircuts were the extremely short kind her parents sometimes made fun of.

She also noticed red spots on the two men's white shirts. The dark man had a slash on one cheek, and blood was oozing from it. He moved carefully, as though in pain. The blond man held one arm against his chest with the other hand.

The two men smiled broadly at her. Even an eight year old could tell that the smiles were forced.

"Hello, Delia," the blond man said. "Welcome home."

"My name's Judy Tarrant," Delia said quickly.

The two men laughed. The one who had spoken before said, "That's okay, Delia. We're friends of your parents. We know your real name."

Friends of her parents always addressed her by her current identity. Now she was sure something wasn't right. "Where are my Mom and Dad?"

"They had to go away for a few days. They asked us to take care of you."

"Will you take me to the march? They said we could go to a march tomorrow."

Both men grimaced. "We'll see about that."

Delia kept her eyes fixed on the men's faces. At the same time, she paid attention to her peripheral vision. It was a trick her father had taught her. He had told her that he had learned it in the war. A lot of her friends' fathers had been in the war, too.

"Sometimes," her father had told her, "you can see more with your peripheral vision than by looking right at something. Don't ignore what you see from the corners of your eyes."

"You mean, like Viet Cong sneaking up on you?"

Her father had smiled. "Could be. Enemies sneaking up on you, yes."

From the corners of her eyes, she saw red splattered on the wall of the dining room behind the two men. She was sure it was blood. She was sure it was her parents' blood and that these two men had killed them.

Her mother had once said to her, "Delia, whatever happens to us, you have to live. Survival is the most important thing. Do whatever you have to. Just survive."

Terrified, grief stricken, Delia maintained a bland exterior and played along. She knew that her parents were lost to her forever. And she knew she must survive.

She was transferred to a foster family who took good, if distracted and detached, care of her. They didn't love her and she didn't love them, but she didn't care about that. She didn't need love. She had hatred.

Her hatred was intense. At times, it overwhelmed her, left her unable to function. It focused on the two men, her parents' killers. Later she began to wonder who was behind the two men. They weren't common thugs, and the murder hadn't been the result of a botched robbery. There had been planning behind it. She knew her parents had enemies, but she had never really understood who those enemies were, or why they were enemies. She hadn't even understood just how dangerous they were.

Her parents had taught her to fear strangers and to keep information to herself. That training stood her in good stead as she grew up.

She was treated well in the succession of foster homes she was placed in. For the most part, she encountered kindness and even affection. She never responded with anything beyond politeness. She couldn't. The image of her parents was always with her. As the years passed, they grew cleaner, purer, more loving, and sweeter in her memories of them. She could trust these versions of them. She could trust no one else.

She concentrated on schoolwork and did exceptionally well. Soon, though, she began to feel impatient. Physics had become her passion, and she resented the time the school system required her to spend on other courses. She wanted to concentrate on physics, and she wanted to do much more advanced work than her suburban Philadelphia high school offered.

"Mr. Courtney, it's not enough."

Courtney, the school's guidance counselor, sighed. This was exactly the kind of kid he wanted to help, but he found Delia exhausting. "Delia, you're already taking senior–level courses, and you're only a freshman. What more can we do?"

"It's not enough," she repeated. "Why won't you let me take

college courses?"

"I've told you before. I don't think that would be a good idea. Even having you in classes with the seniors has been disruptive, and it's not good for your social development. Think how much worse it would be if you were surrounded by college kids."

"If they were smart ones, it would be great."

"Maybe you think so now. Look, Delia, there's another problem, a big one. I told you I'd look into college courses for you, and I did. There are a couple of schools in the area that might be willing to let you take some courses there, but they're private schools, and you'd have to pay the tuition. I'm sure the—" He had been about to say, "I'm sure the people who're taking care of you can't pay that kind of money." Instead, he softened it to, "I don't think you should place that kind of financial burden on your folks."

She understood what he really meant. She was vague on the details and rarely thought about them, but she understood that some state agency paid her foster family to give her food and shelter. She supposed Mr. Courtney was right, and the state wouldn't be willing to pay the extra money for her to take courses at a private college. She was stuck. "Mr. Courtney, what am I going to *do*?"

"I don't know," he said honestly. "I'm sorry."

After dinner, her foster father—he wanted her to call him Dad, but she couldn't—asked her what was wrong.

"Nothing. Tough day at school."

He smiled. "You never have a tough day at school. Unless you mean socially?"

She shook her head. "Nothing. I don't want to talk about it."

"Delia, come on! Give me a chance to help you."

She looked up at him and saw the affection mingled with the exasperation in his face. She felt sorry for him, and for that reason more than any other, she told him about the college courses and the cost of tuition.

"Interesting," he said. Then he started talking about other things, and Delia realized that he wasn't really interested in her problem at all, that he was just pretending to show concern, and now he had forgotten all about it.

The following evening, a stranger showed up at the house. He was tall, broad shouldered, wore a coat and tie, and had his hair cut very short. For an instant, Delia thought he was one of the men who had murdered her parents, and she froze, terrified, unable to move, to speak, to breathe.

Her foster father greeted the man warmly and introduced him to Delia. "This is Mr. Allen. He's with the Subversion Monitoring Council. They have a scholarship program for gifted students. They're going to take care of the problem we talked about yesterday."

Allen smiled at Delia, and the similarity to her parents' murderers disappeared. "Hello, Delia." He voice was mellow and pleasant. "We've been following your progress for quite a while. You're a very promising young lady. We've arranged a place for you at a private high school in California. They specialize in bright students like you."

Delia was confused. "You mean, next year?"

"No, I mean immediately. We'll be leaving right away. You should be able to start your classes tomorrow or the next day."

Her foster mother showed up with a small suitcase. "Here you are, dear," she said. "I think this is everything you brought with you. If I've missed anything—"

"We'll send for it," Allen said quickly. He took the suitcase. He said to Delia's foster mother, "We might have someone else for you in a couple of weeks. I'll see what we have on the list. Usual arrangement."

The two foster parents smiled happily and thanked him.

"Say goodbye to everyone, Delia," Allen said.

Delia glanced at the two adults who had taken care of her for the past year. "Okay," she said. "Bye. Thanks."

Allen had a car waiting at the curb. They drove in silence. That much was a relief to Delia. She felt dazed and disoriented by the suddenness of this change in her life. If Allen had tried to fill the space with the bright chatter adults so often engaged in when confronted by a silent teenager, she thought she would have jumped out of the car.

Allen took them to a small airport where a small jet waited for them. He left her there. She was the only passenger. A woman dressed in plain slacks and blouse met her with a bland, professional smile and showed her to her seat. There was seating for a dozen people, but Delia was the only passenger. The woman who had greeted her before brought her a sandwich, which Delia ate obediently. Then, strangely and suddenly sleepy, she dozed off and didn't wake up till the airplane landed in California.

Another tall, silent man wearing a suit drove her through dark countryside to the school where she would live for the next four years.

It was an old mansion, built eighty years earlier and recently renovated. It was set among acres of beautifully landscaped grounds, surrounded by high walls and locked gates, isolated.

Delia didn't mind the isolation. The coursework was demanding, of college level, and she was allowed to concentrate on the subjects she preferred and excelled at. She was happy enough to be there with the small handful of quiet, withdrawn, serious, brilliant young people who were her fellow students.

She discovered that most of them were from rich families. She gathered that the tuition was very high. She understood that the Subversion Monitoring Council, whatever that was, was paying for her. At first she wondered why. Then she wondered what they expected to get from her in return. She told herself not to worry about that. She would take advantage of what had been given to her and let the invisible forces that controlled the direction of her life carry her along in whatever direction they desired. She didn't know enough yet to try to change any of that. Eventually she would be in a position to take control of her own life.

She graduated at the top of her class. That didn't surprise her. Nor did it surprise her when she was accepted immediately by one of the top university physics departments. Her acceptance letter said that all expenses would be covered, but no scholarship was referred to. She wondered if she was sensing again the invisible hand of the Subversion Monitoring Council, her almost parent, and she wondered if it really would be possible for her to take back control of her life in the future. She feared she was being swept along too fast, caught in rapids too powerful for any human swimmer to fight.

In the summer of 1988, an elderly man whose relatives had placed him in a retirement home in Florida, because his mind had started wandering beyond their limits of tolerance, was given the latest package of newspapers from his Michigan home town. Such packages of the town's weekly paper arrived once a month, much to the nurses' relief. It was the only thing that kept him calm.

He grabbed the first newspaper from the stack and began reading eagerly.

The front page showed a construction site. Men stood around a jumble of what looked like sticks piled on the ground. Below that was a closeup of the pile. The workers' boots showed at the right–hand side of the closeup. Mixed in with the sticks were scraps of cloth. There was a bright reflection from something that had caught the light of the photographer's flash.

The old man took off his glasses and picked up a magnifying glass he kept handy because he needed it often these days. He held it over the reflection and finally made out a ring. He stared at the ring and started crying.

Delia received her Ph.D. in 1989. She was 26 years old. This was the time, she knew, to take control of her life. The offer she received immediately from InterAgency seemed perfect for that purpose. She had never heard of them before, but from the little the recruiter told her, they were a big and well established organization. The salary they mentioned was astonishing. Above all, the research facilities and freedom they offered were far superior to anything she thought she could reasonably expect in the academic world at the beginning of her career.

Within months, she knew that InterAgency was in fact the Subversion Monitoring Council. It had changed its name a year before she completed her dissertation. It didn't take much longer before she realized that she would be in physical danger if she said anything about leaving. She had given up control of her life even more completely than she could have imagined. That should have made her furious and defiant, but she was being given funding and facilities that she could not have dreamed of elsewhere, as well as however many subordinates she asked for, and she was being allowed—encouraged—to pursue some ideas of hers about time travel. If she could go back, back to that day the month before her eighth birthday ...

It was a price worth paying. She would let others control her life now so that she could gain the power to assert so much greater control over the course of events, the power to control the present by changing the past.

When Delia began to feel that her project was a dead end, it was hard for her to accept. Her interests had broadened, and biology drew her increasingly, but biological research lacked the personal connection, the hope—however unrealistic it might have been from the beginning—of changing the past. She knew she had to be hard headed about the matter. If enough time passed with no results, she was sure that InterAgency would cancel the time–travel research project. And if that happened, what would happen to her? She had her suspicions, and they terrified her. But even if her fears for her physical safety were unfounded, even if nothing worse happened than the termination of her employment contract, what would she then do professionally? In the eyes of the outside world, she had no publications. InterAgency would not allow any of its work to be shared outside the organization.

To her enormous relief, when the time-travel project was killed, she was offered an equivalent lead position in an in-house cancer research project.

Vera Ransom, the InterAgency official who came to see her in person to offer her the new job, was surprisingly old, perhaps the oldest woman Delia had yet seen inside InterAgency. Delia had been reporting to Ransom from the beginning of her time at InterAgency but had never met her in person. She had always pictured her as younger, and at first could not square her age and grandmotherly face with the hard coldness she had sensed in her memos and occasional brief telephone calls. Ransom agreed to let Delia bring two of her top people with her, but her request to transfer the rest of her team as well was met with a refusal couched in terms that made her realize she had best not pursue the issue.

Delia's team gave her a small going–away party in the office. Everyone was smiling and laughing. Delia didn't know if they were naïve, or if they were whistling past the graveyard, or if she was simply inventing bogeymen to scare herself with.

She had learned to read between the lines. It was a survival skill in InterAgency. When she received memos commenting on her reports, mentioning the areas of progress and asking about future research directions, she reacted to what she understood to be her superiors' real interests. She could tell that they were intrigued not so much by her team's methods of killing cancer cells but by their occasional success at encouraging healthy cells to remain youthful, to keep dividing indefinitely without turning cancerous. Thinking about Vera Ransom's age, Delia could understand their interest. She changed the focus of her team's work from cancer to tissue rejuvenation. If she could eventually offer her bosses some way to rejuvenate, say, their hearts, then she thought her position would be firm and she would be able to get funding for more interesting research.

She was 31 and not yet worried about larger issues of mortality. To her, death wasn't what happened as the result of day–to–day aging. It was something visited upon one by evil men.

She needed to be in a position of sufficient power that she herself would be safe and could begin to track down two particular evil men. Science was her path to power.

But just as she was making progress, the project was terminated.

Again, it was Vera Ransom who came to see her. She walked slowly and painfully into Delia's office and said, "Shut it down."

"What? Shut what down?"

"You're brilliant, so don't be stupid. The project, Garrison. Shut it down. Close up shop. Right now."

"But we're getting somewhere! We really are. You've seen my reports."

Ransom nodded. "I know. I'm under orders from higher up."

Only now did Delia realize how bitter and angry the older woman was. "Do you have to follow them? Can't you just let us keep going?"

Ransom looked astonished. Then she laughed. "I want to live forever, but failing that, I want to live out my normal life span." She shook her head. "Shut it down, turn everything off, or whatever you have to do. Then I've got another assignment for you." She hesitated, then added reluctantly, "Also orders from above. Someone's watching out for you."

That last statement astonished Delia. It also made her uneasy. Who was watching out for her, and why? She didn't know anyone in the higher levels of InterAgency. That I know of, she thought. Given the degree of secrecy and anonymity maintained throughout the organization, she really had no way of being sure of that. What was the hierarchy, how did it work, who reported to whom? It was all kept secret—absurdly so, in her opinion. She knew who reported to her, and she knew she reported to Ransom, and that was it. Who else reported to Ransom? To whom did Ransom report?

Clearly, this was not the time to ask. For now, she accepted her good luck, or guardian angel, and also accepted her new assignment from Ransom.

It had nothing to do with science.

She found herself behind a desk managing a team of people located all over the world. Day by day, she spent her time shuffling members of her team between different projects and making sure they had what they needed to do their jobs. At that level, it was simple managerial stuff. On another level, though, her assignment was something else entirely. Her teams were shoring up governments in some places, helping to overthrow them in others. They were planting bombs and assassinating policemen. They were buying off reporters and doing away with those who refused to be bought off. They were extending InterAgency's tentacles throughout the world.

Funding came from numerous sources—from crime controlled by InterAgency, from businesses controlled by InterAgency, from national governments, each of which thought that InterAgency was working primarily for it. Delia could see that InterAgency only worked for itself and that its end goal was always control.

During the first few months in the new position, Delia wrestled with her conscience. She had joined the enemy, she had become one of the people her parents had despised, she was doing the kind of work they had spent their lives opposing. They had given their lives to oppose it!

But she was good at it. She amazed herself with just how good. She discovered that she knew exactly where to apply pressure, exactly whom to have assassinated, exactly how to corrupt a government in order to achieve the results she had been ordered to achieve.

It was an intellectual challenge.

In its own way, it was science.

And she was good it. Oh, she was so good at it.

Mom, Dad, she thought, you don't understand. I haven't joined the bad guys. These people we're overthrowing or killing, *they're* the bad guys. I know you didn't believe in killing anyone, but you were wrong. Some people need to be killed, and those are the ones we target. See, Dad? I'm changing the course of history. I'm changing it for the better. And, Mom, things are moving along a predetermined good path. But here's the important thing. InterAgency has amazing archives, records of everything. They get detailed records from government agencies everywhere, and everything gets stored in fully searchable databases. If I can keep working my way up the ladder, keep doing a good job and getting more power and authority as a result, eventually I'll be able to find out who killed you and punish them. Do you see? That's the real reason I'm doing this. It's for a good end.

I think about you all the time. I've never stopped missing

you. I've never stopped hating the two men who killed you. I fantasize about killing them in the most horrible ways I can imagine. You'd be shocked at what I come up with. That's not realistic. The reality is that I may be able to get into a position where I can use other people to kill them.

I still don't even know why you were killed. From what I can remember, I guess you were part of the anti–war movement. Maybe you were too good at what you were doing, and the government had you eliminated. Maybe those two men worked for the government. I don't care. I just want to kill them. I know how to have that done now. So you see, what I've been doing, it's really in a good cause. In the long run, I'm doing the right thing. Can you understand that?

She listened for their answer but heard nothing.

At first, she couldn't see the records she was sure she needed.

It was unbearably frustrating to get so close and then to be blocked from the next step because she wasn't at a high enough level within InterAgency. As far as she could tell, there was little rhyme or reason to it. She could view some database records, but she couldn't access others that seemed much the same as those she could view. She could see some parts of a record but not other parts, and which parts were visible and which invisible varied from one record to another. It all had the haphazard feel of something glued together in haste by a variety of people, without much planning or coordination or communication. A variety of people, she thought, each of whom had been afraid to grant too many permissions, people erring in the direction of too much security rather than too little. People who worked for a neurotic organization and who survived by never taking any chances, never risking offending anyone higher up in the organization.

The haphazardness of the databases worked in her favor. The lack of organization left openings she finally learned to exploit. The only exception she found was that personnel records were well protected. She couldn't access information about anyone at her level or above, including herself.

Many of the records in the database included links to documents, and many of those links had no built-in permission checks and pointed to documents that opened on her screen without any difficulty. Some of those documents were memos written to InterAgency managers. When the images of the memos displayed on her screen, she saw the seals of the CIA and FBI on some. The content was obscure, consisting of references to projects that meant nothing to her. What struck her was the familiarity of their tone, the sense that these were parts of a long chain of communication between equals, between personnel on both sides who were equally involved in ongoing projects.

Other memos had logos she didn't recognize, or no logos at all. They were from a variety of agencies whose names she was not familiar with and of whose existence she had been unaware. The names meant nothing to her. What, for example, did the Defense Intelligence Extraordinary Rendition Bureau do? Or the Exposure Reduction Office? These were comic opera names. An adult couldn't take them seriously.

But they were very serious.

She read the memo from the Exposure Reduction Office and saw her parents' names. The language was simple and straightforward: "IA elimination of Fred and Linda Garrison is hereby authorized."

Beneath that was a handwritten note. "Couple of longtime pains in the neck, but now they're getting dangerous. Thanks for taking care of it for us."

And below that, another note, in a different handwriting: "John Stemple and Kareem al–Bagdadi assigned. Project closed successfully. Agents will be rewarded."

InterAgency. On some level, she had always known it. Her home, her substitute family, her surrogate parents had murdered her eternally loved and yearned–for real parents. That was the devil she had sold her soul to.

I'm trapped now, she thought. The devil has my soul, and now he controls my life.

She couldn't leave InterAgency. No one could. She knew that by now. She couldn't cease doing her job well. That would have the same result as trying to leave.

She thought she no longer cared if she died. Death would at least end her guilt. The devil would no longer control her. But death would also mean that she would never be able to take revenge for her parents' murder. The only way she could see to accomplish that end required that she keep doing her job and doing it well. It was an evil means to a good end. Making that argument sickened her now, but the end still dominated her life, and achieving it was the only way she could see to achieve any kind of peace.

So Delia continued her duties with even more energy and dedication, and InterAgency continued to reward her.

Eleven

The strange, confusing dreams faded. The sun was shining on his face. How had morning come so quickly? He was cold. The covers had slipped off.

Tommy opened his eyes. He was lying on the ground, on his side, his knees drawn up to his chest.

He got to his feet. He was wearing trousers, shoes and socks, and a short–sleeved shirt. He rubbed his arms and moved around trying to warm himself.

He was standing in charcoal. When he moved, it crunched under his feet and a cloud of soot stirred and then blew away in the breeze. Bricks and shattered pieces of wood were scattered around him. The bricks and wood both bore sooty traces of fire. Sunlight reflected from metal and glass mixed in with the debris.

On the dirt in front of him was part of a mummified body.

Tommy bent forward and looked more closely. It was the upper half of a body, sex indeterminate. It was shriveled, little more than darkened skin stretched over bone, but in the sunlight he could see wisps of blond hair still attached to the skull.

Where the hell am I? he wondered.

Rocky ground sloped away before him. Wisps of yellow grass poked up between the stones. An undulating plain stretched away for miles, ending in a range of snow–capped mountains. For a moment, Tommy froze, cold within. Then, knowing—fearing—what he would see, he forced himself to turn around.

Behind him was the sheer face of a red cliff, split by a jagged crack.

Ellen, Tempus, the attack, the machines. Now he remembered it all. He was supposed to be fifty years in the future, but he had assumed that Tempus—the buildings, the people—would still be here, waiting for him. And on some irrational level, he knew he had been assuming that Ellen would be here, too.

There was nothing here. There was nothing to do but move on.

The snowcapped mountains were to the east. Fifty years before, he had seen the sun rise behind them.

The sun wasn't much above those mountains now. He guessed it was about 10 a.m.

Below him, miles away, a cloud of dust moved across the prairie. He had seen the same thing in 1945, when the bus arrived at Tempus, bringing Ellen. Maybe there was a road down there. Maybe he could reach it and get a ride to a town before the sun set and the temperature started dropping.

By the time he reached the place where he had seen the dust, Tommy estimated that it was noon. This must be spring or fall, he thought, because even at its zenith the sun wasn't very high, and the air remained cold. They had said it would be August, but Tommy didn't think it was. He was shivering, and his nose and throat were burning from the dryness. He feared that he wouldn't last much longer if he didn't find shelter, warmth, and water.

The cloud of dust had disappeared. In its place was the glow of artificial lights so strong that he could see them even in daylight. He could hear the occasional roar of a passing car or truck.

He was staggering with fatigue and the draining effect of the cold. He kept tripping over rocks. But he was drawn on by the magic of the light and sound.

What he found was a dirt road passing under a highway. The highway was straighter and flatter and had more lanes than any highway he had ever been on. It reminded him of pictures of Hitler's highway system in Germany. At the intersection was a building he guessed was a gas station, but it was enormous. The concrete plaza seemed endless, the odd–looking pumps innumerable, and the building huge and made so much of glass that its interior was almost embarrassingly open to view.

Inside, behind the counter, a young girl chewed gum vacantly and stared into space.

Suddenly, Tommy felt at home.

Best of all, there was a water fountain just inside the door. It was metal instead of porcelain, and it had a button on top instead of a faucet handle below, but Tommy knew instinctively what it was. The water that came from the spout when he pressed the button was surprisingly cold, as though it had been refrigerated despite the low temperature outside. Tommy didn't mind. He drank steadily from it.

At last he felt ready for something else, something with a kick and some heat. He straightened and said to the girl behind the counter, "Miss, can I get some coffee, or something else hot to drink?"

She gestured with her chin. Tommy found a pot on a hot plate and strangely flexible white cups without handles. He couldn't see sugar or cream, but at this point that scarcely mattered. It was the heat and the invigoration he needed.

He held the cup in both hands and breathed in the steam from the coffee for a while before sipping it. Once he had stopped shivering, he put the cup down and reached into his pocket, bringing out a handful of change. He picked up the coffee and walked back to the counter. "How much is it? A dime?" He looked at the change, wondering how far he'd get in this world on a couple of dollars.

The girl said, "It's fr—" She stared at the money in Tommy's hand, at the gleaming pure silver coins and the wheat pennies, all in mint condition. "Seventy–five cents. Refills are free."

"Seventy–five cents for a cup of coffee?" Jesus Christ, Tommy thought, what happened? He knew about the terrible inflation in Germany before the war. Was this something similar?

Grudgingly, he handed over the amount. This was terrible. How was he going to do anything, now that he was suddenly virtually penniless? How was he going to survive? And why hadn't he thought to take his wallet with him when Dolores and Frank woke him up in the middle of the night?

He was shaking, and not with cold. The coffee spilled on his hand. "Oh, d—" He caught himself. "Darn it."

"You spilled fucking coffee on my fucking floor," the girl said. "Asshole. Now I'll have to clean it up. Shit."

I think I can fit into this world, after all, Tommy thought. "Fuck you, young lady."

He looked around and spotted something that looked vaguely like a telephone. On closer examination, he wasn't sure he was right. For one thing, there was no dial. Then he looked at the rows of shiny metallic buttons on the front of the thing and saw the familiar letters and numbers inscribed on them. Buttons! he thought. Clever.

On a shelf beneath the telephone was a slender telephone directory—something else he recognized from his own time. Tommy looked eagerly in the white pages and then randomly, hopelessly, through the yellow section. There was no listing for Tempus.

He picked up the receiver, put it to his ear, and pressed the button with the large O and the word "Oper" on it. The tone in his ear startled him and then charmed him. It went on for as long as he held the button down. When he let it up, there was a purring sound and then a woman answered. "U S West. How may I help you?"

"What?" Tommy said, startled. "West? What's that?"

"U S West, sir. That's the telephone company. Can I help you with something?"

"What happened to the Bell system?"

There was a puzzled silence. Then she said, "Is there something I can do for you?"

He could hear the impatience in the woman's voice. He didn't want her to hang up on him. "I'm trying to find a telephone number. I guess I need Information."

"Directory Assistance. Please deposit fifty cents, and I'll direct your call."

Tommy fished out what remained of his money and groaned. He fumbled a couple of quarters into the slot marked *25*. After a series of clicks, another voice came on the line. This one was male, which Tommy found more disconcerting than anything else so far.

"Directory Assistance. What city?"

Tommy looked around him. "Damned if I know. Somewhere in the boonies."

"Sir? What city?"

"I told you. I don't know where I am. I'm somewhere in the boonies."

"What city do you need Directory Assistance for, sir?"

"Oh!" Tommy could see that the simplest transactions were going to require not only remarkable amounts of money but also remarkable amounts of time. "Denver. Look in Denver."

"The name?"

"Tempus. It's a company. An organization." It's salvation.

"Sorry, sir. No entry for Tempus in the Denver metro listings. Do you have another search?"

"Another—? No. No, nothing else. Thank you." Nothing else. Tempus was all he had been told to look for. The eternal Tempus, the helping hand that would always be there for all three of them, in each era. And here he was, a mere fifty years later, and it was already gone.

He would have to help himself. Just like always, he thought. He wondered who would help Ellen and Frank.

He went to one of the walls that were all glass and waited for someone to pull in for gas. All he had to do was talk his way into a ride to the nearest big city. Talking his way into things was what he did best.

East or west? He knew he was in Western Colorado, but that told him little, for he was ignorant of American geography. In fact, after the lessons forced into him at Tempus, he knew more about the history and geography of Germany and Russia than those of America. He knew Denver was east of him, though, from what Hughes had said before leaving to pick up Ellen and the other girls. And he also knew from that incident that it was only a few hours away—probably fewer hours now than then, judging from the width of that highway and the speed of the occasional car or truck rushing by.

And what cars! Tommy longed to ride in one, to drive one.

His sense of loss and strangeness was fading away. His excitement was growing.

From time to time, a car would pull into the station and its driver would get out and put gas in the tank. Tommy was intrigued by the fact that they did it themselves instead of waiting for a gas jockey.

No gas jockey, no tip, Tommy thought. That's an improvement.

Some of the drivers came into the station and paid the girl behind the counter, but to Tommy's amazement most of them drove away without paying for their gas at all. He watched more closely and realized that those drivers were inserting something into the gas pump. Dollar bills, he guessed.

The lights above the concrete plaza reminded him of the ones inside Tempus. They made the place as bright as sunlight.

An old car pulled in—old and battered, and yet still strange and futuristic by Tommy's standards. A young woman got out, pushed some buttons on the pump, and inserted the hose into the capless opening on the rear fender. Tommy watched her appreciatively. She wore skintight pants made of some kind of stretchy material that stayed molded to her curves as she moved. She was blonde, strong and athletic, and she reminded Tommy achingly of Ellen.

Tommy pushed his way through the station's doors and strolled over to the girl. "Hi," he said. "Need some help with that?"

She jumped at his voice. "No!"

Tommy persisted. "I could clean your windshield for you. Probably got bugs all over it."

"I said no. Leave me alone!"

Tommy stepped back, driven away by the fear in her face and voice. He was stunned. She was afraid of him? It made no sense.

She yanked the nozzle from her car and dropped it, and then she jumped back into her car, started the engine, and drove from the station, her tires squealing on the concrete.

Tommy stood openmouthed, watching her leave.

Gasoline dribbled from the nozzle and spread slowly across the concrete. Moving automatically, Tommy picked up the hose and managed to get it back in place in its slot in the pump. After a few seconds, there was a whirring sound and a slip of paper extruded itself from a slot in the side of the pump. Tommy tore it off and stared unthinkingly at it. He let it slip from his fingers and watched it flutter to the ground.

Either the young woman was mad or this world was.

Tommy retreated to the warmth of the station and took up his watch again. Just in case it was the world that was mad, he decided he'd wait for a man to pull in for gas before trying again.

It took longer than he anticipated. There were more women driving alone on the highway that he would have expected.

Two men in a pickup truck drove in. Tommy began to open the station door, but when the two men—both young, muscular, wearing t-shirts, jeans, and cowboy boots—stepped from the truck and looked around them, Tommy could tell they were hoping for trouble. He was certain that if he hitched a ride with them, they would do something that would force him to kill them, and he didn't want to start off in the new world that way. So he moved back inside the station and waited while they filled up their truck's gas tank, looked around again, and, looking disappointed, climbed back into the truck and drove away.

Fifteen minutes later, a car pulled in that fascinated him. It was black with discreet gold trimming, and its curves were just as discreet. It murmured wealth and taste. The symbol on the front—a tilted L in a circle—was unfamiliar. A Lincoln, Tommy thought. The Lincoln company must have changed its logo.

The man who got out was around forty. He too stood by his car for a moment and looked around, but it was a friendly look. Tommy watched while he inserted the nozzle and then began cleaning his windshield with the sponge and squeegee stored next to the pump. When the man was fully occupied, Tommy strolled out.

"Say, mister, I'll wash your windshield in exchange for a ride to Denver."

The man looked startled, just as the young woman had, but then he smiled. "Works for me. Make sure you get all the bugs off."

Small though it was, that smile was the first friendly

gesture Tommy had encountered in this strange world.

"My name's Greg," the man said. "What's yours?"

"Tommy. I'm Tommy. Thanks, mister."

Later, when he climbed into the car, Tommy was delighted by the warmth inside and by the feel of the leather seats. As they were accelerating up an entrance ramp onto the highway, Tommy felt himself being forced into the seat. "This is some car!" he said. "What kind of Lincoln is it?"

"Lincoln? Are you kidding? This is a Lexus. An E–400."

"Lexus?" Tommy turned the unfamiliar name over in his mind. It was a name he'd never heard before. "They don't have those where I come from."

"Where's that?"

"Back East. Small town. So where's this Lexus Company?"

"Must be a really small town. Lexus isn't really a company. They're made by Toyota."

"Don't know that one either."

Greg glanced over at him. In the bright glow from the dashboard, Tommy could see his amazement. "You've never heard of Toyota? The biggest car company in Japan? Destroying Detroit almost by itself?" He shook his head.

"A Japanese car? This is a Japanese car?" Tommy shivered in revulsion. He wanted to pull away from all contact with the seat. "They're the enemy!"

Greg snorted. "What, you mean buy American to save American jobs?" He slapped the dashboard. "When America builds a car this good, I'll buy it. That's the way capitalism works."

"No, I mean the war!"

Greg almost lost control of the car. "The war!" he shouted.

"Are you crazy? They dropped the bomb on Hiroshima on the day I was born! That was fifty years ago! The war's been over since long before you existed. Jesus Christ, what're they teaching you kids out there in those farm towns?"

Tommy sensed that he was about to be ordered out of the car. "Sorry, Greg. It's ... my pop. He was in Normandy, and he's never gotten over it. I guess he filled me with a lot of hatred for the Krauts and Nips."

"Jesus! Call them Germans and Japanese, okay? I don't like that kind of language."

"Yeah, sure. You're right. I guess the world has changed."

"Damned straight. Good thing, too."

They drove in silence for a while. The darkness reminded Tommy of the blackness of the night he had sometimes watched from his balcony at Tempus—the polar opposite of the bright, noisy nights where he had grown up. As a kid, he'd spend hours trying to fall asleep despite the constant sounds of human voices and radios and gramophones. In the summer, even a sheet was too much cover. He'd lie naked and sweating. In winter, he'd shiver beneath a single, inadequate cover. No matter how strange this world was and how little he fit in, he was glad to be here instead of there.

Ellen ... Well, that was another matter. For now, he tried to put that aside.

Finally, Greg spoke again. "I guess your dad must have been around my age when you were born."

"About twenty, I think," Tommy said without thinking.

"Twenty! What? How can that be?"

"I mean, my ma was about twenty. She was his second wife." I'm going to have to make up a believable life story for myself, Tommy thought. And then memorize it.

"Lucky guy," Greg muttered. "Well, I guess I can kind of understand your dad's attitude. My dad was in the war, too. He was in the Pacific, and my mom was back home pregnant with me and with a couple of older kids to take care of." He shook his head. "I guess it was pretty rough on both of them. When I was growing up, my brothers and me, we'd try to get him to tell us about the island fighting, but he never would. The only thing he'd say was that he'd seen things and done things that he never wanted to talk about again. I guess you kill men on the other side in a situation like that because you have to or they'll kill you, but you feel guilty about it for the rest of your life."

"I guess so," Tommy said, trying to imagine feeling that way and not succeeding.

"But I'll tell you what," Greg said. "My dad and his friends, they were heroes. They saved the world. They beat the Germans and the Japanese. Just a bunch of American boys, and they did all that. And they were men of their word. They grew up when Americans were honest and upright. People were moral and reliable back then. Nowadays, all that's gone out the window. I don't know what's happened to this country."

"Oh, yeah. Things have really changed since then. My pop was always telling me how everything was a lot better when he was young."

"Wonder what it would be like to go back to those days," Greg said wistfully. "You know, time travel."

Tommy went rigid for a moment. He tried to keep his voice calm. "Travel backward in time? I'd love to do that."

Greg nodded. "Me, too. Like in that sci-fi movie, the one about the Terminator. Except that I wouldn't want to meet the

Terminator. I'd like to meet the babe who was in it, instead. Wish that stuff was real."

"A movie," Tommy said. He relaxed into his seat.

"Yeah. That was a good one."

"I guess I missed it."

"Jesus, that must be a small town! No wonder you're heading for the big city."

"To look for the secret of backward time travel." Tommy laughed to convert it into a joke. "Think it'll ever happen, Greg? You ever heard anything about it?"

"Maybe it'll happen some day. Maybe not. Some guy tried to explain to me once why time travel's scientifically impossible, but I couldn't understand it. Anyway, he seemed to know what he was talking about."

Tommy sighed. So if backward time travel existed in this era, it was a secret. For that matter, if the forward–travel abilities developed by Tempus in the 1940s still existed, that was apparently a secret as well.

"So what're you going to do when you get to Denver?" Greg asked.

"Christ, I don't know. Make my way, somehow. Get a job, I guess, and see what the situation looks like. I've got some friends who're supposed to be showing up in town eventually. Well, they're going to try to make it, anyway. I'd like to be in a position to help them. I also want them to be able to find me."

"That's the spirit!" Greg said. "Job market is hot in Denver right now. A young guy like you should have no problem getting work and moving up. Get yourself some warm clothes first, though. You're lucky it's been so warm out here lately, or you'd be dead already, dressed the way you are."

"Yeah, sure. What about skills? That could be a problem with finding a job." I know how to kill in three languages, Tommy thought. How's the market for that?

But Greg's optimism was undimmed. "Start out unskilled. There's lots of manual temp work. Just keep your eyes open for something better, and it'll come along. Tell you what. There's a temp place out on East Colfax. That's almost on my way. I'll let you off there. Bet you can pick up some work today even. Get in a couple of hours before dark, make a few dollars. Find yourself a room for the night, or at least buy a warm coat at a thrift shop. You'll get your start right away."

"Great! Greg, this is a good year to be alive and in America."

"Damn, Tom, I wish more young people were like you!"

The highway carried them over a rise and suddenly Tommy saw Denver spread out far below, sprawling across the prairie from north to south and east to the horizon. "My God, it's big!" he said.

Greg glanced at him, surprised. "Not compared to the cities back East. You must've seen bigger."

"Sure, but you don't see them," Tommy said quickly. "Not really. The air's too dirty, and you don't get up above them like this."

"Oh." Greg nodded. "Yeah. That's true."

The conversation lagged. Tommy concentrated on what lay ahead. Much of the time, the city was hidden from view and he could see only the surrounding hillsides and the expensive houses crowded onto them. Now and then, the highway turned in such a way that he got another glimpse down to the plains and the city. They were drawing closer to the city all the time, so that with each of these glimpses he could see more of it.

The sun was setting behind them. The mountain valleys were in shadow. Ahead of them, the glass and steel office buildings gleamed in the sun.

He was surprised at the buildings' straight edges and sharp corners and the abundance of glass. He had expected something more like the Empire State Building in this city of the future—more concrete, graceful arcs at the top. And where were the elevated ramps and flying cars?

Disappointed, Tommy looked away from the city and at the dirt and rocks and scrub grass racing by. The ground hasn't changed, he thought. Perhaps the world had changed less in fifty years than everyone back in his time had expected it to.

If it hasn't changed very much, he thought, how likely is it that these people have discovered how to travel backward in time?

Without that discovery, why was he here? What was the point in what he had done, in the risks he had taken, in the separation from Ellen?

Despite those thoughts, as they dropped lower and the city grew nearer and larger and the highway filled with more of this era's sleek, powerful cars, Tommy's pulse raced. This was a world filled with power and opportunity. This was the future, and he was in it.

Twelve

Greg dropped him off on a busy street lined with cheap restaurants and rundown office buildings.

"That's the place to look for work," Greg said, pointing at the one-story office building he had stopped in front of. Groups of men dawdled in front of it. "Watch your back, Tom." He shivered and looked around with fear in his eyes. He seemed eager for Tommy to leave the car.

Tommy got out and stood on the sidewalk, looking around. They had followed a bewildering route along freeways and city streets, and he didn't even have a mental picture as to where in the city he was. He had questions he wanted to ask Greg. Before he could say anything to him, Greg leaned over, said, "Good luck," and pulled the car door closed. He pulled away from the curb into a gap in the traffic and was gone.

This world is kind of like Normandy, Tommy thought. You meet new people, and then they disappear on you before you can get anything useful out of them.

Tommy walked up to one of the men lounging against the side of a building. "Hey, buddy," Tommy said, "is this the right place to look for work?"

"Read the sign, dumbass."

For a moment, Tommy considered injuring the man. But that would probably mean legal problems, just as it would in his own time, and he needed to avoid the law, not draw its attention. So he shrugged and turned away. This world wasn't much like Normandy, after all. Back there, the people who spoke English understood that they were on the same side.

The building he was standing in front of, the one Greg had pointed to, had a sign painted on the window reading

TEMP WORK
NOW HIRING

By God, Tommy thought, I *am* a dumbass. He decided he liked that word.

Inside, the building seemed to be one large room. It was filled with people milling about. Desks lined the walls, and some of the people were lined up in front of the desks. The floors were scratched wood, creaking slightly under the shifting crowd. The air was dusty, and it was hazy with cigarette smoke.

The idea of joining a bunch of beaten–down men lining up obediently before a desk sparked unpleasant memories in Tommy. He looked around.

There were sheets of paper plastered all over the walls. Curious, Tommy walked over and took a closer look.

They were forms of some kind. Thanks to the Army, he had learned to hate forms, but he had also come to appreciate their importance. These forms tuned out be job advertisements.

Tommy's initial excitement quickly turned to despair as he

read one list of required skills after another that he not only didn't have but didn't even recognize. What the hell was a system administrator? Or Unix? The salary ranges for those jobs took his breath away. Christ, a man could spend one year on the job and then retire and live the life of Riley till the end of his days! Then Tommy remembered the cost of coffee and phone calls in this era and realized that even the kind of money he saw on the ads wouldn't last for very long.

Still, the salaries quoted were remarkable. He wondered if he could bluff his way into one of those jobs, the way he had bluffed his way into Tempus. He decided that was a silly idea.

Mixed in with the ads for jobs he knew nothing about were a few for jobs he knew all too well. The Army was recruiting. So was the Air Force—a name that confused him at first, but he decided it must be a new name for the Army Air Corps. So were military forces he had never heard of, but the ads had government seals at the top, making Tommy think that these were also new or newly named U.S. government military organizations. There were some ads offering good pay to men who knew weapons and were willing to work outside the country, and these ads did not have anything on them to indicate that the government was involved. They wanted men with military experience and without families.

Private armies? Tommy thought. That's interesting.

There were quite a few of those. He was both tempted and repelled. It was work he knew and was good at. Presumably it would be dangerous, but he felt sure he could get one of these jobs right away, and then he wouldn't have to worry about money. He'd have some kind of security while he set about finding the secrets he had been sent here to find. Although if these private armies were anything like the government army he had had known, he wouldn't have much opportunity to pursue his mission. He'd be under the control and eye of other people. He'd hate that.

It was something to keep in mind for the future, in case it became necessary. For now, Tommy decided he'd look for normal civilian work.

He read more of the job openings posted on the wall. He couldn't see anything that didn't require special skills—either skills he had never heard of, or skills he possessed but preferred not to use again.

He looked again at the people lined up in front of the desks. Their clothes were dirty and in ill repair. The men and women themselves were dirty and looked physically broken down. He could smell them.

Christ, Tommy thought. They didn't meet the requirements of the jobs on the walls, either. They're all in the same boat as me. That's where I belong, with them.

He felt he had little control over events, little choice regarding his actions. It had been that way ever since he had handed over control of his life to the Army and later to Tempus.

With a sigh, Tommy stepped to the end of one of the lines.

The line moved slowly. There was an occasional mutter of conversation, but for the most part the people around him were silent. Their expressions were dull and resigned. They were, Tommy thought, like debris being carried along by a slow but irresistible river.

He looked at them more closely. Debris: yes, that's what they were. The debris of their world, the worthless garbage that had fallen to the bottom. What of the great opportunities Greg had spoken of? There were opportunities in my world, too, Tommy thought. For those who were able to grasp them or who had opportunity handed to them. For most people, though, the good life was something they saw in the movies. It was probably the same here.

He reached the desk at last. The middleaged woman seated behind the desk pulled a form from the top of a stack beside her right hand, put it down in front of her, and glanced up disinterestedly at Tommy. "Name?"

"I'm hoping for some kind of semi–skilled work. I've been studying system administrator and Unix stuff, and I think I'd like to work my way into that."

"Name?"

"Yeah, I'll get to that. So what kind of work do you have for me?"

"*Name?*"

Bitch, Tommy thought. He smiled as charmingly as he could and said, "Thomas Stillwell. Tommy."

"Thomas Stillwell," she said. She wrote on the form. "Social Security Number?"

"Hell, I don't have one of those."

The woman put her pen down. "Then we don't have any work for you. No one's gonna hire you without that number." Her eyes narrowed slightly. "What are you, some kind of illegal immigrant?"

Right. I'm a refugee from Nazi Germany. "Do I sound like an immigrant?"

She shrugged. "I could care. Come back when you've got an SSN."

"How do I get one?"

Someone behind him said, "Hey, man, move it!"

Tommy turned and looked at the men behind him. None of them met his eye. He turned back to the woman behind the desk and repeated his question.

She seemed suddenly more cooperative. "Go to the Social Security office. There's one downtown. Show them your birth certificate, and they'll probably take care of you. Now, please leave the line. There are people waiting."

Tommy nodded and left the line. Nice to know I can still scare people, he thought.

But he wouldn't be able to scare the government.

He vaguely remembered when the government had started issuing Social Security numbers. He must have been around twelve at the time. It wasn't the sort of thing he had paid attention to at that age, but he still remembered his father railing against the scheme in general and Roosevelt in particular. As far as his father was concerned, Roosevelt was an agent of the Bolsheviks and the international Jewish bankers, and the new Social Security numbers were part of a Jewish–Communist plot to control every aspect of every American's life. Rosenstein, as his father had always insisted on calling the president, was a traitor and should be taken out and hanged. Tommy's father would never give in. He would never have one of those numbers. And neither would any member of his family.

Thanks, Dad, Tommy thought.

Not that it would have made any difference if Tommy had had a Social Security number. He couldn't use the same number now. Or his real birth certificate. Imagine the alarm bells either of those would set off now! He would be pegged as a hoodlum who had stolen the papers from an old man or a dead man.

So he was stuck.

He looked toward the job ads on the wall and was briefly tempted. No. He was here to stop the killing, not to add to it.

Tommy left the building with no idea where to go or what to do. On the sidewalk outside, he stood and looked up and down the street. One direction was as good as another—all downhill, all downstream.

"Hey, man. Looks like you didn't find anything in there."

Tommy looked the man up and down. He had been aware of his approach but had dismissed him as not being a threat. Now he looked at him more carefully.

The man's clothes were newer and cleaner than the clothing of those inside the office Tommy had just left or the clothes of the men lounging against the wall of the building and watching Tommy with dull interest.

"Nothing up my alley," Tommy said.

The other man grinned. "Nothing up your alley," he repeated. "Yeah, I know how that goes when you're between jobs. Maybe I can help you."

"I don't rob banks."

The other man laughed. "Nothing illegal. Ordinary work."

"Not advertised in there?" Tommy nodded toward the office behind him.

"That's right. Not advertised anywhere."

"So what's the catch?"

He shrugged. "No catch. You're young, you look healthy. You come out of there with that look on your face that tells me there's some kind of legal problem that keeps them from giving you work. Immigration problems, criminal record. Something. Thing is, I don't care. I've got people who want workers, and they don't care, either."

"So, no Social Security Number?"

The other man laughed. "Is that your problem? You worried about your future?"

Tommy shook his head. "The future isn't real. There's only the present."

"That's right." He looked at his watch. "So, what do you say?"

"What's the pay like?"

For the first time, the other man looked angry. "It's whatever your boss decides to pay you. Make up your mind."

You mean, *if* he decides to pay me, Tommy thought. Some kind of crappy work for crappy money. He knew had no choice, that it was this or being back in uniform, killing people. He was in the grip of events, of currents beyond his control. He hadn't gone forward in history; history had taken control of his life. He hated it, but he was powerless, and he would never escape.

"Understood. I'm in."

Sometimes, when he looked around at this bright city with its gleaming, futuristic buildings and the healthy young people hurrying by, so self-absorbed, so self-important, none of it seemed real. 1945 was real. 1995 was a dream. In a dream, killing meant nothing. You could kill dream people without any guilt.

He tried not to think about that. There were boxes to be loaded and unloaded, dishes to be washed, meager sums of money to be earned.

It kept him fed and it bought him a room stinking of urine and feces in an old building on 23rd, just north of downtown.

He'd probably have been better off sleeping under a bridge, as so many other men in his situation did, but he wanted an address with his name attached to it. A telephone number would have been even better, but that was financially impossible. The address would have to do. It would be a way for them to find him—his time-traveling friends, his rescuers.

He could do nothing in 1995. His mission was dead. Rescue was all he looked forward to now—rescue and return to his own time and to Ellen.

Rescue required survival. That was his focus.

His hands grew callused and his patience short. The money—paid to him every day after work—would have been a small fortune in his own time, but here it barely sufficed to keep him fed and clothed. Sometimes, he couldn't make it stretch to cover food and had to eat at a nearby mission—food he paid for by listening to sermons and signing whatever pledge was put in front of him.

There was a TV set at the mission. Usually, it was tuned to a religious channel, but sometimes, when the staff members weren't in the room, the mission's "clients" changed the channel, searching hopefully for sports and usually settling for news. Pictures of disasters and wars elsewhere seemed to comfort them even while it brought out a human, sympathetic side that Tommy didn't see in them otherwise.

1995 was a world at war. There was no large war, especially not by the standards of a man who had been in the midst of World War Two not long before. There weren't even many medium-sized wars. But watching the news, Tommy could tell what the citizens of this era perhaps could not, that small wars abounded. These wars were small in terms of geography and the numbers of soldiers involved, but they were long lasting and dirty. And they were everywhere. Usually, they weren't called wars. Instead, they were police actions or government crackdowns against terrorists or drug lords or anti–government guerillas—evil forces somehow linked together into a shadowy, worldwide conspiracy against order and decency.

Tommy knew better. He also knew that what he saw on the news explained the job ads for private soldiers. Mercenaries, they called them now.

He had seen Tempus as his chance to escape from Hell. Tempus had sent him forward in time to a world where Hell was part of the fabric of existence.

There were nights, before he went to sleep, when Tommy did something akin to praying—not prayers to an imagined God, but thoughts sent out into the timestream: Ellen, Frank, anyone, for God's sake, come here and rescue me!

If you can.

It was 6:00 o'clock. Tommy carried the wooden crate from the back of the truck trailer, down the ramp, and into the furniture warehouse. He held it in front of him, his arms around it, fingers laced under it, bending backward to keep his balance. It was a warm day and Tommy was sweating, but he wore the coat he had been given at a mission on 18th Street. Otherwise, as he had learned quickly, his forearms would be filled with splinters.

The warehouse echoed with the voices of the other men. Outside, the roar of truck traffic on the nearby Interstate was constant. The air was filled with the stink of exhaust fumes and unwashed bodies. Tommy noticed none of it. His attention was on the work most immediately, and then on the fifty dollars he had coming to him for his ten-hour day.

Tommy's legs were shaking with fatigue. He didn't seem to be getting used to this work or getting stronger from it. It was breaking him down.

He staggered over to the pile of crates he had already unloaded and stacked. Gasping, he put the crate he was carrying down next to the pile with a crash, then turned and sat on the box. He ought to pick it up and put it atop the others, but he didn't think he could.

He sat there for a long time. His head drooped until his chin rested on his chest. He began to dream—of Ellen, as always.

Someone yelled.

Tommy jerked awake and fell off the crate, onto the concrete floor.

He heard the box crack. Something bounced onto the floor, ringing. It was a mallet, heavy enough to have broken Tommy's head.

"Jesus Christ! You crazy? You coulda killed him!" It was Chuck, the supervisor for Tommy's team. He was looking up at a catwalk above them, yelling, his face pale with shock. In the harsh light, sweat gleamed on his forehead.

Tommy looked up to see a man looking down at them from the catwalk. The brilliant lights were just above the catwalk, behind the man, casting his face into shadow. He yelled down, "Sorry! Accident! Is everyone all right?"

Chuck shouted, "What?" In a lower tone, he added, "God damned immigrants."

Only then did Tommy realize that the man above had spoken Russian.

A chill ran down Tommy's spine.

The man above threw up his hands and moved back, fading into the shadows. Tommy heard his footsteps as he ran along the catwalk, and then even that disappeared.

"Fucking foreigners," Chuck said. "They're all day workers. They pick up their cash and they're gone. No addresses. I don't even know who that guy was. You recognize him?"

Tommy shook his head. "Never seen him before." But he knows me. That's why he's here, in this place and time: to kill me.

"You okay? Maybe you should get looked over, just in case."

Tommy was surprised and touched by the supervisor's concern. "No, I'm fine. Is it okay if I collect my pay and leave now? I don't think I can do any more."

"Hey, yeah, sure. Of course. I should get you to sign a release first, though. A waiver of indemnity, or whatever they call it."

Tommy laughed. So much for Chuck's concern. "No problem."

Accompanied by Chuck, Tommy went to the office and signed the waiver. He collected his day's pay and left. The address he had written on the waiver would be valid until he got back to his room and packed his few belongings in the backpack that was his only piece of luggage.

There was no more kindness or concern in this age than in his own. There was no great war raging in Europe and Africa and Asia, but men had no more love for their brothers now than in 1945. As always, Tommy was on his own and in danger. Forget the fixed address, forget the rescuers from the timestream. He had to move and keep moving. He had to spend no more than a day or two at a job. It was terrible to think that Ellen or Frank wouldn't be able to find him, but it was even more terrible to think that by staying too long in one place he would make it easy for time–traveling Soviet agents to find and kill him before rescue could arrive.

He was walking rapidly along the sidewalk on Curtis Street, headed home, when it struck him: It would be impossible for his rescuers to find him, so he would have to find them. Somehow, he had to become more transient in order to protect himself, but at the same time he had to acquire sources of information so that he would know when Frank or Ellen or someone else from Tempus arrived.

Even if they didn't find out how to travel backward in time and come looking for him, he knew exactly when and where Ellen and Frank would arrive. He knew from his own experience that Tempus's forward time travel worked. That meant that Ellen would arrive at that site in western Colorado in 2045, and Frank would arrive there in 2095.

Tommy would be dead long before Frank's arrival, but if he took care of himself, he had a good chance of surviving to greet Ellen.

Yeah, he told himself, and she'll still be 22, but you'll be 71!

He could imagine the scene: Ellen as fresh as beautiful as he remembered her, standing confused on that barren hillside. Tommy coming toward her with his arms open wide for an embrace. Ellen recoiling, unable to disguise her revulsion.

Seeing that look on her face would kill him. Better to kill himself now and never experience that.

Well, I'll deal with that problem later, he decided. For now, I've got to take care of each day as it comes.

Tommy spent the first few hours of that night leaning against a tree in a downtown park. It was cold, but he had spent colder nights sleeping in the open in Normandy.

To his right, at the south end of the park, the rounded top of the new central library building was an ominous silhouette against the stars. Facing him across a stretch of green was the lighted dome of the state capitol. It occurred to him that unlike the office towers in the business center or the new library, the capitol's dome must have been there, looking exactly the same, in 1945. He chewed this idea over drowsily. He began to dream of youth and age, of timelessness and decay.

A movement startled him awake.

Someone had tugged at his backpack. Tommy came to his feet yelling even before he was fully awake. The sound of someone running faded away into the night.

Dangers all around in this world, Tommy thought. Thieves from this time, Soviet agents from his own. If the agents came across him sleeping out here, that would be the end.

For the rest of the night, he walked.

He felt half asleep when he reported for work at the temp agency the next morning. He was shivering, and his legs felt like lead. He forced himself to move briskly and look strong and energetic. He couldn't risk being passed over for the day.

He got another assignment unloading boxes at a loading dock and managed to make it through the day. But by quitting time, he could barely stand.

As the men were lining up to receive their day's pay, Tommy was overcome by dizziness. He staggered and almost fell against the man behind him. The other men moved away uneasily as though afraid of catching something from him. "Just tired," Tommy said. "It's okay. Just tired."

"Watch that drinking," one of the other men said. "Don't do it until after they've paid you, or they won't want you back tomorrow."

"Just tired," Tommy repeated. "Couldn't sleep on the street. Walked all night."

One of the men put his hand on Tommy's shoulder and said with concern, "Try the shelters. You can spend the night, clean yourself up in the morning."

Another man laughed. "Yeah, and wake up with all your stuff stolen. And maybe a knife in you."

Tommy felt a hand in his hip pocket. The touch was deft and light, well done, but Tommy had grown up around much defter pickpockets. He spun around, grabbed the man's wrist, bent it back. The pickpocket shouted in pain and anger. Tommy's wallet dropped to the floor.

Tommy pushed the other man away and bent quickly and scooped up his wallet. He realized that the other men in line had formed a circle around him and the would–be pickpocket. Larry was the man's name. Tommy knew that much about him. He was large and beefy, towering over Tommy.

Tommy was fully awake now. He felt alive in a way he hadn't since that moment in Normandy when he had killed the young German. He didn't have a rifle this time, but he had something better for this situation—the deadly skills Tempus had trained into him.

Larry saw something in Tommy that made him back away and try to escape, but the circle of men wouldn't let him through. He moved sideways, trying to find an opening, but keeping his face toward Tommy all the while.

Tommy turned slowly, easily, light on the balls of his feet. His arms hung relaxed by his side. He smiled at Larry. "If you can take my wallet now, you can have it."

Larry seemed to shrink. "Please! I didn't mean anything!"

Suddenly none of it meant anything. Tommy could kill this man easily, but then what? This wasn't Normandy during war time. This was America, this was peacetime, and this was an age when records were kept fanatically and the law was everywhere.

Tommy relaxed. He waved his hand. "Let him go."

The circle of men opened immediately. Larry ran through the opening and kept running.

The terrible fatigue came rushing back. The brief rush of adrenalin had pushed his problem aside for a moment, but it hadn't solved anything.

The man who had suggested the shelter earlier—Rob, that was his name, Tommy remembered—said, "Man, I've never seen anyone scare Larry before. Hey, man, I rent a one–room place on Colfax. It's got a couch. You could sleep on it tonight." His face was filled with admiration.

Someone else said, "Hell, you can stay with me. I've got a couch, too. I'll take the couch, and you can have my bed."

Others chimed in, wanting him to stay with them instead.

Tommy looked around at them. He had seem the same look of sheepish admiration in the faces of other boys when he was growing up. He had learned early that they would instinctively follow the one among them who was daring and aggressive. He had seen that again in Normandy. It was fortunate, he thought, that some things didn't change.

To Rob he said, "Thanks. I appreciate the offer. I'll take you up on it." A good leader always rewarded the foremost among his followers. To the others, he said, "I'll take you all up on, one night at a time, so I won't impose on anyone. Just till I get the money together for a place of my own." A good leader didn't neglect the rest of his followers.

This would fit in well with his need to move around and his need for safe shelter. That and the temporary work would take care of his immediate needs for now. He'd be living day to day, but he also needed to start planning ahead.

Thirteen

What had happened to Tempus? Knowing the answer would make no difference in Tommy's life, but he felt an urgent need to know.

On a weekday when he had no work, Tommy walked south through downtown Denver, headed for the main library. He had been sleeping on the couch in the two-room apartment of one of the men he worked with, one of his new followers. It was probably time to move on, and perhaps he should have been using this free time to look for another place to stay. He had decided to accept the risk and look for information instead.

Autumn was beginning. The leaves on the saplings lining the street he was walking along were turning yellow. It was a pleasant time to be out walking. Tommy slowed down and tried to forget about his situation, about Tempus, about Soviet assassins. He tried to enjoy the crisp, cool, dry air. He looked at the young trees and the young women walking by and thought that it was good to be alive and young himself.

All that was missing was Ellen. He tried to push that thought away.

The main building of the Denver Public Library, south of

downtown, had just reopened after major renovation. He had to skirt construction and enter through a new side annex, but Tommy was delighted with the size and newness and cleanliness of the place. Life seemed generally brighter today.

He went to the desk marked *Information*. The young man behind it glanced at Tommy and, before Tommy could say anything, pointed and said, "Restrooms are that way. You're not allowed to wash yourself in them."

"Thanks for the information," Tommy said. "But I wanted to know where the newspaper archives are."

"Oh, newspapers." The young man's expression became a bit less hostile. A dirty bum who read newspapers was a small step up from being utter filth. "Third floor."

Tommy looked over his shoulder at the staircase in the center in the room.

"Staircase only goes to the second floor. You'll have to take the elevator."

An elevator to go up two floors, Tommy thought. His father had complained about the decadent world of the 1930s and 1940s and how the country had deteriorated since his boyhood. Tommy could just imagine what he would be saying now. Maybe he *is* saying it, Tommy thought. Maybe he's still alive. His father would be close to 100, but Tommy had always thought he was such a mean bastard that even the Devil wouldn't want him in Hell, so maybe he was still stuck up here on earth, making everyone around him miserable.

Jesus, he thought, I could look the ice man up, just so I could spit in his evil, old face.

On the third floor, Tommy found the newspaper section, but he couldn't see any place where old editions were stored. He asked at another desk, this one manned by a pretty young woman. Tommy turned on the charm, but he could tell that all she could see was a dirty, beaten-down man who looked like he lived on the streets.

"I'm looking for your old newspapers," he said to her. "I need to find out about something that happened in Colorado in 1945. In February."

"That's all on microform. I'll retrieve it for you, and you can use one of the readers over there."

"What? I'm sorry, Miss. I'm from a small town, and I don't know what you're talking about."

For a moment, he feared she'd lose patience with him. Instead, he had apparently touched on something that interested her. She became enthusiastic as she found the microforms for the period he wanted and then showed him how to insert them into the reader and search through them.

He watched her adjusting the machine. There was a slight smile on her face. She was clean and pretty and suddenly he yearned for her. Then he saw the newspaper page displayed on the screen in front of him, February 4, 1945, and this ghost world and all its ghost people disappeared and he was jerked back into his world, the real world, the world of 1945.

Before him was a photograph of a banquet table. In the center of the frame was Roosevelt. To his left, Churchill, wearing a naval uniform. They were turned slightly toward each other. Tommy thought Churchill was speaking quietly and Roosevelt was listening while seeming to be directing his attention elsewhere. Stalin sat on Roosevelt's other side, also in uniform. These were the rulers of the world, the real rulers of the real world. The caption read CONFERENCE IN YALTA.

While these men ate and drank and divided up the world, elsewhere Tommy's comrades struggled and died. On the same page, a story told of the expulsion of the Germans from Belgium. The Allies pressed east toward the German frontier, suffering heavy casualties as they advanced. Tommy felt relief that he was no longer there, mingled with guilt that he was not with his buddies.

This was self-indulgence. He had to move ahead to February 8, the day he had jumped forward, and try to find out what had happened to Tempus when the Soviet agents invaded it.

He advanced the images quickly until he reached February 8.

Once again, the news from the front held him. Allied troops were beginning to enter Germany from the west. The Soviets were already well inside the Fatherland.

Soviets! That brought him back to his purpose, and he scanned the newspaper quickly. He found nothing that seemed relevant.

Tommy ground his teeth. Why had he thought he would find anything? The secrecy Tempus had surrounded itself with would have kept any word of the attack from getting out.

He jumped to the February 9th edition of the newspaper.

More news about the advance into Germany and the steady destruction of the Japanese forces in the Pacific. Tommy suddenly had little interest in any of that. He was focused on Tempus.

He read through that edition quickly. Again, nothing.

February 10th. More of the same. Germany was collapsing. Japan was being forced back. It was history. Since jumping forward, he had heard and read enough about the end of the war to know what had happened. Those events still seemed like the real world, far more real than this one that surrounded him, but they were a sideshow to the what mattered most now. Tempus. What about Tempus? There was nothing.

One more day. He'd try one more day. Then he'd have to give up. He'd have to accept that he would probably never know what had happened.

February 11, 1945. The war seemed to be as good as over, although Tommy knew that many more good men would die before the leaders gave up. Good men on both sides, he thought, surprising himself.

He shook his head and began to read the paper quickly, hopelessly.

Again, nothing.

Tommy closed his eyes and squeezed his hands into fists. He sat that way for a while, muscles tight, shaking with tension. Then he consciously, deliberately tried to relax. He opened his fists and willed his hands and arms to relax. He opened his eyes and stared at the newspaper page displayed before him. He flipped back to the first page and stared at it for a while.

And then finally he saw a small item in the lower right-hand corner of the front page that he had not noticed the first time.

The headline was MYSTERIOUS EXPLOSION AND FIRE ON WESTERN SLOPE.

He read the article, muttering the words without realizing he was doing so. "A private airplane enthusiast from Grand Junction reports sighting a series of tremendous explosions and a fierce fire in an uninhabited area some miles north of the town of Milton."

Tommy frowned. Milton. He didn't remember that name. But then, he hadn't known anything about the geography surrounding Tempus.

The article talked about mysterious military aircraft keeping planes away and local rumors about some kind of secret government work in the area.

There was nothing more.

So all I really know, Tommy thought, is that the Soviets really did infiltrate Tempus and set off explosives. But I knew that before.

He knew something else, but he was reluctant to admit it.

What he had glimpsed in 1945 before jumping forward in time and what he had found when he arrived in 1995, combined with what he had just read and his inability to contact Tempus, told him that Tempus had been destroyed on that February day. There must have been no survivors. Any other Tempus offices must also have been destroyed, probably in a carefully planned, simultaneous attack.

It was all gone, as dead as the Third Reich and Churchill and Roosevelt and Stalin and everything else from that era.

He was alone.

It was about two miles from the library to the temporary employment office where Greg had let him out of the car when he first arrived.

He wasn't interested in anything the people behind the desks might have to offer him. It was the job notices on the walls he was there for—specifically, for the ones that would pay him to kill these ghost people.

This time, he noticed something in the ads that he hadn't noticed before. More than half of them had the same contact telephone number. Most of the rest of them gave a telephone number that began with 800 and had too many digits. Obviously, the telephone system had changed a lot since his time. After a while, he concluded that there were two main companies in the business of hiring mercenaries. The larger one had many different telephone numbers in its office, but they all began with 800. The excess number of digits annoyed him. Also, he appreciated the simplicity of a company that had everyone call the same main number. They were probably quite a bit smaller than the other place. That appealed to him. He'd call them first.

Now all he had to do was talk his way in. He didn't have to worry about meaningless jargon like *system administrator*. These people wanted skills that he definitely had. What he was worried about was what they would think of him when he showed up for an interview looking like a bum instead of a soldier.

What would he do if they asked him about his prior military service? Oh, yeah, I fought in Normandy in World War Two. I'm older than I look.

The gift of the gab, he told himself. I've got it. That's one of the main reasons Tempus wanted me. So now I'll use it. I'm smarter than any of these damned ghosts.

Tommy remembered seeing a pay phone a few doors down from the employment agency. He looked at one of the ads again to make sure he had the telephone number memorized, and then he left, fingering the coins in his pocket as he walked.

He identified a quarter by its feel and pulled it out of his pocket. The money of this time still intrigued him. The coins were all the right size, but they looked so odd to him. They seemed like foreign money, as though they were left over from his short time in England and France.

He didn't know how lucky he was that the payphone worked. Even with his cynicism and his dissatisfaction with this era, he would have been surprised to learn how common vandalism of pay phones was.

A woman answered while the first ring was still buzzing in Tommy's ear. "InterAgency."

"I'm calling about a job. I saw an ad on the wall of a temporary employment agency."

"Job code?"

"I don't know. It was the one where you said you wanted people who know how to kill and keep their mouths shut."

"None of our ads say that."

"Sure they do. They all do."

There was a long pause, and then she said, "Your name?"

"Stillwell. Tommy Stillwell."

The woman responded with an address in downtown Denver. "Can you be there at 2:00 o'clock this afternoon?"

"I can be there in ten minutes."

"Sir, I asked you if you can be there at 2:00 o'clock this afternoon."

Tommy thought about the meager amount of money in his pocket, about his empty stomach, and about how long it was until 2:00 o'clock. "And I told you I can be there in ten minutes. I want to start working right away."

"One moment, please."

There was a click, and Tommy thought he had overstepped

and that she had hung up. But then he heard music, the pap that this era fed over telephone lines at the slightest excuse.

There was another click. The same woman said, "Your eagerness is commendable, sir. Be at the address I gave you in ten minutes, and someone will be waiting for you."

Some things don't change, Tommy thought as he headed west toward downtown. The squeaky wheel still gets the grease, and bureaucrats still back down if you stand up to them.

He felt better than he had in months. He had spent his time here so far being passive, acted upon by this confusing world. Now he was taking control of his life again.

Tommy smiled. It was a beautiful day. The skyscrapers of downtown—highrises, they called them nowadays—were ahead of and below him. He was walking down a long hill, heading west into downtown Denver. To his left was the state capitol. To his right, a river of cars rushed along the street— new, shiny, expensive, and, strangest of all, mostly Japanese and German. He glimpsed the drivers' faces as they passed. Some frowned, but most seemed content. He'd have all of that some day, the money and power. If he was fated to spend the rest of his life in this era, then he'd spend it well. He'd be on top.

A few yards ahead of him, one of the eastward-rushing cars swerved from the stream of traffic and bounced onto the sidewalk. It roared toward him, picking up speed. Tommy stood frozen in surprise. Someone yelled. Tommy threw himself to the left and rolled onto the capitol lawn.

The car screeched to a stop on the sidewalk beside him. Tommy rose slowly to his feet. He was shaking. The driver stared at him for a long moment. Then, with another screech of tires, the car sped away, down the sidewalk, then bumped over the curb, rejoined the flow of traffic, and disappeared.

"Where the hell are the cops, man? I pay my taxes! Where the hell are the cops?" The man who was yelling was standing near Tommy on the sidewalk, face white with fear. His hair was long and greasy, and his clothes and skin were gray with ancient dirt.

Jesus, Tommy thought, I looked almost that bad a month ago. A few months more, and I would have looked like him. "Cops can't be everywhere," Tommy said. "Anyway, he's gone now. Did he look like a Russian to you?"

"What?" The bum looked bewildered. "Who?"

"The driver. He looked Russian to me."

"You're crazy, man." The bum took a few steps backward, then turned and walked rapidly away, glancing over his shoulder every few seconds as though to make sure Tommy wasn't following him.

"He looked Russian to me," Tommy repeated. The Soviet Union had disappeared a few years before Tommy's arrival in this era, and modern Russians were more concerned with simple survival than world conquest. Maybe today's Russians didn't even have a distinctive look, but Communist agents in Tommy's day did. So he had been told, anyway. It was a heavy-jowled, expressionless look, and the face of the driver, when he stared at Tommy through the passenger–side window, had looked just like that.

Perhaps it was nothing, just an accident, a driver momentarily losing control of his car. Or perhaps it was a Soviet agent, sent forward in time, trying to eliminate his American competitor.

Tommy started walking downhill again, toward downtown,

but now he kept as far from the rushing traffic as he could, and he tried to be aware of each and every car as it roared by.

The address he had been given over the phone was that of a gleaming black office building that occupied most of a block on the pedestrian mall, right where 16th Street began to descend into Lower Downtown. Tommy paused to look around, to sense the power and wealth embodied in the glass and steel and concrete. He watched the healthy, athletic young people moving along the mall and through the building's doorways, and he felt their distance and insubstantiality, these ghosts of the future.

He shook his head. "I'm part of this now," he muttered, and entered the building.

The door of Suite 3201 was inconspicuous and blank except for the number on it, no different from the other doors lining the hallway. The sign on the wall beside it read simply *InterAgency*.

The office inside was small and surprisingly plain. Facing the door was a gray metal desk much like those Tommy had seen in the Army fifty years before. It gave the room a feeling of familiarity.

Beyond that desk was another similar desk, also facing the door. A middleaged woman sat at the front desk, watching him. A slightly younger man sat at the rear desk, also watching him. There was a chair beside the woman's desk but no other furniture in the room and no hint that any work was done in it. Both desks had what Tommy now knew was a computer, but neither the man nor the woman was doing anything with it. They were watching him as though they had nothing better to do than wait for him.

"I'm Tommy Stillwell. I called earlier."

"Sit down." The woman gestured to the chair next to her desk. "I have to ask you a few questions." She took a sheet of paper and a pen from a drawer of her desk. "Date and place of birth?"

"This is a waste of time," Tommy said. "I'm not going to give you any information about me beyond my name. It was clear from your ad what you wanted. I can do that kind of work. That's all you need to know about me."

Tommy noticed the man at the other desk looking back and forth between him and the computer screen. The woman turned around and looked at the man as well. He nodded slightly at her.

She opened the drawer again and put the paper and pen away. "You're in. My colleague will get you started."

Tommy smiled. "That's it? You're taking my word about what I know?"

"We know what we need to know about you," the man said.

At that moment, Tommy felt sure that he had done the right thing and that he was in the right place. It felt like the last piece of the jigsaw puzzle sliding into place. At the same time, he realized that this recruitment had been strangely like his recruitment into Tempus.

The similarity continued. Within hours after his acceptance, Tommy was on a plane. This one was far larger, faster, and quieter than the one that had carried him from Normandy to Colorado, and it was filled with other men dressed the way he was, but it too was taking him from one strange, dangerous, alien world to another.

This time, though, he was flying from a land at peace to one at war.

He had been given fresh clothing—strange clothes, a dull green covered with irregularly shaped patches of darker green. The other men with him on the plane referred to them as BDUs. The eerie thing was that Tommy had seen similar clothing once before, in Normandy, when a captured German soldier was being shipped through on the way to England. Waffen SS, someone had told him, speaking in a tone of awe, as though the German were something superhuman.

They had each been given a strange, short, stocky rifle— "Hecklers" according to one of Tommy's comrades, a man with a British accent—and a heavy backpack. Only Tommy had needed instruction in the use of the weapon.

An older man, dressed the same way as the rest of them, stood up at the front of the plane's cabin and said, "My name is Griswold. I'm in command. I have no rank, but you'll call me 'Sir.' I have no subordinates, no second-in-command. If anything happens to me, you're all dead meat, so do your best to keep me alive. InterAgency has been hired to wipe out a nest of narcotics traffickers. The host government isn't happy about our presence, but they know better than to interfere."

Someone asked, "What's our transportation?"

Griswold grinned. "You're riding it. Friendlies have prepared a landing strip for us. We'll land and stroll off this plane and complete our mission, and then we'll leave the same way we came in. Cakewalk. Do a good job, and InterAgency will reward you."

Tommy called out, "Hey, Sarge, what happens if we do a bad job?"

Griswold glared at him. "Call me 'Sir.' If you do a bad job, you'll never get a chance to know it."

They landed at an airstrip carved from the jungle, a dirt runway surrounded by an acre of cleared land.

Griswold was the first one out. He pushed open the door in the plane's fuselage, which was hinged at the bottom and now provided a ramp from the plane down to the ground. By the time Tommy reached the open door, Griswold was already on the ground, yelling for the rest of them to hurry up.

Tommy ignored him. He stood at the top of the ramp, looking around in fascination. The air was like warm water, filled with smells he couldn't identify. Under it all was the sweet, nauseating stench of decay. Human, animal, vegetable? He couldn't tell. The wall of vegetation at the edge of the airfield was greener than anything he had ever seen before. Insects buzzed around him. Birds—maybe they were birds—screeched somewhere in the greenery. The bright sunlight was a physical thing, a weight on him.

The Briton who had earlier identified his weapon for him pushed past Tommy and then also stopped. "Big space they prepared," he said. "They probably have to clear away the new growth every day. A lot of expense and trouble. We should be in the narco business."

Griswold yelled at both of them, and the Briton grinned at Tommy and turned to go down the ramp. Other men also pushed past Tommy and started down toward the ground.

Something stung Tommy on the cheek. He slapped at it reflexively. There was blood on the palm of his hand, a lot of it.

What the hell kind of mosquitoes do they have here? he wondered.

The man in front of Tommy sank onto the ramp. He sprawled on his back at Tommy's feet, his eyes staring, blood welling from his chest. Something pinged against the fuselage of the plane.

The engines roared into life.

"Get down!" Griswold shouted. "Off the ramp, God damn it!"

Tommy and the others on the ramp huddled down, trying to make themselves as small as possible, but the plane was moving, dragging the ramp with it.

One of the men on the ramp jerked, grunted, collapsed.

Tommy grabbed the railing, swung over it, and dropped to the ground. He landed on his side in deep mud. Even with the mud as a cushion, the impact stunned him. He lay there, gasping for breath, hoping he hadn't broken anything.

A shadow passed over him—the ramp, still being pulled by the plane. The wheels at the end of the ramp ploughed through the mud inches from his head. He could hear something rattling against the sides of the ramp and the plane.

Bullets, he thought. The Soviet assassins. They've found me again.

He tilted his head back to follow the plane as it tried to take off. Despite the dangling ramp, it lifted a few feet off the ground. Then one of the engines exploded. The wing broke off at the burning engine. The plane tilted, fell. It slid across the muddy field into the barrier of trees and burst into flames. Tommy and the other men watched as though paralyzed. He could feel the heat of the fire. The roar of the flames drowned out any screams.

Some of the men on the ramp had survived. A half dozen figures, silhouetted against the flames, came running toward Tommy and the others. Two of them pitched forward and lay still. The other four made it all the way and flung themselves into the mud near Tommy. They were crying. One of them moaned, "Griswold, you fuck."

Ignoring the bullets and the crying and the curses, Griswold was busy assembling his survivors in the shelter of a pile of dirt left over from the clearing of the runway.

Tommy watched Griswold with interest. He watched the men glaring at Griswold with even more interest.

Tommy slid over next to Griswold. "Sir, how're we going to get out when we're done?"

"I've made radio contact with InterAgency. There's an extraction team on its way. We've got about eight hours."

"That better be a big team, with something better than what we flew in on."

Griswold glared at him. "Shut up. InterAgency knows best."

Jesus, Tommy thought, what kind of idiots am I working for?

Finally, Griswold looked around at the men who were still breathing. He nodded. "Not bad. I've had worse insertions." He gestured over his shoulder with his thumb at the edge of the clearing containing the landing strip. "See the forest wall? That's where all the firing's been coming from. Hit it with everything you've got. Now."

It was what they had been waiting for, what they needed— the chance to hit back, to feel they had some control, to inflict pain and death. Every man who could still do so emptied his weapon at the blank wall of green.

It was like some kind of terrible scythe, Tommy thought. A scythe made up of innumerable small pieces of metal. An immense blade before which the forest exploded into a mist of wooden splinters. The mist was green and brown and red.

Through the thunder of the firing, Tommy thought he

heard screams. The red is blood, he thought. The blood of those who attacked us. God, if we'd had weapons like these in Normandy, the Germans wouldn't have even tried to fight off the invasion! If I could go back to 1945 just with these, it would be enough.

The thunder died away. The mist settled to the ground. The jungle wall was still there, but the nearer trees were gone. It was as if the wall had moved backward, like a living thing stepping back from a terrifying foe.

Animal sounds began again. Mixed with them was sobbing that Tommy was sure was human.

Griswold said, "All right!" He named three men. He pointed toward the shattered tree stumps. "Go out there, find a couple who're still alive, and bring them back here. I need information."

Bending low, the three men ran in short sprints toward the minimal shelter of what was left of the first line of trees. After a few minutes they were back, carrying a couple of limp shapes with them.

They dropped their burdens on the ground in front of Griswold. The men crowded around to see. Two boys lay on the ground, shirtless, barefoot, wearing only dirty, torn jeans. One of them gasped constantly for breath. His face was pale. With his right hand he gripped his left upper arm. His left arm ended at the elbow in a ragged tangle of red. Shards of bone stuck out from the wound and blood trickled from it. The flow increased as the boy's grip on his arm weakened. The other boy seemed unharmed, but he curled himself into a ball and whined—whether from pain or fear, Tommy couldn't tell.

He wondered how old the boys were. They looked about 15 or 16, but he suspected they were older. They might have been around the same age as the young German Tommy had shot by the roadside in Normandy. This time, he felt pity, and he hoped that neither of these boys had a girl waiting somewhere for him.

One of the men who had brought the boys back held up a rifle that looked ancient even to Tommy. "This was the only weapon I found, sir."

"Fucking commies." It was Griswold. "They ought to arm their men better than that. Shows what scum they are."

"Men?" Tommy said. "They look like kids to me."

"And I say they're fucking commies, and we're here to kill them."

"You said we were here to fight narcotics traffickers."

"You can call them whatever you want. There's a camp of them less than a mile from here. Our job is to eliminate them. These prisoners"—he kicked the boy who was curled up and whining, and the boy curled up into an even tighter ball, but he stopped making any sound—"are gonna verify the location for us."

"They're kids," Tommy repeated. "Looks like one of them's dead already." The boy with the severed arm now lay still on his back, both arms by his sides. He stared wide eyed up into the sky. The chopped–off end of his arm no longer bled.

Griswold cursed. "Fucking commie. You're right. Well, we've still got the other one." He drew his knife from the sheath on his belt and knelt down, grinning.

"Sarge," Tommy said, emphasizing the word.

Griswold straightened up quickly and spun around. He held the knife out ahead of him and glared at Tommy. "I told you to call me–" He looked at Tommy for a while and lowered his knife. "What?"

"The enemy was waiting for us. They knew we were coming. Going on with this mission would be suicide. I think we need to worry more about surviving right here until the extraction team arrives. And we'd better hope they've got the brains to come for us in something that won't be so easily shot down."

The men around them muttered agreement.

Griswold said, "You think that, huh? Well, I think that InterAgency knows a lot more than you do, and I think that they're gonna kick you out on your ass when we get back and I tell them about your insubordination. I also think you must have lied about your previous experience. You should have stayed wherever you were before you joined up with InterAgency."

Yeah, Tommy thought. I wish I was back in Normandy. And that you were there with me, walking ahead of me, with no one else around, you jackass.

Griswold nodded in satisfaction when Tommy said nothing. He turned back to the boy on the ground and knelt beside him.

Tommy turned away. He couldn't stop what was going to happen, and he didn't want to see it. He could hear it, though: Griswold's voice growling questions in Spanish, the boy's responses, at first brief and uncooperative. Then the boy's shrieks of pain. Then he answered Griswold's questions, crying, begging for mercy, telling his torturer what he wanted to know. He screamed again, the scream ending in a loud gurgling.

Tommy turned back to see the boy convulsing. The convulsions stopped and he lay still. Griswold had slit his throat.

Griswold wiped his knife on the boy's jeans, then straightened and returned the knife to its sheath. He looked happy. "That way." He pointed toward the jungle. "Just a couple of hundred meters. Just like InterAgency told me. See? They know best."

"Who prepared the runway for us?" Tommy asked.

"Some InterAgency people, I guess."

"And the commie narcotics traffickers just let them do it?"

"They did it at night, you asshole."

God Almighty, Tommy thought. He wondered who was really fighting whom in this strange world. Who had sent them here? Who had set them up? Who had put this fool in charge? He doubted if he'd ever know what was really going on. It didn't seem likely that he'd survive the day.

Griswold stared at the forest wall. He squinted. He posed like something from a Nazi poster or a Hollywood Western. "We're moving out. Time for some killing. Stillwell, take point."

Shit, Tommy thought. Stillwell, slit your wrists. That would probably hurt less. Well, what the hell. I'm not really here, anyway. I'm just a visitor. They're all ghosts. Maybe their bullets are ghosts, too.

He touched his cheek. It had stopped bleeding. Except for that bullet, he thought.

"Right shoulder arms," he muttered, and he moved out from behind the protection of the heaped-up dirt and stepped into the open, marching along as though he were in a post-war victory parade. Back straight, eyes fixed straight ahead, he marched as well as he could over the wet, uneven ground. He could sense his comrades behind him, zig-zagging forward a few feet at a time.

There seemed to be no fire from the enemy. Tommy could hear the soft thudding of his boots in the mud and the heavy breathing of the other men behind him. He became aware of animal sounds again. Some of them were bird calls, or maybe they were monkeys. He heard occasional screams and wondered if they came from the throats of humans or of big cats. Maybe elephants, he thought. Maybe they'd be less dangerous than big cats. Or humans.

There weren't any elephants here, were there? He realized he was recalling images from a Tarzan movie he had seen before going onto the troop ship. Something about Nazis in the jungle. He had mainly wanted to see Maureen O'Sullivan in that skimpy outfit again, but Jane wasn't even in the movie. Never mind the elephants, he thought. I should be worrying more about poisonous insects and snakes and bullets.

But still there were no bullets. He reached the shelter of the trees and collapsed, sitting down on the wet ground and leaning back against a giant tree. His clothes were soaked with sweat.

The hell with insects and snakes, he thought. I'm still alive. These ghosts can't touch me.

The other men caught up and gathered around him. Even without looking, Tommy could sense Griswold's hostility and the admiration of the rest of the men.

"Man," one of them said, "that was like magic. Stillwell, you're—"

"Shut up," Griswold said in a low voice. "You're telling the enemy where we are."

Tommy laughed. "You think that's a mystery to them?"

Griswold rubbed the hilt of his knife.

Tommy looked at him and smiled. "Careful, Sarge."

Griswold took his hand from his knife. "Follow me. Single file. Quietly. We've got killing to do."

None of the men moved.

Griswold glared at them. "Stay with me, or you're all dead."

"Stay with you, and we're dead for sure," one of the men said. "Stillwell is right. They know exactly where we are. They were waiting for us. This mission's blown. We need to go back to the landing strip and wait for extraction. Stillwell can get us back there alive."

Tommy was surprised by how quickly Griswold moved. He covered the distance to the man who had spoken with one long step and smashed his fist into the man's face.

The man fell on his back and lay arched over his pack, semiconscious, blood streaming from his face.

"I don't give second chances," Griswold said. He pulled the knife from his belt and bent down.

Tommy fired.

Griswold's chest blossomed red. He staggered back a couple of steps and sat down heavily on the ground. He stared at Tommy and tried to say something.

Two of the other men fired.

Griswold jerked and collapsed.

"Damn those commies," Tommy said into the sudden quiet.

"Back to the landing strip, sir?"

They were all looking to him for direction. Tommy slipped into command with a feeling of rightness and relief. "Yeah. We'll have to wait it out and hope Griswold was telling the truth about the extraction team." He pointed to the man Griswold had hit. The man was trying to sit up and not succeeding. "Couple of you help him. Maybe if they see we're leaving, they won't shoot at us."

No one shot at them as they made their way back. Tommy walked ahead as easily and openly as he had when covering the same ground going in the opposite direction, and this time the men followed his example.

Maybe those two kids we killed were the whole enemy army, Tommy thought. No, too much firing for that. Maybe we killed all of the others when we returned fire. Or maybe they just left. Yeah, that could be it. They saw what a fool Griswold was, and they decided they didn't need to bother defending themselves against us.

Griswold had been telling the truth. The extraction team consisted of two men flying a plane just like the one that had brought them. Fortunately, this time there was no fire from the surrounding jungle.

Tommy's opinion of his new employer continued to go down. Was the shoddiness and carelessness of this operation an anomaly? Or was it due to a shortage of funds? Or of brains? Whatever the case, if he ever got the chance to set up missions like this one, he'd do a much better job of it.

If he survived to get the chance.

Tommy looked around the men in the plane with him. Now that they were a few thousand feet in the air, they were finally relaxing—talking, smoking, trying to crack jokes.

What would happen when they were debriefed? It would be easy for them to blame Tommy alone for Griswold's death. What then? A firing squad? Not even that much formality? A bullet in the back of the head, maybe. Tommy thought that was more likely.

They were taken to an InterAgency base in some hot, muggy, swampy place. Tommy had no idea if they were somewhere in the southern United States or in South America or Africa or somewhere in Asia. He couldn't get off the base to find out. When he tried, he was turned back by very large guards.

This happened while he was waiting his turn to be debriefed. His comrades were being questioned one at a time inside an isolated hut.

Too late, Tommy realized that he hadn't talked to them about a common version of what had happened on their mission—and more to the point, what had happened to Griswold.

When he was called into the hut in his turn, he found himself alone with three men in civilian clothing. Two of them were standing, and the third sat at a small desk with a computer in front of him. Those damned things are everywhere in this world, Tommy thought, focusing his anger on the computer as a way of controlling his sudden fear.

To his astonishment, they broke into smiles, and the seated man stood and held out his hand.

"Mr. Stillwell," he said, shaking Tommy's hand vigorously. "For the last few hours, we've been hearing about your coolness under fire and how you saved the day when Griswold got himself killed by the enemy."

One of the other two laughed. "Saved us the trouble. Frankly, Griswold had screwed up a couple of missions before, and this was his last chance."

The man who had shaken Tommy's hand said, "All of your companions said they'd be like to serve under your command on their next mission. We've talked it over, and we're prepared to offer you a promotion to team lead. We'd like you to prepare to take the same group on a mission in a couple of days."

Tommy wondered how the system of ranks used in

InterAgency corresponded to the military ranks he was familiar with. "Team lead. Is that what Griswold was?"

"He was project level. We have rules about how far you can jump at a time. After a couple of successful missions, we'll talk about it again. Do you accept?"

"Sure. Who do I have to kill?"

After a frozen moment, the three men laughed.

The answer was, "A lot of people." Male and female, young and old, in isolated villages and urban slums, armed and unarmed, resisting fiercely or dying helplessly.

Tommy never asked who they were or why InterAgency had decided they must die, let alone what authority InterAgency had to make such a decision. What government was InterAgency working for? Or was it operating on its own? What war or wars was he part of? Where did the money come from to pay for the missions and to cover Tommy's frequent bonuses? Was he killing his country's enemies? Was he a mercenary, leased by the government? Had InterAgency rented him and his men out to mobsters, so that he was a soldier in a gang war?

Was the war between factions within InterAgency? On one mission, he suspected that was the case. He was given photographs of two men and told where to find them. When he and his men showed up, the targets—both tall and competent looking, both wearing suits, one very blond and the other very dark—greeted them as though they thought Tommy and his team were there to help them. He killed them both quickly before they could realize their mistake and defend themselves. But he couldn't shake the memory of their welcoming smiles.

When he reported routinely on the success of the

mission—such successes and such reports had become routine for him by now—he received a request for more details. That was unusual. In particular, he was asked whether the two men's deaths had been quick and easy or slow and painful.

Tommy stared at the sheet of fax paper for quite a while, puzzled by the question and not sure whether to tell the truth. He had been given no instructions about how to kill the men. Indeed, he hadn't even been explicitly told to kill them—just given their photographs and location, and he had understood what that meant. He decided that someone wanted to hear that the men had suffered, or he would not have been asked the question. He wrote a brief reply saying that one had died in a matter of minutes but that the other had taken an hour to die and had been screaming all the time.

That should cover all the bases, he thought.

He reread the report a couple of times before faxing it back. It seemed brief, emotionless, to the point. Killing kept getting easier.

What moral right did he have to take these lives? The right of survival, he told himself. With a growing feeling of detachment and emptiness, he saw his victims increasingly as ghosts of the future, citizens of an unreal time and place. West Africa, Central America, South East Asia—the places all came to look the same, and so did the people. After Tommy and his men passed through, they were all corpses anyway.

Promotions and pay increases came regularly. He was given letters of praise, copies of which, he was told, were being placed in his personnel file. He was a model employee.

On a day when he was relaxing at one of the company's

base camps, recovering from a mission, he was summoned to the small building that housed the camp's administration. A fairly high InterAgency official named Sam Feldman wanted to see him.

Outside the building were men wearing sweat-stained uniforms, but inside it, men and women wearing business suits bustled about in an air-conditioned chill. Tommy found it uncomfortable. Much as he disliked the heavy, damp air outside, this seemed unnatural. It was like being shut up in a refrigerator.

He found the office he had been summoned to. It wasn't hard to do, for the building was small. He was beginning to shiver. He was eager to take care of whatever bureaucratic annoyance he was going to be subjected to this time. The sooner he could get this done with, the sooner he could get outside again. *And the sooner I'll be killing again,* he thought. He tried to push that thought aside.

He knocked on the door and entered without waiting for a response. Minute by minute, he was growing more physically uncomfortable and more annoyed.

Another desk, another computer, another woman in a business suit.

He wanted to smash all those damned machines. "Stillwell," he said. "Tell your boss I'm here."

She raised her eyebrows. "My boss?" She was a few years older than he was, he guessed, and very attractive. He wouldn't mind asking her out, if there were anywhere to take a girl in these camps. He already knew there wasn't, either in the camp or for many miles in any direction outside the camp. He'd be happy to skip the asking-out stage, but he suspected she wouldn't respond to an overly direct approach.

"Yeah, Feldman. Get a move on, honey. Tell him I'm here and I'm in a hurry."

"Honey?"

Belatedly, he noticed the nameplate on the desk. It read SAMANTHA FELDMAN—REGIONAL DIRECTOR. He also realized that there was no other door in the room than the one he had entered through. Well, damn, he thought. He'd never get used to women being in these positions of power. It still seemed unnatural to him.

"Sorry, ma'am. I'm Stillwell, and you wanted to see me."

She chuckled, and Tommy found her all the more attractive. Maybe he should try the direct approach after all. She hadn't become a regional director by being timid. She was probably pretty tough and experienced.

"Fortunately for you," she said, "the request actually came to me from much higher up. Otherwise, after that behavior, I'd have you taken out in the jungle and shot."

She looked at her computer screen. "Although that would be a waste. You've served InterAgency with distinction. South America. Africa. Asia." She nodded. "Not bad. Looks like someone in New York has decided you're too valuable to risk out in the field."

"Someone?"

"Delia Garrison. She's high up. She wants to see you in New York. You'll be leaving here around midnight tonight."

Tommy glanced at his watch. "Too bad there's no canteen here. I'd ask you to have a drink with me after I finish packing, to celebrate my escaping being taken out in the jungle and shot."

She smiled. For a brief moment, she looked young and

vulnerable. "Come back here after you pack, and I'll show you where the executives go after hours."

Tommy saluted smartly. "Yes, ma'am."

She smiled again, and this time she looked neither young nor vulnerable. "You're going to go far in InterAgency."

Fourteen

Vera Ransom disappeared. Retired, Delia hoped.

She fantasized that InterAgency owned secure locations, perhaps beautiful Pacific islands, where people like Vera were allowed to spend their old age. She feared that, her usefulness over, Ransom had been consigned to an unmarked grave.

She was offered Ransom's job and took it. She doubted if she had the option of refusing. The change meant that she had many more people reporting to her—more teams in more countries assigned to even more morally dubious missions. More moral compromises for me, she thought. The only thing that seemed to be decreasing was what was left of her conscience.

She now reported to someone named Martinez. She didn't know his first name. She also didn't know whom he reported to.

It was Martinez who passed on to her an order from higher up. "Much higher up," he said with emphasis.

The order was unlike any she had been given before. This time, she wasn't told to overthrow a government or push into a position of power someone whose soul InterAgency had bought. She was given a name, Thomas Stillwell, and a photograph. She was told that he would be looking for unskilled labor in Denver and that he would come to an InterAgency office. He had skills InterAgency could use, and she was to recruit him for the organization.

"Sir," she said to Martinez, "this seems like a roundabout way for someone to get a friend or relative into InterAgency. If someone wants me to give this man a job, why don't they just send him to me, and I'll find a place for him?"

Martinez looked uneasy. "It's unusual, but those are the orders, Garrison. Just do it."

"What if he doesn't show up where he's supposed to?" She glanced at the paper in her hand. "Looking for unskilled work in Denver. Maybe that's what someone told him to do, but maybe he'll change his mind. I don't want to be held responsible in that case."

"You'll be held responsible if you don't follow orders. You should know that by now."

"What are these skills he has? What work is he supposed to end up doing for us?"

"He's a killer. A soldier and a killer. That's all I was told. Garrison, you now know as much as I do about this man. Follow your instincts. They've been good so far."

"Yes, Mr. Martinez."

Martinez was a nice enough man, Delia thought. He seemed a bit more easygoing than others in authority at InterAgency. But he wasn't strong. He was easily cowed by those above him, and she knew she couldn't count on him for protection. If her instincts led her in the wrong direction, she alone would pay the price.

She sent an alert to certain members of her team to be on

the lookout for the man named Stillwell and tried to put the matter out of her mind. Another strange InterAgency game was under way, and she had learned that she would drive herself crazy if she tried to unravel its twists and turns. The wisest and safest course was to act out her assigned role in the play and hope that she was just a minor character, one who would still be alive when the curtain fell.

Delia wasn't surprised when word came to her that Thomas Stillwell had followed the script.

A killer, she thought, and shivered. InterAgency always needs more of those. Good ones, anyway. I need good ones working for me. The inept ones endanger me.

One of the killers working for her, a team leader named Griswold, was proving to be one of the inept ones. He had become a danger to his comrades and to the missions he was sent on, and thus to her. He had been promoted by Ransom, and Delia had inherited him. Looking over his record, Delia thought that Ransom had promoted him because of his bloody record as a killer, and not because of any leadership talents. Or perhaps he had had some personal hold over Ransom.

The reason didn't matter now. She had to decide what to do about him.

A test, she thought. One final chance for the man. It will be a test both for him and for this new man, Stillwell.

She gave orders, set up a mission. Griswold was in charge, and Thomas Stillwell was assigned to his team. They would be walking into a trap. How they handled it would be the test.

They might all fail the test and die, she thought. An entire team wiped out, just to get rid of one man.

No, two men. Griswold, who was already a problem for her, and this new man, somehow connected to someone in InterAgency above Martinez's level, and therefore quite possibly a danger to her. No one in InterAgency would mourn Griswold's loss, but the new man might be a different matter. Should she try to protect him? No, whoever was behind his being recruited had specified that his skill was killing, so they had to know that Delia would assign him duties that would put him in danger. It was possible that the mysterious sponsor also wanted Stillwell tested.

Stillwell survived and Griswold didn't.

That was one problem solved, anyway.

Half the team was lost. Those who made it back gave enthusiastic reports about Stillwell. It seemed that he had taken charge and saved the survivors. He was fearless and competent, and his men admired and respected him. Apparently, unlike Griswold, there was more to him than the ability to kill.

Maybe he's the tool I've been looking for, she thought.

She was sure now that someone was using her to move Stillwell in some desired direction. If she made the wrong move, her usefulness could end quickly. She no longer cared about that. At last, her long–held goal was in sight. One of her own teams wouldn't have had a chance, but this man was different.

She watched his progress for quite a while without interfering, and then she intervened and had him assigned to a very specific mission.

At first, when Tommy's report was forwarded to her, Delia was afraid to read it. She put it aside for days and tried to ignore it. It sat on her desk, at the bottom of a stack of papers. She was always aware of it.

At last, she pulled it from the bottom of the stack and unfolded it.

Handwritten! That was strange. Why hadn't he typed it, or even sent her an e-mail? Increasingly, her subordinates were communicating with her that way, and she encouraged it.

At least it was legible. He wrote carefully and well, like someone who had been taught penmanship as a child. That was rare, and for a moment Delia wondered about his background. But then she read what he had written and forgot everything else.

It was done.

One man had died quickly, but the other had screamed for an hour.

Which one had suffered? Stillwell's report didn't specify. She remembered them both so clearly, the blond one and the dark one, Stemple and al-Bagdadi. Which one had been spared pain by being killed quickly? They had both been hurt on that day her parents died. She was sure her father had injured them when they attacked him, but it hadn't been enough.

It still wasn't enough. She had wanted both of them to suffer, but now she wished she had been there to see it. She wished she could have caused the agony herself, with her own hands.

She put her head in her hands, her elbows resting on the hard wood of her desk. She wanted to cry, but she couldn't. She felt empty. Those men were dead at last, but InterAgency lived, and she would never be able to destroy it.

What would she do with herself now?

Fifteen

They gave him civilian clothes and put him on a commercial flight.

When Tommy arrived at JFK Airport, he looked like the other travelers. If he gawked a bit in amazement at the huge, bustling city around him, that didn't draw attention either. Newly arrived gawkers were a common sight, and the natives ignored them.

The address he had been given was in a high-rise office building, a featureless black cube in Lower Manhattan. He took an elevator to the 32nd floor and again found himself facing a door that was unmarked except for the suite number and a small sign reading *InterAgency*. The similarity to the Denver office ended there. Beyond the door he found himself facing a window behind which sat a receptionist, a young woman with a calm, emotionless face. Further entry was through a gray door that he guessed was metal. There was no handle on that door.

The window was solid, and it was thick enough to distort the image of the young woman sitting behind it. Bullet and blast proof, Tommy guessed. "Welcome to InterAgency. May I help you?" Her voice came through invisible speakers.

It struck Tommy that she, and whatever offices lay behind the handleless door, were completely isolated from him.

He looked around. The door through which he had entered had no handle on the inside, either. He was completely isolated, too. He glanced up and then at the walls. They seemed blank, featureless except for a couple of small abstract artworks, but he had no doubt that he would be in mortal danger if he said or did the wrong thing.

Trying hard to keep his voice even and calm, he said, "I'm Thomas Stillwell. I have an appointment with Delia Garrison."

The receptionist looked at him and then at something below the level of the window, then back at him again. Finally she nodded. Her hand moved.

Tommy tensed, wanting to run, not knowing where he could run to.

The door in front of him clicked and swung open.

"Third door on the right, Mr. Stillwell." There was a trace of a smirk in her voice. He thought it was pleasure at the fear he had been unable to hide. But when he looked at her, he saw nothing, just the same placidity as before.

Beyond the door lay a hallway lined with unmarked doors. Tommy was unsurprised. By now, nameplates would have surprised him. These doors had handles. He thought of trying the handles on some door other than the third one on the right but decided not to risk it.

The third door on the right opened into a large office containing desks and busy, frowning men and women. A woman behind one of the desks pointed to a door in the far wall. "Through that door, Mr. Stillwell."

It all seemed too ordinary for what he knew this

organization to be. He walked across the office—nervous, watching with peripheral vision, wondering if these people really were the mere office workers they seemed to be—and knocked on the door the woman had pointed to. The door opened, and he was face to face with Dolores Lujan.

He stared at her for a long moment. And then he understood. "You came forward, too!"

"What? You're Thomas Stillwell, aren't you?"

"Sure am. I'm Tommy. And you're Dolores Lujan."

"You've confused me with someone else. I'm Delia Garrison. I had you brought here to see me. Come in, please."

At her gesture, he took the seat next to her desk. She closed the door and then sat behind the desk and concentrated for a long time on the screen of her computer.

Tommy tried not to stare at her, but it was hard not to. Her resemblance to Dolores Lujan was astonishing. Her appearance, her voice, her gestures, all precisely duplicated Dolores's. Studying her, he realized that she was a few years older than Dolores when he'd parted from her in 1945. Older, more worn, even more serious and worried.

She looked up at him suddenly, and he looked away quickly, feeling guilty.

"I don't like being stared at, Stillwell—"

"I'm sorry," Tommy said. "You have this amazing resemblance to a woman I knew ... a few years ago."

"The one whose name you called me by when you came in?"

Tommy nodded.

"An interesting coincidence." She seemed uninterested,

though.

"You don't have a twin sister? Or maybe a cousin who looks just like you?"

"No," Delia said. "The reason I had you brought here, Stillwell—"

"Maybe your grandmother," Tommy said. "If she looked just like you, you could have some distant cousin who also did, and you might not even know it." She had to be Dolores's descendant. So complete a resemblance couldn't be just coincidence. There had to be a connection, and that made her his only link with the past—with Ellen, with Frank, with Tempus.

Delia was growing increasingly annoyed. "No. Drop the issue, Stillwell, or I'll decide I made a mistake in sending for you."

"Sorry. My apologies." Dead end. Tommy felt frantic at the tantalizing possibility of a link to Tempus, but he knew he must try to appear calm.

Delia made a gesture of dismissal. Tommy couldn't tell if she really was putting aside his questioning. She was impenetrable, inaccessible. In that, too, she was just like Dolores.

While she appeared to be staring at her computer, Delia had been running through a mental list of her rivals inside InterAgency, wondering which one of them Stillwell worked for. She had ordered him brought to her partly out of an irrational desire to face her possible enemy. But more than that, she had to see, in the flesh, this remarkable killer who had killed her parents' murderers. She might be risking her life by letting him inside the cordon of her guards, but she had to see him in person.

I take risks all the time, she thought. I'm surrounded by competent killers, and any of them could be subverted. No one is faithful. No one stays with you. Everyone leaves you or is taken from you eventually.

The first surprise had been how small the fearsome killer was.

He was roughly her own height, and she suspected he didn't weigh much more than she did. She had seen his photograph and knew what he looked like, but unconsciously she had expected him to be huge and physically intimidating.

The second surprise was that she found his looks pleasant. Not only didn't he make any threatening moves, he seemed entirely non–threatening.

Maybe that's his secret, she thought. Maybe that's how he gets close to his victims.

"As I was about to say," she said, "I've been following your career for the last eighteen months. You've done very well for us. The men we hire are tough and they survive, but few of them show concern for the men under them, and not enough of them have the ability to take command in a crisis. We saw that on your very first mission."

Tommy smiled. "Some of that was circumstances. Griswold was a born loser. You people didn't realize that when you put him in charge of that mission. He went through all the motions, but he didn't understand the men under him."

"Apparently you did."

"I knew that none of them cared about InterAgency or the mission any more than I did. We just wanted to survive and get paid. That's all war is—survival. The people on the home front are the ones who talk about the goals and the big ideas. The GIs in the trenches just want to keep their heads down and make it through."

"But you finished the mission successfully after Griswold was killed. And the men followed you, even though they didn't have to."

"We knew we wouldn't get paid if we didn't finish the mission. Real war is a matter of survival. This kind of war is a matter of survival and getting paid."

"And you've survived for eighteen months," Delia said. "Day by day, the odds are never very good in your line of work. If I send you back, you probably won't survive for another eighteen months."

"Yeah," Tommy said. "That thought has crossed my mind."

"How much do you know about InterAgency?"

"Your checks don't bounce." At her look of annoyance, Tommy added quickly, "I know that IA hired me when I was in trouble, and you've treated me well." Except for sending me places where people are trying to kill me, he thought. "And I'm grateful that you've given me a chance to see New York."

"It's an interesting town," she said absently. She thought it was time to change the direction of the conversation suddenly and see if she could catch him off guard. She had to know who had sent him. "Did you ever wonder why you were hired so quickly and easily?"

He was surprised by the question. "From time to time. Why was I?"

She watched him carefully. "I was told to expect you. I was given your name and a photograph. That was about three or four months before you contacted us."

Tommy felt a chill. That was when I arrived in this era, he thought. That was why they took me onboard so quickly and acted as if they knew all they needed to know about me. Christ, who knew I was coming? "Who told you that?"

For just a moment, he took command of the conversation. She had had to work so hard to learn how to impose her will on others, but it seemed to come naturally to him. "You forget your position, Stillwell. And mine." He had seemed genuinely surprised and caught off guard, Delia thought. She didn't know what to make of that.

"Sorry, ma'am. But what you said threw me for a loop."

"I don't know where the order originated. From high up, I think. Possibly even from one of the chiefs. I'd like you to tell me who it was. Who are you working for, and what are your orders regarding me?"

"Jesus! I'm not working for anyone! I mean, I'm working for InterAgency, but that's all. When I first got hired, I didn't even know what InterAgency was. I sure as hell didn't know anyone in it. I was in Denver looking for work, any kind of work. I saw an ad and I answered it."

He wasn't acting. She was sure of it.

But someone above her *had* known he'd be looking for work in Denver and that he'd approach InterAgency. If Stillwell was telling the truth, then someone could foretell the future.

That's not possible! she told herself. You know that's absurd.

But if it *is* true ...

How could she protect herself from someone like that?

Tommy saw the fear in her eyes. It wasn't fear of him. He was sure of that. It was fear of whoever had known ahead of time that he'd be showing up. This organization he had joined was even nastier than he had realized. Hell, he thought, it's even worse than the U.S. Army.

In this case, though, she wasn't the one who ought be afraid. He was. He knew who would have known about him in advance. There was only one kind of person who could have that knowledge, the same kind who had almost managed to blow him and Frank and Ellen up back at Tempus in 1945: a Soviet agent.

Getting himself to a high position in InterAgency and then putting the organization on the alert for Tommy would be a good way to flush Tommy out into the open. That must mean that the Soviet agent had jumped forward to a point earlier in time than Tommy had, because it would have taken years to rise to the top of this paranoid organization. Or maybe the man hadn't jumped at all. Maybe he'd been infiltrated into the West after the war and had been working his way up the ladder since InterAgency first came into existence, whenever that was.

But, Tommy asked himself, how did he know my identity? From the team that broke into Tempus, of course! They didn't manage to stop us from being sent forward, but they could have found all the records. Or they could have tortured Dolores into telling them what they wanted to know.

The image of Dolores being tortured and then no doubt killed was a wrenching one. Watching Delia, her near double, made it even worse.

I can't let myself think about that, he told himself. Not now. His immediate problem was the "chief" who had given the order to watch for him. Who was he, what name was he living under, and how was Tommy to protect himself from him?

Delia said, "All right. Whoever sent down that order about you hasn't sent another one. I don't know if he wanted you to prove yourself on missions, but if so, you've certainly done that. I think you'd be more valuable here at HQ now than out in the field. You have too much potential to risk having you get killed."

"Killing's all I know. I've come to hate it, but I'm good at it. What would I do here? File papers for you?"

"File papers?" She frowned. "That's an old-fashioned idea. We file our data here." She tapped her monitor. "Clerical work would be a waste of your talents. I need ... " She hesitated for a long time. "Before I say anything about that, I have to ask you again how much you know about this organization. Don't hide anything from me."

"I'm not hiding anything. I told you everything I know about InterAgency. Oh, I also know that I hate the way you guys put a capital letter in the middle of a word."

She smiled slightly. "And that's it?"

"Yep."

"Here's some background, then. This is what you're permitted to know. InterAgency is an independent organization. We are supranational. We are not part of any government, although our funds come from a variety of national governments. The United States government is the largest contributor, something around thirty percent."

"You sound like the United Nations."

Delia looked startled at the comparison. "I suppose we do, a bit. We work much more behind the scenes than the U.N., though, and with much less oversight." She paused. "Actually, no oversight. We do work with the U.N. occasionally."

"There was a U.N. military attaché assigned to my team in

Senegal last winter."

"We let them send observers sometimes."

"This guy fired a lot of bullets for an observer."

"Perhaps he was in training."

"Perhaps there's stuff you're not telling me."

"There's a lot I'm not telling you, Stillwell. Once again you're making me wonder if I've made a mistake about you."

Tommy ran his hand across his mouth, imitating the motion of closing a zipper.

Again, she smiled slightly. "Good. I'll continue. Our funds are free from oversight by any parliament or congress. Each of us within the organization is answerable directly to his or her superior. It's pyramidal, something like the feudal system."

Sounds like the *Führerprinzip*, Tommy thought. Worked okay for Adolf.

"At the top is a Board of Directors, the people I referred to earlier as our chiefs. I know very little about them. I do know that they coordinate our actions directly with the various agencies that provide our funds."

Tommy raised his hand.

Delia smiled again. "Yes, Tommy?"

"These agencies that provide the funds, those would be people like the OSS?"

"OSS?" she said, puzzled.

"Sorry. I meant the CIA."

"Possibly. That's my guess, too. But no one's told me. That's not really important to us, to people at our level. We get our orders from our superiors, and we report back to them. That's all we need to know. Our superiors also choose who gets promoted. Openings are infrequent at my level and above, so promotions are rare and there's fierce competition for them. This is where you come in." She paused again, choosing her words, then said, "I need a bodyguard."

Tommy whistled. "Competition is that fierce?"

"Perhaps. I don't know that for sure. I do know that there have been some surprising deaths, and in each case the victim was vying with someone else for an opening."

"You could take yourself out of the running. Make it clear that you're satisfied where you are. Then no one would bother you."

She looked at him directly for a change. "But I'm not satisfied where I am. I want to get to the top. I want to be one of the chiefs."

"How do you know you can trust me? Maybe I really am in the pay of a rival. Maybe I'm a trained assassin."

"Surely not. If you were, I'd be dead by now."

Tommy laughed. "My God, you're a cool cucumber!"

"Thank you. That's the job. Do you accept?"

I wonder if I'll be in even more danger here than in the field, Tommy thought. No, I'll be closer to my enemy here. I'll have a better chance of finding out who he is before he does ... whatever it is he's planning.

Why had the Soviet agent done nothing so far? Tommy had been exposed for quite a while. That was a mystery, and his need to solve it gave Tommy another reason to be here at the center instead of out on the fringes of the organization.

There was also the possibility, while he was here, of getting to Delia Garrison's personnel records. Perhaps he could find out something about her mother or grandmother. "Sounds like you really need a small army. Or at least a team of bodyguards."

"That's not feasible at my level. There's also the matter of trusting a team of that sort. So far, I've only decided I can trust you."

"How about the people in that room outside?"

"Oh, I trust them. All of them. Completely."

"Good. Some of them look young and fit. Would you mind if I trained a couple of them? Just some basic skills. It's not safe to depend entirely on one man. No matter how good he is at killing," he added.

Delia thought for a moment. "All right. You can do that. So do you accept the job?"

"Is there a raise involved?"

"There's safety and free room and board. You'll have an apartment right here in this building."

"Do you live here?"

She shook her head. "I have an apartment outside. I commute."

Making my job that much harder, he thought. "I'll move into your place." At her raised eyebrows, he added, "I'll sleep on the couch. We'll both be safer."

Delia sighed. "I suppose you're right. But I have a spare bedroom. You won't need to sleep on the couch."

"Good. About the raise?"

"I'll see what I can do. I can't promise anything, only that I'll put a request in."

"Good enough. I accept your offer."

He relaxed—for the first time, he thought, since he had taken off in that airplane with Griswold. At last he felt that he was getting somewhere, making some kind of progress. He was no longer frozen in place, timeless, timebound.

Sixteen

Tommy and Delia fell quickly into a routine. In many respects, it was no different from the ritualized life of any city-dwelling office worker.

They commuted by rail from her apartment to a downtown station and walked the few blocks to the InterAgency building. They took an elevator up to her office and spent the day there, except for a brief lunch break in the company cafeteria. The cafeteria was neutral ground, Delia assured him. They were safe there. She may have thought so, but after what she had told him about promotion within InterAgency, Tommy doubted if they were safe anywhere.

At the end of the day, they joined the crowds leaving the building and commuted back out to her apartment, where they spent the evenings in their separate rooms, Tommy reading voraciously about the history of the preceding fifty years or exercising, trying to keep his deadly skills fresh despite the lack of a sparring partner, Delia doing he knew not what.

Unsafe and uneasy as he felt inside the InterAgency building, Tommy felt even less safe outside it. When they were pushing their way along a crowded sidewalk, and even when they were in Delia's apartment, he felt threatened. Every stranger was a potential assassin. Delia assured him that InterAgency had unwritten rules, and they were safer outside the building than inside it. He doubted if Soviet agents would follow those rules, but she wasn't willing to move to an apartment inside the InterAgency building.

On his first day on the job, Delia told the workers in the outer office who Tommy was and explained his wish to train some of them so that they could help him protect her if necessary. There were only two volunteers, one male and one female, both young and athletic. The other workers avoided Tommy's eyes from then on.

Did they not want to get involved, preferring to immerse themselves in bureaucratic detail work and avoid the reality behind their work? Were they afraid of Tommy? Afraid of being infected with the reality of violence and death he had brought into their otherwise regulated days? Tommy pondered these questions for a very brief time and then put them aside as irrelevant. His immediate concern was training his two volunteers and protecting Delia.

They were Jeff Holtzman and Christine Awada, both in their mid–twenties, both lifetime athletes. Hardbodies, as they called such people in this era. Cheerful, healthy, and tanned, they were probably more suited to an urban beach than the urban jungle, but Tommy was willing to see what he could do with them. Fortunately, they were quick learners and enthusiastic. They seemed to prefer working out with Tommy to the deskwork they were paid to do.

Neither had fired a gun of any kind before. Tommy thought of teaching them to use the Heckler he had been introduced to on his first mission. It was the Heckler–Koch G36 C, but Tommy still called it a Heckler. It was the standard weapon for InterAgency's soldiers, and Tommy had formed an attachment to it after that first exposure.

He decided the Heckler would be overkill for what these two would be doing. He discovered that InterAgency had a requisition form for handguns—a death menu, he thought. One of the pistols on the list was a Browning 9mm. In England, during the preparation for the Normandy invasion, a member of the Free French had shown Tommy an almost identical weapon and had let him fire it. It had felt perfect to him. And it would be perfect for Jeff and Christine, he thought—unobtrusive, reliable, simple, and not too intimidating for someone not used to shooting.

He need not have worried about the last part. They both took to the shooting and the Brownings quickly. As with the fighting skills he taught them, they were naturally talented.

Natural killers, Tommy thought. I guess I attract them.

The attraction was stronger than he had realized. One of his training sessions with Christine ended with another session in the bed in her small apartment, during which she taught him some new skills.

Despite the delights of her extraordinary body, and despite his need for the release, the relationship was against Tommy's better judgment. Quite soon, he could tell that Christine was becoming emotionally attached to him. He didn't want to hurt her, but sooner or later he knew he would. But he couldn't stay away.

At first, despite the presence of Jeff and Christine in the outer office, Tommy was on the alert all the time, watching for an attack on Delia, waiting for one on himself. He spent most of the workday at a small desk in Delia's office, watching the door, waiting for assassins to burst in, and feeling silly. His only real break was the training sessions and the hour or two in bed with Christine. He ended each day exhausted and yearning for sleep.

As the days and then weeks passed and his two students progressed, he began to relax. Increasingly, he thought that Delia had imagined the danger she was in. He was ready to believe that being an executive at InterAgency was a dangerous job. He had seen enough of the organization's workings and attitudes from the bottom to be convinced of that. But he wondered if Delia was important enough for anyone to want to kill her.

He began to feel restless. "I need some work," he told Delia.

She seemed surprised. "You are working. You're guarding me."

Tommy shook his head. "I'm sitting here all day. I'm not guarding you, I'm waiting to guard you. And while I'm waiting, I'm going nuts. Maybe filing papers isn't such a bad idea. Oh, I forgot. You don't do that any more."

Delia thought for a moment. "Lately, I've been doing a lot of data mining—trying to get into databases in IA and elsewhere to find out whatever I can about certain other people in the organization."

"Your rivals? The ones you think might try to have you killed?"

She hesitated. "I suppose I ought to be open with you. Yes, that's right. Those are the people I'm trying to investigate. But I'm not getting anywhere. I'm locked out of too many places. I don't have the skills to break in, and I'm afraid to bring in someone who does have the skills because I don't know whom I can trust. How do you think you'd do with it?"

Tommy had a flash of memory—of himself trying to fool Hughes into believing that he knew German. He didn't want to try the same trick with Delia, even assuming he could pull it off. "I don't know anything about computers."

"At your age! That's very unusual."

"I'm from a small town. We just had books. And we filed papers."

Delia shrugged. "In that case, I don't see how you can help me. You'll just have to keep sitting there waiting to guard me. If you go nuts, do it quietly."

A joke! Tommy thought. That's amazing. Or maybe it wasn't a joke. Maybe she meant it seriously. But nuttiness, he thought, was a real danger, if he had to keep sitting there day after day, hour after hour, doing nothing with his mind.

He thought about Delia's reference to being locked out. He understood what that meant in the case of information stored on paper. You could be locked out of a room, or filing cabinets might be locked. Tommy assumed something equivalent must apply to information stored on computers.

He had always hated locks that kept him from getting at things he wanted. It was instinctive with him to find a way to unlock them. It annoyed him to think that he had just run into some new kind of lock, the nature of which he didn't even understand, which was keeping him from something vital to him. If he could learn how to use computers, while Delia thought he was looking up information on her rivals, maybe he'd be able to gain access to Delia's personal data.

Maybe he could even use a computer to track down the

Soviet agent at the top levels of InterAgency.

"I'd like to learn about computers," he said to Delia, "so that I can help you. I know I don't know anything now, but I can learn. At one time, I didn't know how to kill people, either. I'm a fast learner."

Tommy had to start at the very bottom, with basic computer literacy. This required a computer, and when one was being set up on his desk for him, he learned that Delia had her own team of computer technicians and other support people.

"It's the pyramid organization," she explained. "Of course it would be more efficient to have a central pool of technical personnel to handle this sort of duty for everyone, but no one would trust them. All of these people report to me. I chose them all, and I trust them all. I don't have anyone sophisticated enough to do the data mining I talked about. That just wouldn't be safe. Someone like that would be able to fool me too easily into trusting them."

"How do you know you can keep trusting your people after you hire them? Do you monitor them all? Spy on them somehow, to make sure they haven't been subverted?"

Delia refused to answer that question. Tommy took that for a yes.

Tommy surprised himself by how quickly he learned computers.

Getting over the initial hump—becoming accustomed to the idea of this strange machine that he'd never so much as heard of before his time jump, and then learning the most rudimentary aspects of making it obey his will—was the most difficult part. The first attempts to stretch his mind to encompass all the new concepts was almost physically painful. It became easier with repetition, and in time his progress became rapid.

He learned how to access the few internal InterAgency databases he was allowed to read, how to log into the external commercial databases for which InterAgency had a corporate account, and how to surf the new World Wide Web. It excited him in a way that was entirely new. It was as though the computer screen was a magic doorway into a limitless new world.

It was a world of information, misinformation, and disinformation, of intelligent, informed opinion and laughable ignorance and stupidity, of admirable sentiment and contemptible prejudice. It was the human comedy, but infinitely accessible.

It was intoxicating, but after indulging for a week or two in intoxication, Tommy became singleminded again and concentrated on hard data. In his current life, information was his weapon, and he wanted something as reliable as his M–1 had been in Normandy.

Delia was a distraction. She seemed to spend a lot of her time on the telephone. She spoke too quietly for Tommy to make out the words unless he concentrated, which he felt would be unethical, but the background murmur became an ever greater distraction nonetheless.

He was aware of the irony. He intended to delve into her personal background, but at the same time he avoided listening to her conversations. For some reason he couldn't put his finger on, information in databases seemed impersonal and noninvasive, whereas voiced conversations were very personal matters.

There were a couple of small storage rooms leading off the outer office. Tommy felt sufficiently confident about Delia's safety that he moved his desk and computer into one of the storage rooms. It was windowless and stuffy, made even stuffier because he kept the door closed, but he didn't mind. It was roomy by his standards, and he spent his days so immersed in his data quest that he paid no attention to his physical surroundings.

He also spent a lot of time devouring history and current events. Where others might see a succession of unrelated or only partially related events, Tommy, armed with what he already knew about InterAgency, saw a frightening pattern.

Almost everywhere, on every continent, at every level, he saw InterAgency's hand.

Or was his imagination getting the better of him?

I'm too close to this, he thought one day. Thinking too much about it. It's driving me nuts, just like I told Delia. InterAgency isn't omnipotent. I thought Tempus was omnipotent, too. But nothing's omnipotent. No being, no supernatural power. There's just the river of time and human events carrying us all along. I've got to think about myself, about Ellen. About Frank. That's what's real. Everything here, all these people—they're phantoms.

On the other side of his office door, one of the phantoms screamed. There was the unmistakable *brrrp* of automatic weapons fire.

Tommy dropped from his chair to the floor and rolled under his desk. His office door slammed open. A roaring chatter filled the air. Chips flew from the walls and ricocheted around the room. Tommy squeezed into a ball, trying to protect his head with his arms.

Someone walked behind his desk. He could see only the feet and legs. A woman—sandals, bare legs, a short skirt. "Tommy!" It was Christine's voice.

Filled with relief, Tommy rolled out from under the desk. He put his hand on the back of his chair and hauled himself to his feet. The training he had given Christine had paid off, after all.

Christine was grinning at him. She was holding a Heckler with easy familiarity.

"Ah, no," Tommy said, filled with sadness.

"Sorry, Tommy," she said, and swung her weapon toward him.

Tommy shoved his chair at her. The edge of the seat caught her in the side of her left knee. Her leg buckled. She fired wildly, the bullets hitting the ceiling. Tommy punched her hard in the side of her head. She dropped her gun and landed on hands and knees and stayed there for a moment, swaying, dazed.

Tommy kicked her as hard as he could, the ball of his foot connecting with her left ear. Something cracked. She sprawled flat and lay unmoving. He scooped up her gun and ran for the door.

The outer office was a jumbled mass of bodies and shattered desks. Blood spattered the walls and ceiling and pooled on the floor. Only one figure was standing, and Tommy was unsurprised to see that it was Jeff and that he carried a gun identical to Christine's.

Jeff was standing in the doorway of Delia's office. The door was open, and Jeff was aiming his gun into the office. Over his shoulder, he said, "Let's do this together."

"Good idea."

Jeff's head jerked toward Tommy. His jaw dropped. "Shit!" He began to turn in Tommy's direction, trying to bring his weapon to bear.

The spray of bullets from Tommy's gun almost decapitated him. Jeff fell limply to the floor. He lay twitching and gurgling for a few seconds, blood pumping from his throat. Finally he lay still and the flow of blood stopped.

Afraid of what he would see, Tommy stepped over Jeff's body and into Delia's office.

Delia sat behind her desk, her face pale. Tommy looked quickly around the office, but there was no one else there. A bit late for that, he told himself. If there was a third one of those bastards already in here, you'd be dead by now.

Tommy went to Delia and put his hand on her shoulder. She let our her breath in a long, shuddering sigh. Then she managed a slight smile and said, "Thank you, Tommy. Are we safe now?"

He smiled back at her, thinking that if she was Dolores Lujan's granddaughter, she was a much stronger woman than her grandmother had been. "I'll check," he said.

Stepping over bodies, he made his way to the door that led into the hallway. He opened it slowly, thankful for the well-oiled hinges. The hallway was empty. Tommy knew that the sounds of firing and screaming would not have penetrated the heavy door and thick outer walls of the office. What surprised him was that there was no one outside waiting for the attack to be over or waiting in case Jeff and Christine called for help.

Confident bastards, he thought. Must have been sure those two would be enough for the job and no backup would be needed.

Or, he thought, they realized that if Jeff and Christine failed, they wouldn't have a chance to call for backup. The mission would either be successful or it would be suicidal.

Tommy closed the hallway door again. There was a deadbolt. He turned it, listening to the bolt sliding smoothly into place. He hoped that Delia's enemy, whoever that was, didn't have a key.

Now he took the time to check the office workers' bodies. They were all dead. Jeff and Christine had displayed a competence and ruthlessness that was beyond what he had trained into them. Not that he needed confirmation after what had happened, but it was now clear to Tommy that the two of them were already trained killers who had been infiltrated into Delia's staff by one of her enemies. They had stepped forward when Tommy had called for guard volunteers to prevent anyone actually loyal to Delia from doing so.

"They were good," he said aloud.

He went into his small office and knelt beside Christine. She was still breathing and had a pulse, although she was unconscious. He felt her head gently. There was a swollen place where he had kicked her, and when he pressed on that, he could feel something giving way under his fingers.

Probably beyond giving me any information, he thought, but I'll have to try.

Delia knelt beside him. "Is she still alive? Did Jeff get her, too?"

"Delia, she was with Jeff. They were operating as a team.

Someone sent them here to kill you. I did this to her when she attacked me."

Only now did Delia show weakness. She trembled and her eyes filled with tears. "Oh, no! I trusted them! They were cleared by IA. Everyone was."

Cleared by someone, Tommy thought. "Delia, I want you to go back in your office. Close the door and ignore any sounds you hear. I'll come and get you when I'm done here."

She looked at him in confusion and then suddenly turned pale again as she understood. "No!"

"It's necessary."

The tears that had been filling her eyes spilled down her cheeks. Silently, she stood up and left.

Tommy waited until he heard her office door close, and then he set to work.

More than an hour later, Tommy entered Delia's office quietly and lowered himself into the chair next to her desk. He sat silently for some time, then said, "It was hard to wake her up. Hard to make her talk. It was hard."

Delia shivered. "And?"

"And now she's dead."

"She didn't tell you anything? There was no point to it, then?"

Tommy looked away. "The point is survival. That's the only point. She said nothing."

For the first time, Delia thought, he looked tired and dispirited. From the moment she'd first seen him, he had seemed to be barely managing to repress a dangerous energy. A dynamo hummed at his core, always just about to spin out of control. That danger and unpredictability had influenced her choice of him as her bodyguard, but they had also made her fear him. He sagged in the chair and for a moment she felt pity.

"She could have said something," Tommy said. "She could have tried to get me to stop. She didn't."

It wasn't true that Christine had said nothing, but it was true that she had told him nothing. At the very end, she had looked into his eyes and whispered, "Lie." And then she had smiled, closed her eyes, and stopped breathing.

Admitting she had been lying about everything? Tommy wondered. Calling me a liar?

Ah, Christine, why didn't you make me stop?

There was another long silence. Then Tommy rose to his feet, straightened, and tried visibly to be his old self. "So we don't know anything, except that you have to recruit a new staff and I have to recruit some people to guard you. This time, I'm going outside InterAgency to do it."

"I don't know if that'll be permitted!"

Tommy grunted. "You'll have to figure out how to get it permitted. It's just paperwork. That's what it always is. Every generation, that's all it is. I can think of a couple of guys from the streets, another couple of laborers. From before I was hired by IA. And maybe one or two of the men I served with after I was hired. So some of them will be from inside IA, anyway."

"I told you I wasn't high up enough yet for a private army."

"You're obviously high up enough to need this kind of protection. So this is the way we'll go."

Delia agreed with only partial reluctance, understanding as she did so that she was also agreeing to a shift in power and authority. From now on, whatever their titles might be in the

InterAgency databases, Tommy was really in charge of her organization and she had become his assistant. She didn't entirely regret the change.

Seventeen

Officially, Tommy's title was Security Adviser to Delia Garrison, but, encouraged by Delia, all of her personnel looked to him for orders and direction.

The organization expanded. It hired people who were far better than Tommy could ever hope to be at tracking down desired information in IA's databases. They passed their results on to him. On a sheet of paper Tommy kept always with him, a list of names grew longer.

Tommy spent much of his time recruiting and training Delia's private army—Tommy's army. He was beset by a sense of urgency, of events rushing forward and carrying him along in the flood, in the irresistible current of a mighty river, but he forced himself to move deliberately and to train his people well.

He often wondered just how much time he had. Just a bit under fifty years, he would tell himself during his more cynical moments. Realistically, he had no idea.

Given what he had put in place, an attack was unlikely. Delia and he were now both far more carefully protected than before at the office, at her apartment, and when traveling to and from work. After his experience with Jeff and Christine, he could never let himself be completely sure of the loyalty of the people he hired. At the same time, he couldn't worry about their trustworthiness all the time. He had to put his doubts aside and assume he could trust them, or he would be paralyzed.

His thoughts were often occupied by the nature of the strange organization he and Delia were both part of. What kind of structure was in place above her level? There had been no repercussions, no response of any kind to the bloodshed in her office and to the requested removal of bodies and replacement of damaged equipment. Delia's superior, a man named Martinez, had agreed to all of her requests readily and without question, as though such incidents were a common occurrence in IA.

Perhaps they were. Had Delia reached such a level that further upward movement came only through assassination? Did IA's executives routinely eliminate violently those who stood in their way or were in competition with them for promotion?

Who was at the head of the organization? Who were the mysterious chiefs who sent the rare e-mails? Who was chief among the chiefs? Who had known about his arrival? What plans, what moves, were now underway?

The more he pondered these questions, the more uneasy Tommy grew, the more the hairs at the back of his neck rose, the more nervous he became when he sensed anyone behind him.

In a pyramid of murderers, he told himself, the only way to be safe is to be alone at the very top.

When Tommy looked into the old Tempus site in western Colorado, he was surprised to find that the title to it was held by InterAgency and that it was protected around the clock by a perimeter of IA guards. The perimeter had been established after the explosion in 1945 and manned continuously since then. Their standing orders were to make sure no one entered the site but to hide themselves from anyone coming out of it.

Meaning me, he thought. Someone knew I'd be there. Who? The same person who knew I'd be applying for work at IA, of course. Wheels within wheels ...

He was able to transfer control of the old Tempus site to his own organization without difficulty. He sent a team to relieve the perimeter guards and to remove any bodies, mummified or otherwise. His people were very good at getting rid of bodies.

He also told them to collect everything else on the site— glass, metal, brick, stone, wood—and send it to an IA warehouse. It was possible he'd have a use for it some day.

"I know so little about you," Delia said. "Sometimes that bothers me."

They were sitting in her apartment after finishing dinner, and Delia was feeling unusually relaxed and communicative.

"Cripes! Haven't I proved that I'm trustworthy yet?"

She nodded. "Certainly. Repeatedly. You've proved it repeatedly. The odd thing is that even without that, I'd trust you. I don't know why. People tend to trust you, don't they?"

Tommy realized, with surprise, that she was right. "I guess they do. Maybe they shouldn't."

"But I should?"

"Yeah. You should."

"Why? Never mind." She smiled. "That's what I meant. That's the strange thing. I know you won't betray me."

"Considering the way IA works—"

"Yes. It's a leap of faith on my part to say that I know you won't betray me. There are very few people in IA about whom I can say that."

"I wish I could talk English the way you do."

She laughed. Tommy liked the sound. She had never laughed at first, but she did so much more now. But only when they were alone. She never laughed when others were present.

"I don't know much about you, either," he said. "How did a nice girl like you end up in a place like this?"

"Now you're really asking me to trust you. I might tell you things you could use against me."

Tommy smiled and said nothing.

"Right. I know you won't do that. It's a good thing you made sure there are no bugs in this place. I trust you, but I wouldn't want someone else listening to this."

Someone else was listening, but he already knew the story Delia was about to tell Tommy. He knew it even better than she did.

"I'm not sure how to start."

"How about your name? I don't think I've ever known anyone else named Delia."

"I suppose it's unusual. My parents said they named me after a friend, but it wasn't anyone I ever met. At least, I don't remember meeting her. Maybe it was one of those people who passed through our house when I was a child."

She told him about how her family had always been on the move and how their various homes had always been filled with strangers. After a moment of hesitation, she told him that they had lived under a succession of pseudonyms. "I don't know why

I told you that. When I was a kid, it was a serious secret."

He grinned.

"Right," she said. "Because I trust you."

"Just like your parents must have trusted you."

She nodded. "Yes, they did, even though I was a child. They told me my real name and trusted me to keep it to myself. They even told me their real names, Fred and Linda. They knew I understood not to tell anyone."

"So why the fake names and the constant moving?"

"I didn't really know why at the time, but thinking about it later, I figured it out. My parents were some kind of anti–war activists. There was a lot of that at the time, but my mother and father were very serious about it, and they must have been very effective. They knew they were in danger. Hence the *noms de guerre*. That's not right, is it? What would 'anti–war names' be in French?"

"Cripes, don't ask me. I don't know any French."

"Too bad. France is beautiful. IA sent me there for some training once. I loved it."

"Yeah, I know. Normandy was beautiful." The parts that weren't blown up.

"You've been there? But you didn't learn any French?"

"I was surrounded by Americans. And before that, I was in England, and I was surrounded by Americans and Limeys. Everyone spoke English."

"'Limeys.' I've never heard anyone use that word in real life before."

"Things were old fashioned where I grew up."

"So you went to France but surrounded yourself with English speakers. Typical tourist."

"I was a kid. I was young and stupid. I didn't know what the Hell I was doing."

"What did you do there?"

He shrugged. "Roamed around the countryside. Walked a lot. Looked at stuff." Kept my head down. Shot a guy. "Nothing unusual. Lots of other young guys around me were doing the same thing."

"You should go back, now that you're older."

"Yeah. Probably should. Maybe your parents just imagined they were in danger. What do they say about it now?"

"They were murdered a month before my eighth birthday."

"Jesus! That's terrible!"

"It was."

"What happened to you?"

"They had taught me to survive, and I did." She paused. "I've never talked about this to anyone else. Even after they were gone, I felt they were still with me, guiding me, advising me. Not literally. I don't believe in spirits or life after death. It's just that they were such enormous figures to me, so much larger than life, that it felt as though their essences were persisting somehow, as if they still existed in some sense I couldn't put my finger on."

"I'm surprised that a kid would think that way."

She shrugged. "Maybe that's common with children who have lost their parents. I don't know. As I said, I've never discussed this with anyone else. My father was a very wise and strong man. I mean that he had great emotional and intellectual strength, although he was very strong physically, too. My mother was completely loving. They were devoted to each other. Even as a child, I could see how complete and pure their love was."

"Are you—I'm sorry to ask you about this, but I want to know. Are you sure their murders had anything to do with their anti–war work? Maybe it was something else. Robbery, say."

"Oh, I know what happened. I found out later."

He waited for her to say more. When she didn't, he said, "Sounds like there's another whole story there. Are you going to tell me about it?"

"No. Never." Not what I discovered, she thought, or how I used you to settle that score.

"Okay. Understood. So who took care of you? Family?"

"Foster homes. All paid for by something called the Subversion Monitoring Council. They paid for my education, too."

"Jesus! I mean, what a strange name."

"You know them by a different name. They changed it."

"To what?"

She smiled. "InterAgency."

"So they're still around."

"InterAgency is, obviously. I don't know how far back it goes. I have no idea when the Subversion Monitoring Council came into existence. "

"A long time ago. That would be my guess. So they made sure you got a good education, and then they hired you. There must have been something about you that made InterAgency want you."

"Maybe they felt that my talents would be particularly useful to their research projects."

"So they put you to work on some project right away? What was it?"

"Time travel."

Tommy jumped to his feet. His face was white. He was trembling visibly. "Time travel!" He seemed to be having trouble speaking properly. He breathed heavily for a while. "Time travel!" he said again. "You were trying to find out how to go back to the past!"

Delia shrugged. "The past, the future. Whichever. It all turned out to be a pipe dream, anyway. We never got anywhere with it. Eventually the project was shut down."

Tommy fell back into his chair. He muttered, "Christ."

Delia was astonished by his reaction. All of this was a secret, unknown to anyone outside InterAgency and indeed to almost everyone within it, and she supposed it was an amazing and wonderful idea. Still, she couldn't understand why it had affected Tommy so much.

"You're sure it's dead?" Tommy asked. "It really was shut down?"

There was a pleading tone in his voice, Delia thought. "Oh, yes. It was interesting work, but it became obvious that there was no point in spending more money on it. I didn't blame InterAgency for putting a stop to it. Anyway, I was getting more interested in biology by then. It fascinated me."

Even before she was told that the time–travel project was to be terminated, Delia had begun to think that basic physics research had a limited future. The interest of the scientific community was shifting to biology. That would not have been her first choice for an alternate scientific career. Her other main interest, besides physics, was archeology. The human past and the attempts to uncover and understand it had always intrigued her. She was fascinated by the ways in which the past shaped the present and the present shaped the future. But the interest and the money were moving to biology, certainly not to archeology. Moreover, the more she looked into current biological research, the more she saw interesting problems that she thought she could apply her physics background to fruitfully.

"So InterAgency let you change careers?"

"Change focus, I'd say, not careers. They let me do that. They had invested enough in me by then, and they valued my abilities enough, that they didn't want to lose me. That's what I like to think, anyway."

"What happened to the rest of the team?"

"Oh ..." She gestured vaguely. "Transferred to other lines of research."

Or so she hoped whenever she thought about them. She had often wondered what had happened to those whom InterAgency no longer needed. Were they allowed to walk out of the organization with all of their knowledge about what went on inside it? How close had she come to finding out the answer to that question?

"So what kind of biology work did they have you do?" Tommy asked.

"Apoptosis."

"I'm trying to think of a funny comeback, but I can't."

Delia felt annoyed, but she forced herself to smile and pretend to be amused. "Programmed cell death. Any normal cell in the body dies after it has reproduced by splitting a certain number of times. Cancer cells don't do that. Understanding what controls apoptosis might tell us how to make cancer cells subject to it, too. That would give us a way to cure cancer. Or at least to control it, to make it a treatable, chronic illness instead of a terminal one. I think a lot of the top management in InterAgency were getting old enough at that time to worry about cancer."

Tommy shrugged. "No point in worrying about it. You either get it or you don't. If you get it, you'll probably die, but maybe you won't. There's nothing you can do either way."

A fatalist, Delia thought. She would not have assumed that about him. She would have thought he was the kind of man who is determined to control events, not be controlled by them.

Her mother had been a fatalist, too. Delia had heard her talk of time as a great river, implacable, impersonal, and too mighty for humans to affect. Individuals, mankind, the universe itself were carried along in the river's current. Individuals could do little or nothing to affect their own course. Even as a child, that view had bothered her. She had preferred her father's opinion, that the great men of history had been able to control the flow of events. Now she clung to his viewpoint the way she had once clung to him.

"You just have to get on with your life the best way you can, while you can," Tommy said. He seemed to be thinking aloud, oblivious to his surroundings or Delia's presence.

While you can, Delia thought. That was the clue. That, she suspected, was the real reason upper management had supported her research in the early days. They were all old and getting older. Perhaps they simply didn't want to die.

She suspected there was something more subtle involved, though. For decades, they had been increasingly in control of world events, and they didn't want to give that up. Age itself was a threat. As they grew older, the rulers of InterAgency grew weaker, less supple mentally as well as physically, less able to control their turf and defend themselves against their peers and the hungry lower levels of the organization. If not immortality, then at least they all wanted to remain strong and vigorous till the end. Her research had seemed to promise that.

Then the promise was not fulfilled, and that project had been terminated, too, and Delia had been moved into a low-level management position. It had been made clear to her that this new career path was her future.

"The irony," she told Tommy in a later conversation, "was that I was beginning to see hints of something when the project was killed. The right direction, the right way to take the research. I had started to think about life extension instead of cancer, and I was making some progress."

"Life extension? What does that mean?"

"Increasing the human lifespan. Possibly even rejuvenation. Eternal life." She shrugged. "I don't know. Something of that kind. I was only just beginning to see the faintest outlines of it, so at that point I couldn't say exactly where it would all lead."

"Too bad they killed the project when they did."

"Yes. Too bad. Well, I've become used to this management work. It's turned out to be more interesting than I expected."

Tommy laughed. "Overthrowing governments and setting up assassinations?"

Delia shivered. She didn't care for the direction the conversation was taking. "I do a lot of good," she said. "The higher I rise in the organization, the more good I can do. Recruiting you was a good thing, wasn't it? What would have happened to you if we hadn't pulled you in?"

"Bad things. Have you ever found out who sent you that memo about me? The one telling you and the rest of InterAgency to keep an eye out for me?"

She noted his tension as he asked that question. She wondered why he was so worried about something minor that had happened years earlier. "I have no idea. But I've come to think that it's nothing to worry about. Upper–level management has a lot of sources of information that I don't know anything about. I suppose someone was keeping an eye on you because you showed promise earlier. You told me you grew up in an isolated small town, but I bet someone there was working for InterAgency. I bet we have people like that all over the world keeping an eye on promising young talent for us. You should be flattered."

"Yeah. You're probably right. That's probably all it was."

He kept frowning, though. Delia looked at the wrinkles on his forehead and thought about the aging process. How wrinkled was her own forehead nowadays? She looked in the mirror as little as possible. She hated any sign of aging, whether in herself or anyone else. It was a reminder of the iron grip of time, and that was something she loathed.

Would she prefer to be young again? She often thought about that, and she wasn't sure of the answer. When she was young, she had learned quickly that men were strongly attracted to her. It had frightened her. She had welcomed the lessening of sexual advances from men as she had grown older, although she wasn't sure how much of the lessening was due to her aging and how much to her rise in InterAgency and the fear her position inspired in men in the agency. If she could get her youth back and yet be unattractive to men—that would be ideal.

Perhaps at some time in the future, if she came to trust Tommy more fully, she'd tell him that she hadn't entirely given up on her research. Once she had reached a high enough management level and had enough autonomy and command of a sufficiently large budget, she had created her own small research staff and had set them to work on apoptosis. They were sworn to secrecy, and they understood what the penalty would be if they violated their oath.

Eighteen

Eventually, the list on Tommy's sheet of paper ceased growing longer and began to shorten.

Delia was unaware of all of this, or so he hoped. His people were never obtrusive. One of them would pass him in the office and mutter something—a word, a phrase, just enough to allow Tommy to cross off another name.

Years passed.

Delia's competitors vanished, and she rose steadily up IA's slippery, bloody ladder. Tommy rose with her, always at her right hand, ever more thoroughly in charge. As Delia spent ever more time on her scientific work, increasingly Tommy's role changed from passing on orders to giving them.

In the autumn of 2007, Delia did something—Tommy had no idea just what—and their relative positions were made formal. Now it was officially Tommy whose rise continued. The two of them moved into their new roles easily. Their organization hummed along smoothly, unperturbed by the nominal change.

InterAgency grew in wealth and power, and so did Tommy's organization. He commanded armies—armed and uniformed men in the field, agents behind the scenes, important members of supposedly independent national governments. More and more, the world's governments and supranational organizations were puppets manipulated by InterAgency, which meant by Tommy and his peers and superiors, all of them following orders filtered down the pyramid from the mysterious top level.

Tommy's people assassinated his enemies and foiled their attempts to assassinate Tommy, and he continued to rise in rank and power.

Years passed. Decades passed. Thoughts of Tempus faded away. His original mission seemed foolish, irrelevant—not even real, a fantasy, a story, a strange fiction. He would never return to 1945. Finally, he accepted that. In time, he realized that he would avoid such a "rescue" even if it were possible. His life in the here and now was far better than it had been back then. Despite the effects of physical age and the stress of his life, he would never return to those days of powerlessness and subordination.

There was only one thing from the past he couldn't forget, didn't want to forget, and that was Ellen.

He held onto her memory with all his might. But inevitably, details faded. The time came when he could no longer reconstruct her face or her body accurately in his mind. Still the idea of Ellen persisted, the woman above all others, his soul mate.

The mate of my soul as it was back then, he thought. Or as she thought it was. There were parts I would never have shown her, even if we could have spent our lives together.

He knew he could never show her what his soul had

become since he arrived in this world. She would be repelled.

He looked at himself in the mirror, at the seams and wrinkles, the grim expression, the sagging jowls, the gray, thinning hair.

She'd be repelled by what I've become physically, too. But even if I looked just the way I used to, she couldn't love me as I am now. She'd hate me.

These thoughts came to him when he let his guard down, when his fierce concentration on his job and survival lessened for a moment. They were always there, hovering in the background, watching him, waiting for an opening in his armor. They robbed him of his strength and will and purpose and filled him with grief.

No! he told himself. No. This is reality. That other world no longer exists. None of it is real any more.

And then one day he looked at the calendar and was astonished.

Nineteen

The emptiness of the temporal crossroads gave way to a faint rushing sound, like the whisper of a nearby creek. She was standing on a hillside and staring mindlessly at sunlight on a distant range of mountains.

Only now did Ellen realize that she had been able to see nothing before, even though she had been aware of vast rivers of ...

Of what?

It was a dream, fading in the morning light, tantalizing, ungraspable. There was no rushing water in this barren place.

She could tell it was morning by the position of the sun. She turned around, unsurprised to see the cliff face with its jagged crack.

But there were no buildings around her. The hillside was bare, as though Tempus had never been.

The rushing sound was real. There was a highway of some kind visible on the plains, well beyond where the fence and guard towers of Tempus had once stood. Cars moved along it in both directions. She stared at the traffic, trying to make out the shapes of the individual vehicles, but it was too far and they moved too fast. Suddenly she felt disoriented, dizzy. She thought she could estimate how far away the highway was, but if she was right about the distance, then those cars were traveling at amazing speeds.

Frank could probably calculate the speed, she thought. Maybe Tommy could, too.

"Tommy," she said. Where was he?

Why wasn't he here?

She shook herself. She couldn't stand here worrying. She had to get on with it.

The highway seemed the logical place. She starting walking down the hill toward it.

Hidden from her sight among the rocks and pebbles on the hillside, tiny cameras followed her progress. Microwave generators focused on her, keeping her warm despite an ambient air temperature that was only a few degrees above freezing. A rescue squad hidden nearby watched their monitors silently, ready to race to her side if she were threatened. Even further away, an old man sat in a darkened room and watched her moving image, life sized on a wall screen, while tears ran down his cheeks.

Ellen walked down the hill toward the highway. She was almost surprised that she could move so easily, that everything felt the same as before. One hundred years before. She had spent a timeless eternity on the voyage, but for her only a split second had passed since Dolores had activated the strange machinery.

Somewhere on this hillside, she thought.

She stopped and looked around again for some sign of what had been, but she could see nothing. Remnants of terracing, perhaps—a flattening of the natural contours that had made the great, spread–out Tempus building possible. She couldn't be sure even of that. She might just be imagining it. In this climate, where vegetation was sparse and rain a rarity, major terracing would have survived.

What had happened? To Tempus, to all of the people, to Tommy? Where had it all gone?

She started moving down the hill again.

As she drew near the highway, she could make out the shape of the speeding cars at last. They were all low, curved, dark colored, and seemed identical. She wished one would stop so that she could examine it more carefully. For that matter, she wished they'd all stop. She could feel the wind of their passage from thirty or forty feet away, and it made her nervous, as though they could suck her in and squash her.

At last the flow of traffic ended. The last car rushed past her, dwindled in the distance, disappeared.

Ellen could hear nothing now. The air was still. There was no sound of traffic at all. She was alone on the prairie.

She approached the edge of the highway, fearful but curious.

Unlike the roads of her time, this one was smooth, its surface as featureless as the cars. There wasn't even a stripe painted down the middle. She was astonished at that, considering the speed of the cars. How did the drivers manage to stay on the right side of the road? The surface was a neutral gray, and the sunlight gleamed on it as though on metal. Its edge was sharp and clean, like a line drawn with a ruler. The empty road was like a straight, flat, gray ribbon vanishing into the distance in both directions.

Ellen heard a low humming. She looked up quickly, scanned the sky, then the prairie in all directions. Finally, far off to her left, she saw something small and dark, growing steadily as it approached her. The humming, she realized, was coming from the highway.

The object was a car coming toward her. She stepped back quickly in alarm, but as it came nearer, the car slowed. Finally, even with her, it stopped. The door on her side swung open.

"Hi! Saw you standing there. Need a ride?"

Ellen stepped forward. The car was low enough that she had to bend forward to see the driver. It was an older man, portly, cheerful, white haired—a bit like Santa Claus without his beard, she thought. She smiled at him. "I would, but I don't really know where I'm going."

He laughed. "Just like the rest of us. I'm headed for Denver. Climb in, if you want. You'll catch cold standing out here dressed that way."

"Denver," she said doubtfully. She hadn't even thought yet about where she should go. Find the secret of reverse time travel. Find futuristic weapons. Those were nice and vague. Find Tommy. Just as vague.

"Right," the man said, "Denver. Major city, center for the information industry and the space industry. Good place to find a job. Fine library system. Good place to look for information about historical events or even long-lost friends."

Suddenly Ellen became aware of the cold. As if her thought had caused it, the temperature began to drop.

"Sounds good to me. I'll accept your offer." Climbing into the car required a surprising degree of athleticism. In her day, you stepped on a car's runningboard and then stepped inside and sat down. With this one, she had to bend her knees first, hold onto the roof, and then slide in. "Tight fit!" she said. At least it was warm inside the car. Once she was in place, she realized that the seat was slowly adjusting itself to her shape and length. It held her with an almost embarrassing intimacy. "This is ... very comfortable."

The driver shrugged. "Standard issue. Ah, when I was a boy, you still had variety. You could get a car that matched your personality. Things are much more uniform nowadays. I don't like it, but most folks seem pretty happy with the situation."

A strip of cloth extruded from the top of the door, slid diagonally downward across her chest, and attached itself to the seat to her left. Another strip crawled from right to left across her stomach and also attached itself to the seat. She was reminded suddenly of a boy she had dated only once in high school.

Was this guy some kind of loon? Ellen tested the straps. They seemed loose enough. She was sure she'd be able to get out any time she wanted to. Not to mention that the driver was old and out of shape and, thanks to her training at Tempus, she knew she could handle him easily if he tried any funny business.

Driver? But there was no steering wheel in front of him! There was just a dashboard, with no kind of hand controls she could see.

He turned to the dashboard and said, "Denver." The car started moving, and he turned his attention to Ellen. "My name's Greg. What's yours?"

She shouted at him, "Jesus! Watch the road!"

He grinned at her. "The road's watching us."

The car accelerated smoothly and then moved along the

highway at a steady pace. "We're safe?"

"Safer than we would be if I tried to control this thing myself at this speed. No one gets killed in traffic accidents nowadays. Not on these roads, anyway. Now you can tell me your name."

"Ellen. Ellen Maxwell. Pleased to meet you, Greg."

His eyes twinkled. He looked more like Santa Claus than ever. "I bet you're from a small town."

"Why do you say that?"

"Well, you see, in some small towns, they don't have the guide roads yet, so they still drive old cars. That's about the only place you can still find those old ones. So I figured you must have spent your life in a such a place, and even though you know all about how the guide roads work from watching TV and movies, you reacted automatically with fear when the road took control of the car. Am I right?"

"Uh, yes, you're absolutely right."

"Fortunately, by the time we reach Denver, you'll be so used to this kind of traveling that you won't react to it. Which is a good thing, because otherwise people would notice, and you probably don't want to draw lots of attention to yourself."

"That's true."

"Tell you what, Ellen. I like to talk. I even like to tell people stuff they already know. So you just relax in that comfortable seat, and the road will do the driving, and I'll talk about this and that. You can tell me to shut up at any time, and I will, but I hope you won't, because talking like this is my pleasure." He chuckled. "Think of it as the price you have to pay for the ride. Okay?"

"Sure. Go ahead." Just another old geezer who got a kick out of talking to a pretty girl. Maybe she'd learn something by listening, though. And in the meantime, she could watch the scenery.

She wondered if they were following in reverse the route the Tempus bus had taken when it brought her from Denver. She knew she wouldn't be able to tell. The mountainsides, the trees, the rocks beside the road, the small streams that ran beside the road here and there—it all looked the same. It probably was all the same, she thought. A century meant nothing here. She tried to comfort herself with the thought that that giant rock they were passing by was probably there, looking exactly the same, when she had last seen Tommy. But instead of linking her to him, it reminded her how fearfully separated they were from each other.

They climbed steadily, the sun moving higher ahead of them.

One thing had changed since her time. The road was filled with cars on both sides, a steady stream headed east and west. And they drove at terrifying speeds with only inches between Greg's car and the ones ahead of it and behind it. The cars on the other side of the road were a blur. To her own surprise, after a few minutes she stopped expecting to be involved in a horrible crash. She started to find the speed exhilarating. So what if they're going a hundred miles an hour, or even more, she asked herself. I've just gone a hundred years in a fraction of a second!

"I love it out here," Greg said. "Too many people, though. Bet it was nice out here a hundred years ago. Not so many people. A lot less traffic. Cars you drove yourself. Do you ever think about that? About what things were like a hundred years ago?"

"Different from now." She was feeling uncomfortable. Why

was this guy talking about the time she had come from? Did he know the truth about her? She told herself she was being silly. Maybe he just likes history, she thought. Like Frank.

"Oh, yeah," he said. "Real different. A hundred years ago, they were still fighting the Second World War. Now the British Empire's gone, the French Empire's gone, the Soviet Union's gone."

"The Soviet Union's gone," Ellen repeated in wonder.

"Yeah, and Russia broke up into pieces, and the European countries are combined into a kind of United States, and there are people in space, and China is trying to take over Mars. Japan's our ally, now. They're also one of our major trading partners. You'll see Japanese products and Japanese tourists all over the place. Especially Japanese cars. Like the one you're in right now. Their main problem is that they're worried about the Chinese marching in and taking over some day, the way they did in Siberia. Oh, yeah, it's an interesting time to be alive."

Ellen's head was spinning. One thing Greg had said had caught hold of her, though. "Space," she murmured. "There are men in space."

"Oh, yeah. Lots of them. Most people don't think much about it. They think space is boring. Sounds like you're different."

"How can anyone think it's boring? Especially space travel! I dreamed about that when I was a kid. I read every space story I could get my hands on. I daydreamed constantly about being in one of those stories."

"Well, I guess things must be different in small towns, like the one you grew up in. I guess you must have been reading old stories, from back in the days before we had real space travel, before it was common. Old fiction, right?"

"Right," Ellen said hastily. "Yes, that's right."

"That's what I figured. Well, people may be bored by space, but they can't ignore it. It's where everything is starting to happen. Governments, corporations—everyone's tied up in it. You could almost believe there was one group behind it all, controlling everything, taking over space. Well, except for the Chinese. They're independent of everyone else. For now, anyway."

"One group? I don't understand."

"Oh, I guess I'm exaggerating. I'm getting paranoid in my old age. I do know there's an organization named InterSpace that seems to have its hand in a lot of the space work. They're some sort of umbrella agency. But they're probably not really behind everything. Maybe they're just a kind of employment agency for the people doing the work in space. If I were young and looking for a job, that's where I'd go. They have communication booths all over the place. Some people call them infobooths. Some say access booths. I'll show you one when we get to Denver. They're voice activated. You just speak to the booth. I don't know if you had that kind yet where you grew up. You'll find yourself talking to a person, but you have to remember that they're not really people. They're just computer programs. They're artificial."

Artificial people? Ellen thought. She had read stories about such things when she was a kid. It was hard to believe that they really existed, even though she was now in the future. She had a more pressing matter to think about, though. "I am going to have to look for work," she said. "I'm trying to get in touch with some friends, but I don't know how long it's going to take to find them. In the meantime, I'll need to make money. I'm a really good typist."

Greg laughed. "Yeah, well, that would have been really useful a hundred years ago, but no one does that nowadays."

Again that reference to a hundred years ago, seeming to come out of the blue. Ellen tensed, then tried to relax. She looked sideways at Greg. He was an old man, overweight and out of shape.

"If you go looking for a job," Greg said, "don't even mention the typing. It sounds like a nice hobby, but you don't want people thinking there's something strange about you. I don't think you'll have a problem finding work. Space work. They're screaming for people. Hell, employers here on Earth are screaming, too, because the best people are taking space jobs. Also the second–best and third–best people."

By now, they were beginning to descend the east face of the Rockies. The car was in shadow, but ahead and below the plains glowed in the sunlight. Ellen could see the light reflecting like a million stars.

Denver, she thought. It's the buildings in Denver. It's their windows reflecting the sun. But how big it is!

The city had spread enormously across the plains since she had seen it months—no, a century—ago. Even here in the mountains, they were now driving through what looked like a suburb.

Greg watched her as she stared out her window. "Space," he said. "That's what built this. Denver's one of the main centers of the industry. I'm telling you, that's where you should look for work. You're young and healthy and eager, and they'll train you. The pay's great, and as for job security"—he laughed—"the work'll be there for centuries. We're just getting started. Right now, we're still limited to the Solar System, but you just know that's going to change eventually. I bet they're working on a way to get to the stars right now."

They were both silent for a while. Ellen watched the ever denser cityscape outside the car as they descended out of the mountains and onto the flat lands. Her mind was filled with thoughts of space, with images from the stories she'd read so long ago. And with memories of Tommy.

"A hundred years ago," Greg said suddenly. "I've read about those times. Kind of primitive, but kind of interesting, too. I wouldn't mind going back there, if there was some way to do that. Too bad there isn't."

He said nothing more. Ellen sensed that he was waiting for her to say something. Finally, she said, "Are you sure there isn't?"

"Nah. There are stories about time travel, but it's all fiction. There's no such thing in the real world. No one could keep that secret. Nope. We're stuck right here in our own time. No going back, and we can only go forwards one day at a time. Make the best of things. That's what I always say."

Ellen stared out the window and said nothing.

"By the way, you said you were trying to look up some old friends. The communication booths I mentioned, most of them you can use to access newspaper archives and to search for people. You just speak to the virtual helper and ask it your questions. Keep that in mind."

Before Ellen could answer, Greg said, "There's one! Park at the jobs infobooth," he said, speaking to the dashboard.

The car slowed rapidly to a stop, then slid sideways into a

space at the curb.

"Okay," Greg said. "Remember everything I told you. You're young and eager and talented, and this world wants and needs you."

"It's ... " She tried again. "It doesn't look like the ones at home. I don't know about this."

"Oh, you probably still had one of the early models. Those were tricky. That one over there is entirely voice operated, like I told you. When you go inside it, you'll be facing a black wall. Just speak to it. You won't have any trouble. Good luck, Ellen."

"Thanks," she said. "Thanks for the ride and the advice. And all that information."

"You're quite welcome." He watched her benignly as she climbed out of his car and closed the door behind herself. She bent down to wave at him. He waved back, and then she could see him saying something to the dashboard. The car moved sideways away from the curb, back out into traffic, which paused to let it in. Then the traffic flow resumed, carrying Greg's car away.

Wanting a last glimpse of him, of this first person to befriend her here, Ellen stared through the car's rear window. Greg was a silhouette, just another driver, no longer a friend. His car moved away from her, and then she could no longer see him inside it. It was a bustling area. People were pushing by her, and the stream of cars was constant. Soon she was unable to pick Greg's car out from the rest.

She walked over to the booth. There were two side walls but no door or roof, so it provided far less shelter than the telephone booths of her day and cut out less of the surrounding noise.

The wall she was facing was featureless and black. Feeling silly, Ellen cleared her throat and said, "Er, hello?"

The black wall vanished, replaced by a handsome young man floating against a white background. Despite Greg's preparation, Ellen grabbed at one of the side walls, overcome with vertigo. She also found herself drawn to the young man's good looks and warm smile. "How may I help you?" he said.

"Are you ... Gee, I'm sorry! This is insulting, but I have to ask. Are you real?"

He shook his head. "I'm a virtual helper. Helping you is my pleasure. How may I help you?"

"I'm looking for work. I was told that ... " She tried to remember the name. "InterSpace. InterSpace might be hiring. Space work of some kind. I've worked on an assembly line, and I've been trained in office work...." Her voice trailed off. She thought of the advanced scientific wonders that must be common in this age, especially in space, and what she had said seemed silly to her.

The virtual helper hadn't reacted. For a moment, his face had gone slack, losing its simulated spark of human vitality. It was as though he was listening to something she couldn't hear. His sudden lack of humanity sent a chill down her spine. Then life returned to his face and he smiled at her, and again she found herself responding to him as she would have to an attractive young man.

"There are positions available at Interspace," he said. "They're low level, but training is available for those interested in advancement."

"That sounds like me!" Ellen said happily. "What do I need to do?"

"There's an InterSpace office not far from your present location. I can tell you how to get there."

"Can I get there on foot?" She had no money for any kind of public transportation, and the odds were against another lucky chance encounter with someone like Greg.

"On foot, if you prefer. The distance is 1.13 miles. Most people would consider that too far to walk."

Ellen laughed. "Most people must be real weaklings in this—in this city."

"The people in this city rank at or near the top of most measurements of physical fitness for Americans."

Then the rest of them must be really weak, Ellen thought. They must not have any strength or self-discipline at all. She kept the thought to herself. Even though she realized the feeling was irrational, she didn't want to offend this man—this being, this artificial creature, whatever he really was.

"I hope this isn't going to require any paperwork," Ellen said. "You see, I'm from a small town originally, and one day the City Hall building burned down and all the records were lost. Even my high school diploma and grades." Which they were storing there for some unbelievable reason, she thought. Once again, her own words sounded silly.

The virtual helper stared at her with what seemed like disapproval and distrust. She wondered if that meant he could feel emotions. She also wondered if she had managed to get herself in trouble.

"What is your name?" His voice was cold.

"Ellen Maxwell. Do you ever date ordinary people?" Tommy rubbed off on me, she thought.

He stared blankly at her. As it had before, his face lost its human spirit and he seemed to be paying attention to something or someone else. "I have no physical being," he said. "I'm a visual image created and controlled by software. Your name will be sufficient. I have notified the InterSpace office to expect you. They will administer tests to determine your capabilities and potential. I'm instructed to tell you that what matters is what you can do in the future, not what you have done in the past."

"That's funny. My brother used to say something like that."

"Perhaps your brother would also be interested in joining Interspace."

Ellen shook her head. "He died in the war." She froze, shocked by her own carelessness.

But the virtual helper looked sympathetic, or was being made to appear sympathetic by the software he had said controlled him, whatever software was. "I offer you my sympathies, Ellen Maxwell. We all hope that the benefits of our expansion into space will eventually bring an end to war on Earth, and no families will suffer the loss you have suffered."

It sounded like a canned speech, Ellen thought, but her eyes filled with tears suddenly. She had lost everything—her brother, her family, Tommy, her world. What had she done to herself? Why had she agreed to any of it? Tempus was mad.

"And now I'll tell you how to walk to the InterSpace office."

"Oh. Yes, please. Thank you." I'm here now, she told herself. I'm not going to kill myself, so I've got to get on with it and make the best of the situation. Greg was just some old guy with an eye for a pretty girl. What did he know? I'll continue with my mission. I'll find what I came here for.

The route to the InterSpace office was direct and simple, fortunately. She was sure she would have become lost otherwise.

She was astonished by the crowds on the sidewalks and the denseness of the traffic in the streets. She had noticed the growth in the city's size before, while driving down into it in Greg's car, but this brought that growth home to her. This was nothing like the small, sleepy place she had been driven through by Hughes a hundred years ago. Greg had said that the space industry was behind this growth. She supposed it was also behind the serious expressions on the faces of the pedestrians, the earnest conversations, the distracted looks, the expensive clothes, the general air of prosperity and bustle.

The virtual helper's directions led her to an office building with little to distinguish it from its neighbors except for the stream of people entering and exiting through the glass doors that lined its front.

Ellen joined one of the lines of people entering the building. Inside, she stopped, bewildered by the noise and movement, the voices echoing from the marble walls.

The purposeful bustle and the underlying focused tension reminded her of Tempus and of the munitions factory. She was, she thought, feeling the organized energy of a large number of people with a unifying mission. She liked the sense that all of them had been brought together to work toward a higher goal, a goal she applauded. But she was acutely aware that she wasn't in Tempus or the munitions factory, that she was in a place almost as alien to her as space itself.

She saw a man in uniform behind a curved marble desk ahead of her and went up to him gratefully. She thought he was about Greg's age, but unlike Greg, this man was distant and unwelcoming.

"I was told to come here about employment," she said.

"Your name?"

You people like asking that, she thought. "Ellen Maxwell."

His attitude changed. He smiled and said, "Welcome to InterSpace, Ellen Maxwell. They're expecting you. Room 540. Use that elevator bank." He pointed.

Welcome to the club, she thought.

The elevator carried her to the fifth floor with surprising speed. Someone was waiting for her there and hurried her down a hallway to a large room where she was subjected to a series of physical examinations. She was probed and measured by humans and machines, and she could not have said which group was more detached and dispassionate.

Then came verbal tests administered by machines. They seemed to be designed to gauge her mental agility and adaptability and her ability to learn quickly rather than to measure her knowledge.

A woman led her from that room to an office across the hallway. It was a large office, filled with desks behind which sat frowning, concentrating people—concentrating, as far as Ellen could tell, on something hovering above their desks, something invisible to Ellen but apparently engrossing to them. A man behind one of the desks beckoned her over and offered her a job at InterSpace as though it was something he had done a dozen times already that day and expected to do a dozen more before heading home. When she accepted enthusiastically, he nodded and then waved a small beeping, blinking object in front of her face.

He stared at the space above his desk and seemed surprised for a moment. "That's interesting," he muttered. "No record." He shrugged, not really interested at all. "Go back down to the building's front lobby," he told Ellen. "In a few minutes, a van will be leaving for the complex. There'll be a group of you ready to go by then. You'll be assembling down there."

"The complex?"

He looked at her in surprise. "The IS complex, of course. East of the city. You'll be staying there while you train. Looks like someone already opened an IS account for you and deposited your first paycheck in it. Good luck." He turned his attention back to the invisible something hovering above his desk, and she ceased to exist for him.

Not all that different from Rosie the Riveter, she thought. Except that now I'll be working to build things, not blow them up.

The complex was enormous but not particularly complex.

It covered a huge area of land east of Denver. It was a self-contained city, with streets laid out in a simply numbered grid system that bore no relationship to the street numbering and naming conventions of the city next door to it. It had shops and entertainment centers, buildings that contained classrooms, buildings that housed the fifty thousand or so people living on the complex at any given time, and other buildings whose function Ellen never did learn.

When she and a group of other recruits were brought to the complex by the van on her first day, they were taken to the building they would all be staying in. A genial older man greeted them. He was white haired and twinkly eyed, and, like Greg, he made Ellen think of Santa Claus.

"I'm Wally," he told the dozen slightly dazed young men

and women. "I'm the supervisor of this building. That means I'm here to help you feel comfortable and to take care of your needs. I guess I'm kind of like your grandfather." He chuckled.

Ellen could sense the people around her relaxing. How different this was, she thought, from Hughes and his welcome to Tempus.

But at Tempus, Tommy had been there to greet her on her first day.

She looked around at her new companions. Not a Tommy among them.

One of her fellow recruits, a young man, said, "I have needs I don't think you can take care of, Grandpa."

There was an embarrassed silence, but then Wally laughed loudly, and the whole group followed suit. "Oh, I know, Michael Obeid," Wally said. "I used to be young." He chuckled and looked off into space as though indulging in a memory. "That's why we give you a few free days, Michael. Your training won't begin until the end of the week. In the meantime, I want you all to wander around the complex and make yourselves at home. Enjoy everything we have to offer here. It's a free country. You kids are our hope for the future, and come the end of the week, we're going to be working you really hard, but we want you to have fun, too."

Ellen tried to imagine Hughes saying that to the group he had brought to Tempus, and she smiled at the image.

"So we can go anywhere we like?"

It was Obeid, the same young man who had spoken before. Ellen looked him over. He might be worth getting to know, she thought.

"No, I didn't say that. You can go anywhere you're allowed

to go. If you can open a door, you're allowed to go in there. If the door won't open for you, that means the place is off–limits."

The others nodded as though this was all quite normal. Ellen looked around at them and was surprised. Didn't they have any curiosity?

"Wally," she said, "what if I want to go back into the city for a while?"

Wally frowned. He stared at her. "Well, Ellen Maxwell, there is a public transport station on the complex, and from there you can take a train into downtown Denver. But we discourage you from doing that at this stage of your IS career. Later, when you've been in training for a while, feel free to take the occasional short trip into the city. But at this point, we want you to think of IS and your training cadre as your family."

"I need to look someone up. An old friend. I think he might be in Denver."

Wally frowned again. "Ellen, we think you'll find that all your real friends are right here, in IS. However, we do have excellent research facilities right here on the complex. IS has the best facilities of every sort you'll find anywhere. You can do your searching for your former acquaintance right here on the complex. IS prefers that you stay on the complex, and as we say here, IS knows best."

Ellen spent her free days exploring the complex and looking for information about Tommy.

The complex was vast, but the parts that were not out of bounds weren't of much interest to her. The information she was looking for didn't seem to exist.

There were infobooths all over the complex much like the

one she had used in the city, although the simulated humans living in them—that's how she thought of it—didn't seem as friendly or warm or, well, human as the ones in the public booths. They could answer her questions about world history or current politics or science or art or technology, but they knew nothing about a young man named Tommy Stillwell who had arrived in Denver fifty years earlier. They could dredge up old records about Napoleon and Hitler, but they could find nothing about Tommy.

She despaired at first. Was this the end of it? Was she here and cut off forever from her world and from her hopes of finding Tommy again?

Classes began, and she threw herself into them. She felt like an ignorant child compared to the others. So much had happened during the last hundred years, so much new technology had appeared. Just to keep up in class, she had to teach herself things the others took for granted and had been familiar with all their lives. That was the only time she found herself appreciating the capabilities of the IS information booths.

Classroom lectures gave way to hands–on training for the kind of tech work she'd be doing in space if she were chosen to go there. That astonishing future waited for those who proved themselves here on the ground. Ellen was determined to be one of them.

She *would* find Tommy. She had survived her trip, so Tommy must have survived his. If he had made it alive to 1995, she knew he would have survived thereafter. He wasn't the kind to give in or be defeated. The records that would lead her to him must exist. IS just wasn't as good at tracking down information as it thought it was.

Twenty

On a weekend, Ellen headed for the city.

It was Saturday morning, bright and sunny and already warm. She wore shorts, a tank top, and sandals—standard clothing for her generation in the summer in this time and place. She still felt uncomfortable exposing so much of herself to the view of others, but she couldn't deny the pride and pleasure she felt at the yearning glances of men. She wished the women of this era wouldn't look at her so hostilely, though. It wasn't her fault that she was so much leaner than they were and moved so much more vigorously.

She made her way across the complex quickly, hoping she wouldn't run into any of the people she'd met during the week. But as she strode along a pathway between green, close-cropped lawns, she heard someone calling her name.

It was a voice she knew. She picked up the pace, but Hal's legs were longer than hers, and he was determined. Resigned, she slowed and let him catch up with her.

"Ellen!" He was gasping for breath but trying not to show it. She sensed that he was embarrassed by her obviously greater fitness. "Where you headed? I'll walk with you."

"I'm going off the complex for a while."

Hal put on the combination frightened and worried look that Ellen had already learned to expect. "You really shouldn't, you know."

"Why not? It's a free country."

"It certainly is! Freest in the world! But, you know ... Have you read your employee orientation handbook yet? They explain it all in there."

Ellen hadn't stopped walking during the conversation. Now she picked up speed again. "Sure, sure. We're all one big happy family. I'm already missing the wider world, and I want to go to the main public access booth to look something up."

"You can look up anything in one of our own infobooths, right here on the complex."

"Not quite anything."

"Anything you need."

"No, anything InterSpace says I need."

"IS knows best." He said it without pausing to think.

"Hal, I know what's best for me. No one else does."

"But—Okay. I'll come with you."

"You don't have to."

"It's no trouble at all."

Ellen sighed. She stopped and turned to face Hal. "I wanted to go by myself. I wanted to see a bit more of the city."

"But you don't know your way around! You'll get lost."

She laughed. "I'm a big girl. And I have a good sense of direction. I'll be fine. I'll see you on Monday."

"You really don't want me to go with you?" He looked down at the ground and then glanced up at her.

"Jesus," Ellen muttered. She hated it when a man behaved

like a puppy dog. When a puppy behaved that way, she wanted to pick it up and mother it. When a man did it, she wanted to kick him.

She found herself suddenly thinking of Frank and thinking that she had in effect kicked him, even though he hadn't tried that look on her. This guy was no Frank, but Frank wasn't around. His very absence made her want to apologize to Frank for hurting him, and yet for all she knew she'd never have that chance. "All right, Hal. If you want to come with me, you can."

"I do want to. Great! Thanks." He grinned from ear to ear.

Despite herself, Ellen laughed, amused by his boyish enthusiasm. He was a nice looking fellow, and pleasant enough company when he tried, and emotionally safer than Mike Obeid. She missed Tommy fiercely, emotionally and physically. She missed Frank, too—not his body or his love, of course, but his steadiness and strength and warmth. Hal didn't measure up to either of them, but she didn't have either of them, and Hal was here.

It was a short trip into town by rail—ten minutes from the station at the western edge of the InterSpace complex to the eastern edge of downtown Denver. It would have been even easier to make the trip had the rail line extended further into the IS complex. She suspected that that was why it didn't.

Ellen turned to stare out the window behind her at the landscape and buildings rushing by. She was thrown into the past, into another similar train trip. "Do you know if the old train station downtown is still in use?" she asked Hal. "If we stay on the train, do we end up there?"

"Damned if I know," he said. "You could ask when you get

to the infobooth. I've only been on this train a couple of times before, and I didn't go all the way into downtown."

"Why not?"

"No need to. Didn't want to, either. Look, I've been at IS for more than a year, and in all that time, I've only needed to go off the complex twice. I went just as far as I had to, that's all."

It didn't really matter about the old train station, even if it was still being used, she told herself. That other world was a hundred years in the past, on the other side of an unbridgeable divide, a chasm that grew wider with every day that passed. Information and future plans—those were the most important things now. "Where's the nearest main public booth?" she asked Hal.

"I don't know that, either," he said, his voice betraying his annoyance. "Ask the train."

"What?"

"That town you came from must sure be small." He raised his voice. "Train, what's the first stop within ten minutes' walk of a main public access booth?"

A voice from somewhere in the ceiling said, "The Broadway stop. One minute, six seconds."

It was a male voice, pleasant, and to Ellen's ears it sounded real, not in any way mechanical.

"You mean one minute from here, or a one-minute walk to the booth?" Hal's annoyance was even greater. "Stupid machine."

"It's now fifty-eight seconds from here. Walk south two blocks on Broadway from the stop."

"I didn't ask you for that part, machine."

Ellen said, "Thank you, Train."

"You're welcome."

Hal looked startled. "They never say that to me!"

The infobooth was just off the sidewalk, at the edge of a small park. It was the same sort of roofless, open structure Ellen had used on her first day. When she stepped into it, Hal tried to crowd in with her. Ellen pushed him away and pointed to the lawn next to the booth. "Stay."

The black wall in front of her vanished, replaced by an image of the same young man who had appeared the first time. He smiled the same warm smile. "How may I help you, Ellen Maxwell?"

"You remember my name!"

"Of course. How my I help you?"

I wish you were real, Ellen thought. "I'm trying to find someone, a man named Tommy Stillwell. Thomas Stillwell, I mean."

"That information produces an excessive number of results. Please limit the search by adding more details."

Ellen gave the machine a brief description of Tommy, then added, "He might have arrived in Denver in 1995. He was twenty-one years old."

"There are employment records for a man matching those parameters in 1995. He held temporary jobs in Denver from February through April. There are no records of him after May of that year."

"He's alive!"

"He was alive in June 1995," the virtual helper corrected her dispassionately.

Ellen leaned against the wall for support. He had arrived,

he had been here, maybe not far from where she was now.

"Are you sure you can't trace him after 1995?"

"Of course I'm sure."

What about Tempus? Tommy would have tried to contact Tempus. That would be a link to him.

"I'm also trying to find a company, an organization, named Tempus. They were in business somewhere in western Colorado during World War Two."

"I can find no records of such a company or organization. Is that all?"

"Wait! I know there was some sort of shooting or something there. It happened on February 8, 1945. People were killed. There must be a record of that!"

"I can find no record of such an event. There was one unexplained episode of violence on that date in the area you specified. Would you like to see that record?"

"Please!"

The virtual helper vanished, replaced by a newspaper floating in the void where he had been. Ellen reached instinctively for the paper. She stopped herself in mid–motion and looked around quickly to see if anyone had noticed. The few pedestrians passing by were paying no attention to her. Hal was bending over and looking with interest at something in the lawn.

The newspaper was the *Rocky Mountain News* from Sunday, February 11, 1945. She remembered seeing the same newspaper for sale in Union Station when she arrived in Denver in 1944. This issue had probably been written by the same reporters and printed by the same printers as that one. She longed to hold it, this link with that lost past that still seemed like the present to her.

Most of the front page was filled with war news. Some sort of big meeting between Roosevelt, Churchill, and Stalin had ended. The Allies—and the Soviets—were overrunning Germany. The Canadian army had just captured Cleve. Why did that sound familiar to her? She remembered Frank mentioning it. It had some connection to an English king, but she couldn't remember what. But that was ancient history. This was happening now. No, it isn't, she reminded herself. It's also ancient history. But suddenly it didn't seem that way. It seemed like fresh news, vital news.

She felt dizzy. She grabbed at the wall of the booth on her right and held it for a while, squeezing her eyes shut.

When she opened them again, a small item in the lower right-hand corner of the newspaper page was blinking bright red a few times to draw her attention. She read:

MYSTERIOUS EXPLOSION
AND FIRE ON WESTERN SLOPE

A private airplane enthusiast from Grand Junction reports sighting a tremendous explosion and fierce fire in an uninhabited area some miles north of the town of Milton. Our informant, who prefers not to be identified, says that he saw the event from some miles distant but did not attempt to fly closer because on a previous occasion, when he had tried to approach that area, he was warned away by what seemed to be military aircraft lacking identifying marks.

Rumors have persisted for some time in

towns in the area of a secret government installation somewhere in the region, performing work of a classified nature.

Repeated calls to the War Department by this reporter have gone unanswered.

The virtual helper appeared again. "Will that be all, Ellen Maxwell?"

She was stunned. What could that fire and explosion have been but the aftermath of the battle whose beginning she had seen?

She didn't know what to do, what avenue to explore next.

One possibility occurred to her, a slender one. "Maybe there are records of Tempus somewhere else," she said. Her tone was almost pleading. "I know about their site in western Colorado, but maybe their headquarters were somewhere else. Can you look for—"

"As I said, there are no records of such a company or organization." He spoke slowly and with emphasis, staring into her eyes. "It is fruitless to pursue this matter further."

He seemed so real at that moment. How did she know he wasn't? How would she be able to tell the difference between a real human being and a computer construct? Computers were still strange and mysterious machines to her, seemingly limitless in power, capable of anything.

Not that that mattered. The warning she had just been given was real and clear.

"Thank you," she said. "I have no further queries."

The wall in front of her turned black and silent again.

Ellen backed out of the booth. She felt aimless. She had

spent almost a week in this time filled with purpose and determination, but now she felt lost. What was there for her to do now? Settle into InterSpace and try to feel at home in this bizarre world? She was a century out of her time. Even if Tommy was still alive, how could she hope to find him?

Fifty years from now, she thought, Frank will arrive. And so what? He'll be in the same fix I'm in now.

"Hey, look at this!" It was Hal, pointing at the ground. In front of him was a small stone with a metal plaque fixed to it. "Says here that this was the site of the main library until they finally tore it down thirty years ago. I learned about those buildings in school. Big places filled with stuff printed on paper. What a waste of space!"

"Libraries ... " Ellen remembered how often she had escaped into the library as a child. "They're nice places."

"You still had one in that town you grew up in?" He shook his head in amazement. "Glad I grew up in a city. You're like my dad. He couldn't stop talking about how great things were when he was young. Libraries, especially. The day we learned about them in school, I came home and told him. I thought he'd laugh, but instead he got real sad and talked about how he loved the library when he was a kid and how upset he was when they started shutting them down."

"I'd like to meet him."

"Well, he's dead. Died about ten years ago."

"I'm so sorry!" Impulsively, she put her hand on his arm. "What happened?"

"He was murdered."

"My God, that's awful! Who did it?"

Hal shrugged. "They never found out. Just some crazy man,

I guess. Shot him while he was walking into his office building. The guy ran away. So, you ready to go back to the complex, finally? Did you find out whatever it was that was so important?"

She took her hand off his arm again. "Yes, I'm ready to go back."

The train back to the IS complex was almost empty. Ellen sat next to a window, and Hal sat next to her, on the aisle seat. As the train started moving, Hal said thoughtfully, "Yeah, my dad. He was okay. Except that he kept talking about how much better everything was when he was young. Got on my nerves. He told me he used to have a little gadget he could hold in one hand, and it did everything a main public access booth can do."

"Did you ask him what happened to his little gadget?"

"Yeah, I did. He said that one day UNOT announced some kind of protocol change in the Net so that those things wouldn't work any more, and they sent people around to collect the gadgets. He said they claimed it was to improve the Net, but he couldn't see any improvement. He said things got worse, not better. He said that happened when I was about five. I don't remember any of it, of course. I asked my history teacher about it one day. He said my dad was right, those gadgets had existed, but my dad was exaggerating. They weren't really all that good. The booths are a lot better. I told that to my dad when I got home, and he got angry. Just kept on about how much better things were before."

Ellen was about to ask Hal what UNOT was when she noticed that one of the other passengers, a broad-shouldered, middle-aged man, was staring at her intently.

There were only two other people in the car with them, and both of them were lost in their own dreams. The man who was staring at her was sitting half the car away, facing in Ellen's direction. His stare was fixed and unblinking. The only movement in his face was his slowly broadening smile. It was a predatory smile, not a friendly one.

He rose from his seat and stepped out into the aisle and began to walk slowly toward her. His eyes never left her face.

She noted how smoothly he stood up and how easily he balanced against the sway of the train. She had noted his broad shoulders when he was sitting. Now she could tell that he was tall and powerfully built. He licked his lips quickly.

Ellen said sharply to Hal, "Let me out!"

"What?"

"Let me out. Get out of my way."

"What? We're not there yet!"

The man was close enough now that Ellen felt the first stirrings of panic at being trapped. She shoved Hal hard. He slid sideways and almost fell into the aisle, catching himself just in time. "Hey! What—"

Ellen pushed past him and out into the aisle. Now that she had room to move, her panic vanished and her Tempus training took over. She stood comfortably, knees slightly bent, right leg toward her opponent, chin tucked in, shoulders rounded, arms up and hands balled into fists.

The big man laughed and fell into a sloppy parody of her pose. "Ha! A fighter!"

Could he really be so untrained? Or was he trying to mislead her? Ellen waited for his next move.

He threw a clumsy punch with his right fist, looping and

wide, exposing his face completely. His head was up, his chin out.

For an instant, she hesitated, fearing that he was good enough to look bad. Then she hit hard with a straight right that connected solidly with his chin.

He sat down heavily on the floor, looking dazed. He shook his head and looked up at her with sudden fear. For a moment, she could smell his sweat, and then the odor was whisked away by the train's air conditioning.

He muttered something, scuttled backward a few feet in panic, stood up, and ran to the nearest door. The train was slowing for its next stop. He stood at the door, watching her, shrinking back as though afraid she would come after him. As soon as the train stopped, he stepped off onto the platform and hurried away.

The door closed and the train began to move, accelerating away from the station.

Ellen became aware that Hal was still saying "What?" and that he had been repeating it throughout the confrontation.

"Did that sound like Russian to you?" she asked.

"What?"

"What he said just before he left. I couldn't quite hear him. Did it sound like Russian?"

"You're crazy! Russian? Here? I don't understand."

"Maybe not. Maybe he was just a drunk. I just thought he was planning something."

"Planning something? You mean—" Hal looked at the now closed door in alarm. "It's a good thing the train slowed when it did and knocked him off his feet. You should have stood behind me! I could have handled him."

Maybe you could have, if he was just some drunk, Ellen thought. If he was a trained Communist agent sent here to get me, he'd have killed you quickly.

Pretty inept for a trained agent, though, she thought. He didn't even see my punch coming. Maybe he's an agent *and* a drunk. The Russians all drink too much, and the poor guy's probably as lost and out of his time as I am. He can't go back home, either.

Maybe he didn't expect me to be so fast.

Frank had complimented her once on her speed. That had been a proud moment for her.

"It's really getting dangerous out here," Hal said. "That's another good reason to stay on the InterSpace complex. I heard there were three rapes and a couple of murders in Denver last year. It's chaos there. It's scary. Could you stay on the complex from now on, please? As a favor to me?"

"Might as well," Ellen said. She made herself smile at Hal, hiding her despair at the loss of her friend, of her lover, of her world.

Twenty–One

He watched the monitor. Wherever he was, a monitor was always there—the size of his hand or covering a wall, the size determined by convenience, but always there. And the beautiful young face was always centered in it, the same young face, his dream and his delight always with him, always remote from him. At night, she filled his dreams, a memory made almost solid, even though this was real and she was there and solid, only a few hundred miles away from him.

Tommy switched his gaze to the mirror. He had almost become used to the face in the mirror. He had almost convinced himself that it wasn't too old a face for her, that she wouldn't mind.

He knew better.

Delia entered without knocking. It was a habit of long duration.

She glanced at the monitor and caught a glimpse of the young woman's face just before Tommy ordered the monitors to go blank. "She reminds me of my mother, this Ellen Maxwell of yours. As far as I can remember anyway." Those faint, fading memories. She had almost stopped trying to clutch at them, to hold onto them.

She wondered about Tommy's obsession with Ellen Maxwell, whoever she was. There were many beautiful young women working for IA and its many front organizations, and Delia assumed that some of them would be willing to sleep with Tommy just because of his position of power, despite his age. But as far as she knew, Tommy had never taken advantage of what might have been offered him. Instead, he watched this girl—watched, but never approached her. Delia suspected that Ellen Maxwell didn't even know Tommy existed.

"Really? So that's what your mother looked like."

"I think so. Something like that. That song you're playing … " She closed her eyes and sang along almost in a whisper, "*We'll meet again, don't know where, don't know when, but I know we'll meet again some sunny day.*" She opened her eyes again and laughed in embarrassment. "I heard that one a lot when I was a kid."

"The old music was the best," Tommy said. "I think I would have liked your parents. I wish I could have met them."

"Yes," Delia said. "I wish that, too."

"So. Something must be wrong."

"I don't come here only if something's wrong."

"Usually," Tommy said.

"You're due for another treatment."

"God, I hate those. I wish you could make it permanent."

"We're working on it."

"And more thorough—more than just stopping the deterioration."

"We're working on that, too."

She hesitated, then decided to go ahead and say it.

"Tommy, why don't you introduce yourself to that girl?" She held her breath, afraid of his reaction.

"She's young and beautiful. I'm an old man."

Delia was caught by surprise. "Maybe that wouldn't matter to her."

"I'm an evil man. She would be repelled by what I've become."

An odd thing for him to say, Delia thought. It implied that the young woman knew what he had been before InterAgency. "We do what we have to do, to survive in this place. That doesn't make us evil."

"Of course it does, Delia. I have so much to atone for." He nodded toward the monitor. "I don't even have the right to be in the same room with her, the way I am now."

Delia thought it was the sort of thing an infatuated boy might say about a girl he adored and had placed on a pedestal. Was this some strange side effect of the treatment? Was it affecting Tommy's mind? She had been using it on herself and her lab team for twenty years, and she hadn't seen any signs of mental effects. The rats that had received the first successful form of the treatment were twenty-five years old now and seemed normal. Tommy had been receiving the treatment for less than a year. But he had always seemed different from anyone else, and she knew that his cells were unusual. Perhaps he was reacting atypically.

She chose her words carefully. "I doubt if she's that naive and unworldly. Give her more credit."

"I know a lot more about her than you realize." He stood up. "Well, let's go downstairs and get this damned treatment taken care of."

As they walked down the hallway together, Delia asked, "How safe are we in here?"

Walls, floor, and ceiling were all a dull gray. The lighting was uniform and subdued with no visible source. Delia always thought it was like being in a metal cage. Sometimes, she felt protected up here. More often, she felt trapped and vulnerable.

Tommy stopped walking and stared at her. "You worry about that? Still?"

"Constantly."

He shook his head and started walking again. "Either you are vulnerable, or you aren't. When your number's up, it's up."

Invisible cameras observed them as they moved. To left and right, and above and below, hallways of whose existence she was unaware paralleled the one they were in. Armed teams paced beside and above and below them, moving at the same rate they did, constantly alert. The walls and floor and ceiling that seemed like solid metal to Delia were transparent from the other side. The men and women accompanying them silently and invisibly were deadly killers even without weapons, even deadlier with them, and all were utterly loyal to Tommy.

"Fatalism," Delia said. "It always surprises me, coming from you. You've always seemed like the sort of man who takes action and tries to control events."

"I'm a fatalist, but I'm not a fool. We're safe. You're remembering Jeff and Christine."

"I've never been able to forget them."

"That's good. It will keep you from trusting people."

"I don't want to not trust people, Tommy. People are good inside. Most people, anyway. I truly believe that."

He shook his head again. "No. People aren't good or evil

inside. They're just puppets. Fate uses them for good or evil purposes of its own. They don't have any say in the matter. They think they do, but they're fooling themselves."

Enemies made constant attempts on his life. They were all from within InterAgency, he was sure, for no outside killer would be able to penetrate even the edges of the agency, let alone reach Tommy. He lived in this building. On his rare trips outside, he was protected by teams paralleling his routes just as he was inside the building. It was a prison of his own making, a claustrophobic life, but it was safe. Unable to subvert his people or reach him physically, Tommy's enemies tried to eavesdrop on his conversations. They never succeeded. Like their teams of assassins, all such attempts were intercepted and terminated by Tommy's efficient, deadly specialists.

They had reached the elevator at the end of the hall. The door opened as they approached.

Tommy and Delia stepped inside, and Delia said, "Clinic level."

Even his own people couldn't hear what he said to Delia here. Nor would any of them try. They were prevented by their intense loyalty and by the knowledge that their own comrades watched them constantly.

The elevator began its long descent. Tommy said, "Take it from me, we're quite safe. Time is a lot more dangerous to us than people are."

"Time?"

"Age. You told me this treatment isn't really permanent. It stops working eventually."

"In rats. I'm not sure about humans, and especially you."

"What, I'm unusual somehow?"

"I've been examining that tissue sample I took from you last week."

"Yeah, I'll never forget it."

"I was proud of you. You were very grown up about it. Seriously, though, your chromosomes have the longest telomeres I've ever seen."

"No woman has ever said that to me before."

"I'm sure that's true. Do you have unusually long-lived relatives?"

He thought for a moment. "Don't think so. Pretty average, so far as I know."

"How odd. I'd ask if anything very unusual had happened to you, but I can't think of anything that would have that effect."

"I wonder if that would be a good pickup line in a bar. 'Say, I've got really long telathings.'"

"Telomeres. I suppose it would depend on the kind of girl you were trying to pick up."

Suddenly, the conversation was making Delia uneasy. To her relief, the elevator stopped. "Here we are," she said. "If you're a good boy and don't cry, we'll give you a lollipop afterwards. Butterscotch."

Tommy laughed. "My favorite!" He strode down the short hallway and into the white room at the end. He was smiling. No matter how much he hated the treatment itself, he loved what it did for him.

The waiting medical team stiffened to attention when he entered the room.

"Hello, youngsters!" Tommy said loudly. "Relax, everybody. Let's get to it."

They seemed at ease right away and set about their tasks

without hurry or wasted motion. Watching from the doorway, Delia was proud of them. She was also amazed yet again by Tommy's ability to win people's confidence and loyalty. He might think he was evil, but she was sure that the world needed him.

Twenty-Two

"I'm afraid to even look," Ellen said. "I know my name isn't on the list." She didn't really believe that. She felt confident that she had been selected for space duty. She was pretending mainly to make Hal feel happier. At the least, she hoped it would make him shut up about his own entirely justified fears of not making the cut.

At least it's not like Tempus, she thought. They're not going to take Hal out behind a hill and shoot him. They'll just drop him from the program. And I won't have him tagging along after me. A nice, clean break.

They had finally reached the front of the crowd and could see the list of names taped to the wall. It seemed a primitive way to do it, Ellen thought. Or maybe it was just a cold way to do it.

As she had expected, her name was near the top. As she had not expected and was dismayed to see, Hal's name was also on the list. His was the last one, but he was there. He had made the cut, and he would be accompanying her to space.

"Yaaah! Hee aah!"

It was Hal, jumping up and down and shouting and making a fool of himself, as usual. Ellen couldn't help but laugh, despite herself. She hoped that if she tried, she'd be able to keep finding him amusing.

"She looks happy," Tommy said. "I did the right thing. She'll be safer with him there. God, what a drip he is, though. Couldn't she do better?"

Delia looked from the monitor to him and then back to the monitor again. She thought she detected more resignation than happiness in Ellen's face, but she wouldn't tell Tommy that.

"Do her good to forget about the past and get on with her new life," Tommy said. "Maybe she already has. Anyway, she'll be safe in space."

"Somewhat. InterSpace is run by InterAgency, after all."

"Sure, but they leave the spacemen alone. They're too valuable. Have you ever listened to the conversations some of them have, up there on their space stations and ships?"

Delia shook her head. She would never be comfortable with eavesdropping, and she only did it if she felt it was necessary for her own safety.

"You should. It's interesting. More interesting than what people talk about down here on Earth, that's for sure. They're intelligent people up there."

"Of course. They're the best we have. The cream of the crop."

"Yeah," Tommy said, "but it's more than that. They're subversives. They're openly anti–government. They discuss all kinds of alternate politics and economics. Fascinating stuff."

"I've heard about that. IA doesn't mind as long as they only talk that way in space. It's the price we pay to get the best work out of our best people. But you know, some of them have trouble keeping their mouths shut when they come back down. They develop dangerous habits up there."

"I'll make sure she's safe. Does she still remind you of your mother?"

Delia nodded. "I could almost believe she's a reincarnation of her."

"I'm surprised that a biologist would believe in reincarnation."

"Oh, I don't. Sometimes I wish I could, though. It's hard to accept that the past and the people I loved are lost to me forever." I wish I could go back and change things, she thought. I wish I could save them.

"The past is set in stone," Tommy said. He might have been responding to her thoughts, but he was staring at the monitor, lost in thoughts of his own. "Good or bad, it can't be changed. We can only change the future."

He pushed himself to his feet. "My knees hurt. I guess that's my future. And I have a meeting. That's also my future."

"I'll leave. But if your knees hurt, why don't you sit down."

"Because every time I do, I have this stupid fear that I'll never stand up again."

"You have some very strange ideas."

"Maybe it's something to do with my telathings."

After Delia had left, though, he did sit down again. This meeting would probably go on for quite a while, and if he stood for too long, the constant ache in his lower back would become agony.

He let the monitor showing Ellen continue to track her. The wall in front of him gave way to a small conference room in Atlanta. Three men were seated at a round table. They all faced him. When his magnified image appeared in front of them, they stiffened as though coming to attention. "Gentlemen," Tommy said, "let's begin. Halverson, why don't you go first."

"Yes, sir. Thank you sir." The man's face glowed, while his two companions looked deflated. They hadn't yet realized that Tommy determined the order of precedence randomly each week and it didn't indicate who was higher in his favor. "The religious leaders are all on board now, sir."

"What about the one you mentioned last week? You said he was a problem."

"No longer a problem, sir."

"Ah. And you're sure they all understand who's really in charge?"

"Yes, sir."

After being marginalized by the social revolt earlier in the century, they were now willing to accept IA as their master in return for being given a seat in government again. All you have to do with anyone, Tommy thought, is make a big enough offer. "All right. Let's get into the details."

The details flowed in. Halverson and the other two were conduits, each representing his own large organization and presenting its information to Tommy. It was the larger picture that Tommy really wanted, more than the details, and the picture was of growing control of governments, corporations, and powerful social institutions and growing division and weakness among those institutions and governments that still offered opposition. Even the Chinese wall was finally cracking. Tommy could foresee a time when IA's control would be complete.

But I'll still be at the second level within IA, he thought. Maybe not even that. I don't really know.

Who was above him? And what were their goals? Once they had unchallenged control of the world, what then?

Twenty–Three

"Catch!"

Ellen turned toward Mike in time to see the clamp tumbling slowly toward her, flashing in the sunlight. She reached clumsily for it, missed. It hit her shoulder—she could feel the *thump*—and bounced off, spinning irretrievably away, disappearing against the brilliant field of stars.

"Oops! Another fifty bucks down the drain. Or wherever."

Ellen laughed. She could imagine Tommy doing something like that, and then joking in the same way about his own irresponsibility.

Hal's voice filled her helmet. "Christ, people, we're over budget on this project already. Will you quit playing games?"

He was right, of course. Mike had drifted close enough for her to make out his grin through the shaded glass, and she found herself grinning in response. "Take a breather, Hal," she said. "We're serious enough. Come on, Mike."

It took an hour of fumbling and cursing, trapped in suits that seemed to get hotter and stuffier and clumsier as they worked, before the tear in the station's skin was clamped tightly enough. They applied a temporary seal, a strip of thick rubber with vacuum-safe glue on one side, over the clamps. Then they floated next to the repair for another two hours while the section on the other side of the outer wall was slowly pressurized.

The seal seemed to be holding. The next step—the permanent repair job—would be up to another crew, wearing lighter suits, working on the inside of the station.

Ellen and Mike could just possibly have managed to do their job from the inside, as well, but Ellen had wanted to see the stars.

She had come to space five years ago to see the stars, to be free of Earth, to fulfill her childhood dream. To be there, just to be there. But in practice, too much of the time she might as well have stayed on Earth. What windows there were on most of the stations were too small and too thick to satisfy her. The drawings in the books and magazines she had read as a kid had been more exciting than what she could see through that thick glass.

On most of the stations she had worked on, the gravity was less than one g, but it was always there, nonetheless—enough to counter the feeling of being in space, but not enough to keep her from losing bone mass and muscle tone, no matter how hard she worked out in the station gyms.

And working out was all she could do. She couldn't find anyone to spar with her. It wasn't because of her sex, which would have been the problem in the era she had grown up in. Rather it was because no one seemed interested in studying or practicing any kind of self-defense.

She had offered to teach a few people, like Hal, to fight. Hal's reaction was typical. "Why would I want to learn something like that?"

"To defend yourself against an attacker. That's why it's called 'self-defense.'"

"That's what we have police for."

"The police can't always be there. Remember that time in the train in Denver, right after we met? That man who was about to attack me?"

Hal shook his head. "I don't remember that at all."

She tried to remind him, but his puzzlement turned to fear, so she gave up.

At Ellen's urging, they had both transferred recently to this zero-g research station. It was the zero g she wanted, and the physical exertion of the work. It was low-level work, mostly maintenance and repair, and she and Hal were at the bottom of the station totem pole, treated like dirt by most of the resident scientists. Whereas she looked at their pale, soft bodies, compared them to Tommy and Frank and herself, and felt superior.

In zero-g, she finally felt that she was in space. After more than five years working for InterSpace, almost all of that time spent in orbit, at last she really felt like a spaceman.

Hal, she suspected, hated it. He tolerated the lack of gravity and the condescension of the scientists just to be with her. She ought to be flattered, she thought. Increasingly, she was annoyed.

She was aware of the sweat drenching her inside the suit. "Seal's okay," she said. "Let's go inside. I need a shower."

"Me too," Mike said. "I'll join you."

Ellen laughed. "Dream on, sailor. You'll wait until I'm finished and dressed."

Hal said nothing, which filled Ellen with guilt. She wished he would say something. She wished he'd fight for her. Not physically, but why couldn't he at least put Mike in his place with a few strong words?

Tommy ... well, Tommy, she suspected, would have ripped Mike's helmet off and let him suffocate in the vacuum.

The irony was that Mike reminded her occasionally of Tommy. During that moment of horseplay, for example. And at other times, as well. He looked at her with the same kind of frank sexual desire as Tommy had, the kind of look that Hal was as incapable of as Frank had been. It excited her, whereas the hurt–puppy look annoyed her.

Inside the station, they floated in the tiny space that served as their common room. The surface dwellers down on Earth believed space workers lived in luxury. In fact, for all its money and power, InterSpace was miserly with personal facilities. The three of them bumped into each other constantly as they struggled to extract themselves from their bulky vacuum suits, maneuvering as best they could.

"Hate zero g," Hal grunted. "Be glad to get back down to gravity."

"Gravity kills spacemen," Mike said.

Hal muttered something and continued to wrestle with his suit.

Ellen was done first, stripped down to panties and halter top. She grabbed a wall handle. Mike, still struggling with his boots but otherwise naked except for underpants, stopped and stared at her. She held his glance for a moment, annoyed at herself for doing so. He raised his eyebrows. Ellen shook her head and launched herself toward the shower stall.

Hal hadn't noticed the exchange. Just as well, Ellen thought as she soaped herself.

The stall was a narrow cylinder, even more difficult to maneuver in than the common room. A river of air washed over her. Water sprayed in at one end of the cylinder, was carried down the cylinder's length by the flow of air, and was sucked into a drain at the other. Rather, most of it ended up in the drain. Inevitably, a certain amount always escaped and ended up as microscopic spheres drifting in the air of the common room. It was a foolish, inefficient way to clean oneself in zero g, but InterSpace's orbital workers had managed so far to resist any movement to replace the showers with superior waterless alternatives. The psychological comfort of a shower was irreplaceable.

But it was cramped and awkward. If she ever did give in and let Mike into the shower with her ... Ellen laughed. The image of the two of them trying to have sex in this tiny space was more amusing than arousing.

Well, no, she thought, you're being dishonest with yourself. Of course it's arousing. Mike is an exciting guy. Much more so than Hal. Which is of course what makes Hal so much safer than Mike.

She paused in her scrubbing and floated unmoving, letting the air and water wash down the length of her body.

She could admit the truth to herself, but she didn't like dwelling on it. These people, this place, this world—they had become real. The world she had come from was turning into a dream. She wanted human contact, wanted sex, needed emotional warmth and comfort, but she was aware of the need to avoid anything too real, too intense, any relationship that would make this world more solid and substantial at the expense of that other one, that one lost to her in the past, that world where Tommy still lived.

She sighed, turned the water off, and floated drying in the flow of air. Rosie the Riveter would have been thrilled at the idea of building and repairing space stations, but Rosie was used to being able to go home to her husband and kids at night.

Well, kids, anyway, she reminded herself. Rosie's husband would have been away at the war. Or maybe dead. Where's Tommy now? It's like he's away at the war. Is he still alive? I don't even know what "still" means! What happened to him? Oh, Tommy!

She felt tears swelling in her eyes. She squeezed her eyes shut, rubbed the tears away with the heels of her hands, took a deep breath.

Less than fifty years, now, she reminded herself. Then Frank will be showing up. I can make it.

When they were all showered and dressed in clean clothing, they made their way through the ramshackle structure to a large module that served as a dining hall. Zero-g food was rarely appetizing, but there were other people here and the illusion at least of warmth and a normal life.

Twenty–Four

The station was huge behind them, a vast structure, a strange assemblage of struts and cylinders and spheres, with numerous separate modules accompanying it in orbit. She could see suited figures floating within the structure, welding torches winking against the blackness, tugs approaching the station and departing from it. It was 25 times as big now as when she had arrived at it. Coming back to it after a few months away, so that she could catch the shuttle down to Earth, she had been astonished at how big it was.

And a lot of that increase in size is due to me, Ellen thought. To my work. Whatever else I do or don't do, I've contributed that much to this world in the past five years.

She had been a time traveler, jumping forward decades. She had traveled hundreds of miles on the surface of the Earth. Somehow, that all seemed trivial compared to the years she had spent in this structure, far bigger than anything else in Earth orbit other than the Moon itself.

I was standing at the gateway to the universe, she thought.

She sat half turned in her seat, staring back through the porthole, until the ship's changing attitude took the station out of sight behind its wing.

She turned to her companion. "Glad to be going back to gravity at last?"

Hal looked queasy. "I'm feeling uncomfortable already. Maybe this wasn't such a good idea."

Ellen sighed. No, maybe it wasn't such a good idea. In five years in space, she'd lived with four different men, and finally, giving in to his begging, she'd returned to Hal. She'd even let him invite himself on her vacation on Earth. Six months of paid vacation ... Time enough to get used to gravity again, but would it be time enough to get used to Hal?

When they landed in Salt Lake City and tried to stand up from their seats to leave the ship, Ellen was horrified. She had been working hard physically for five years! She had been exercising religiously in the station's gym for the past week, preparing for the return to gravity. Now she could scarcely support her own weight, and she could feel everything, every part of her body, being pulled downward—her breasts, her head, even, she could have sworn, her internal organs. This was intolerable! Six months of this? How would she endure six hours? Six minutes? How would she be able to sleep tonight without suffocating?

Fortunately, Hal started whining at that point. Ellen forced herself to her feet, stepped out into the aisle, and started walking toward the exit. "Oh, come on," she snapped at him. "Don't be such a weakling. You've been complaining about zero g for years."

He struggled to follow her, gasping and wheezing. "Gravity kills spacemen," he managed to say.

"If gravity doesn't, maybe I will," Ellen said. At Hal's look of alarm, she said quickly, "That's a joke. Come on."

She'd seen the numbers, though. Space workers who retired to Earth tended to die prematurely, often within a year or two of coming home. Someone had told her that it was because the unaccustomed stresses of gravity wore their bodies out. Spending years in zero g was fundamentally weakening and destructive. Indeed, the longer a spaceman spent in space before retirement, the sooner he was likely to die after returning to Earth.

"Look," she said, "we're just here for a vacation. We're not retiring. There's a long time to go before that, for both of us. We'll get used to this, we'll have a good time, and then we'll go back home. Back up to the station, I mean. You'll be fine."

They took the train from the spaceport into the city and then rented a private car for the trip into the mountains.

Traffic was heavy all the way, but Ellen didn't mind that. She couldn't get enough of the greenery, the mountainsides, the sky—the openness. There were no manmade walls hemming her in. In space, she had been limited, confined. Much as she loved being in space, she was surprised to realize that here on Earth she felt free.

Physically free, anyway, she thought, glancing over at Hal. He was leaning against his door, sleeping, oblivious to the beauty around them.

He's tired, she told herself. He has a right to be. I would be, too, if I weren't so excited.

The similarity to another trip into the mountains, more than a hundred years earlier, occurred to her. Then, the car had been moving westward, whereas now she was headed east. Then, she had been on the way to Tempus and the unknown, in a strange vehicle driven by a human being. Now, she was on her way to a campground, headed into the not–very–unknown, in a car driven by a computer. But now, as then, she was in a foreign world where her neighbors seemed to be at home but she felt alien.

The car left the broad, multi–lane highway and turned onto a two–lane road that headed sharply upward. Even here, the traffic was heavy. It stayed heavy all the way to the campground.

And into it. The advertisement she had looked at online had persuaded Ellen to make a reservation here, but the photos in the ad had depicted a pristine, isolated place, a mountain garden spot populated only by wildlife AND YOU! The reality was a squalid row of numbered cabins filled with tired parents, yelling children, and a few bewildered, hostile pet dogs.

They got out of the car and stared around them.

"Shit," Ellen said.

Hal brightened. "This looks pretty good! I was afraid we'd be stuck out in the middle of nowhere. Come on!" Suddenly comfortable in Earth gravity, he picked up his bag and headed for their cabin.

Hal slept like a baby that night and awoke fresh and cheerful and ready for a day of mountain adventures, which for him seemed to mean sitting in the sun in front of the cabin and chatting with the other vacationers. Ellen slept fitfully, bothered by the gravity, the heat at first and then late at night the chill, the dryness, the dogs barking, the wind, the birds, the darkness and then the dawn—by everything that wasn't space.

This is ridiculous, she kept telling herself. I lived on Earth for most of my life! I've only been in space for the last five.

But that didn't help her sleep.

She ate breakfast in the campground's dining hall along with a scattering of other campers. It reminded her a bit of dining halls in orbit, of the dining hall at the InterSpace training complex outside Denver, and even of the Tempus dining hall. The rambunctious children were a difference, though.

The food was almost as tasteless as the meals in space, which surprised her. She remembered Earth food as much tastier—fresher, more varied. Maybe my memory isn't all that good, she told herself. Maybe I've been romanticizing Earth during the last five years without realizing it. The food down here can't really have changed.

Behind the campground, on three sides, were steep, wooded hillsides. In the fourth direction was the road they had taken to get here. After breakfast, Ellen walked to the end of the row of cabins and went behind them, hoping to find a hiking path up one of the hillsides that was tame enough for her space-weakened muscles. Instead, she found stinking piles of trash buzzing with flies and a high chain-link fence that separated her from the hillsides.

Annoyed, she went back the way she had come and then walked a short distance down the road. She left the road and entered the trees, but the fence was there, as well. She crossed the road and tried the woods on the other side. Again, she encountered the fence.

Her annoyance was increasing by the minute.

Earlier, at breakfast, she had noticed an infobooth in a corner of the dining room. That had bothered her at the time. It had seemed inappropriate in a place that was supposed to provide escape from normal urban life.

She returned to the dining room. A bored teenaged boy

was standing in the booth. He surrendered it with ill grace when Ellen promised that she only wanted it for a few minutes. She stepped into the alcove and experienced again the dizzying sensation of her first infobooth encounter. She was floating in space, in an empty universe far less real and far more disconcerting than the real one she had spent so much time floating in during the past five years.

Floating in front of her was a young woman, attractive to the moderate degree standard with virtual assistants. "Ellen Maxwell. Welcome back from space. We hope you're enjoying your vacation."

"Not very much, actually. I can't get out of this so-called campground. There's a fence around the whole place."

The young woman nodded. "Of course. It's for your protection. The world is a much more dangerous place than when you were growing up."

Ellen thought of her siblings and her parents and felt angry. Is this what she had come down to Earth for, to be patronized by an ignorant girl who wasn't even real? What did this bitch know?

She thinks she knows that I was born in 2023 or thereabouts, Ellen reminded herself. "Maybe it's for my protection," she said, "but it makes for a boring vacation. Space is boring enough. I was hoping for some excitement, some variety, not just more of being shut inside a small space."

"You have accumulated six months of paid vacation. You are in an idyllic mountain spot with your lover. Most women would consider that quite exciting."

Maybe if it were Tommy ...

Astonished, Ellen realized that she had stopped thinking of

Tommy some time ago. The love of her life, the love that spanned time, the love she had once been sure would be found again somewhere, somewhen, and would last forever, had become just another memory of just another man.

No, not just another man: far more than any of the other men. But nonetheless a man she knew, knew in her heart, knew in a way she hadn't wanted to admit to herself before, she'd never see again.

"What would you like to do?" the virtual assistant prompted. "I can arrange for you to cut your vacation short and go back to work in space. Perhaps at some future time, you could try another vacation on Earth."

"I'm not ready to go back. Suggest another alternative. Something else for me to do now."

She could almost have imagined that the virtual assistant shrugged. "If you don't want to go back to space, and if you aren't happy with the degree of wilderness adventure that is available to you, then I can only suggest touring the sights of some urban center."

People crowded together in a small space? It wasn't an appealing prospect. And yet in reality a big city was more open and unlimited than this supposed wilderness escape site had turned out to be. "Not a bad idea. Very clever of you. You have a lot of insight into human beings."

"Thank you," the virtual assistant said gravely. "That is one of the functions my designers labored to instill in me."

"Who are your designers? They sound interesting. I'd like to meet them."

"I'm sorry, that information is prohibited."

Ellen sighed. Maybe she could search for that information

once she got back to space. There was much less blocking up there. She heard an exasperated sigh behind her and turned to see the teenager walking toward the exit, shaking his head in an exaggerated display of annoyance. She turned her attention back to the virtual assistant. "Suggest a city for touring, then."

"Your request is far too general. The number of cities in the world that human beings find interesting is very great. Please add some limiting criteria."

"Okay, then. Cities within three hours of here."

"Salt Lake City is the closest. Then Phoenix, Denver, Albuquerque. Those are the largest. Should I continue with a list of smaller cities?"

Ellen felt tired, and not just from gravity and lack of sleep. "Oh, hell. Salt Lake City. Send a car to take me back there. If I get bored, I'll just go back to the station, after all."

"May I offer an observation of a psychological nature?"

"Sure."

"Your experience is a common one with space workers. They find the physical stress of Earth gravity unpleasant and the crowding and high population here on the surface also stressful. They are usually eager to come here for their vacations, and then very soon they are eager to leave and go back into space."

"Gravity bores spacemen?"

"Your car will be arriving in thirty minutes. Please be ready in front of the dining room."

Ellen realized she had fallen again into the trap of trying to have a conversation with the virtual assistant as if it were a real human being. That was a mistake that someone born and brought up in this time wouldn't make. I'll probably never get over that habit, Ellen thought. They seem so real, so sympathetic. Much more so than most of the real human beings here. Maybe I'll never feel at home here, no matter how long I stay. Which will probably be the rest of my life. I need a companion from my own era. I need ...

Tommy, of course.

She repacked her few belongings and was waiting for the car fifteen minutes after leaving the infobooth.

Hal broke off his conversation with one of the other campers and strolled over to her lazily. "This is the life!" he said. "I'm never going to want to go back. What are you doing?"

"Leaving."

"What? Why?" The whine was already back in his voice.

"Because—" She imagined the argument with him. "Never mind why. I'll see you back on the station. Have a nice time."

A torrent of words flowed from him. She heard none of them. An invisible wall separated them. A hundred–years wall, she thought. I can't hear him over the distance of a century.

Her attention drifted away from him and toward the road. She was unaware when he gave up and stamped away, back to the group he had left lounging under a tree.

When she was in the car, headed back down the mountain toward Salt Lake City, Ellen said, "I'd like to do some sightseeing. Are you able to take me to the major tourist spots?"

"I have that capability," the car said. "I can access data sources on the subject and determine the most frequently visited sites in Salt Lake City in decreasing order."

Ellen chuckled. In the space adventure stories she had read as a kid, a robot would have said something just like that. "That sounds right."

"I can also make a hotel reservation for you as we travel

and take you to the hotel first."

"No, take me to the top tourist spot first." I won't need a hotel room. I'll probably spend five minutes gawking and then go to the spaceport and catch the first rocket home.

Twenty-Five

"Where are we?" Ellen asked the car.

"This is historic Temple Square. Before you is the six-spired granite Salt Lake Temple, and next to it is the famous Tabernacle, home of the famous Mormon Tabernacle Choir and—"

"Yeah, yeah, okay. I read about all of this when I was a kid."

"It has been famous for a long time."

"Lots of people walking around."

"It's the most frequently visited tourist site in the city."

"Of course. As you promised. Wait here for me. I'm going to walk around a bit."

When she got out of the car, she realized that the air conditioning had misled her. The heat was intense and the sunlight blinding. She didn't think her space-weakened legs would be up to much walking after all.

She squinted up at the light-brown sky. Bet it was blue a hundred years ago, she thought. But the heat was probably worse back then, without this layer. She coughed, then shook her head ruefully. Every cloud had its muddy lining.

There were tree-shaded walkways, and she headed for one

of those. It led past a reflecting pool, beyond which were the Temple and the Tabernacle, the giant gold angel atop the latter brilliant in the sun. Ellen paused in the shade and stared through the trees at the two buildings, trying to derive a tourist's pleasure from the act. They remained buildings—large and imposing, but lifeless, and far less significant in her mind than the various orbiting habitats she had helped build.

She heard chanting. Because of the trees, she couldn't see far down the curving pathway. The chanting seemed to come from the direction she had been heading in before, somewhere beyond the curve. Intrigued, she started walking that way again.

The pathway ended in a large, sunny plaza directly in front of the Tabernacle. In the center of the broad space was a small crowd of young people holding signs. What had seemed to be religious chanting when she was far away now resolved into the synchronized shouting of slogans.

She was too far away to make out the words or read the signs. She noticed a line of policemen just beyond the demonstrators, separating them from the Tabernacle. The police wore flak jackets and helmets with plastic visors and held plastic shields up in front of them with one hand and long, straight black sticks in the other. They were watching the demonstrators but not moving. More policemen came from somewhere beyond the Tabernacle and joined the still, silent line.

Ellen stood watching indecisively. She wasn't sure what to make of any of this. Other space workers had told her about demonstrations on Earth, although she'd never seen anything about them on the news.

Curiosity overcame caution, and she stepped from the

shade of the trees and walked—slowly, hesitantly—across the sun-bright concrete until she was close enough to read the signs and understand the shouted words.

The signs varied, but two designs seemed to be the most common. One type had a large picture of the Tabernacle inside a red circle with a red diagonal stripe across it. The other consisted of one word, in large, red letters: DISESTABLISH.

Now that she could see the signs, she realized that the crowd was chanting the same word: "Disestablish! Disestablish!" After a few minutes, at some signal she couldn't detect, they switched to "No state church! No state church!"

Ellen touched the arm of one of the demonstrators, a young man, not coincidentally one of the few she considered attractive. "Excuse me." Her voice was drowned out by the chants. The young man ignored her. She raised her voice. "Excuse me!" She shook his arm. This time he noticed her. "What are you demonstrating for?"

"Against," he shouted back. "Against a state church."

"There's a state church?"

He looked at her oddly. "Where do you come from? Yeah, Latter Day Saints. State church of Utah. Tomorrow we're traveling to Baltimore. Same cause. Roman Catholic church."

Ellen shook her head in amazement. She had no idea any of this was going on. "I've been in space for five years."

"That explains it. State church legislation only got really going about four years ago." He looked at her more carefully. The severity, almost anger, faded from his face and he smiled. "I'm Matt." He held out his hand.

"Ellen." She grasped his hand firmly and shook it vigorously—a habit which had started as something unconscious but which she now did partly deliberately, as a test. Matt passed the test. His surprise changed to a look of admiration.

"So what about the Constitution?" Ellen asked. "I thought it prohibited any kind of state church."

Matt gave her another odd look. "You sure you've only been in space for five years?"

Ellen wondered if she could use her standard raised-in-a-small-town cover story, but she suspected it wouldn't work in this case. The wall between church and state had never counted for much in small towns in her century, and she doubted if that had changed.

While she was considering her answer, one of Matt's comrades shouted, "The cops! Look!"

The police line had begun to move. The center stepped slowly toward the young demonstrators, while the wings spread out and began to encircle them.

The demonstrators moved closer together. Their chanting stopped.

"Shit!" Matt said. "What are those bastards up to?" He stepped away from Ellen and away from his comrades. He waved his arms and shouted to the police. "Hey! We've got a permit! We're following the rules!"

The police ignored him and continued moving. There were enough of them, Ellen guessed, to completely encircle the demonstrators with a line two or three deep.

And the circle was closing rapidly.

Ellen felt a touch of panic. "Come on!" She grabbed Matt's arm and began pulling him toward the rapidly narrowing opening in the police circle. "All of you! Come on!"

She let go of Matt's arm and started running. She could hear running steps behind her, sense a crowd of bodies. She didn't know if it was the demonstrators or the police, and she didn't care. All that mattered was getting free, out into the open, away from these armored figures and the clubs they held up above their heads.

She heard screams behind her and ran faster. From the corner of her eye, she saw a dark figure raising its hand, bringing it down, striking. She ducked, dodged aside, leaped forward.

And was free.

Ahead of her was the empty plaza, and then the trees. She kept running until she was past the trees and once again on the pathway she had taken to get here. She had to stop. She was exhausted, gasping for breath.

She turned to look back. In the center of the plaza, a tightening circle of policemen, their backs to her, pressed forward. Their arms rose and fell. She heard screams. Blood ran between the policemen's feet and trickled across the concrete.

She heard bangs. Shots, those were shots, she was sure of it.

Sickened, Ellen shrank back into the cover of the trees. Others figures were fleeing the scene, running from the plaza and vanishing between the buildings. She heard more shots, and then more armored police appeared from the directions in which the demonstrators had been fleeing.

Time to leave, Ellen told herself. Definitely time to leave. She turned away from the scene. Matt was standing almost behind her. His mouth hung open, his eyes were wide. He was staring at the violence in the plaza. He seemed unaware of her presence or even on of the danger they were both still in.

"Get out of here," she told him.

He looked at her uncomprehendingly.

Another voice spoke, a familiar one. "Ellen Maxwell, can you hear me? Please enter and I will take you to a safer place to continue your tour."

Her car was moving carefully down the pathway from the parking lot, coming toward her. It was still some distance away, unable to detect her in the shadow of the trees. Ellen laughed explosively. "Mary had a little lamb!"

Before she could move toward the car, Matt grabbed her shoulder and stopped her. "Look!"

More uniformed figures had appeared, moving between the trees. They surrounded the car and pointed their batons at it. Flames roared from the ends of their batons. The car jerked like a living creature. The windows and headlights shattered.

Matt pulled at Ellen again, and they backed away carefully and then started running again. Behind them, the sound of firing was continuous.

The car's cameras showed one brief shot of Ellen and Matt running away down the path, and then the monitors went blank. Sound transmission persisted for a few more seconds, but all the people in the control room could hear was shots being fired, the banging of batons against the car's body, and an occasional yell or laugh. Finally, the sounds stopped as well.

Tommy leaned forward. "Follow her! Protect her!"

In Temple Square in Salt Lake City, a policeman who had been standing on the pathway apart from the others and had watched Ellen and Matt run away nodded and set off after them.

Ellen sighed. Sometimes, often, she thought that her generation must have been the last one with brains. Matt and his contemporaries, who could have been her however–many–times–great grandchildren, were so remarkably naive.

"If what I said is true," she pointed out, "it's already too late. So we might as well stay here." She pointed at a framed photograph on one wall. "Who's that?"

Matt shrugged. "No idea. This house has been in Tamara's family for generations, so that's probably some ancestor of hers. Genealogy is very important in this town." He squinted at the photograph. "I bet that thing's a hundred years old."

"A hundred years old," Ellen muttered.

Ellen stepped closer and carefully examined the young man in the photograph. He wore an Army uniform. The photograph could well have been taken on the day she stepped into the time machine in Colorado. The young man could have been a soldier home on leave from the fighting in Europe or the Pacific or North Africa. He could have been her contemporary. He could ...

The world shifted, spun, and she had to hold onto the wall for support.

He might have been a comrade–in–arms of Tommy's. He might have been in Normandy with Tommy. Or in Italy with Frank. Or on that damned island with her brother.

She looked at the young man in the photograph, his Army cap at a rakish angle on the side of his head, a self–confident grin on his face, and Tommy sprang to life before her, cocky, wonderful, wanting her. She ached for him.

My God, she thought, what's happened to me? It's been five years already!

I didn't forget, she thought. I just ... I just put it all aside.

Matt was increasingly nervous. "We can't stay here. We've got to go."

I've got to go, Ellen thought. Back to space. I can't stay with this man. I'm not safe. It's not healthy here. "Gravity kills spacemen," she said, thinking aloud.

"Of course it does," Matt said. "That's because those guys have so much freedom up there. They come down to Earth and they see the way things are here, and they're shocked. Then they want to do something about it, and they kill them."

"What are you talking about?"

"That's why there are so many spacemen in the resistance. They come down on vacation or to retire, and instead they join up. Engineers, physicists. We've got lots of them. They kill them when they can, of course. The government, I mean," he added. "Or the people who're behind the government. The people who really control the government."

"Physicists?" Ellen had caught the important word, the one that had everything to do with her.

"Oh, sure. I could introduce—" Matt paused and stared at her for a while. "You're in the movement now, you know. After what you did back there in Temple Square, helping a known resister escape the police, they'll be after you, too. You have to be in. If you're not ..." He paused, took a deep breath. "If you say you don't want to join up after all, then you're a security threat and I'm required to kill you. Please say you're with us."

Ellen looked at him, so earnest, trying to look threatening, managing only to look wistful and needy. She suppressed her urge to laugh. "After what I saw today? Of course I'm with you. What about those physicists? What are they doing in the movement?"

Matt looked relieved. "I don't know what they're doing," he admitted. "Some kind of work to help us, I guess. Now that you're in, I'll introduce you to some of them, and you can ask them yourself."

Five years in the space program, supposedly the most advanced engineering undertaking in mankind's history, and she hadn't met anyone who was working on anything more blue-sky than improving specific impulse. Maybe this would turn out to be just as disappointing. Or maybe not. Maybe she'd finally meet people who were working on time travel.

I won't get my hopes up, she assured herself. What're the chances that anyone in this pitiful group of sign-carriers is comparable to the team Tempus created? But I'll stay with this fearsome revolutionary for a while, anyway. Just to see what I can find out.

strain.

"So now where are we going?"

"Following an old trail."

They were moving in a cloud of dust, and the car was bouncing madly and rolling from side to side. Their conversation was punctuated with grunts.

"Better be following something," Ellen said. "We're gonna end up in a gully. Matt! Slow down!"

"Oh, all right."

He pressed some of the buttons, and the car slowed to a crawl. Conversation became easier.

"Maybe now we have a chance of making it," Ellen said. "For God's sake, someone tell me where we're going! This is ridiculous."

"Following this trail," Matt said. "That's all we know. The committee is waiting for us."

In yet another safe house, Ellen thought.

The car stopped abruptly. "Did you do that on purpose," Ellen asked Matt, "or did the power die?"

He didn't answer her question. "We're here," he said.

Ellen climbed out of the car, stretched, breathed deeply. The dryness bit at her throat and the back of her nose. She didn't care about that. The familiarity of the dry, cold air exhilarated her. It made her feel closer to what had once been, to Tommy.

To what might be again, she told herself.

The sun was setting behind a distant mesa and the temperature was dropping and the light was fading rapidly. She turned, looking for the safe house. Instead, in the dimness, she made out a cliff with a great crack down its face.

Her heart leapt into her throat. Oh my God, she thought, I'm here! I'm back, I'm almost back!

The cliff made her feel close to Tommy again. She could almost pretend that he was watching her, ready to protect her.

At Tommy's headquarters, the screens showed only the open space where Tempus had once stood, empty of life.

Lynn grabbed her arm and pulled her forward, in the direction of the cliff. "Come on! We have to show we're reliable." She seemed frightened.

"It's all right," Ellen said. "We're safe now. Where's the house?"

"What house? There isn't any house."

Three men waited for them. They sat in folding chairs set up on the stony ground. A lamp on the ground in front of them created a circle of light, creating darkness beyond. The three were bland and expressionless. They were also all dressed in suits, which astonished Ellen. No one in the underground, in her experience so far, dressed formally. Why, she thought, it's the anti-government managerial class!

Facing the three chairs was another, unoccupied one. Ellen assumed that she was supposed to sit in that one and answer their questions.

She undid her jacket and draped it over the back of the chair and then sat down. "Let's begin, gentlemen," she told them. "What do you want to know?"

For a moment, the three seemed taken aback by her forwardness. She knew that they had expected her to be intimidated. Not me, she thought, with a pride that momentarily embarrassed her. I'm from Tempus.

"We've been looking into your background," one of the

three men said. "We can trace you back to 2045, and then we run into a dead end. You showed up out of nowhere, you joined the Resistance, you know a dangerous amount about us. Now we want to know where you came from and who you're working for."

Ellen's defiance and feelings of strength deserted her. This was not at all what she'd expected. She felt defenseless and threatened. She glanced over her shoulder and saw her four companions watching her with hostility. Even Matt no longer seemed warm and friendly. And Lynn—wispy, forgetful, inept Lynn—had a hard and very competent look on her face and a pistol in her hand, pointing at Ellen's face.

"I've told you before. Rather I've told Matt. I came from a small town, and I went to Denver in 2045 to look for work."

"Nonsense," the man said. "There's no town so small that it wouldn't have records of your birth and schooling. We've searched. There's nothing. This name you use, this identity, it sprang into existence in 2045. Clearly it was manufactured for you. It was part of a scheme to infiltrate our organization. Tell us the truth, and we'll make it quick and easy for you."

Ellen couldn't speak. Her throat was too dry. Her tongue stuck to the roof of her mouth. Her thoughts were spinning in random directions. She had no idea what to say, what words would save her life.

Off to her left, someone gasped. Ellen looked in that direction. A woman stood at the edge of the circle of light. She seemed oddly familiar.

Ellen stared at the woman, and the woman stared back at her as though entranced.

My God, Ellen thought, it's me!

The woman looked just like her. She even wore clothes just like those Ellen was wearing.

Behind her, she heard Matt say, "Ellen?"

Ellen turned around in her chair. Matt stepped toward the newcomer, then stopped, confused, and looked back at Ellen. "Ellen?" he repeated.

Lynn's arm had dropped to her side. Her gun pointed at the ground. She held it loosely, as though unaware of it. She looked back and forth from Ellen to the strange woman. "What the hell?"

The man who had asked all the questions stood up. He pointed at the woman. "Grab her!"

Before any of them could move, the woman shouted Ellen's name. She leaped across the space, bent forward, put one arm around Ellen's waist, and pulled her to her feet.

Too amazed to do anything, Ellen stared into the face only inches from hers. It's me, she kept thinking. It's me!

Brilliant light suddenly bathed the area. A giant voice boomed, "You're under arrest! Put down your weapons!"

Ellen saw Lynn raise her gun and then fall limply to the ground, her chest blossoming red. Matt's head exploded.

Something whipped by Ellen's face. An enormous blow hit her. She heard a distant, roaring sound, the rushing of mighty waters, and the world ended.

Twenty–Seven

Notification arrived at Tommy's office in the form of a thick, brown envelope delivered via the internal InterAgency system. There was no return code. Attempts to determine its origin were fruitless. After careful examination, the package was opened. The contents were also examined carefully. Tommy's experts decided that none of the contents was explosive or poisoned or otherwise dangerous, and finally the package was placed on Tommy's desk for his examination.

The experts had read the letter as part of their examination—normal operating procedure, and in accordance with Tommy's standing orders—so even though they didn't understand the personal references, they could tell that the package was intended to hit Tommy like a bomb psychologically, and they warned everyone else to be prepared.

Even so, the cry of grief from this man who was normally so tightly controlled astonished everyone within earshot.

Delia had just arrived at the office. She heard Tommy's cry and came at a run. She found Tommy sitting behind his desk, his mouth open, his face white. He was panting, desperate for breath, and his face was covered with sweat. The envelope was on his desk in front of him. It had held two items, and both were also on the desk, beside the envelope. One was a one–page letter, simple, no letterhead. The other was a small square of plastic enclosing something flat and reddish.

"Tommy, what's wrong, what's happened?"

He seemed incapable of speech. He pointed at the letter. His hand shook. Delia was struck by how old and frail he suddenly looked.

She picked the letter up. It was a police report, dry, official, straightforward. It described an attempted arrest of a group of anti–government activists in a rural area in western Colorado and the enormous explosion that had ended the operation. It referred to the small amount of recovered identifying human tissue recovered from the site, including the enclosed retinal tissue of one Ellen Maxwell, one of the activists.

"Oh, God," Delia whispered.

"I tried to protect her," he said. "You know I tried."

He was standing again. His jaw was clenched and his back straight. It was a hint of the younger Tommy.

"I know you did, Tommy. But it was impossible. She must have become involved with some underground group after the riot in Salt Lake City, when we lost her. Once that happened, it was too late. Not even you could have protected her, even if you had known where she was."

He knew she was right. That last glimpse he had had of Ellen, seen from the car's viewpoint, of her running away down a tree–shaded pathway, that was the moment at which she had passed from reality, the last moment he could possibly have brought her in under his protection.

I used to think she was lost to me because of the barriers of age and evil, he thought. *That I could only watch over her from a distance. Now I've failed even in that, and now she's truly lost to me because of the barrier of death. There might be a cure for age, but there's no cure for death.*

He turned toward the desk. His glance fell on the square of plastic, and he shivered. Almost visibly, he exerted control. Pointing to the piece of plastic, he said to Delia, "Have that analyzed and make sure it really is ... that it really is Ellen's retina." *But he knew it was.*

Grimacing with distaste, Delia pushed the piece of plastic back inside the envelope. *At least,* she thought, *this will get it out of Tommy's sight. And out of his mind, eventually.* "You're going to be okay, aren't you?"

Tommy smiled at her. It was a fond smile, a gentle smile. "Never again." *But I'll survive. I always do.* "This police report. Trace it back for me. See if you can find out who sent it." He knew it would be a dead end, though. Someone much above him in InterAgency was behind it. Maybe it was a warning, or maybe it was a reminder of who was in control. It was someone with the ability to blind his sensors, so that he had seen none of it— the meeting, the police attack, the explosion. It was someone who had known in advance that Tommy would arrive in 1995.

Twenty–Eight

"I see you've hired a physicist. This Iselin kid. Eddie. I'm surprised."

"You're keeping track of who I hire? I'm surprised you have the time for that." Delia stirred uneasily.

"Only the interesting ones," Tommy said. "The kid's brilliant, but I thought you were done with physics research."

"I am. He reminded me of myself when I was his age. I wanted someone who could take over my team and my projects at some point, and my instincts told me that he was the right choice for that. Look, I'm 119 years old. I told you I don't know if this rejuvenation process will work indefinitely. At some point, it might stop."

"Then you'll die, and you won't be worrying about your team and your projects."

"But I worry about them now! I worry about what will happen to them without me. There's an old saying: 'In a civilized society, old men plant trees whose shade they know they won't live to enjoy.'"

"You're not living in a civilized society. You're living in InterAgency. There's another old saying: 'Old men start wars for young men to die in.' That's us."

"I have a responsibility to the future."

And I used to think I had a responsibility to the past, Tommy thought. Now my responsibility is to power and staying alive and getting to the top.

But the conversation stayed with him.

He kept an eye on Eddie Iselin. Over time, Delia shifted much of the management of her research team to Eddie and spent her own time secluded in her lab. Tommy suspected she was happier than she had been in years.

Eventually, Tommy decided that Iselin was trustworthy. In 2087, three years after Delia had hired Iselin, Tommy paid him a visit.

Eddie Iselin was a tall, slender man with light–brown hair. He was barely past thirty but already going bald. His office was small and contained only a desk, his chair, and a single chair for a visitor. There was only one piece of art on his wall, a large, framed photograph of a giant rock sticking out of the water just off a rocky coastline.

"Beautiful snapshot," Tommy said, looking at the photograph. He had entered silently, unannounced. He had ordered everyone in the outer office to leave, and they had done so quickly, fear in their eyes.

Eddie had been engrossed in the computer display hovering above his desk. He looked away from it slowly and reluctantly. When he registered who Tommy was, he gasped and jumped to his feet. "Mr. Stillwell! Sir! This is an honor! I had no idea—Can I get you something? Coffee? Water? Um, wine?"

Tommy laughed. "Don't try so hard. I don't want anything. Sit down." He waited until Eddie did so, and then he sat in the visitor's chair.

"Did Delia—did Madame Anderson ever tell you that she once worked on time travel?" Tommy watched him carefully, interested in his reaction.

"She did. She said it was a long time ago." Eddie seemed calm again. He spoke conversationally, and his face showed little emotion.

Tommy nodded approvingly. Delia had good judgment, it seemed. "Unfortunately, her superiors ordered her to shut the project down." He caught the flicker of surprise on Eddie's face and smiled. "I wasn't her superior at the time. I would have told her to keep on trying."

"Really, sir? It's impossible, you know."

"Time travel?"

Eddie nodded. "Oh, yes. It's a fascinating idea, of course. I'm sure we'd all love to go back to some interesting time in history."

"Like World War Two, you mean?"

Eddie shuddered. "No! Certainly not then. No, I'd like to go back to the Seventeenth Century. That's when the modern world really began. Imagine being able to speak to Isaac Newton! Or even further back. I'd love to spend some time with Aristotle."

"You speak ancient Greek, do you?"

"Well, no. That would be a problem, wouldn't it? I'm sure I'd look out of place, too. Trying to fit into another time without drawing everyone's attention would be impossible."

"Yep. I bet it would be."

"But that's not what I meant." By now, Eddie seemed to have forgotten that he was talking to one of the rulers of InterAgency. He was in his element, and for the moment, he was the superior. "I mean that it couldn't happen. It's simply not possible. It doesn't even make sense. It's a question of mathematical physics—I mean ... "

"That's all right, Eddie. I'm not offended. I'll take your word for it. Except that you're wrong."

"Oh, really? Sir?"

"I managed to track down a couple of members of Madame Anderson's old team. Turns out they kept working on the problem in their spare time."

Part of that was true. He had dug up the names, but the records of the team's members indicated that all of them had died shortly after the project was abandoned. Only Delia had been spared.

"Against orders, sir?"

"Yes. Not very smart of them. Anyway, they took a new approach in their private research." He told Eddie what he could remember from Dolores Lujan's lectures in 1945. "I didn't really understand what they were saying, as you can probably tell, but that's the way I remember it."

Eddie frowned. "To be honest sir, all of these metaphors about a river and upstream and downstream energy—it sounds like what you hear from scientifically illiterate people who're convinced that they've solved all the problems that real physicists can't."

"Maybe they were trying to put it in terms I'd understand. Anyway, they had some success. They claimed that they were able to go forward in time a few days. Not backward, though, for some reason."

"Amazing! I'd like to talk to them. I'd like more details."

"Unfortunately, they both died soon after they talked to me.

Someone must have found out about our conversation. It's a good thing that I'm a much more powerful man now, and that you work for me, isn't it?"

"Yes, sir, it certainly is."

"I did find their equipment. Someone had tried to destroy it. I've had it stored in a warehouse for a long time. I'll have it delivered to you. Maybe it'll help. Put as many people to work on this project as you want. Order whatever equipment you need. Don't worry about the budget. Make sure you swear all your people to secrecy, and keep your own lips zipped. I'd rather you didn't mention any of this to Madame Anderson. Not yet."

Eddie stared at him for a moment. "Sir, at first I thought this was a casual conversation. Obviously, I was wrong. This is a very high-priority project, isn't it?"

"The highest. I don't have time for casual conversations."

One year passed, then two. Tommy began to fear that the long shot had not paid off. He had been foolish to think that telling Eddie some garbled, half-remembered version of the work done at Tempus and giving him that tangled mass of metal and glass recovered from the hillside would lead to him and his team rediscovering the secret of time travel.

Yet Eddie was still working on the problem. His quarterly budget requests were enormous, and his staff had expanded significantly.

Maybe he's using all that money and manpower for something else, Tommy thought. Something that interests him more. Maybe he's playing me for a sucker. No, not Eddie. That's a mug's game, and Eddie's not a mug.

In the autumn of 2094, Iselin came to see Tommy. His face had lost its boyish look, and he had lost more hair.

Maybe I should tell Delia to use her rejuvenation thing on him, Tommy thought. He's too valuable to lose. Maybe it's time to start using it on all our most important people. They'd blab about it to their friends, though.

"You said it was important, Eddie. Have a seat."

Iselin sat in the visitor's chair in front of Tommy's desk. "Fairly important, sir." He was trying to be reserved and low key, but he couldn't contain himself. "We did it! We can travel in time!" He grinned, and the boyish look was back. "Forwards and backwards."

"Backwards?" Tommy gripped the edge of his desk. His heart was hammering. He could hardly force words out. "We can go back in time?"

"Sure. It was easy. Once we could go forwards, we were able to go back as well. It just took a lot more energy. That was probably the problem those other guys had. A few years ago, they wouldn't have been able to generate enough energy. Upstream energy." He grinned again. "That's your terminology. I'm sticking with it. Actually, I'm surprised they were able to do anything, working in private. It requires a lot of equipment and energy and money. Maybe that's how they attracted the wrong kind of attention. It probably wasn't because of your conversation with them. You don't have any reason to feel guilty about that, sir."

"Ah. Thanks. 2051. Can you send someone back that far yet?"

"Uh, we've only been working in the range of minutes, so far."

"But you could scale it up, right? It just takes more energy, right?"

"A lot more energy, sir. Fortunately, it's not a linear relationship. That's what the math says, anyway. Also, we haven't actually experimented with people yet. Just instruments of various kinds. I don't know if any of this is safe for living things."

"It is. I know that much."

For a moment, Iselin displayed both surprise and skepticism. Then his expression became bland again.

The kid's learned, Tommy thought. Maybe he'll survive. "Figure out how much energy you'd need to send a man back to 2051. Then build whatever you need to generate it. We're going to need to start using your equipment very soon."

"Yes, sir. Whatever you say, of course. There are dangers you should be aware of, though."

Tommy sighed. "Go ahead. Tell me about them."

"Well, I'd have to explain how it all works, first. That could take some time."

Tommy flashed back to the classroom lectures at Tempus in 1945, and he grimaced. "I don't have much time."

"Perhaps I could write it up," Eddie said quickly. "I could summarize it better that way. I could probably send something to you by tomorrow morning."

"All right. I'll try to read it. Keep it very simple."

Eddie almost smiled. "I was planning to, sir."

Eddie's writeup was waiting for Tommy when he arrived the next morning. Tommy settled himself in front of the dense lines of text hovering above his desk and steeled himself for what he was sure would be a tedious and difficult task.

The property we sense as "time" is dynamic, not static, but is embedded in a static four-dimensional matrix. Outside that flow, time is undefined.

"Oh, boy," Tommy muttered.

Our model indicates that initially space–time consisted of a string of nodes—tightly wrapped loci of time and space, four dimensions reduced to one. The separation of these nodes from each other was defined by the difference in the cross–stream state. This situation was static, unchanging; time was not defined or meaningful. At the moment of the Big Bang, one of the nodes was abruptly converted into movement along one dimension, creating the flow of time. Time as we know it is that flow, and time has meaning only within our stream. Outside the stream—in the "cross–stream" direction— time is presumably undefined, and only the other, unchanging nodes exist.

Everything within the flow is constantly carried forward by it, but an object's precise position within the stream is determined by its stream–potential, where lower potential corresponds to a downstream position and higher potential to an upstream one. Stream–potential has no relationship to physical position; changing one does not change the other. Time travel requires that the subject jump ahead in the stream or backward in it. That is, his stream–potential must be decreased or increased.

Thus, the mathematical problem is reduced to a simpler engineering one.

However, the engineering problem is certainly non-trivial. The energy required to move a human being any considerable distance upstream is prodigious—far beyond our current capabilities, in fact. However, although our model implies that the energy levels of the timestream should be independent of physical location, we have discovered a curious exception. An instrument we placed on the Chinese space station last year detected an anomaly in timestream energy in western Colorado. We believe that at that one point, and only there, we will be able to send a human subject upstream by the distance you stipulated.

I must add that the existence of such an anomaly is troubling and undermines our confidence in our model.

Tommy smiled. He had no doubt that the point in question was at the base of a sandstone cliff with a great crack down its face. When it sent people forward in time, Tempus created the anomaly. He wondered if that was why the first travelers sent forward by Tempus had experienced such stress. Perhaps they had been forcing their way through some kind of resistance as they created the anomaly. Maybe that's all bull, Tommy thought, and I should leave that stuff to the double-domes.

Our energy-based model implies potential dangers for a human subject. While stream-potential energy is a function of an object's position in the stream, it is not necessarily an inherently stable property. Adding energy to an object to transfer it upstream—i.e., to send it back in time—would probably render its energy state unstable and attractive. That is, suppose that two objects, Alpha and Beta, have identical mass, but Alpha's stream-potential energy is less stable than Beta's. Now suppose that Alpha and Beta come into close contact. Under certain conditions, for example if thermal or kinetic energy were injected from an outside source, some of Beta's stream–potential energy could transfer to Alpha, resulting in Beta being thrown downstream.

Similarly, analogous to certain restrictions in quantum mechanics, two objects cannot occupy the same timestream state, where that state is defined by timestream energy and physical identity. Practically speaking, that means that a human being cannot jump backwards or forwards and then live in a time in which a physically identical version of himself is already living. Certainly he would have to avoid close physical proximity. The resulting instability in the timestream state of each would destroy one or both of the versions.

One of my researchers believes that the mathematics of the model implies that the timestream itself can be made unstable by the injection of too much energy. He sees indications that it is possible to create a loop, a condition where the flow is locally reversed and doubled back to encounter itself at an earlier point—that is, an upstream position. In such a case, the loop will either repeat itself endlessly or will simply cease to exist. In practical terms, this could mean that some series of events that we know actually happened would, to those trapped in it, happen over and over again, eternally. Or it could mean that the events, and all the people and places involved, will vanish from the four–dimensional cosmos. They will never have been.

Tommy sat staring through the screen, no longer reading.

The next day, he set in motion the process of building his new headquarters underground in western Colorado.

Twenty–Nine

He blinked in surprise, confused at finding himself outside in brilliant sunlight.

He frowned, looked at his surroundings. Where was he, where were—

Then he remembered. And understood.

The sun was at its zenith, but the air was chilly and a cold wind was blowing. Frank was oblivious to the cold. He looked around in wonder. He was on a rocky hillside with no sign that anything manmade had ever stood there. But towering over him was a familiar cliff face with a great crack down it.

He heard a sound, a faint rushing, that grew then faded away. He peered into the distance, out over the dusty plain, squinting in the brilliant sunlight. The sound came again. He saw what looked like a black snake speeding across the prairie from west to east. It passed behind a fold in the land, and the sound faded away.

Then there was silence again. Even the breeze had stopped.

"Hi. I didn't see you there."

Frank whirled around. A man stood a couple of feet away. Startled, Frank said, "Where the hell did you come from?"

The other man laughed. "I've been here all along. You were so busy looking off into the distance, you didn't see me. Question is, where did *you* come from? One moment you weren't here, next moment you were. Very strange."

"I—I was out hiking. I just climbed up the hill from over that way." Frank pointed vaguely to the west. He was annoyed that he'd been put on the defensive. He also felt threatened, both by the man's nearness and by the suddenness of his appearance. Then Frank looked the man over more carefully and relaxed. The man must be at least fifty years old. His hair was gray, almost white, his jowls sagged, and he had a paunch.

The older man took a step closer and held out his right hand. "I'm Greg."

Frank responded. Greg's grip was stronger than he had expected, which alarmed him anew. But Greg held the grip for only a second and then let go, and the whole incident seemed natural and unthreatening.

"Frank. My name's Frank."

"Nice to meet you, Frank. You must be cold, dressed like that." He gestured toward Frank's short sleeved shirt and ordinary slacks.

"You must be colder." Frank inclined his head toward Greg's shorts and sandals. He felt tense and suspicious again.

Greg laughed. "Hell, I'm never cold. I'm immune to the weather. Cold, heat, snow, rain, gloom of night. None of it matters to me. I'm just made that way."

Frank was suddenly aware of the cold. "Nice meeting you, Greg. I'd better be going now. I parked pretty far away."

"Parked, huh? You mean a car?"

"Sure. Of course."

"Now, that's unusual," Greg said. "When people come out here, they always take the Salt Lake–Denver train. They just signal for a stop along the way. No one owns a car. Well, except for a few rich, eccentric antique collectors. And they don't drive their cars. Too expensive to drive. No suitable roads, either. Not nowadays."

Christ, Frank thought, I can't even get through my first simple conversation without making all kinds of mistakes. This world is too foreign to me. I'll never survive. I'll expose myself immediately. Maybe I already have. I still don't know who this guy really is.

Greg snapped his fingers suddenly. "Now I get it! I should have realized it before. You're one of those retro guys. What do they call themselves? Retrospectors. Yeah, that's it. Those people who dress like they're living in a previous century, and they adopt the speech patterns and slang of another time. Do the whole thing. Always stay in character. Now, most of them seem to prefer the 18th century, or even earlier than that, but there are a few who stick with the 20th. That's what you're doing, right? Around the mid–20th century, am I right? That would explain your clothes and the way you speak and acting like you own a car."

"Right," Frank said quickly. "You're exactly right." He could scarcely believe his luck, but he wasn't going to look this gift horse in the mouth.

Greg rattled on like a much older man, talking to himself more than to an audience. "I know there are a lot of retrospectors in Denver, so I suppose that's where you're from. A lot of them actually work for InterSpace. That's the space agency," he added helpfully. "The people who run the space program. Their headquarters are in Denver, and it's where they have most of their employees, except for their main launch center in Africa. I suppose those folks concentrate on all that ultra–modern technical stuff, late 21st–century superscience, and then during their free time they need to get away from all that and retreat to a simpler time in the past."

He began walking down the hillside. "Come on," Greg said over his shoulder. "I'm heading for the train so I can go back home to Denver. We'll travel together." Despite his age and girth, he walked easily, untroubled by the uneven ground and breathing easily. "InterSpace is a pretty good place to work, I hear. A safe place to, heh, park yourself." He shrugged. "Safer than down here, anyway. Things happen to people down here."

"What was that?"

"I don't know, sir. Maybe just a glitch. Looks all right now."

"Hey! Hold on! What kind of things happen to people?"

Greg stopped and turned to look at Frank for a moment. Then he shrugged again and resumed walking. "Things. This can be a dangerous world. Politics, the law—a lot has changed in the last 150 years."

A chill ran down Frank's spine. "Wait!" he shouted.

Greg turned around again, a puzzled expression on his face. "Something wrong?"

"Why did you say that? About how much things have changed since 1945?"

"I didn't say since 1945. I said the last 150 years. And I said that because of the way you're dressed. Some of you retrospectors get a bit carried away. So I've heard, anyway. I mean, you kind of forget which century you're really in. So I thought maybe I should remind you."

Frank breathed deeply, trying to still the trembling that had suddenly come over him. "Right, sorry. Of course. I was ... I guess I was thinking of something else."

"That's okay. Are you nervous about something, Frank?"

Yeah, I'm nervous that a time–traveling Russian agent is waiting here to assassinate me. "Nothing in particular, no."

"Good."

They resumed walking. Greg resumed talking. He rambled on about the world of 2095. He talked about contemporary work, slang, laws, and much more. It was an intensive course in living and surviving in this era. Frank concentrated on every word.

Eventually they came to what seemed to be a road—a black ribbon, flat and utterly nonreflecting, stretching from the horizon in the west to the mountains in the east. By now, Greg had switched to complaining about how the world had changed in his lifetime. Cars had vanished, small towns had vanished, everyone lived in the big cities and the cities were spreading out over what was left of the farmland. "It was a lot better when I was a boy, I can tell you," he said. "Of course, that was a long, long time ago."

There was no sign of a railway that Frank could see. He wondered how far they'd have to walk to get to the station. It also struck him as odd that there'd be a station out here in this emptiness. "The train ... ?" he said, trying to keep his question safely vague.

Greg glanced at the back of his hand. "It'll be along in a few minutes. Don't worry."

Greg continued with his curious lecture, but Frank's attention began to wander. My God, he thought, I'm really here!

I'm 150 years in the future!

Everything he had known was gone, even the building he had called home for the last few months. The mountains and the rocky prairie looked the same, but everything else had changed.

What had happened in the final stages of the war? And after 150 years, did it really matter? He did a quick mental calculation and realized to his amazement that to the people of this time, World War II was as far in the past as the Napoleonic wars or the American Revolution were to him.

A distant rushing sound interrupted his thoughts. It sounded like a river rushing through a rocky canyon somewhere far away across the prairie. He shifted uneasily.

The sound grew louder. It came from his left, the west. He looked in that direction and saw a black object far in the distance, almost at the limit of visibility. It grew in size steadily as he watched. Now he could see a dust cloud hovering above it.

"We'll only have about 30 seconds to climb on," Greg said. "I remember when the train would wait for a whole minute, maybe even two, but they say there are too many people along the way now, too many stops, so they had to cut down on the wait time to keep to their schedule." He shook his head disapprovingly. "The world just keeps speeding up. Everyone's in a hurry."

By the time he finished speaking, the black object had grown into what even Frank knew must be a train. Except for being black, it could have been an unusually sleek subway train from his own time. And except for its looking continuous, with no sign of a gap between cars, if it was even divided into cars. And except for its traveling along what looked like a road for cars.

The rushing sound grew to a roar with the train's approach. A wind blew around them. Dust filled the air, and pebbles bounced across the ground.

"I hate that," Greg said. "I wish they'd do something about it."

The train slowed rapidly to a stop before them. Its surface looked solid black, with no sign of windows or doors. Part of the surface separated from the rest suddenly and slid to one side, revealing the interior.

"Come on!" Greg said. He stepped—almost leaped—through the opening.

This is worse than the Italian campaign, Frank thought.

He jumped after Greg, landing awkwardly inside the train. The door swished shut just behind him, brushing his leg.

Inside, the train was brightly lit. From the outside, the sides of the train had been solid black, but from the inside the walls were transparent and Frank had a panoramic view of the prairie.

There was a central aisle with seats on either side. He couldn't see any division into individual cars. The aisle stretched away in both directions without a break.

The train began moving, accelerating quickly. Frank staggered, almost fell. A hand gripped his arm and held him up. "Easy there!" It was Greg, grinning at him.

Greg pulled Frank after him toward a pair of empty seats. Frank fell into the seat gratefully.

Beside him, beyond the invisible wall of the train, the prairie rushed by with increasing speed. The train's walls were flexible as well as transparent. It snaked around curves and over ridges, slowing for nothing. It moved across the prairie with astonishing speed, still accelerating.

Greg tilted his head and spoke to the transparent ceiling. "Denver. Main station. Both of us." He turned to Frank. "That's okay for you? The main station?"

Frank waved his hand. "Uh, yeah. Sure."

Greg spoke to the ceiling again. "Right. Main station for both of us."

Coming from above, a voice replied. "Thank you." It was a woman's voice. It sounded like Ellen's.

Ellen, Frank thought. Christ, where is she? Is she here somewhere? Fifty years older! She'll be married, maybe a great-grandmother. Not really Ellen any more. And Tommy. God, he got here 100 years ago. He must have died years ago. I'm alone. I don't belong here.

He looked around in sudden alarm, but no one was paying any attention to him.

His fellow passengers were a mixture—men and women, various races, all ages. They were dressed much the same, in loose, long-sleeved shirts and trousers or shorts, most of it a dull light brown. Their shoes were the same color and looked to Frank like moccasins or slippers.

They were old, tired, and worn, these people. It wasn't just his clothing that made Frank stand out. It was also his youth, his height, and his vigor. He tried to shrink down into his seat. He tugged at the cuff of his shirtsleeve, pulling it down so that it covered his large, conspicuous watch.

But he wasn't the only one wearing a large watch or leather shoes. There were a few men dressed much the way he was, and a few women wearing dresses. Their fellow passengers ignored them, just as they ignored Frank.

They're retrospectors, Frank realized. No one pays any attention to them. So no one's going to pay any attention to me, either. Relax, he told himself. Watch the scenery.

Outside, beyond the invisible walls, the flat prairie was changing to rolling hills as the train began to climb into the mountains.

It was beautiful. He had thought so when he first arrived at Tempus, and he thought so now. That it hadn't changed in 150 years was comforting. Greg was still talking, but Frank tried to ignore him.

The train rushed through a long, narrow, stunningly beautiful river valley, moving high up along one of the valley walls. He looked down through the transparent floor and saw the river far below him, a narrow torrent of green water and white foam confined between rocky banks. It was as though he were flying above the river and there was nothing to keep him from falling into it. "Ace," he whispered.

He remembered the beautiful Irish Setter barking frantically and tumbling out of the canoe. A flash of that bright orange–red coat, and then the dog was swallowed by the raging water. The river tore the paddle from his hands, and the canoe raced with the flood, out of control, carrying the eleven–year–old boy away and holding his dog behind. He remembered his father running along the bank, trying to keep up, face white with fear, yelling words Frank couldn't hear over the roar. Then an eddy, some kind of turbulence, caught him, and the canoe floated sideways into a quiet spot and nosed gently against the bank. His father leaped into the water, grabbed the canoe with both hands, and hauled it out of the water, canoe and boy, with frantic strength. Later, they backtracked and found Ace half buried in the mud at the edge of the river, dead, his beautiful fur covered with drying mud.

Frank gripped the arms of his seat tightly and forced himself to breathe slowly and deeply.

Greg's voice forced its way into his awareness. "I remember the first time I rode on one of these things. It was scary. But they build them well." He leaned over in front of Frank and rapped his knuckles firmly on the invisible wall.

The sound of Greg's knuckles hitting the wall was muted, almost inaudible, but it made the walls seem solid and protecting. Frank's racing heart slowed.

"Of course," Greg said, "young people like you, you're used to it. It doesn't mean anything to you. But I still feel a bit tense on a stretch like this." He raised his head and addressed the ceiling again. "How long to our stop?"

"Approximately 17 minutes."

This time, it sounded even more like Ellen's voice. Frank gritted his teeth. I'll have to avoid these trains, he thought.

He felt pressure in his ears. He yawned widely, trying to get relief. The train was beginning to descend. Frank could see mountaintops and valleys to his side, but he couldn't see ahead. He hoped he'd be able to catch a glimpse of the city as they descended into it. He had enjoyed that sight before, the one time he had been driven from Tempus to Denver on a trip for supplies, and he guessed the train must be following much the same route as the Tempus car had. He wondered if the city had grown much since the 1940s. Then he realized that he had been staring at houses and streets and schools and shopping areas crowded along the sides of the mountains without really registering their presence.

What would have made the city grow so much? InterSpace. Greg had said it was headquartered in Denver.

Greg was right. He'd look for work there. The idea of actually going into space—it was fascinating, it was breathtaking. It would also have nothing to do with his mission. Or would it? Surely InterSpace was at the forefront of this era's technology, so if the secret of backward time travel existed anywhere, it should be there.

But how could he get inside it? The place must be guarded in ways he couldn't even imagine. The security would probably make the security at Tempus look childish. Maybe they needed workers of some kind. I'd be qualified to be a janitor, he thought, and that's probably about it.

"You know," he said to Greg, "you were right about my not having a car. I just said that because I was embarrassed. I think a retrospector should have an old car."

"Yep. Some of them do."

"But that's much too rich for my blood. In fact, I'm going to have to start thinking about doing something for ready cash pretty soon now. I inherited money from my folks, but that's running low. Would you happen to know if InterSpace is hiring these days? Or anyone else in Denver?"

Greg scratched his chin. "Gee, I dunno. InterSpace is pretty hungry for people most of the time. There's just so much going on out there, as you know. Colonies on various planets and moons. Orbital stations. All that stuff. Thing is, though, I don't know if they're quite as hungry as they used to be. I remember when I was a boy I used to hear people saying that if you needed a job it didn't really matter what kind of skills you had. As long as you weren't old or sick, you could go to Denver and get on with InterSpace. But that was ..." He paused for a moment. "Fifty years ago."

A chill ran down Frank's spine. Once again he had the feeling that had struck him right at the beginning—that Greg knew something about Frank and his past. Fifty years ago was when Ellen had arrived here. Greg had mentioned that number in a way that seemed deliberate to Frank.

Frank shivered slightly, uncontrollably. He felt a pressure on the skin at the back of his neck, as though he were being watched. He forced himself not to turn around and look.

"Still," Greg said, "it's worth a try."

Sir, it's not us. We've lost control.

"You know where the InterSpace recruiting offices are in downtown Denver, right?"

Frank shook his head. "No idea."

Greg stared at him. "I got the impression you were from Denver."

"No. No, I'm ... I'm just kind of wandering around the country. Living on the money my folks left me, as I said. Just passing through." I'm getting really good at lying, Frank thought.

"Hm." Greg stared at him for a moment longer, then looked away. "Well, it's probably simplest if I show you where they are, then."

Why is he acting that way?

Something was probing our system, sir. We've blocked it. We're fine now.

The stare had unnerved Frank all over again. Maybe he wasn't getting good at lying after all. He watched the scenery and said nothing more, and to his relief, Greg fell silent at last.

The train began a rapid, curving descent. On some of the

curves, he could see the city below. Once again it struck him that he was following much the same route as he had so long ago, but now the city covered the eastern plains out to the horizon and as far as he could see to north and south. The many open spaces he remembered from his own day were gone. He also remembered some lakes and reservoirs, and they too had vanished. Buildings covered everything. Lights twinkled across the city as the afternoon waned into evening. Those would once have seemed welcoming, but not now. What had once been a small, friendly city was now immense, alien, and threatening.

Once the train had dropped all the way down to the plains and he could no longer see the city from above, he began to lose that momentary fear. Now it was just a city, and he could have been on any commuter train in any large city on the East Coast back in his own time.

The train stopped a few times on the way in, the voice from the ceiling announcing the stops. Finally, the voice said, "Denver, Main Station."

Greg jumped to his feet with surprising lightness and strength. "Here we are!" He tugged at Frank's arm.

Frank stood up more slowly. His legs felt stiff and his back hurt slightly after sitting so long in one position without moving. His head felt heavy, and he had the beginnings of a headache. He remembered then that he had had less than three hours of sleep the night before.

Images paraded before him: Tommy and Ellen in bed together, dead bodies in the hallway, the smashed doors, Dolores's anxious face as she struggled with the controls.

Greg pulled at his arm again. "Come on! We need to get out here."

Frank shook his head. The adrenaline's wearing off, he thought. Finally. Now I need a good night's sleep. I want to go to sleep and wake up back in 1945.

Greg and Frank stood outside the train for a moment on a covered platform. The others who had exited with them walked away rapidly down the platform.

Wish I knew where I was going, Frank thought. The mission seemed silly at that moment. Go to the future. Find an item of superscience. Use that item to bring the item itself back home. Pat yourself on the back for a job well done.

The Tempus planners had not anticipated just how large and complex the world of the future would be. Hell, Frank thought, even our own world was too big and complex for such a mission. And yet those Soviet agents were able to break into Tempus, so maybe I'll be able to do the same thing here. If I can figure out where to break into.

"Come on," Greg said again. He started walking. Frank followed him. Greg led the way into the station building. The interior was a large open space filled with purposeful crowds. Loud voices making unintelligible announcements echoed from the walls.

Not everyone was moving. Some were standing still and looking up. Frank followed their gaze and gasped in astonishment. From perhaps twenty feet above the heads of the crowds up to the distant ceiling, the walls were covered with moving pictures in full color. The voices he had thought were making announcements about trains seemed instead to be coming from the moving pictures.

Movies on the wall of a train station? What the hell was this?

Fascinated, Frank stared, his mouth open. He couldn't make head or tails of it. There was too much, too many different things to watch. It formed a jumble in his mind, and he couldn't follow any one set of pictures. He had a general impression of improbably beautiful people, of explosions, sports, war, glimpses of machines moving through space, a tumult of changing images.

"Bread and circuses," Greg muttered. He stood close to Frank. "Come on." He turned away, and Frank hurried to catch up with him. "If you get on with InterSpace," Greg said, "you'll have access to real news. News about politics. Science." He paused, then added, "New technology."

"War," Frank said, almost without thinking.

Greg stopped, turned, grabbed Frank's arm in a powerful, painful grip. "Don't use that word! People don't like to hear it. There isn't any war. Just talk about your job, like most people do. And think about," he shrugged, "you know, your purpose in life. Your mission."

"My *what?*"

But Greg had turned and was hurrying away again. Frank made his way through the crowd, trailing him this time, not trying to walk beside him. Now he was sure something strange was going on, possibly something dangerous to him. But Greg was the only contact he had here now, and he couldn't take the chance of heading off on his own.

He looked around himself, and for a brief moment his self-confidence returned. The area around the train station was filled with buildings dating from the very early 20th century. Abandoned for decades, they had been rediscovered by a generation that found them charming and admired their solid brickwork. Now close to two hundred years old, they were the city's most prestigious business addresses, harboring the priciest offices in town. He might have traveled back to his own childhood and his visits to this city, when he had left the same train station and stood here looking at the same buildings in this familiar, friendly city. He could imagine his grandparents driving up all hurried, flustered, and welcoming, apologizing for being late.

The feeling vanished when he raised his glance and saw, over the roofs of the brick buildings, faceless towers of glass and steel rising far into the alien sky. He stopped walking and stood staring, his mouth open, like any country cousin of his own era spending his first day in the big city.

Greg came back to him, grabbed his arm, and pulled him into motion again. "Come on," Greg said. "You shouldn't draw attention to yourself. No one should," he added quickly. "It's ... well, it's just not a good idea. Come on."

He led Frank into one of the old buildings. In the lobby, the decor continued the recreated charm of an earlier era.

Greg looked around. "That way."

All right. Everything better be smooth from now on. We want to get him safely stored away in space.

No problem, sir.

Frank followed Greg through a pair of heavy glass doors engraved with a logo of a ringed planet circling a star and a spacecraft circling the planet. Beyond the door was a wooden desk, behind which sat a young woman. She was pretty in a low-key, almost bland way.

"My friend here would like to join InterSpace," Greg told the receptionist.

"Interview Room 3," she said. She pointed toward a hallway to her left.

Once again, Greg led the way. He stopped at a door with the numeral 3 on it. "I guess this must be it," he said. "I bet they don't use most of these rooms nowadays. Not like a few years ago. Go ahead." He gave Frank a gentle push. "I know you retrospectors prefer talking to real human beings, but they're so real nowadays, you can just pretend it's human."

"What are you talking about?" Frank said. Part of the wall slid to one side, like the opening in the train. All Frank could see beyond the opening was a small, empty room.

Instead of answering, Greg pushed him through the doorway. Frank stumbled forward. He caught his balance and turned back. He faced a blank wall, with no sign of a door.

"I'll need your ID before we start."

Frank spun around. A man was standing in front of the wall opposite the door. He was as nondescript and threatening as the blank, gray walls, but the hidden entrance he had used could be used by others, and that made Frank feel threatened.

"My—I must have lost it. I've been in the mountains. Probably left it out there. My name's Frank Anderson. What kind of openings do you have?"

The man looked puzzled. "That's impossible. Hold out your hand, please."

"Oh." Some sort of advanced fingerprinting system, Frank thought. "Um, right hand? Left hand? Palm up? Palm down?"

"It makes no difference, of course. Are you well? Are you feeling disoriented? Perhaps you need medical help. Are you required to take regular medication?"

"No, no, that's fine. Just a bit too immersed in my

retrospector role."

"I see. Your hand, please."

Just a formality, Frank thought. I hope.

He raised his right hand, palm forward, as though he were swearing an oath, and waited for the other man to produce some sort of clever gadget to record his fingerprints.

Instead, the man disappeared.

An illusion, Frank thought. He was a damned illusion. What's real here? What a terrible place this is! Maybe none of it's real. Maybe it's a dream. Maybe I'm still at Tempus in 1945 and hallucinating.

Even if it was a dream, he was stuck in it. What would happen now, in this world that seemed like a dream? Something had gone wrong. He had aroused suspicions. The police were probably on their way. He had to get out here, maybe find Greg—assuming he could trust him—and think up some other plan of attack.

He examined the wall he had entered through, but he couldn't find the doorway or any hidden button or lever to make it open. In growing desperation, Frank examined all of the other walls. Nothing. Not even a window. The room was brightly lit, but he couldn't even see any distinct lights on the ceiling. The ceiling above him was smooth and featureless, glowing evenly across its surface.

He could feel his heart rate increasing. His breathing grew faster and shallower. He closed his eyes and tried to calm himself.

He sensed the open doorway and opened his eyes. A man stood in the doorway—tall, strong, hostile. He wore dark blue, loose-fitting pants and shirt. There was a pouch on his left hip, apparently stuck there somehow, for he had no belt. A small red star was on the front of his shirt, centered on his chest.

Jesus, Frank thought, it's worse than I imagined. The Soviets won. They're in control!

"You have no ID," the uniformed man said. "If you have no satisfactory explanation, you'll be eliminated. Come with me." He turned and walked away.

Frank hesitated, then stepped through the doorway. He had expected the corridor beyond to be filled with men in uniforms, but it was empty except for the one man he had already seen. That man now stood a few feet away, looking impatient. "I order you not to hesitate," he said. "Come." He turned and took a few steps, then turned and stopped when he saw that Frank was not following. He glared at Frank. "I can call for help, or I can eliminate you here myself. Very painful for you in both cases. Or you can cooperate and come with me."

Frank straightened. "Oh, I can think of another alternative. You can leave and forget about me." He stepped forward.

The other man stepped back quickly, fumbling for something at his belt. "Help!" he yelled. "Under attack!"

Frank kicked the fumbling hand, heard something crack, followed through with a fist to the man's throat.

He stood over the writhing, choking figure. "Why did you make me do that? Damn you!"

The agonized movements stopped. The other man relaxed slowly and lay still. Frank turned and walked down the hallway toward the reception area—walked swiftly, but didn't run. The dead man's comrades would be on their way, but they had no way of knowing what Frank looked like, so it was important not to attract attention.

He passed through the outer office, nodding at the young woman behind the desk. She looked at him then looked away again, uninterested. He pushed at the heavy double glass doors, relieved that they opened, and even more relieved that they were ordinary doors of the sort he was familiar with.

As he walked across the building lobby toward the front door, a squad of grim-faced men passed him, headed toward the InterSpace office. They were dressed the same way as the man who had threatened to eliminate him earlier, and they trotted in step.

Frank stopped and watched them go by. His curiosity was genuine, but in addition he thought it would look suspicious if he didn't watch them. Surely an ordinary citizen would watch.

Then he turned and walked from the building.

Outside, he breathed more easily. Choosing at random, he turned to his right and started walking, trying to keep the same seemingly unhurried but rapid gait. He saw other people, ordinary civilians as far as he could tell, walking along the sidewalks just as he had seen them before. There were no uniforms. And there was no sign of Greg.

At least he got out. Keep the team out of his sight. What happened in there?

I don't know, sir. They seem to have taken over the building somehow. We lost him and the Greg as soon as they entered.

Letting me know. Making sure I don't forget.

Sir? We should pick him up, sir. Get him to a safe place.

If anyone approaches him, he'll panic. He can handle any of our people, including the ones I trained myself. We'll have to tread carefully.

Frank walked for hours. He turned corners at random, went down alleys, along major streets and minor ones. He was exhausted, light headed from lack of sleep, hours of stress and exertion, and lack of food and water. He had no idea where he was and whether he had managed to elude any pursuit. Sometimes he found himself walking among crowds. At other times he was alone on the sidewalk. Light was fading, the day was ending, and the temperature was dropping. He began to wonder if he'd end this bizarre mission to another time by dying of hunger and exposure behind an apartment building.

He saw large numbers of retrospectors. Some were dressed the way he was, but most of them were wearing much older costumes.

No one wants to live here, he thought. They're all trying to escape into the past. Who can blame them?

From time to time, he thought he recognized a face in the crowd. He thought he had seen certain men and women repeatedly during his strange wondering. But none of them approached him or attempted to stop him, and he decided he must be imagining things.

His mind was wandering. His shoulders drooped, and he could scarcely manage to walk in a straight line. His legs felt too heavy to lift.

I'm at the end, he thought. I'm not going to be able to go on much longer.

What was the point of going on? He was going nowhere, accomplishing nothing. He couldn't live in this world. Might as well stop and let them catch and "eliminate" him.

Hell, he thought, I'll take care of the job for them.

He looked up at one of the great office towers that seemed

to dominate so much of this city in this age. Maybe he could get to the top of one of them and jump off. Float into space. Make an impact on the future.

Not that anyone here would notice or care. Maybe they had some kind of futuristic machine that would come along and scrape up his body and wash the blood off the sidewalk. The people wouldn't do anything. They didn't even look at each other. They walked along with their eyes on the ground. Frank had been looking at them, at the cars, at the buildings, but no one looked back, no one met his eyes.

How different from his own time! That made him feel stranger, more an outsider, than anything else. No smiles, no glances, no casual conversations. It was a very sad place, this glittering world of the future. Maybe they had gained outer space, but they had lost their humanity and warmth.

That's what Dad used to say about the Twenties and Thirties, Frank thought. He used to praise the days before the first war. Gee, maybe traveling in time has made me prematurely middle–aged!

The thought made him chuckle aloud. He stood still on an almost deserted sidewalk in the dusk in a rundown business district in a alien city in an alien century and laughed.

He could sense how the few people passing by made an extra effort not to look at him, not to notice him. "You shouldn't draw attention to yourself," Greg had said. "No one should."

For a moment, his sleepiness and dizziness vanished. He looked around.

A man stood nearby, watching him.

Frank pulled himself to his full height and stared back at the man. He wasn't large, didn't look threatening, didn't seem to be armed, but who knew what kind of weapons this era had, or how easily they could be concealed?

"If you're looking for a shelter," the man said, his voice mild and friendly, "I know of a place."

"A shelter? What are you talking about? I'm just walking around."

The other man smiled. "Yeah, and you look like you've been doing it for a long time. My name's Rob." He held out his hand.

After a long moment of hesitation, Frank took his hand briefly. He let go of it quickly, wanting both hands free.

Rob held both his hands up, palms out. "That's okay. I don't blame you for not trusting me. I'm just a stranger. You don't know me. Look, even retrospectors need food and a place to sleep. Unless they've got time machines and can go back to the times they're dressed for." He laughed loudly. "Which we all know is impossible, right?"

Frank searched the other man's face. In the gathering dark, it was hard to make out his expression clearly. From what Frank could see, it was open, guileless. "Yeah, as far as anyone knows, I guess it is."

"Too bad," Rob said. "I'd like to go back myself. Back to the time you're dressed for. A hundred years ago? Two hundred? Better times than nowadays, I bet. Friendlier times. Safer times. Anyway, the local retrospectors have a building where you can spend the night and get some food. I bet that's the place you were looking for."

"I guess ... I must have missed it. I'm not from around here."

"I figured as much. I guess it's part of that whole network you guys have—the buildings and conventions and festivals. I hear you can spend all your time in those, if you want, and it's like this world doesn't even exist. I could take you there now."

The river was in control again, and he had no real choice but to let it carry him wherever it willed. He was so tired that he no longer felt hungry. All he wanted now was to sleep—to sleep, and to awaken at last in the world he knew, the world of 1945, the real world, to leave this fantasy world behind in its proper place, in the kingdom of nightmares. "Thanks. I'd like that."

"Thank God," Tommy muttered. "Frank, babysitting you is exhausting. You don't know when to give up. That's always been your problem."

He took the helmet off and stood up and stretched. He still found controlling these robots awkward and stressful. He felt as tired as though he really had been the Rob and had really been walking around for hours, shadowing Frank.

Now Frank was stashed and so was the Rob, and it was time to take care of numerous matters he had been neglecting.

First among them: the package.

He had found it on his desk the day before. It was nondescript, mundane, old fashioned, just a thick, sealed manila envelope. But it was on *his* desk, in *his* office—inviolate space, heavily guarded space, possibly the most secure and heavily guarded and inviolate place on Earth. No one but Tommy could have entered that office. Not even his personal bodyguards could have left that package there.

He hadn't touched it. He hadn't even gone near it. As soon as he saw the envelope on his desk, Tommy had backed out and summoned a security team to take it away and test it. The envelope had turned out to be harmless.

Tommy had deduced that much even before he'd called for

security.

Leaving the envelope for him—that had been the message. Someone was telling him that all his security measures meant nothing. To that someone, Tommy's citadel was open and defenseless. That usual someone, the powerful shadow who had always been there. He could have killed Tommy at any time. If there was a further message, then it was probably inside the envelope, and it would be an actual message, not a bomb or a poisonous gas or a virus.

"It's just sheets of paper, sir," the security man said. "With writing on them. Hand writing," he said wonderingly. "We tested the sheets, and they're just paper. It's all entirely harmless."

"What does it say?"

"We would never read it, sir!" The security man seemed shocked at the suggestion. "The top sheet was addressed to you, so I made sure that no one read anything else."

Tommy nodded. "Well done. All right. Give it all to me, and I'll have a look at it."

After the security man had left, Tommy sat at his desk and placed the stack of paper in front of him. This was the entire contents of the envelope, perhaps a couple of hundred sheets of letter–sized paper. It seemed so innocuous.

The top sheet contained one line of writing, block letters that said

TO TOMMY STILLWELL

It had been written by hand, as the security man had said. Odd indeed, Tommy thought. He lifted the sheet and was about to continue when he noticed a new message from Eddie Iselin hovering above his desk.

He scanned it quickly. It was the news he had been waiting for. This took priority over everything else. He dumped the pile of papers in one of the drawers of his desk and headed for Eddie's office.

Thirty

"As you know, Eddie's been following up on your old work on time travel."

"I didn't know that. That's interesting."

Tommy laughed. "Come on, Delia. He told you about it. He asked for my permission first."

For a moment, he saw fear in her face. She stared at him for a while, and then the fear faded away. "I never was much good at this game," she said.

"True. We're both much safer with you doing the technical work and me running the show."

"I guess so. Eddie never gave me any details. He just told me what he was working on. A few months ago, he stopped talking about it. I tried to get more information out of him, but he's really good at keeping secrets. I thought maybe you had found out that Eddie was talking to me about it and told him to stop. But if you knew from the beginning and approved ..." She frowned, and her gaze drifted sideways.

Tommy knew that look. Usually it meant that she was thinking about scientific matters he would have no hope of understanding. This time, she was thinking about politics and subterfuge—Tommy's natural mental realm, and a difficult one for her.

She gasped. "My God! Something's happened, hasn't it? He's had some kind of breakthrough."

"He has. He's done it."

"Time travel? That's wonderful!"

"Yeah. It's the cat's fucking pajamas."

Delia stared at him for a moment, bewildered by his answer. But she turned quickly to the question that really intrigued her. "I wish he'd been keeping me updated. I'd like to know what led him to the answer. I want to know where I was going wrong. I was up against a brick wall."

"Apparently your entire approach was wrong. I didn't tell Eddie to stop sending you reports. He stopped because he didn't want to have tell you that. The kid worships you."

Delia looked embarrassed. "I do want to know what approach he took. I want all the details."

"Don't look at me. I couldn't understand anything he said. Feel free to go see him. You guys can talk math at each other. I'll tell him it's okay. I did give him the basic idea, though. I set him on the right path." He grinned.

"You did that? Tommy, I don't want to hurt your feelings, but—"

"But I'm a scientific ignoramus, and this is work that requires topnotch brainpower."

"I was trying to think of a kinder way to put it."

"Yeah, well, you can always speak your mind with me. You know that."

She shook her head. "I haven't spoken my mind with you for decades."

"Really? Damn, that's depressing. So why are you being frank now?"

"I'm so excited that I lost my sense of caution. What was it you told Eddie?"

"I told him to think of time as a river."

"That's a very old idea, Tommy. It's an ancient way of viewing time."

"I'm an old guy. I'm ancient."

"Of course. We're both old. It's the rejuvenation."

Tommy smiled. "Oh, I'm much more of an old-timer than you realize."

"Tommy, what are you talking about?"

"I'm so glad you've always kept using my name instead of calling me by a title. I think it would have broken my heart if you had done that. You were my first real friend here."

"What? Tommy, you're being completely bewildering."

"That's just the start. It's going to get a lot more bewildering. Everything's about to change. I have a mission for you. You have to accept it. I don't mean that I'm going to force you to accept it, or that there'll be terrible consequences if you don't. I just mean that it has to happen. If you refuse, you can go your way and keep working on whatever research project you want to, but the results will disastrous for all of us. For the world, in fact."

"This is a dialog of non-sequiturs. I feel like I've walked into a nineteenth-century Russian novel."

"I've never read one of those, and now I won't try. Here's the point. I come from a time and place where some very clever people figured out that time is a river, and they also figured out how to skip people down the river, move them forward in time.

That's how they explained it to me. What they couldn't do was add enough energy to people to force them upstream against the current. To send them back in time, in other words. I know they were telling the truth because I was born in 1924, I fought in World War Two, and in 1945 those people sent me forward in time to 1995."

Delia stared at him. Her mouth was open, but she said nothing. He wasn't sure she was breathing.

He stepped around his desk and to her side. "Oh, I forgot to add that one of the people who did all of that and sent me forward in time was Delia Garrison. You."

Tommy caught her as her knees buckled. Her face had turned white.

"I think you should sit down." He helped her to one of the deep armchairs set against one of the walls of his office.

"Would you like something to drink?" he asked her. "Alcohol? Caffeine? Water?"

"You're crazy," she whispered.

"But not a liar. I don't think I was crazy before that jump through time. That probably scrambled some brain cells. I heard the river while I was traveling. I heard it rushing and roaring, like a trapped animal, or maybe just like a river channeled between rocky banks, unable to escape."

"I don't believe any of it."

"Maybe that's how I got my spiffy telathings."

"Telomeres, Tommy. Telomeres. That almost makes sense. Even so, you're asking me to accept a lot."

"I can't prove any of it. Go talk to Eddie. Once you know that he can do it, that it can be done, you'll be more willing to believe that it was done to me. Then come back here, and I'll tell you about your mission."

She was back in his office the next day. She looked her normal self, although Tommy was sure she would never be her normal self again.

"Hey, honcho," she said. "The dolly's back. Are you ready to flap your lips, or do you want me to take a powder?"

Tommy laughed. "I'm glad you're in a better mood. But people didn't really talk that way in my time, at least not outside of gangster movies. Anyway, you're not a dolly. You'd better look that word up again. So. You sound like you believe me."

"It's hard not to. Eddie showed me what his people have achieved. He also told me that it was some ideas from you that set him on the right path. As opposed to ... " She sighed. "This is really hard for me to say. As opposed to the path I had been following. So now I know it's possible. You could be a man from the past, from before I was born. You could even have known my parents when they were children!"

"Strange thought, but I suppose you're right. I didn't know your parents, but I did know that woman you said could almost be a reincarnation of your mother."

"Ellen Maxwell? The young woman who was killed in that explosion all those years ago?"

"Forty–six years ago. Yes, Ellen Maxwell. We ... " He sighed. "We knew each other in 1945. We were both sent forward in time, along with a guy named Frank Anderson."

"You were in love with her."

"In 1945."

"You still are."

"I guess I always will be. For the rest of my very long life. So when you go back, you'll get to see me as a silly, lovestruck boy."

"Lovestruck and a boy, perhaps, but I bet you were never silly. Anyway, even if I did agree to go back, I'd never fit in. The woman who looked like me must have been someone else."

"Oh, yeah? Here's something that'll break you off at the ankles." He slid a sheet of paper across the desk to her.

"Paper," Delia said. "You're one of the few who still use it."

"I'm also one of the few who still write notes by hand. On paper. You must have wondered about that."

Delia looked up at him and then quickly down. She focused her attention on the sheet of paper. "What is this, a page from an old newspaper?"

"Very old. Autumn of 1937."

She read it quickly. "Oh, this is awful! What a terrible story!"

"You once told me that you were afraid all these years at InterAgency had burned away your humanity. See, you were wrong."

"I wasn't wrong. I spent years being a serial killer, but it was always at a distance. The people weren't real to me. And there were too many of them. This girl seems real."

"A single death is a tragedy, a million deaths is a statistic, as Uncle Joe used to say."

"What an unpleasant uncle. I bet you stayed away from him."

"I did my best."

She looked at the sheet of paper again. "It says that the driver reported the accident the next day. He said he had hit and killed two women on a country road, but the police only found one body, that of Esperanza Lujan, a local resident. 'Mrs. Lujan lived with her daughter, Dolores, whom police have not yet been able to locate.'"

She looked up at last. "Why did you show me this?"

"Because of the daughter, Dolores. Interesting person. She was a brilliant student. Loved physics. Graduated from high school a year early. At the time of that accident, she was nineteen and already a sophomore in college and doing very well. She had a full scholarship, but she lived at home because her mother needed her."

"What about her father?"

"Unknown. The newspaper referred to the mother as *Mrs.*, but that was a courtesy. They did that sort of thing back then. Esperanza moved up to Michigan when she was in her twenties and worked in a local dime store. She got pregnant and raised the kid, Dolores, mostly by herself, although locals would sometimes see a man staying at her place. The same man each time, I mean. They thought he was a traveling salesman who refused to marry her for some reason. Maybe it was a racial thing. There was a lot of prejudice in those days."

"A traveling salesman? What in the world is that?"

"I don't think they exist any more. They were guys who spent much of their time driving from town to town, trying to sell whatever product they were hawking. It was tough and lonely, and a lot of them took to drink or womanizing. Or both, I guess. Anyway, that doesn't matter. Whoever Dolores's father was, he's not important."

"You seem to have spent quite a bit of time researching this girl. Did you know her?"

"No. I was never even in that part of the country. Anyway, she was five years older than me."

"I can't get used to this. I look at this," she held up the paper, "this story about something that happened so long ago, and you talk about this girl being only five years older than you. It's just too strange."

Tommy smiled. "Be patient, Delia. It's going to get a lot stranger. Don't you want to know what happened to Dolores, the daughter the police couldn't find?"

"Are you really going to wait till I ask you?"

"Nope. I'm going to tell you whether you ask or not. After the accident was reported to them, the police went out to investigate. That wasn't till the next day, but that was a road that didn't have a lot of traffic, so Esperanza's body was still there. There were a lot of wild animals up there in those days, and the body was partially eaten. That's in the article you're holding, but the way it's worded, you might not realize that that's what they're talking about. Newspapers were very discreet and respectful in those days. There was a lot of dried blood on the road. The policemen on the scene thought that there could have been two victims."

"So where was Dolores's body?" Delia shivered suddenly. "Maybe one of those wild animals carried it away. Good God! I hope she was dead, the poor girl."

"The policemen thought of that. Or maybe she had been hurt and had wandered away in confusion. They searched the nearby fields for a bit but didn't find any trace of her. I don't think they really put much effort into it. Wrong surname and wrong kind of family life. In any case, a few days later, they got an inquiry about her. Dolores had just applied for a job, and the employer wanted to make sure she was clean. The police told them they had nothing negative about her, and they closed the books on the accident. Obviously, Dolores hadn't even been in the area when it happened, and now she was getting on with her life."

"Just like that! That makes her sound heartless."

"I suppose so. Except that about fifty years later, the area where the accident happened was being developed as a new suburb, and the construction crews found a skeleton. Young and female. Dead for a long time, probably decades. The police pathologist could tell that much, but not much more. However, when the story hit the local papers, an old man said it was Dolores. The skeleton had a ring on one finger, and he said he had dated Dolores briefly, and she had been very proud of that ring and had told him it was a gift from her father. The old guy wasn't all there, so no one believed him."

"Well, of course not. We know Dolores was alive because of that employer inquiry."

"Obviously. Not that the police could have done much checking, even if they'd wanted to. That employer was a bit mysterious and hard to track down. And I happen to know that their headquarters and most of their employees got blown up in 1945."

"Good God! Was Dolores one of them?"

"I certainly hope not. All she had to do to escape the explosion was follow my directions."

Delia raised her hands as though in protest and then let them fall in her lap. "Tommy, please. I've always hated game playing. You know that. Just tell me. Just explain all of this."

"Sorry. Okay, here's an important fact. By chance, Dolores looked a lot like you. Somewhat similar in the face, but more than that, the height and weight. Coloring, too. Her mother came from Mexico originally and had very dark hair, almost black, but Dolores's hair was a light brown, very much like yours. Her skin color was close to yours, as far as we can tell. Admittedly, that's guess work to some extent. We only have a few black–and–white photographs of her. I've already mentioned the intellectual similarity—the scientific brilliance, the love of physics. The main difference between you now and her then is that she was nineteen, and you look middle–aged."

Delia looked away. "We've talked about that before."

"I know. You feel more comfortable flying under the radar. You don't want to be attractive to men anymore. But you made the breakthrough in that treatment of yours years ago. You've kept me looking and feeling like a young man for the last twenty years, so I know you could do the same for yourself if you wanted to."

"I don't want to."

"I want you to. I want you to adjust your rejuvenation process so that you'll look nineteen."

"It doesn't work that way. I've explained it to you. The best it can do is put you in optimal physical condition. That means you'll look like you're in your mid–twenties. I can make myself look this way by not applying it optimally, but I can't somehow return myself to some point in my youth earlier than that optimal age. Mid–twenties would probably be the best I could hope for."

"Mid–twenties will have to do, then. Young people tended to look a bit older then than they do now. Here's the plan. We're going to send you back in time to 1937. You're the one who's going to apply for that job. That body they found in the 1980s, that *was* Dolores. I don't know what happened to her. Maybe she was badly hurt in the accident and wandered away and died in the fields. Or maybe an animal found her and dragged her off. That doesn't matter. What does matter is that the poor kid died out there that night."

"And now you want me to go back in time. To make myself younger and then to go back in time." She shivered.

He wondered which one of those two frightened her more. "Yeah, that's it. Piece of cake."

"It would be so hard. Everything was so primitive."

"Yeah, we were primitives. We had just finished killing tens of millions of each other, all over the world. But it was in a good cause. They told us that fairly often."

"Now you want to send me back into that madness."

"You'll spend all your time in the States. The madness was elsewhere. Anyway, you have to do it because it was done, because it happened. We have to make sure that everything happens the way it already did and that nothing changes. You remember how, when we first met, I was sure you were Dolores Lujan?"

Delia gasped. "Oh, God! I'd forgotten about that! You kept going on about it."

"Because I recognized you. You were an older version of the girl I met back in 1945. You were there, Delia. You and me and Ellen and Frank. We were all there together. If you don't do this, then that won't happen. Everything will change. History will change. I can't risk that."

"I need time to do the math. What Eddie achieved changes everything. I want to dig up my old work and reevaluate it."

Tommy shook his head. "I don't have time for that."

"That's absurd, Tommy. Time is exactly what you do have.

It doesn't matter whether I go back now or if I wait for a few months or a few years and then go back. The result will be the same."

"Well, here's the deal. You'll do it my way, or you'll have no access to Eddie and his equipment." He couldn't afford to let her wait. The longer she thought about it, the more likely she was to discover objections and to insist that he modify his plans. Give her time, and she'd be insisting that they send someone back to get Dolores Lujan and her mother out of the way of that car. And of course she'd want to save her parents. Nothing could be allowed to change. He couldn't waste time having that argument with her. "You have to be there to save our lives. We know the building was destroyed, blown up, killing everyone inside it. That happened. We can't change that. I also know that my two friends and I escaped because you got us out of there in time by sending us forward." He laughed and added, "In time."

"What about me? How will I escape?"

"The same way. I'm sending two men back. One of them is going with you. After you send Frank and Ellen and me forward, you'll send those two men back here, and then you'll send yourself back here, as well."

"Ellen Maxwell. I'll be sending her forward so that she can be murdered."

"There's a way around that. You'll have to trust me. Someone else died, not her. When you come back here, to 2097, she'll be waiting for you, along with Frank. You know how dangerous this world is. They'll need you. They'll need your protection."

"You could do a better job of protecting them than I could."

"I won't be here. They'll never even see me. You won't see

me again, either."

"Where will you be?"

"Taking back control of my life. That's all I'll tell you."

"You're asking for so much trust!"

"I always have. And I've never let you down."

In spite of what Tommy had said, Delia couldn't be sent back immediately. Her further rejuvenation would take time, and she had to be given the information she needed to fit into another era.

"You're better off than I was," Tommy told her. "We know a lot about 1937—history, events, how people lived, even the slang they used and the music they listened to. We also know a lot about one specific person, Dolores Lujan. When they were training me at Tempus in 1945, they didn't know what I'd find in 1995. They said they were making educated guesses, but that was crap. They were way off. You could have told me the facts, but that would have exposed you. And it would have changed things. I arrived in 1995 with that worthless crap they told me, and you mustn't change that. You'll have to stick to what the so-called experts at Tempus tell you to say.

"Here's one thing I can tell you. I had to learn this the hard way. When you get there, to 1937, pretend you're in a dangerous foreign country, a place where people only seem to be speaking English. In reality, they're communicating in some kind of code that you don't understand. Keep your eyes open and your mouth shut."

"I wish you were coming with me. I feel like I'll need a bodyguard."

"You'll be okay."

"How can you know that?"

"Because you *were* okay. Because it already happened back then. You're just going back to make sure it happens the way it did, to make sure nothing changes."

"Yes, all right. I've already given you my word that I won't try to change events. Still, I'm not looking forward to the actual trip. Eddie thinks that because of the amount of stream potential energy I'll be absorbing, it could be physically stressful, even painful, in ways we can't even predict."

"We can predict that you'll get there safely."

"Because you saw me there."

"Exactly. And you looked just fine. Anyway, Julie will protect you."

"Who?"

"Giuliano Fiorentino. He prefers 'Julie.' The man who's going back with you. You can trust him."

"I can trust him to be your man?"

Tommy smiled. "You can trust him to follow my orders like they came from God. He'll stay with you till you get the job Dolores was applying for."

"What a sad name the poor girl had!"

"How so?"

"It's Spanish for sorrows."

"Well, it'll be your name soon. Her mother told someone that she named her daughter after a river near the town she came from. She was probably homesick."

"Tommy, what was it like, traveling in time? You said something about hearing the river trying to escape."

"I guess I was trying too hard to be poetic. I can't really describe it. It seemed to go on forever and to last for no time at all. It felt like I was standing in some enormous, flat, open space. I couldn't see anything. I could just sense the distances around me. There was this tremendous sound, and I had a feeling ... " A feeling that everything was possible, that events could go in any direction, that he was at the crossroads of an infinite number of paths. "I had a feeling that I had no control over where I was going, that everything was predetermined, that I was being carried along, and there was nothing I could do about it."

"I suppose I was hoping to hear something else. I still think the past is malleable."

"Sorry to disappoint you."

For the first time, Tommy began to worry about what she would experience during her trip. If she felt the same sense of infinite possibility, would she be able to keep her word to him? He knew how important honesty was to her, but if she saw or felt something during her trip back that made her think she could change history, then when she had the chance to actually do so, would she be able to resist? He could trust her desire to be honest, but how far could he trust her self–control?

I have no choice, he thought. It's too late to try to add safeguards. Maybe she's the weak link in my plans, but I'll have to take the chance. She'll go back and then I'll just wait and see if the world changes in some strange way. Assuming I'll be aware of it, even if it does.

It was the sort of speculation he hated, and he always tried to avoid it. He shook his head, as if to shake the thoughts away.

"Is something wrong? Tommy, are you all right?"

"I'm fine." He smiled at her. Soon she would leave, and he would never see her again. He wondered why their decades of friendship and working together hadn't changed into something more. He said, "It's time for you to go back to class and learn more about the good old days."

"I've been learning about all the war and genocide. What was so good about those days?"

"I was young. That's what was so good about them." I was in love. I was fully alive. Most of all, I had no idea what was going to happen next.

Three weeks after the initial conversation, Tommy was in Eddie Iselin's lab watching Delia standing on a platform under a glowing glass tube that reminded him disturbingly of the equipment in a room in Tempus in 1945.

Delia seemed lost in her thoughts. Julie Fiorentino stood beside her. He was a short man, only slightly taller than Delia, dark, slender, and alert—a contrast with tall, blond, broad-shouldered, seemingly stoic and detached Hank Morrison, whom Tommy had seen vanish from this platform a day earlier.

"Julie," Tommy said, "remember, you'll be arriving at night. The site will be empty. There'll be a couple of night watchmen. Maybe dogs."

"We'll avoid the watchmen. I'll take care of the dogs."

Delia started suddenly, as though emerging from a dream, and looked around her. She stared at Fiorentino for a long while, thinking about what Tommy had told her about his mission and Morrison's. "You won't hurt the dogs," she said.

"Madam Garrison, if one of them attacks us—"

"Then you'll bleed. You will not hurt the dogs."

Fiorentino looked at the floor. "Yes, ma'am."

Tommy wanted to say something to Delia, but nothing came to him. He felt oddly dull and detached, as though this were a minor event, nothing momentous, a simple departure in space instead of time. He turned to Eddie and said, "You may fire when ready."

He turned back, expecting to see the two of them fade into nothingness. Instead, the platform was empty. Delia was already on her way.

He wondered what she was feeling at that moment. Did going back feel different from going forward?

I guess I'll know soon, he told himself.

Gorman was waiting for him.

The doctor hesitated, holding the anesthetic disk. "I have to ask you this one last time, sir. Are you sure you want us to proceed? Do you have any doubts at all? I apologize, but I'm your doctor, and I have to ask you this."

Tommy smiled to allay the man's obvious fears. "It's all right, Alex. I don't have a single doubt. Do you? I'm told that you're probably the best man in the world to do this work. Do you have any doubts about your abilities?"

Gorman stiffened. "Not at all, sir. We can do what you said you wanted. My team and I can do it."

"If you're worried about your own safety in case something goes wrong, don't be. Madame Garrison will be here shortly, and she'll be in charge during my absence or if I'm incapacitated. I've left her a detailed message explaining everything and telling her that you're operating under my orders."

"Sir, my only fears are for you. As I told you before, this surgery will change you from the core of your body to the skin. Bone structure, hormones, retinas, reduction in body mass—we'll be virtually taking you apart and putting you back together as a different person. I couldn't find anything like it in the literature. Individual aspects of this have been done to other people, certainly, but no one has undergone the entire ensemble of changes you've mandated. There'll be a lot of pain and a long, difficult recovery. That's the part I worry about the most. You simply have to spend at least three months under our care after we're finished in here."

"I've already told you that's not possible. What I have to do after you've finished with me won't take very long." Only minutes to atone, he thought. Only minutes to stop being a puppet. And then there'll be no more pain.

Tommy hoisted himself onto the operating table and lay on his back. In the tone of command that had become second nature to him, he said, "Do it. Now."

Gorman stepped forward and pressed the disk to Tommy's temple. Tommy's thoughts became random, scattered. He heard a rushing sound, as though he were already standing beside the great river, but it was softer than he remembered, quieter.

At last, he, and not the river, was in control.

Thirty-One

The rushing sound seemed to last forever. She could see nothing. A huge pressure on her back forced her forward through something that pushed back and resisted.

For a moment, the resistance increased, and then it diminished. It increased a second time, becoming almost painful. She felt she was being crushed between the force pushing her forward and the one trying to stop her.

Unknowingly, she had traveled past two explosions, the first in 2051 and the second and larger one in 1945, both of which had released great bursts of temporal energy in the downstream direction.

At last the pressure faded away. She had moved past both events.

And into blinding sunlight and the roar of engine noise. Metal clanged against metal and men shouted.

Next to her, Fiorentino said, "Shit."

Delia looked around in confusion. A giant machine rumbled by, inches from her face. The air was filled with dust.

"Come on!" Fiorentino grabbed her arm and pulled her away and behind a small shack.

"I don't understand," Delia said. "Tommy said we'd arrive in the middle of the night and no one would be here."

"Someone was wrong. Give me a minute, Madame Garrison. Let me think."

He was being abrupt, acting as though he were in charge. A day earlier, Delia would have been angered and might have had him disciplined, but in this environment, she was happy to let him assume control.

"Okay," he said, "we still have to get out of this place. We thought we'd only have to deal with one or two night watchmen, not all these guys. Stick close to me. We've got to stay under cover. We'll have to move in short runs. I see the next position." He pointed. "Count of three, we run."

He didn't get the chance to start counting.

"Hey! "

They spun around. A man wearing overalls was glaring at them. "Who the hell are you? I don't know you." A whistle dangled from a string around his neck. He fumbled for it and raised it to his mouth.

Fiorentino moved with a speed that astonished Delia. His arm a blur, he punched the workman in the diaphragm.

The man crumpled and fell to the ground. Delia glimpsed his bulging eyes and the veins bulging in his neck as he fought for breath.

"Shit," Fiorentino said again. "Okay."

He bent down and grabbed the shirt collar of the writhing man in one hand and his belt in the other. He straightened, picking the man up easily. Carrying him, he stepped from behind the shack and threw the man out into the open.

Delia heard a loud thump and shouts. "What—?"

"Truck. Come on. They're not looking." Fiorentino grabbed her hand and started walking quickly, not quite running, pulling her along behind him.

Delia tried to turn and look behind her. She caught a glimpse of a pickup truck and a group of men gathered in front of it. She stumbled and turned her attention to the uneven ground. Fiorentino's grip on her hand was unbreakable. She half ran, half walked, trying to keep up with him.

He pulled her down behind the shelter of a pile of lumber to avoid a group of men who ran past, shouting.

"You killed that man," Delia said. "You didn't have to."

"Yeah, I did. He would have started the alarm going. Anyway, what do you care? It's not like he was a dog."

"How dare you!"

He stared at her. There was not a trace of fear or deference in his face. "Madame Garrison," he said, the standard term of respect sounding strangely dismissive, "you can have me punished later. For now, my duty is to get you to Denver alive. If I fail, Mr. Stillwell will do worse things to me than you ever could. So let's pretend that I'm the boss for the moment. For both our sakes."

Delia nodded without saying anything. He was right. But he would regret this.

The distraction of the accident worked in their favor. The path to the fence was clear, and the open gate was unguarded.

Fiorentino sneered at that. "Mr. Stillwell would never have allowed this to happen," he said as they walked off the site and down the hillside. "Their security is crap. Guards don't abandon their post."

"Lucky for us they did."

"Lucky for them."

Now that they were walking at a normal pace, Delia turned around to look behind her.

She couldn't see any of the new construction, just the cloud of dust above the construction site. What had been built so far was still too low to the ground to be visible at this distance. She could see the sandstone cliff behind the site, though, and the dark crack in its face.

"My God," she said. "It's real." She had looked at that same cliff face during a brief walk above ground just that morning. This morning one hundred and fifty–some years from now, she reminded herself.

Fiorentino followed her gaze. "Oh, that. Yeah, I guess it is. Come on. The road shouldn't be far."

Tommy had given Fiorentino detailed directions— especially detailed, because he had thought they'd be here in the middle of the night, finding their way with a flashlight. He'd also thought they'd have to wait till daylight to get a ride to Denver. "On the bright side," he had told Fiorentino, "people were much less suspicious. They gave rides to strangers waiting beside the road out in the middle of nowhere, and they didn't assume the strangers were dangerous. Which is pretty funny, considering how dangerous one of you is."

"Which one is that, sir?" Fiorentino had asked, and Tommy had laughed.

They found the road where Tommy had said it would be. It was two lanes, paved, oddly narrow to their eyes. Fiorentino worried about how they would manage in the summer sun, without shelter or water. There didn't seem to be much out here, he thought, other than the Tempus construction site. How much traffic could there be? He felt disloyal doubting Tommy's planning, but he did wonder if his boss had thought about every important detail. Maybe the road was paved because there was a lot of traffic. Or maybe it was paved just for the use of Tempus. Tommy had warned him not to hitch a ride with any of the vehicles from the construction site. "It could be a problem if they see your face," Tommy had told him. "It could be fatal later if they see Madame Garrison' face. You wouldn't want that."

"No sir! I wouldn't want that!"

Fiorentino looked around him. There was no cover other than a nearby, shallow gully. He guessed that if he saw something coming toward them that looked like a vehicle from the construction site, he'd have to grab Delia and try to hide them both in that gully. Rattlesnakes, he thought. And Madame Garrison already furious with me. Two deadly threats.

He needn't have worried. A farmer in a pickup truck came by after they'd been waiting for about half an hour. He took them less than fifty miles, but that brought them to a small town. From there, the traffic heading east was heavier, and they were able to get to Denver in two more stages.

The contemporary currency Tommy had provided them with seemed to be completely convincing. They rented rooms under an assumed name, posing as brother and sister. Fiorentino began the first stages of his recruiting, while Delia waited as patiently as she could for the message from Morrison.

The call came two months later. The big, clumsy telephone distorted and muffled the voice, but she understood the message.

"It's over. No more Dolores."

That poor girl, she thought. A child of sorrows.

When Fiorentino came back that evening, she told him. "Good," he said. "We're on schedule."

"You'll find them a curious trio," Hughes said. "Intellectually lacking, unfortunately, except in the case of Anderson. He, however, suffers from lack of imagination. Try to reserve judgment, and keep your explanations simple. Stillwell especially has trouble with complex notions. Despite that, I do think we chose well with these three."

"I'm eager to meet them."

"Come along, then." Hughes opened the classroom door and ushered her in.

Delia stepped quickly through the doorway, staring with fascination at the three people seated in the room.

They looked back at her with equal interest, and in that moment, she knew.

Frank was staring at her intently, frowning slightly. She felt something pass between them, an almost telepathic jolt of recognition, almost as though he knew it too, and she felt panic.

How could this be? It was impossible, but she had no doubt. I can't handle this, she thought.

Worse was to come. The next day, Frank followed her after class and asked her for a date. Delia was filled with revulsion. She said something vague about being friends and hurried away.

Her revulsion gave way to anger. How could he have done this to her? How could he have soiled her memories?

The night before their scheduled jump in time, Delia showed the three of them the equipment that would be used to send them forward and showed each of them where to stand. When the time came, they would be in a greater hurry than they now realized. She hoped that preparing them in advance would diminish the chance of dangerous confusion. Things would be confusing enough.

She supposed that she was also hoping that seeing the actual equipment would give them a healthy shock. Perhaps realizing that they would be heading into the future, into three separate futures, in only hours would destroy what was between Ellen and Tommy.

It seemed to have the opposite effect, and when she objected, it was Frank who told her to leave Ellen and Tommy alone. "They've got other things to think about," he said to her.

You fool! she thought. How could you be so stupid and so weak?

Delia didn't try to sleep that night. Fully dressed, she sat in the dark on the bed in the small room assigned to her, straining to listen to every sound in the hallway outside. Occasionally, she heard someone walk past or a door open or close. She heard such sounds every night and normally ignored them, but now she jumped at each one.

When they finally did arrive, they made no noise.

The light on her ceiling flicked on, almost blinding her. A tall, blond man stood in front of her. He stared at her in surprise, as though he had just realized something. Then his expression went neutral. He spoke in a low voice. "Madame Garrison, I'm Hank Morrison. I'm Julie's co-leader."

"You're early."

He shook his head. "I'm right on time. We've been disabling

security. It was even easier than Mr. Stillwell said. You need to get going."

"You're not wearing a uniform. You look like an ordinary civilian. I thought you were supposed to be Soviet agents."

He smiled. "We'd be pretty bad Soviet agents if we came in wearing Soviet army uniforms." His smile vanished. "You do need to do your part now, Madame Garrison."

She wanted to say, I've been doing my part since before you were born. Instead, she nodded, pushed herself to her feet, and headed for the door. She felt as though her shoes were filled with lead. Now that the time had come, she wanted to delay the final moments.

She woke Frank first and told him the prearranged story. Then they went to collect Tommy.

They found him in bed with Ellen. Delia stared at the two of them, stunned. This couldn't be. This wasn't supposed to have happened. "This is all wrong," Delia said. They had changed the flow of time. The Tommy who had lectured her about the danger of changing history had himself done just that. And that future Tommy had known about this. Or he hadn't known, because none of this had happened in the past he had experienced. Which was it? And what could she do to correct things? "I don't understand this," she said.

"Jesus, does that matter now?" Frank said. "Come on, Dolores!"

Perhaps he was right. Morrison and Fiorentino weren't hesitating, she was sure.

She led them back to the room containing the temporal equipment, pretending to be cautious along the way. She didn't have to pretend to be afraid. It wasn't Soviet agents she was afraid of, but the consequences of what Tommy and Ellen had done.

As they went, Delia turned to look over her shoulder frequently. She expected to see Morrison or Fiorentino tracking them, or men she would somehow know were theirs, but the corridor behind was as empty as it was ahead. She began to fear that something had gone wrong. What if they had been killed or captured?

Maybe they were chased off, she thought. Tempus's guards look competent to me. Maybe Tommy's boys aren't as tough as they like to think.

But then they reached the metal double doors guarding the section of the complex housing the time–travel equipment. The two Tempus Security men guarding the doors had not been tough enough. Both were dead—recently killed, according to Frank—and the doors themselves had been blown open.

"Oh, my God," Delia whispered, "they got here ahead of us!" They hadn't even bothered following her. They had stuck to their schedule, assuming that she would be on schedule, too.

The rest of the way seemed to be clear. They could hear noises in the distance—gunfire, Delia thought—but they encountered no one.

They reached the door to the room containing the equipment. Delia unlocked the door and they entered. Everything looked unharmed, just as they had left it hours before. She moved to the podium–like control panel. The panel was live and the power levels were correct. Thank God, she thought. Now they can go forward.

The reality of what was about to happen seemed to have finally struck the three travelers as well. Tommy and Ellen were pressed against each other, kissing, holding each other tightly.

Damn you both, Delia thought.

Something hit the heavy wooden door behind her. "My God!" Delia said. "Hurry!"

The three of them ran to their positions.

Delia checked everything quickly. Something hit the door behind her again, and this time she heard the wood crack.

She glanced up at the three of them. Frank was staring at her. I could change plans now, she thought. I could save Ellen.

She knew she couldn't. She activated the equipment and watched the three of them vanish.

Behind her, the door split open finally, and she turned to face the intruders.

"Madame Garrison," Julie Fiorentino said. "Everything's on schedule?"

"On my end."

"On ours, too," Hank Morrison said. "The timers are set. The first one goes off—" he looked at his watch "—three and half minutes from now. Are we supposed to stand in those circles?"

"What about your men?"

"They did what we hired and trained them for," Morrison said. "We can't take them back with us."

Meaning that he and Fiorentino had killed them all. "I see." They were just another pair of IA killers, no different from the two who had murdered her parents.

She adjusted the settings in front of her. "Yes, that's right. Stand in those circles. Whichever ones you want. You're both going to the same place."

She watched them vanish on their short trip—their trip

three minutes into the future, into the heart of the explosion.

Then she adjusted the downstream energy level for her destination and stepped into the same circle Frank had used and waited for her trip to begin.

Thirty–Two

The rush and roar of the river was all around her again, but it seemed calmer than before. Delia had the sense of standing in a vast open space where all roads crossed, where all things were possible. For an instant, she felt caught in something, turbulence, an eddy, a whirl, time looping back on itself. She thought she glimpsed a woman, strangely familiar, caught in place on a river's bank while she glided past.

Then she left the woman behind. It was all far behind her, and she was standing in a familiar room.

Eight years earlier, Eddie and his team and Tommy had all been here, watching her as she waited for her jump back to 1937 to begin. For them, only a few days should have passed. She had expected someone to be waiting for her, but the room was empty.

Outside, the hallway was also empty. She glanced up at the time and date displayed on the wall. After years of looking at mechanical analog clocks, that glowing digital display was disconcerting.

What the display told her was even more disconcerting. It was the middle of the night, a day and a half before she had expected to return. It was that turbulence, she thought. That sense of a loop. Whatever it really was, it somehow increased my stream energy level. This is interesting. I'll have to discuss it with Eddie.

Yearning for the familiar, she hurried to her office. The Message Waiting chime confused her at first. Then she remembered what it was and sat down at her desk to listen to Tommy's long, unusually rambling and emotional message.

Alex Gorman lifted the disk from Tommy's temple and stepped back. He stared at the still form of this immensely powerful man. How small and weak he looked now!

"Sir?" It was one of his assistants. "Doctor Gorman, the patient is ready."

"Yes." But the surgeon isn't, Gorman thought. To take a knife to Stillwell, and to do such drastic work on him … He couldn't quite bring himself to begin. If something went wrong, Stillwell's orders that he perform this surgery, and the witnesses to the giving of those orders, wouldn't protect him.

But I can't take the chance of delegating this to someone less experienced, he thought. Stillwell trusts me.

"Well," he said aloud, "let's begin."

"*No!*"

"What?" Gorman spun around. "Madame Garrison! What are you—Madame, you're not sterile!"

"Then you'd better not cut anyone," Delia said. "There's been a change in plans. You won't be operating on Mr. Stillwell after all."

Gorman stiffened. "I'm under orders from Mr. Stillwell."

"And I'm countermanding them. While he's unconscious,

I'm in charge."

"Madame Garrison, I think it best that I wake Mr. Stillwell up and let him settle this."

"I hereby order you not to wake him up."

Gorman sensed the fear emanating from his team. It mirrored what he himself felt. He also sensed that they were trying to step back from him, to dissociate themselves from the power play that seemed to be underway.

"Identity of most recent arrival," he said.

From the ceiling, a dispassionate voice said, "Delia Garrison."

"I apologize, Madame. I had to be sure."

"Of course," Delia said. "You did the right thing. How long will Mr. Stillwell be asleep?"

"At least 24 hours. The surgery will take at least 12 hours. We have rotating teams, but I'll be supervising at all times."

Gorman was suddenly overwhelmed with a sense of fatalism. It must be a coup. Garrison's people had taken control, and she was here to kill Stillwell while he slept. After that, she would probably have her people kill the surgical team.

"I'm glad I got here in time to stop you. Please have Mr. Stillwell taken somewhere so that he can continue to sleep till he wakes up. All of you, you'll still be performing the planned surgery, but on a different patient."

"Madame Garrison, I don't understand."

"Not yet, of course. Here." She handed him a small cube. "That contains all the physical data you'll need for the new patient, as well as the patient's identity. I think that after you read that, you'll agree that the surgery will be quite a bit less radical than it would have been for Mr. Stillwell. It should also take less time. While you're preparing, I'll leave a message for Mr. Stillwell for when he wakes up. I'll make sure he doesn't blame you for anything. Have everything ready for your new patient by the time I return. I'll give you an hour."

The pain was far worse than she had admitted in the message she had left for Tommy. It was hard to move, hard even to breathe. Some primitive part of Delia screamed in pain and begged for time—time to recover, time to creep away and hide and think of nothing.

But there was no time. With all the time in the universe at her disposal, fate pressed upon her and demanded that she act immediately.

"What's the holdup?" she asked. Her voice sounded strange in her own ears. Of course she knew it was no longer her own voice, but the oddness surprised her.

"Ma'am," Eddie Iselin said, "it's the danger. We're worried about you."

What a shame I won't able to watch his career, she thought. "I'm all right, Eddie. I'm feeling better all the time."

He shook his head. "That's not what I'm talking about. It's the stream state. At some point, you may occupy the same stream state you did before, on your previous trip. We have no idea what that would mean."

"Interesting," Delia said. "I'd love to discuss it with you, but there's no time. I'll have to take the chance. Now move!"

It came out as a barked command. The team rushed to obey. No matter how she had changed, she still acted in Tommy's name. An order from her was an order from Tommy Stillwell, and no one dared disobey that.

It saddened her to think that this dangerous aspect would be how they remembered her. She smiled at Eddie as he threw the switches. She wanted them to remember her smiling.

Again, Delia was aware of the vast roar of the river of time, the incalculable temporal flow of the universe.

Again, once it ended, Delia wasn't sure she had experienced it.

She had been in a room, in bright lights. Now she stood on rocky ground. It was late evening, and a chilly breeze touched her face.

The pain from the surgery returned. It filled her entirely. She held her breath and tried not to move, as though the pain were something outside her, a force attacking her, and if she didn't attract its attention, it might pass her by.

In her right hand, she clutched a small device designed to generate a minute but carefully calculated burst of stream energy. It had been prepared for Tommy. Delia gripped it tightly. Thank God she hadn't dropped it in that first moment of pain and disorientation.

There was darkness behind her and a bright light in front. Within the circle of the light there was a small group of people, some seated and some standing. They hadn't noticed her. They were too engrossed in their conversation.

One of the group was Ellen Maxwell. She looked little changed from the younger woman Delia had last seen only hours before. Childhood memories flooded back. Delia stood, staring at her, unable to move.

Delia forced herself to look at the others. They seemed young and innocent. She couldn't hear their words, but she could see the passion and conviction in their faces and gestures. They were going to change the world. They were going to save mankind. Here, in this empty space in the middle of nowhere, they thought they were solidifying their plan to change history.

But first they were going to kill Ellen.

Beyond the light, hiding in the darkness, were heavily armed police. They knew about this meeting ahead of time, Delia thought. They must have completely infiltrated these revolutionaries. She imagined them waiting tensely for a signal, weapons at the ready. In a few seconds, the bloodshed would begin.

Still Delia was frozen in place. None of this seemed real. She felt as though she were watching a recording of an ancient event and not the real thing. For a moment, she tried to convince herself that indeed this wasn't real, that if she did nothing, if she didn't disrupt events by projecting herself into this historical scene, then the slaughter wouldn't happen and Ellen would live.

Pain suddenly shot through her, and she gasped aloud.

The people in the darkness turned toward her. They raised their weapons, but at the sight of a second Ellen, they stopped in confusion. "Ellen?" one of them said.

Delia shouted, "Ellen!" She ran forward, pulled Ellen to her feet, and pressed herself against her. Her left arm around Ellen's waist, she held her tightly. Breast to breast, eye to eye—their heights identical, their weights identical, their retinal patterns identical.

Bright lights came on. Booming voices yelled incomprehensibly. Something stung Delia's cheek. She fumbled with the device in her right hand. Her thumb found the button, and she pressed it.

An incendiary grenade bounced onto the lighted ground. It exploded in a flash of fierce, white light and terrible heat. The energy of the explosion combined with and reinforced the release of the immense temporal potential energy Delia had been imbued with. The huge energy wave echoed back to the explosion in 1945 on the same spot, in what had then been Tempus. Vast distortions eddied back and forth in the timestream.

All of that energy focused on Delia.

She experienced an instant of terrible pain, and then a long, timeless, static moment of awareness. She had saved Ellen, and now she was free. Delia sensed a loop closing off on itself, cutting itself off from the main flow and ceasing all movement. She heard the rushing of the mighty river and felt her consciousness sinking into its banks. The river no longer gripped her. She felt it moving on, leaving her behind. And then she felt nothing.

Thirty-Three

Eddie Iselin frowned as Delia flickered briefly and then resolidified.

"Damn," he said. "It didn't work. I don't think it's safe to try this again, ma'am."

She looked around in confusion. "What? Who are you? What's happened to me?"

"What happened to you is just what you ordered. You're disoriented, ma'am. You'll have to take the time to recover before you decide what to do next." He added quickly, "That's just my suggestion, of course."

The woman's knees buckled and she sat down heavily on the floor. She looked around again. "Where is everyone? What did you do with them?"

One of the other members of the team said uneasily, "We're all still here, ma'am. Can't you see us?"

She looked up at him. "I can see you, you bastard. What did you do with my friends?"

Jesus, Eddie thought. Her mind's gone. The surgery and the time travel—the combination was too much.

He couldn't risk handling this situation. He had to go to the top for orders now. "Back off, everyone." He turned back to the woman sitting on the floor. "We're also your friends, ma'am. Delia," he added, hoping his use of her first name would bring her back to herself, or at least calm her.

"What's that? What you just called me?"

"Your name, ma'am. Delia is your name."

She scrambled to her feet. Her jaw was clenched. "My name is Ellen Maxwell. You know that already. You're not going to get any information out of me."

This is more than confusion, Eddie thought. She must have brain damage. Christ, now what? Calm her down. That's the first thing.

He smiled as friendly a smile as he could manage. "That's all right. You don't have to say anything to us. An old friend of yours wants to talk to you."

When consciousness returned, Tommy's first reaction was surprise at the lack of pain.

He remembered soldiers screaming in pain. Shouldn't he be screaming?

The white ceiling swam into focus. Tommy flexed his right fist cautiously, expecting the pain to begin with the movement. Nothing.

He raised his arm, expecting it to be smooth and feminine. It was a still a man's arm.

He sat up in bed, flung back the covers. He was still naked, still a man. Nothing at all had changed.

Tommy leaped out of bed and began shouting. "Gorman! Gorman! Where the hell are you? Gorman!"

A nurse rushed into the room, a young woman Tommy

remembered seeing just before he went under. "Sir, what's—Sir, you're naked."

Tommy bellowed, "That doesn't matter! Why am I still a man? Where's Gorman?"

Gorman, it turned out, was at home asleep, recovering from a long and arduous surgery performed by him and his team.

Tommy gave orders for Gorman to be brought to his office immediately. Then he dressed and went to the office to wait.

The Message Waiting chime sounded as Tommy entered his office. "What is it?" he snapped.

"You have a message marked urgent from Delia Garrison. You also have ten other messages, none urgent."

Tommy hesitated. Nothing could be more urgent than finding out what had gone wrong. This job and all the waiting messages already seemed distant, part of a life he had been about to leave.

But it would take a while for his people to fetch Gorman, so he might as well listen to the urgent message while he waited. "Play the urgent one."

"Tommy," Delia's voice said, "I'm sorry that I've robbed you of the chance to sacrifice yourself. I countermanded your orders to Alex. Don't blame him. You gave me that authority, and Alex didn't know there was any reason not to obey me."

"Pause!" Tommy shouted. "Damn it!" He brought himself under control. "Suspend my previous order. Leave Gorman alone."

"Alex Gorman is already on his way here, Mr. Stillwell, accompanied by two of your guardsmen."

Tommy sighed. "Tell them to take him home again. Tell him

he can go back to sleep. If he's able to. Resume Delia's message."

"Your plan's safe," Delia said. "I want to assure you of that, Tommy. The rescue will still happen, but I'll be the one doing it."

"Damn it," Tommy said. He wanted to go somewhere, do something. He wanted to stop Delia. He knew that was impossible. She was beyond his reach now. Whether she had succeeded or failed, it was too late for him to interfere.

Why had she done it? He would never have expected this of her.

"You're unconscious right now and will be for a few more hours," she said, "The surgery will be performed on me instead of on you. It should actually be quite a bit simpler and less extensive for me. Even so, I can admit to you that I'm afraid it will be painful. 'Afraid' is the right word. I'm not a courageous person."

Tommy laughed aloud. How she underestimated herself!

"You're needed much more than I am, Tommy. I couldn't let you sacrifice yourself. The rescue has to take place, but I'm the logical person to do it. You're the logical person to protect my parents. That's right: my parents. I knew the moment I saw them. All my childhood memories returned. I saw them again in my mind exactly as they were, and I saw them in front of me in that classroom. Frank Anderson and Ellen Maxwell were my parents. How can this be? I don't understand it. It must be some strange anomaly in the timestream. I just know it's true. I also know that because I sent them forward to 2045 and 2095, they won't ever live in the 1960s. I changed the timestream. You said it couldn't be done, but I did it. So now they'll never be my parents. I won't ever have existed. It's one of Eddie's closed loops, I think. But I do exist. Isn't that strange? I exist, and I have a purpose: to save my mother. I don't know how the three of you will work your relationships out. I'm glad I won't have to see that. I'm leaving now. Good luck, my dear friend."

Christ, Delia, Tommy thought. You fool. Couldn't we have discussed this first?

No, he realized, they could not have. He had made up his mind, and he would not have been willing to listen to any arguments from her. She knew him well.

He had always thought her to be utterly mentally stable. Who could have guessed at this underlying madness? What had made her decide that Frank and Ellen were her parents? I'll never know, he thought. I'll never talk to Delia again.

He hadn't trusted anyone but himself for the mission to rescue Ellen. What were the odds that Delia had succeeded? Not good, he thought.

If she had failed ...

Just thinking of the possibility made him shake.

And what about the future? He hadn't planned beyond this point. He hadn't expected to exist beyond this point. His redemption was to have been his escape.

Escape not just from time, he thought, but from duties large and small. Like that long, written message addressed to him that had shown up so disturbingly on his desk. It had just changed from something he could ignore to something he had to deal with.

He took it out of the desk drawer and glanced at his name written in block letters on the top sheet. Then he put that sheet to one side and looked at the handwriting that covered the second page. He recognized that handwriting, and the recognition stunned him. Bewildered, he began to read.

Now that you've finally found the time to read this, you've got a lot to memorize.

Let's start with this. Hughes was not talking on the phone when I arrived.

Tommy read for hours. Bewilderment gave way to disbelief, disbelief to anger, anger to acceptance and resignation.

I was never in control, Tommy thought. My enemy, that evil bastard who I thought was controlling everything—even he wasn't really in control. Delia just proved it. Time is in control. It always was.

But how can I do what he says I have to? How can he ask that much of me? How can I ask that of myself?

"Sir? Mr. Stillwell?"

Tommy looked up. The blank wall to the right of his office door had become a window into another room. Tommy recognized it as Delia's office. Eddie Iselin stood there. From his end, Eddie was looking at a blank wall.

"Yes, Eddie? What is it?"

"It's Madame Garrison, sir. There's a problem."

"She's here? She didn't go back, after all? Thank God!"

Eddie shook his head. "She did go back, sir. Then she returned immediately, but in a very confused state. She doesn't recognize any of us, and she insists that her name is Ellen something."

"Ellen Maxwell?"

"Yes, that's right! Is that someone she knew?"

"Ellen Maxwell," Tommy repeated. "God."

"I thought if I brought Madame Garrison to you, sir, and you talked with her, maybe that would make her snap out of it."

"No! Christ, no." His heart was pounding. She had done it! Delia had done what he had planned to do, and Ellen had been thrown forward in her place.

And now? Now he had no choice. He had no control. His duty and his sacrifice were not yet over. The worst was ahead of him.

"Not yet," he told Eddie. "I won't be able to see her for a few days."

"But, sir—!"

Tommy waved his hand dismissively and then remembered that Eddie couldn't see him. "I'll send some people to take charge of her. Don't worry. You did well."

"Yes, sir! Thank you, sir!"

"Did you help Delia with this mission of hers?"

"Yes, sir," Eddie said proudly. "I'm the only one she trusted with it. I sent her back."

"I see. I'm going to need you to do that duty again. For now, I'm putting you in charge of her group."

"Thank you, sir. But that's probably not necessary. I'm sure Madame Garrison will be herself again in no time at all."

"I like your loyalty, Eddie. Let's say that you're in charge until Delia is herself again." Plan on a long tour of duty, he thought.

The thick package of notes and instructions Tommy had found on his desk had included the complete medical records Gorman would need. Tommy sent those off to the doctor and included a note telling Gorman that he wanted everything done by evening.

Logically, he knew that he could allow days for this. There was no deadline or time limit. But he sensed the roar of events rushing upon him, of days long past that would not wait. If he did not control the turbulent current now, it would race out of his control and carry him away toward disaster.

He awoke after the surgery feeling groggy and wanting to scream from the pain. It was far worse than he had anticipated. And yet Delia just went ahead in spite of it, he thought.

Despite Gorman's objections, he forced himself from his bed and to his feet, dressed, and ordered two people brought to him.

They entered his office together, holding hands. They stopped at the sight of him, identical looks of amazement on their faces.

Ellen was the one who spoke at last. "Hughes! You're here!"

Tommy stared at Ellen and Frank, delighting in their reality. He wanted to throw his arms around Ellen. Hell, he wanted to hug both of them. He wanted to say that he had thought the three of them would never be together again. But to them, thanks to Gorman's skill, he was Lyman Hughes.

"Yes, Maxwell, I'm here. I had to come forward, too, just after the two of you did. Everything went terribly wrong. All our plans have changed. Please, sit down." He gestured towards two chairs in front of his desk.

"What do you know about Tommy?" Ellen said immediately. "We're both here, Frank and me. Where's Tommy?"

Tommy sighed. "I'm sorry, Maxwell. I have very limited influence here, in this time. I've been trying to find out what happened to your friend Stillwell, but there don't seem to be any records. I fear he must have died many years ago and left no trace."

"No! Not Tommy! Not my Tommy!"

Tommy noticed how Frank stiffened when she said that.

"He's a survivor," she said. "He'd have made every effort to be here to meet me."

"Think, Maxwell. Stillwell was 21 years of age when we sent him forward to 1995. 1995! A hundred years ago!"

"Oh, God." Ellen turned pale and sagged against Frank for support.

Frank glared at Tommy. "Hughes, you're as heartless as ever."

Tommy shook his head. "I'm a realist, Anderson."

"That has nothing to do with it! Christ, man, have a heart. Look at her. Have some pity!"

Tommy couldn't meet Frank's eye. He looked at the floor. "Please sit down." He waited until they had finally done so, and then he returned to the chair behind his desk. "Pity won't change reality, Anderson," he said. "I do have pity. For her, for you. For Stillwell. But I have to fight against it. I can't let that rule me. Reality is pitiless. Time is pitiless. Time will destroy me if I give way to pity."

Frank said, "Why should I care what you say?"

"I'm your only hope. I'm your only chance to reclaim your lives."

That got through to both of them. Ellen seemed to regain control of herself. She straightened and looked at Tommy, her jaw clenched, her shoulders back.

Oh, God, Tommy thought. How can I do this?

"What do you mean?" Ellen asked.

Tommy said, "What's the last thing you remember before you woke up here, in this time?"

Ellen frowned in concentration. "It's all confused. I'm not sure."

"What year was it?"

"2051. I remember that. It was 2051. I came back from space, and I got involved ... with some people."

"That was more than forty years ago. I'm sorry, but they're all dead. You're the only one who survived the explosion."

"The explosion," Ellen repeated, staring at him. "Tempus."

"No, not that explosion. The one that happened when you and your friends were having your meeting."

"Yes! I was at a meeting in western Colorado!"

"Where Tempus used to be."

"You really do know all about it, don't you?"

Frank said, "That's why we can't trust him. Don't say any more."

Tommy glared at him. He felt angry at the need to keep acting, and angry at how much more difficult Frank was making everything. "I'm the one who saved her, Anderson. My agent. The woman I sent back in time." He turned back to Ellen. "Do you remember her? The woman who saved you?"

"The woman ... Oh, my God, yes! She—she was me. I mean, she looked just like me. She was in the room with us, shouting my name. It's all so confused. It's all jumbled up. She ran forward and hugged me. I remember how strange that felt. It seemed so familiar, as if she was my sister or an old friend. She really did look just like me. Or maybe that's just part of my confusion." She shook her head. "I don't know. People were shouting, and someone started shooting my friends." She paused again, then said, "And that woman, she hugged me so tight. Then there was an explosion. And then suddenly I was here, in this place. Oh, God, they're all dead, aren't they? Was that really more than forty years ago?"

Frank moved his chair closer to Ellen's and put his arm over her shoulder, but she shrugged it away.

"I'm all right," she said. "I'm fine on my own."

"Everything's gone," Frank told her. "We only have each other now."

"Maybe not," Tommy said. "The situation is more complicated than you know." He sighed and massaged his temples. "I scarcely know where to begin."

"1945," Frank said, his voice filled with hostility. "Start there."

Tommy smiled. "All right. In 1945, you and Anderson and Stillwell were sent forward in time, and Tempus was destroyed in a series of explosions."

"An explosion," Ellen repeated. "I remember explosions. I heard shouts and gunshots, and there were bodies."

Frank said, "How do we know it was real? Any of it? Maybe it was all staged somehow. Maybe we were drugged. I don't trust this bastard. I never did. Maybe the whole story about time travel was nonsense that Hughes made up for some reason of his own, and this is still 1945, and we're on some kind of big stage, like in a Hollywood movie."

"That would have to be one humdinger of a stage, Frank," Ellen said. "I was in space. I know that was real."

Frank stared at her. "You said that before. You really meant it? You were out there?"

Ellen nodded. "I was out there. Beyond the atmosphere, in orbit, looking down at Earth. I spent years there. It's no Hollywood set."

"All right."

The way he deferred to her astonished Tommy. From the moment they'd met, he'd seen Frank as remarkably strong and self-confident. On some level, Tommy had resented and envied him for it. But when Frank was with Ellen, he became secondary, dependent. Tommy wasn't sure if that would be a good or a bad thing when it came to the life that lay ahead of them, but he was sure that it was out of his hands now. They were all in the hands of time now.

"The main explosions came a few minutes after you left." Tommy said. "I had planned to stay at Tempus and continue to direct affairs there, but when Tempus was invaded, I saw only one escape route. That was to follow you. I arrived almost twenty years ago. I've since been able to determine that Tempus was entirely destroyed. There were no survivors."

"What about Dolores?" Frank asked.

Ellen reached over and squeezed his hand.

"I don't know," Tommy said. "She operated the machine while I jumped forward. I ordered her to follow me, but I don't know if she did." Do you really want to know? Tommy thought. That she jumped back in time to save Ellen and died doing it? "That woman who saved you," he said to Ellen. "She's the reason you're here and alive."

"I understand that. I'm grateful to her, of course. I'd like to thank her."

"She's dead." It finally seemed real, now that he said it. "She went there to save you, but she had to sacrifice herself to do so. Her stream energy transferred to you and threw you forward, and that's the only reason you're alive and here. Her name was Delia. Delia Garrison. Remember that name. Never forget her."

His intensity surprised Ellen. She couldn't imagine Hughes being emotionally involved with any woman, and yet he clearly had been with this Delia. "You've been busy since you got here," she said.

"Oh, yes. I've been establishing myself. I fell in with a subversive organization opposed to the government."

Frank snickered, and Tommy said, "I suppose it's amusing. I used to be on the inside. But this isn't the government we knew. There's something behind it, something in control, something big. I suspect it controls most of the world's governments."

"Bullshit," Frank said. "How much do you expect us to swallow?"

"No, Frank," Ellen said, "it's true. The group I was with, we were fighting the same thing. I could sense it back then. It was something huge and nameless."

"Not nameless," Tommy said. "Their name is the Subversion Monitoring Council. SMC."

"That's your outfit!" Frank said. "You told us about them. That's what Tempus used to be called."

"Yes, and it used to be my outfit. Someone or some group seized control of SMC. That's why they destroyed Tempus—to get us out of the way. As far as I've been able to determine, the people I used to work with in SMC died not long after Tempus was destroyed. The new masters kept the SMC name and organization, but they changed their goal to conquering America and the world rather than saving it. They're enormous now, and enormously powerful."

"If they're so powerful," Frank said to Tommy, "why haven't they destroyed you? How big is your organization?"

"Big enough to survive, but fortunately not big enough to have attracted their attention. Yet. Some day, that will change, and then no one will stand between them and complete control."

Ellen said, "The people I was with held demonstrations and committed little acts of sabotage. They weren't really doing anything."

"You're right. They were ineffective. But that's because it was too late. If we could only go back to 1945 and stop the enemy before they got properly started."

"That sounds familiar," Frank said. "It's the same thing you were telling us back at Tempus."

"In effect, it is. The principle is sound. Only the target is different."

"So your little bunch of rebels has a way to travel back in time? That's how you sent that woman back to rescue Ellen?"

"Delia Garrison," Ellen said. "That was her name."

"Yes," Tommy said, "that was her name. Yes, Frank. We've done more than Tempus could, thanks to the technology available now."

"You could send us back to find Tommy!" Ellen said.

No one can find Tommy, he thought. "We can go back, but only in a limited and constrained way. Please don't get your hopes up. I won't pretend to understand this, because I'm not a physicist. I'm relying entirely on what my people tell me. That explosion you escaped from resonated in some manner with the time-travel effects, with the energies that were being imparted to you at the moment of your departure. Its effects linger in the timestream. That explosion that almost killed Ellen happened in the same physical location, and it too resonates with the original explosion at Tempus. What it means is that we can send you back in time to the moment of either of those explosions. With the application of sufficient amounts of energy, which were not achievable in our time but are in this, we can send you back to a few minutes *before* the explosion that destroyed Tempus."

They were staring at him intently.

"Before—!" Ellen said.

"A few minutes," Frank said.

"That would be enough," Ellen said. Enough for her to pull Tommy away—away from the explosion, from the building, from the damnable time machine itself.

"Yes," Frank said. "Enough." Enough for him to ensure Dolores's escape.

"Enough," Tommy said, seeing the lives that lay ahead of the three of them. "You want to do this?"

"Yes!" they said together.

"It might be dangerous. It might be fatal. Let me emphasize that. This could kill both of you."

"I don't care," Ellen said.

"We'll do it," Frank said. "Let's get to it. Send us back."

"Not right away. You have a bigger mission than rescuing your friend. I'm sending you back so that you can fight the takeover of America and the world. You'll need to be prepared. There's a lot of information we have to give you first."

"The way you did at Tempus?" Frank said with a sneer. "Give us classes about what to expect, and then none of it will turn out to be of any use because you don't know what you're talking about? Like that?"

"This time, we *do* we know what we're talking about. This time, it won't be guesswork. This time, Frank Anderson," he stared at him, "it will be history."

"Christ," Frank muttered.

"You'll be back in a classroom," Tommy told him, "but you won't be given training in how to kill people. And there won't be any language lessons."

"Thank God for that," Ellen said.

"No more attempts to prevent the Bolshevik Revolution?" Frank asked.

"No more," Tommy said. "That's beyond our abilities, anyway. There's only one place we can send you to. One point in time. Where it all started."

"It'll almost be like we never went forward at all," Ellen said.

"It'll be the way it should have been," Frank said.

"We'll have to come up with new identities for you," Tommy said. "New names, at least."

"Garrison," Ellen said immediately. "I have a first name picked out already, and Garrison is the surname I want. See? I *am* going to remember her name."

"Yes, of course," Tommy said. "Perfect choice." If only I could have avoided all of this, he thought. If only I had died in the explosion in 2051, and not Delia.

They stood side by side on the platform. Frank stared at the ground, eager to leave this unreal world. Ellen looked around intently. She was, Tommy thought, trying to absorb everything before leaving.

Tommy watched Ellen just as intently. He was also trying to cement the memory of what he saw. This would have to last him for the rest of his life. He could live without this world, but having found her again, how could he live without her?

Ellen looked at him suddenly. He hadn't expected it. He forced himself into the cool detachment of Hughes, the lack of feeling of that human monster, but he feared that she had caught a glimpse of his anguish.

He could still revert to the selfish young man she had fallen in love with. He could save her, keep her here, keep her for himself and condemn everyone else. He could forget all these notions of duty. How he yearned for her!

"Ready, sir."

Tommy looked at Eddie Iselin. The young man was seated at the console, watching Tommy. He must have been bewildered by the change in Tommy's appearance, but he had accepted the DNA identification and seemed to have adjusted quickly and completely. He must have done the same with Delia after her surgical transformation, Tommy thought.

"Get on with it," Tommy said. He turned his attention back to Frank and Ellen.

Frank looked at him finally. Frank smiled slightly and gave a deliberately sloppy salute.

Ellen stared at Tommy. She frowned and started to say something.

The two of them vanished.

Tommy thought he heard a faint sigh. Had he sighed? Had Ellen? Was it a hint, a leaking through, of the rushing sound he remembered from his own trip through time? I must have imagined it, he thought.

"They're on their way, sir," Eddie Iselin said. "To the morning of February 10, 1945. As you ordered."

When the ruins right where we're standing now will be safe, but no officials will have arrived to investigate yet, Tommy thought. And they'll be too late to "rescue" Tommy and possibly change the past. "Thank you, Eddie. Good job. How long will it take you to get the equipment ready to do this again?"

"Again, sir? Uh, an hour. Maybe less."

"Good. Let me know when you're done."

"You'll be sending more people back to the same time as those two, sir?"

"Not the same time. A few days later. And there'll only be one passenger."

Two hours later, Tommy stood where Frank and Ellen had been standing when they vanished. He was dressed in clothes appropriate to the time he was heading for. He had considered taking a variety of equipment with him—the miniaturized, powerful gadgets of this era—but he had decided against most of it. He wanted to fit in as well as he had the first time, when he had been a true citizen of the 1940s.

He did, however, have with him a modern pistol and a small package that, to the natives of the time he was headed for, would look like a book wrapped for mailing.

"Ready, sir. You're sure—?"

"Yes, Eddie. I'm sure. Don't worry about yourselves. You'll be taken care of." He tried to smile reassuringly at Iselin. "Fire when ready, Gridley."

"Sir?"

"Do it, Eddie."

The roaring current pulled him in, and Tommy disappeared.

Eddie Iselin and his team stared at the empty spot. "Eddie," one of his men said, "it's going to get bad. You know how we'll be taken care of. I think we'd better get the hell out of this building while we still can."

"I'd like you to stay."

They spun around. Standing in the doorway, smiling at them, was the man they had just seen vanish. But he was different in one way: his clothing was modern.

Tommy walked into the room. "I did what I needed to do and came back."

"I hope you don't mind if I verify your ID, sir."

"You damn well better," Tommy said.

"DNA ID of person who last entered the room," Eddie said.

From above, a voice said, "Thomas Stillwell. Your boss," the computer added unnecessarily.

Tommy waited for Eddie to speak. He knew Eddie was longing to ask him just how he had come back from the distant past. If he did ask, Tommy wasn't sure what he would say. There would be more advancement ahead for Eddie, though, if he schooled himself not to ask.

After a long moment, Eddie said, "Welcome back, sir."

"Good. Thank you."

"Sir," Eddie said, "what happens now?"

Tommy looked around the room and then at the place where Eddie and the others had seen him vanish. He smiled. "Now the future begins."

Thirty–Four

Two huge explosions in the same physical location but separated by decades, one in 1945 and the other in 2051, both occurring in conjunction with the accumulation and release of timestream potentials, had muddied the river and caused ripples and swells, eddies and loops, in its flow. Nothing could ever be powerful enough to change its course, but locally the current became turbulent, flickered sideways, flowed more rapidly or more slowly.

It was enough to introduce errors into Iselin's calculations and the calibration of his machine. Set against the vast flow of the river, the errors were trivial.

The roaring of a mighty river faded and gave way to the sighing of the western wind.

They were standing amidst smoking ruins. A jumble of broken machinery surrounded them. The upper half of a man's body lay in front of them. His eyes were wide with surprise.

Frank brushed his shoe across the ashes he stood on and saw part of a yellow circle.

They were too late.

"Why is it now?" Frank whispered.

Hughes always lied, Ellen thought. "Come on."

They searched but found no one alive, only bodies. Some had been burned, but others had been murdered. They recognized some of the faces, but others were strangers. There was no sign of Tommy or Dolores.

Eventually they gave up and made their way out of the ruins. They began to walk down the empty hillside.

Ellen sensed someone watching her. She stopped and turned around. She looked back at the dark cleft in the face of the cliff. It seemed cold, uncaring.

No one's watching me, she thought. Nothing in this world cares about me.

Frank had been waiting for her. Now they began walking again, down the hillside and away.

These were the things that Frank and Ellen believed they knew about their world.

They knew that Tommy would appear in fifty years. I'll be an old, old woman, Ellen thought. But I'll be here. Even when time and closeness did their work and her friendship with Frank moved on to physical intimacy, she never let herself feel romantic love for him. That would have been disloyal.

They knew that the celebrations over the surrenders of Germany and Japan were premature and misguided. Other dangers were on the horizon. The Cold War was already beginning, and a series of hot wars was coming soon.

Most important, they knew that a sinister organization was growing in power and influence and was asserting control over national and world events.

"There must be others who know what's going on," Frank said. "We can't be the only ones."

"Sure we could," Ellen said.

"Then it's hopeless. We can't fight the kind of outfit Hughes described all by ourselves."

"So we'll find allies," Ellen said.

"You just said we're alone!"

"No, I said we *could be* alone. What are you going to do, give up right away, at the beginning? We have a long way to go. We'll look. Maybe we'll find some friends."

"What if we don't?"

"Then we'll fight on our own. I'm not going to give up. I never give up."

True enough, Frank thought. You never do. You'll fight on, and I'll be there with you.

He knew that. Whatever happened, however hopeless it was, Frank knew he wanted only to be there with Ellen. If it came to that, he'd die with her.

Or Tommy will show up, he thought, and I'll die without her.

It was the sweltering summer of 1945. Japan had just surrendered. Frank and Ellen were sharing a tiny apartment on Adelaide Street in Detroit. It had running water—cold water only. The landlord thought they were a married couple, but the bedroom was Ellen's, and Frank slept on the couch. She liked to joke that he had more room than she did. She was convinced that their apartment had started out as part of a larger apartment, subdivided during some earlier population boom, and that the bedroom had begun life as a closet.

What counted was that, thanks to her secretarial job, they

could afford the rent, and they had a six-month lease. They had signed it in July, a month before the atomic bombs were dropped on Japan. Everyone knew that once the soldiers came flooding home again, rents would start to shoot up.

"And jobs will disappear, too," Frank said. "There's a shortage of able-bodied men now, but that won't last. I have to look for work now."

"Your job is to make contacts, Frank. We can get along on my salary for now. Concentrate on building a network. We're going to need one."

"I've been trying. I talk to people in the street. I'm getting nowhere. Most people think everything's going to be rosy now that the war's over. There'll be peace and prosperity everywhere."

"I don't think everyone feels that way. A girl at work told me there's going to be some kind of workers' rally this weekend at Circus Park. I have to work on Saturday. You should probably go."

"Workers' rally? Christ, it sounds like something from the Soviet Union."

"I think it's defense workers."

"Hmm. Okay, that's interesting."

Defense plants were being shut down abruptly and the workers were being fired wholesale. Throughout the war, workers of all kinds had labored feverishly for the war effort, foregoing both raises and strikes. Even the American Communist Party had argued against strikes. Now the war was over, and the workers' reward was mass unemployment. Frank knew he'd be able to find lots of angry and resentful people at the upcoming rally. He wondered, though, if he'd find the kind of allies he and Ellen were looking for. A business boom would come in time, and then those fired workers would get new, good jobs, and they'd forget their anger and fear.

No, he thought, they won't forget their fear. Their fear of losing their jobs again will make them quiet and cooperative the next time around.

Going to the rally would be a waste of time. He couldn't say that to Ellen, though. He couldn't let her see him as weak and dispirited. "Sure," he said. "That's a great idea. I'll go to the rally and talk to people."

It was what he had feared. The rally consisted of a large mass of men strolling around aimlessly or sitting passively in the oppressive heat.

All the faces Frank saw were white. If there were any black workers at the rally, they were keeping themselves apart. Or being forced to keep apart, Frank thought. It was only two years since the race riots. A lot of that violence had happened not far from here. It would take longer than two years for the wounds of that time to heal, if they ever did. As long as the blacks and the whites fought each other, they couldn't unite to fight the common enemy.

I'm just one man, Frank thought. How can I get people to overcome their hatred of each other and then convince them that their real enemy is a shadowy organization they don't even know exists?

There was a constant low background noise, the blended murmur of innumerable low conversations. Occasionally there was a shout as someone called out to a friend. Frank almost expected to see games of catch, but he supposed the heat was too great. Or perhaps all these men were too dispirited. They were here, but he suspected that coming to this rally was as much as they were capable of doing.

A lot of the men were taking advantage of the shade of the park's big trees. Because of the humidity, it wasn't that much cooler under the trees, but at least the thick canopy of leaves protected them from the fierce sun.

Most of the men he saw wore work coveralls. He guessed that some of them had come here straight from the factories— those who were lucky enough to still have jobs. A few men were dressed in a variety of military uniforms or parts of uniforms, from khaki to blue denim.

There didn't seem to be much point in walking in the sun. Frank had no idea what he was looking for. None of these beaten-down men was a likely recruit for the ill-defined organization he and Ellen were hoping to put together.

He stepped into the shade of one of the large trees. The men already there made way for him while managing not to seem welcoming. They seemed to know that he wasn't one of them.

In spite of the heat, some of the men were wearing the olive drab jackets of army field uniforms. It made Frank feel even hotter and sweatier to look at them.

One of the men turned to say something to another, and the patch on his jacket shoulder caught Frank's eye. Diagonal blue stripes on a white background. "3rd Infantry," Frank said aloud. For a moment, he was back in Italy, before Tempus, before any of it.

The man swung around to look at him. He stared at Frank with a mixture of surprise and wariness. Then he laughed aloud and rushed toward Frank, his right hand out. "Lieutenant! Shit, I thought you were dead!"

"Bellman!"

They shook hands vigorously. "I don't think I'm dead," Frank said. "I'm not always sure, though."

A crowd had gathered around them, and they laughed when Frank said that. "Know what you mean, brother," one of them said.

"I'm glad you made it," Frank said to Bellman.

"Yeah. I was one of the lucky ones. A lot of the guys you knew bought the farm. It was bad." His face shut down for a moment, excluding Frank from the community he had once been part of. Then Bellman made himself smile again. "Hey, guys, this is Frank Anderson, best officer I ever served under and best soldier I ever served with."

That seemed to be the password. The others shook Frank's hand and slapped him on the back and told him their names. A lot of them had served in the war, and, thanks to Bellman, he was accepted as one of them.

"So what happened to you, Lieutenant?" Bellman asked. "You got called back to headquarters, and then we never saw you again. I figured you got transferred somewhere, and I always wondered if you made it."

"I never did figure it out," Frank said. "They told me I was going to be trained for some kind of mission. So they sent me stateside and started teaching me German, but then the war ended, so they said thank you and told me to go out and explore the world. Which I'm still doing." The lying came so easily, even when he was lying to a man he had once trusted with his life and would never have lied to back then. But none of this seemed quite real. Much of the time, Frank felt as though he was a visitor passing through this world, on his way to a strange and unbelievable future. Bellman wasn't really the man he had served with in North Africa and Sicily and Italy because he wasn't really that Frank Anderson.

Bellman nodded. "Yeah, that's right. That's what they did to all of us. Good job. Thanks for helping to beat Adolf and his pals. Thanks for all the blood. Now go away."

"Yeah, go away," one of the other men said. "We've got money to make. Time to shut down the factories. Here's a blanket to keep you alive when you're sleeping on the streets."

"They gave you a blanket?" one of the men said. "Damn, that's a better deal than I got!" They all laughed.

"Maybe the Communists have got the right idea," Bellman said. "Break into those big houses and take the blankets."

"Nah," someone said. "Take the houses."

"And their wives and daughters." There was a loud response to that.

Frank said, "We don't want a revolution in this country. It just ends in blood and chaos. If you want justice, you have to organize for it. You have to be united."

Bellman smiled. "You kept us from doing stupid things in Italy, too, Lieutenant. It's good to have you back. So what should we do?"

"You have to strike at the forces that really control this country," Frank said. "But not by invading their houses or harming their families. That would just start something that would get out of hand and end up destroying all of us. You have to attack the root of their control." He was feeling his way. He didn't know what the right words were. He was afraid of being dismissed as a kook or worse. Some of the men listening to him might think he was some sort of foreign agent or fifth columnist and get the police. He was afraid that he had already said too much. It would be safer to make his speeches to individuals he thought he could trust, not groups.

While Frank was trying to choose his next words, one of the men said loudly, "The factories! That's where guys like General Motors get their power!"

"Shut down the factories!" someone else shouted.

"No," Frank said, "that's not—" But his voice was drowned out. The crowd started moving, walking fast, then running. They were leaving the park, crowds of the men, as the fever spread.

"We'd have whipped them into shape in the 3rd." It was Bellman. He was still there, watching the others leave with a cynical look on his face. "Good thing our guys didn't go off half–cocked like that back in Italy, right, Lieutenant? We'd all be in German POW camps right now, and Hitler would be sitting in the White House."

"I'm glad you didn't go with them."

Bellman shook his head. "They're just wasting their time. Even if they do shut down the car factories, that won't change anything. You were really talking about something else, weren't you?"

Frank smiled. "I'll tell you all about it, if you'll stop calling me Lieutenant."

It's only one recruit, Frank thought, but that's how you start building an army.

It was one of those rare September days when the Houston sky was clear instead of hazy, the air was cool, and the humidity was low. Two men stood beside a dirt road thirty miles south of the city. They wore light jackets and turned their collars up against the morning chill. They watched an immense construction project under way on the other side of the road. Beyond a high fence, giant machines roared across a flat field and clouds of dust hung in the air.

"Lotta money being made here," Holmen said.

"In Houston, you mean?"

"Sure, in Houston. But I mean down here. Because of this." He nodded toward the clattering machines. "The contractors are raking it in, but the people who're really making a killing are the guys who owned all this land. The government paid top dollar for it."

"Yeah, well." Frank was losing interest. It had been exciting at first to think that he was watching the construction of what would be the headquarters for manned space flight. But after a half hour or so, it had become just another big construction project.

"There was nothing here before," Holmen said. "Just cows. There's oil refineries and fishing villages over there," he pointed toward the southeast, "on the other side of the lake. Even some pretty decent places to eat. About as much civilization as you can find between Houston and Galveston. But not here. Some guys bought up all this land and then got their buddy Johnson to build all this. They made a killing."

"So why are we down here?" Frank asked. He wanted to get back in Holmen's car and be driven back up to Houston so that he could get some sleep. "Why did you insist on coming out here to talk?"

"It's not safe anywhere in the city. I'm afraid to say

anything when I'm there. I know they're listening."

"Yeah," Frank said grudgingly. "Probably."

"Down here, to someone driving by or flying over, we're just two guys gawking at the big construction machines. If they try to eavesdrop on us, they won't be able to hear us over the noise. There's no machinery that can do that."

"Let's hope not," Frank said. They were both almost shouting, and Frank already felt hoarse. He was surprised that Holmen wasn't having more trouble, given that he was doing most of the talking. "So what's the information you have for me?"

"The president's coming down here to Texas. They want to help out Connally."

"So?"

"He's not going to leave. Not alive. That's the information."

"Shit. How reliable is that?"

"It comes from one of our people. He's the only one we've managed to get inside the SMC."

"I didn't know you'd done that! I'd like to meet him."

"That won't work out." Holmen looked uncomfortable. "Fact is, I haven't been able to get in touch with him for a couple of days. I think maybe they figured out he was some kind of spy."

"Then you're in danger, too."

"He'd never talk," Holmen said proudly. "We were in Korea together. Ray was the best."

Frank noticed the past tense but said nothing about it. "Kennedy's no hero. He's not on our side. Why would they want to eliminate him?"

"According to Ray, Kennedy's been talking to the Russians.

They're trying to help him cool things down in South Viet Nam."

"The Bolsheviks? The Soviets?"

"Yeah. SMC doesn't want the U.S. and the U.S.S.R. to get together in any way. I think there's more to it than that, though. SMC is trying to build up a power base in this part of the country. They don't want someone like JFK in the White House, slowing them down."

"Why'd you want to me to know about this? What can I do about it?"

"Nothing. We can't stop it. I just wanted you to be ready. Spread the word. This is the beginning of some real bad stuff."

More like a continuation than a beginning, Frank thought. "I've got to get back to Houston," he told Holmen. "Get a bit of sleep and then start driving. Maybe I can get back to Phoenix before tomorrow night."

"Man, that's pushing it. It takes me two days to make that trip. What's the hurry? Stay here and meet some of the other local people."

"My wife's due any day. I want to be there for the birth."

"Well, shit. You should have sent someone else down here."

"There wasn't anyone else available." There had been a dozen people in the movement in Phoenix, but one by one they had either dropped out or disappeared.

"Boy or girl?" Holmen said suddenly. "What are you hoping for?"

"Hell, I don't care. So long as the kid's healthy. That's all that matters."

"You got a name picked out?"

"Tommy, if it's a boy." Tommy, the man I'll never be, the man I'll always be just a substitute for, the man Ellen is still waiting for.

"I used to want a couple of sons," Holmen said, "but now I'd rather have daughters. No one's going to take your daughters away from you and put uniforms on them and send them to some hell hole to get killed."

Frank stared at him. "They're going to turn *this* into a hell hole. Then it won't matter if you have sons or daughters. They'll just kill everyone."

Thirty-Five

Ellen gave birth while Frank was still on his way back from Houston. He had wanted her to go to a hospital, but she had refused to take the risk. "It could expose the rest of you," she had said. "I'll take my chances. At the worst, the baby and I will die, but you three will be alive."

So she was in the small house outside town where Harriet and Rosa, the other remaining members of the movement in Phoenix, lived. To all outward appearances, they were two harmless and apolitical middle-aged women, interested only in raising chickens and pigs.

Which fortunately meant they were used to dealing with blood and birth. Ellen had a hard birth, with no drugs to ease it. She managed to maintain a stoic silence throughout the ordeal, and when it was over, Harriet patted her head approvingly while Rosa removed the bloody sheets.

Harriet held the newborn girl for a few minutes and then sighed and gave the baby to Ellen. "Did you and Frank talk about a name?"

Ellen smiled at her daughter. "Delia."

Rosa had come back into the room. "Delia?"

"I'm naming her after a woman who will save my life some day," Ellen said.

She remembered vividly that instant of agony, of being torn apart. She had felt something similar for the last few hours. That time, a life had been destroyed. This time, a new life had appeared.

"That's too mysterious for me," Harriet said. "Did you and Frank talk it over beforehand?"

Ellen laughed. "You're so traditional! We talked about names, and he had no objection." He never objects, she thought. Not to anything.

She had told him ahead of time that the child would be named after Delia if it was a girl and that it would be named Tommy if it was a boy. Frank had smiled and agreed. Ellen knew that he was so happy to be with her that he would agree to anything, just so long as she stayed. The knowledge made her feel guilty at times. She had liked and admired Frank from the beginning and, in a way, had finally come to love him. And yet, if Tommy were to magically show up here, in this place and time, the young Tommy, alive and well, she had no idea what she would do.

She looked down at the baby in her arms and tried not to think of such things. If she and Frank and the friends who still remained in their network could somehow succeed, then this child would grow up in a safe, secure, and peaceful world and with luck could avoid being forced to hurt other people. In that world, Tommy would survive.

And my daughter will be older than him, Ellen thought.

It was close to midnight when Frank arrived. Ellen and the baby had been asleep for hours. Frank stood in the doorway of the room, watching the two of them, and felt happier than he ever had. Harriet and Rosa brought in some bedding for him, and he arranged it on the floor next to the bed his wife and daughter slept in. He slept so deeply that night that he didn't hear the baby waking up repeatedly and being nursed by Ellen. Through her own exhaustion, Ellen felt comforted by Frank's presence. Perhaps the worst was over now, she thought.

Early in the morning, while Ellen and the baby still slept, Rosa tiptoed into the room, shook Frank awake, and gestured for him to follow her out into the kitchen.

Harriet was standing by the telephone on the kitchen wall. "Holmen's been shot," she said. "His brother called. He got home and found him dead. He said they're all terrified, and they want to know what they should do."

"Scatter," Frank said immediately. "Get out, go to different places, get in touch later." This is the beginning of some real bad stuff, Holmen had said. Frank had assumed he'd have more time before it began. "You two as well, I'm afraid."

"To hell with that," Harriet said. "I'm not leaving this place."

Rosa stood next to her and took her hand. "And I'm not leaving Harriet."

"These are killers. They'll do to you what they did to Holmen."

"Then we'll die together," Harriet said.

"We'd die inside if we had to leave this place," Rosa said. "Anyway, they probably won't bother us. We're just a couple of old dykes. We're no danger to them."

Frank wanted to say that that description alone made them a danger to the kind of people they were dealing with, but he knew there was no point in arguing with them. He had seen that expression on their faces before. He forced himself to smile. "Do I have to give you a direct order?"

They both laughed. Harriet stepped forward and patted his cheek. "Order away, dear."

She looked over Frank's shoulder. "Get back in bed!"

"Order away," Ellen said. She was standing in the doorway of the bedroom, leaning against the side of the entrance for support. Her face was pale and lined with fatigue, but she spoke calmly, and her voice was surprisingly strong. "Frank, the best protection for Harriet and Rosa is us not being here to draw attention to them. I'll make sure I have everything I need for the baby. You take care of everything else. We need to be on the road as soon as possible."

"That's ridiculous," Harriet said angrily. "You can't travel yet."

Rosa said, "She's right. You need to rest for a few days. The baby, too."

Frank didn't say anything. He shared Harriet and Rosa's concerns, but he knew that Ellen was right. Not only did they have to leave in order to protect Harriet and Rosa, they had to get on the move for their own safety as well.

"This is what I signed up for," Ellen said. "This is the way it has to be."

There were more protests from the two older women, but they gave way and started helping her and Frank collect what they needed. Gloom settled over them. They limited their conversation to practical matters, to detail: Do you want to take this? How about this? You're right—this is too big; leave it behind.

They left at noon. It was sunny, the humidity was around

40 percent, and the temperature was headed toward 90—a normal day. They all tried to act as though this was a normal goodbye—a leave taking before a short trip, with a reunion sure to follow not too far in the future. They all knew they would probably never see each other again.

A year after the Kennedy assassination, Frank and Ellen started trying to put their network back together again. The web of contacts reestablished itself slowly, drawing in survivors and new recruits. Some of the old members had vanished beyond finding. Some were known to be dead. Not long after Frank and Ellen fled Arizona, Harriet and Rosa's house was destroyed by a natural-gas explosion. The two women's bodies were found inside by firefighters after the flames had died down. Frank remembered quite clearly that the old house had had no heating beyond a couple of wood stoves, no cooling of any kind, and only an electric stove in the kitchen.

But the network endured, a thing with a life of its own. Just like the enemy they fought, it had a being that was more than the collection of human beings who made it up. People drifted away from it and sometimes returned years later. Some died—or, more often, were murdered. New recruits entered. The network lived on.

They'll get me, too, Frank thought. No matter how careful we are, they'll catch up with us eventually.

That thought was always there, in the background, darkening even his happiest moments. He thought he could accept that inevitability as long as he knew that Ellen would survive—or at least that Delia would.

He tried to convince himself that even their survival wasn't truly important. What really mattered, he wanted to believe, was that the network continued to survive.

In that sense, Frank was succeeding. He sometimes wondered, though, if they were really accomplishing anything. The acts of sabotage and infiltration sometimes seemed so trivial to him. There were times when he looked at his organization of idealists and self–styled warriors and saw only a sad group of social outcasts lost in a violent fantasy. It often seemed to him that they were opposed by immense forces that countered their small efforts at every turn and kept the great river he had told Delia about from changing, forces that made sure the world grew ever more corrupt, despotic, violent, and sinister.

One day, a month before Delia's eighth birthday, Frank found two strange men in his living room. He knew immediately what they were, and he reacted quickly.

But he was out of practice, and they were younger and faster.

Thirty-Six

Hughes left Tempus during the night of February 7, 1945. He was driven to Lowry field in Denver, where an airplane was waiting to fly him to Washington. His airplane took off about dawn. Two hours into the flight, the pilot received an urgent message for his lone passenger. Hughes came forward to the cockpit. He sat in the copilot's chair and put on the man's headphones. He gasped and turned pale. Then he ordered the pilot to turn back to Denver immediately.

As they flew, messages kept coming in, and the magnitude of the disaster became clear. After the first message, Hughes had radioed ahead to order that a car be waiting to take him directly to Tempus. Now he countermanded that order. He knew there was no point in making the long drive halfway across the state. The small Tempus building in Denver would have to serve as his headquarters for the moment. It was only half a mile or so from the Oxford hotel. If he had to bring in temporary staff, he could put them up there.

The Tempus building was one story, divided into four offices. The largest office had three desks in it, one of which Hughes normally used on the rare occasions when he worked there. It would do for now. New funds, new budgets, and a new building were his second priority.

His first priority was to find out who had destroyed the base in western Colorado and whether he was in danger from them. Then he had to assemble a team and send them west to see what had survived.

Hughes was alone in the room. This building was guarded around the clock, but the handful of Tempus office workers employed here hadn't yet arrived at work. Not that there would be much point in their coming to work now. They were support staff for the huge installation that had just been destroyed. It would be a few days before he had new orders for them.

Hughes stepped out of the office and went to the building's small lobby, where the night guard's desk was located. The guard had been leaning back in his desk chair. Now he leaped to his feet and stood at attention. To the casual eye, his uniform looked like an MP's. Hughes's eyes, of course, were never casual.

"Is anyone else in the building?" Hughes asked.

"No, sir. Your driver left a few minutes ago. He said you had told him to go home and wait for orders."

Hughes nodded. "Quite right. I'm taking over the large office. I'm going to be very busy on the telephone, and I don't want to be disturbed. No one else is to be allowed in the building today. I'll call my driver when I'm ready to leave. Pass that on to the daytime guard team when they show up."

"Yes, sir."

A thought struck Hughes. He glanced at the wall clock and frowned. "When is the daytime guard team supposed to be on duty?"

"They should have been—I mean, they should be here any

minute, sir."

Hughes smiled slightly. "Loyalty to a comrade is commendable, but your highest loyalty is to Tempus. Don't lie to me again."

"N–no, sir."

"Carry on." He returned to his office feeling satisfied with that last bit of work. It made an auspicious start to the day.

The two daytime guards arrived five minutes late. They were talking loudly and feeling cheerful.

"Man, it was about 70 degrees at my house today! It's supposed to be winter. After I got up, I sat outside and had a couple of beers."

"A couple?"

They both laughed.

Their cheerfulness died when the man they were relieving warned them that Hughes had noticed their lateness. They settled into position in the lobby—one behind the desk, the other in a chair beside the door—with serious, even frightened, expressions.

The door to the large office remained closed. The two guards were grateful for that. That office was well soundproofed, and they could hear nothing that Hughes might be saying on the telephone behind that closed door. That was fine with them.

When they came back on duty the next morning, the guard they relieved told them that the door had remained locked all night. "Guy doesn't eat, and he doesn't go to the toilet."

"Maybe he's doing it in there."

"Who cares? Just so long as we don't have to clean it up."

At around two in the afternoon, there was a knock on the

front door. "One of the desk jockeys didn't get the message about staying home," the guard behind the desk said. The other man nodded, stood, and looked through the door's peephole.

"What the hell?" he said. "It's Hughes!"

They looked at the closed door of Hughes's office and then at each other.

"How did he get out?"

"Bet he left when Karl was still on duty. Bet that fucker fell asleep, and Hughes walked right past him."

The knock came again. It seemed impatient and angry this time.

The man behind the desk stepped out and stood at attention. The other man opened the door and then stood at attention, as well.

Hughes stepped into the room. He was carrying a small package under one arm.

"Good afternoon, Mr. Hughes!"

"Good afternoon, sir!"

Hughes nodded. "Gentlemen. As you were. Please be sure to record precisely the time of my arrival." He headed for the door to his office. He opened it, stepped inside, and shut it behind him.

The guards wilted in relief. Despite the chilly air, they were both sweating. The guard manning the desk looked at the wall clock and wrote the time carefully in the register book that lay open on the desk.

The other guard said, "Why—?"

The man behind the desk shrugged. "Don't ask questions."

Inside the large office, Hughes had completed a long phone call and was finishing the last of a few pages of notes when he heard the door of his office click shut. He looked up and was astonished to see a stranger in his office.

The newcomer stood leaning back against the office door, his right hand in his pocket, his left holding a package of some kind. He smiled at Hughes. "Good morning, Lyman Hughes."

Hughes stared back, his confusion growing. "Who are you? I know you."

"You should, after all the trouble my surgeons went to."

"Surgeons? What?" Hughes began to rise from his chair. At last he realized why the face he was staring at looked so familiar. It was his face. "Oh, my God!" He collapsed back into his chair. "Who are you?"

"Thomas Stillwell," the other man said. "Tommy to my friends."

Hughes moved quickly, pulling open the drawer of his desk.

Tommy was faster. His right hand came out of his pocket holding a small, silent, deadly pistol that wouldn't be developed for a few more decades. He fired once. The bullet tore through Hughes's throat, killing the shout he had been about to utter and severing his spinal cord.

Hughes collapsed limply in his chair, blinking, trying to breathe. Tommy stepped forward and leaned over the dying man. "I owe you this so many times over," he said. "Pity I can only kill you once." He aimed carefully at the middle of Hughes's forehead and fired again.

Tommy looked briefly at Hughes's wide-eyed, blank stare and then at the wall behind the corpse, and he grimaced in disgust. The splattering of blood and brains would have been far worse if he had been using a contemporary pistol and ammunition, but still it was bad enough.

He had dealt with worse, though, and he had come prepared.

Tommy placed the package he had been holding on the desk and pressed his palm against it. It sprang open, unfolding to many times its original size. Fully deployed, it became a rectangular container of dull gray a few inches larger than the desk on all four sides.

Tommy reached inside and drew out a small cloth. He stepped around the desk and wiped the cloth over the largest and most visible splotches of blood and other human tissue on the wall and floor. They disappeared, absorbed by the cloth. The marks that were left behind would not attract notice unless someone were looking specifically for them. Nor would the medical and police technology available in 1945 be able to identify them as having come from Hughes.

He looked at the result of his work and was satisfied. If there was one type of technology IA had developed to a really advanced degree, he thought, it was devices and materials for getting rid of human bodies. Along with ways to kill people in the first place.

Will develop, he corrected himself, not had developed.

He placed the cloth carefully under the back of Hughes's head, where the exit wound still oozed. His left hand, he slid under Hughes's thighs. He picked the dead man up awkwardly. Hughes was heavier than he had expected.

He manipulated the corpse into the expanded container. Despite Tommy's care, some of the man's blood had spilled on him. He pulled another cloth from the container and wiped himself with it vigorously, almost frantically.

At last he could see no blood on himself. He dropped that cloth into the container as well. Then he pulled the sides inward until they met over the dead man. Finally, Tommy was able to use his palm print to start the container closing.

The container closed more slowly than it had opened. Clouds of steam issued from it as it closed.

Tommy stepped back in disgust, even though he knew that the steam was pure water. If he had had the equipment to capture it and convert it back to liquid water, he could have drunk it safely. The thought made his stomach churn.

Eventually the container was back to its original form, although considerably bulkier and fifty pounds heavier. Tommy put it in the desk's deep bottom drawer. Only his palm print would open the container properly. The equipment necessary to force it open wouldn't be developed for a century or more. The innocuous package could sit in the desk safely for decades, or even centuries. What was left of Lyman Hughes would stay there as unchanging as if he were lying on the far side of the moon.

Tommy sat down at the desk and picked up the notes Hughes had been working on. He skimmed them quickly. He had read them before, downloaded from the archives.

Tommy flipped through the pages until he found the first blank one. Then he picked up Hughes's pen—his pen, now—and wrote in block letters in the center of the sheet

TO TOMMY STILLWELL

Then he found another blank sheet and wrote,

Now that you've finally found the time to read

this, you've got a lot to memorize.

Let's start with this. Hughes was not talking on the phone when I arrived. This is crucial. You don't want him to say something to someone else when he sees you in his office. Check the visitor log from the guard table outside the door of this office to get the exact time of my arrival.

It was the first of many notes Tommy would write to himself during the coming years.

He thought about writing of his arrival in the smoking ruins, of the shock of seeing what was left of Hank Morrison there, of the agony of hiding while he watched Frank and Ellen walk away down the hillside. But he had to write exactly what he knew he had already written.

He wrote for a while and then pushed the papers aside. It was time to take care of Hughes's small group of associates in Virginia. A few of them were young enough to have a good chance of still being alive in 1995. Any of them might decide to resurrect the work on time travel, while keeping it a secret from Hughes. Fortunately, the records Tommy had looked at before coming back to 1945 showed that they would all die accidentally during the coming months.

Thirty-Seven

Tommy had the name, the face, the body, and the fingerprints of Lyman Hughes. He also had his position as one of the small group of men at the top of the Subversion Monitoring Council. Soon, he was alone at the top.

Years passed. The Subversion Monitoring Council grew steadily. Its influence and wealth grew. Its ruling class grew, most of them recruited or promoted by Tommy himself. The top levels were personally loyal to Hughes, although Tommy knew how fragile those loyalties were and what kind of people these were.

Knowing the future, he was fatalistic. Nonetheless, he created a corps of personal guards, a tough, skilled, deadly group. And he watched his back.

Two men entered Tommy's office. Both were young, tall, broad-shouldered. One had brown skin and dark, short, wiry hair. The other was pink skinned with blond hair that was also short. They wore identical dark suits and ties. Except for their differences in coloring, they were interchangeable. They were two more of the competent killers who worked for what was now called InterAgency.

They were deferential, even awestruck. They looked at the floor, at the walls, anywhere but at the face of the terrifying legend in front of them.

Tommy stared at them, struck by remembered sights and smells. And screams.

Delia, he thought, you used me. But it's okay.

As the silence lengthened, the two men finally gained the courage to look at Tommy. "Sir?" one of them said. "You sent for us?"

Tommy nodded. "Yes. Sorry. I was preoccupied."

There were two chairs set in front of his desk, but Tommy didn't tell the men to sit down. He didn't want them touching anything in his office that they didn't have to. Instead, he stood up. He leaned forward and held out a sheet of paper. "Read this."

The dark one, al–Bagdadi, took it from him. The two of them read it together.

"Looks straightforward," the blond one, Stemple, said. "Simple elimination."

"Simple," Tommy said. "There's a child involved, however."

Al–Bagdadi shrugged. "We've done those."

"Yes. I know your records. However, you won't do anything to this child."

"It's no problem for us, sir," Stemple said eagerly. "Kids are quick and easy."

Tommy stared at him. "I am ordering you not to harm the child."

The two men shrank back. "Yes, sir!" they said simultaneously.

"All right. Take that memo. It's your copy. It has the

address and identifies the two adults you're to take care of for our government friends. Be prepared. These two won't be as easy as you probably expect. Especially the man. He's very good."

Stemple regained his composure. "We're better, sir. Always."

Tommy's throat closed and he couldn't speak or breathe. After a few seconds, he continued, "Do this tomorrow. It's a school day. The parents will be at home. No one else will be there. Go there early, while the child is still in school. She mustn't see any of this. Get there around noon. They leave the back door unlocked. It lets you into the kitchen. On the far side of the kitchen is an archway that leads into the dining room. The woman will be upstairs. The man will come into the dining room when you're there. They won't be anticipating anything."

He wasn't aware of the looks of awe they exchanged. They had just witnessed Hughes's legendary knowledge of events before they happened. They'd tell others about it afterwards, and the legend would grow.

"You'll tell the child that you're friends of her parents and that you know her real name. You'll tell her that her parents had to leave unexpectedly and asked you to take care of her. They do often go away for a while, and friends of theirs take care of the child for them." He told them the child's real name and gave them an address. "You'll take her there. That's a foster family we employ. You'll transfer custody to them. Questions?"

"No sir," Stemple said. "We'll do a good job for you, sir."

Al–Bagdadi said, "Thank for the opportunity to serve you, sir."

Tommy kept his emotions under control until they had left

the office and shut the door behind them. Then he collapsed into his chair, weak, helpless.

He pulled the original of the memo from the Exposure Reduction Office toward him and wrote a note at the bottom:

> *John Stemple and Kareem al–Bagdadi assigned. Project closed successfully.*

After a pause, he added:

> *Agents will be rewarded.*

It would take more than twenty years, but eventually they would encounter Tommy Stillwell again and be appropriately rewarded.

He remembered that he had had no idea if the two men he killed, one of them slowly and agonizingly, had deserved what he had done to them. He had simply followed orders, trying not to feel anything while doing so. Now he could exonerate himself.

Or can I? I followed my orders and killed two men just because I was told to. I didn't even ask if they deserved it. How am I different from them? They're going off to do exactly the same thing, except that this time the orders come from me.

Because they're doing it voluntarily, he thought, and they're enjoying it. I did what history said had to be done, and I didn't enjoy it.

No, that's not true. I didn't enjoy it, but I didn't hate it, either. I told myself they were ghosts, like everyone else in the future, so that killing them didn't matter. And I didn't know at the time that I was playing a part in keeping the timestream in its course. I thought I was acting as a free agent. I killed them just to get ahead in InterAgency.

He shivered. There would be so much more of this—year after year, decade after decade, until he reached that point where all was not predetermined and he could no longer see ahead. There would be so many more deaths, of the innocent and the guilty, single deaths and mass murder, and he would be the cause of all of it, the instigator, the planner, because he had no choice.

InterAgency grew still more in size and influence. Its name was commonly shortened to IA. Its real power was known only inside the agency, and only at higher management levels.

It was a pyramid whose base kept spreading and whose weight upon the earth increased constantly. All the lines of authority met at the apex of the pyramid, in the hands of one man, Lyman Hughes.

Decades passed, but he remained, ever young, ever changeless, ever more dominating. To those few just below the apex who dealt directly with him, he was a terrifying, supernatural figure. Some of them wondered if he was even human. Was he a robot? An alien? Or were they dealing with a series of clones? They kept their speculations to themselves. It seemed wise.

Hughes watched history rush by. He was above it, apart from it, manipulating it, utterly controlled by it.

In 1990, he moved the core of his operation to his new headquarters, inside a mountain, far from any city.

In 1995, he watched Tommy Stillwell arrive and be met by a jovial passerby named Greg.

Hughes stared at the young man as he traveled to Denver in Greg's car. He remembered those events vividly, and yet it didn't seem that he was watching himself experience those events. Rather, it was as though he were watching someone else reenacting his memories.

That young Tommy wasn't the same young man he had been. It was a different young man named Tommy Stillwell. This wasn't his own past. It was the present. It just mimicked his past in every detail. For a dangerous moment, it seemed foolish to think that this reenactment must continue to be precise in every detail. Why shouldn't he step aside and let that young man go his own way and make his own life? Why force him to experience the pain and loss he could not forget?

But he knew better. He sighed and continued with his duty. He alerted a handful of people in IA, telling them to expect the young man and to hire him. A nudge here, a nudge there. He made sure that young Tommy's life followed the path ordained for it, the path he had already followed more than a hundred years earlier.

At about the time the younger Tommy was flying to South America under Griswold's command, on his first mission for InterAgency, Hughes told his people to track down Jeff Holtzman and Christine Awada.

They found Jeff already working for InterAgency as a soldier in one of its many small armies. He was a competent and enthusiastic killer. He's me, Hughes thought, reading the report. He shivered.

Now he understood why Jeff had been so easy for Tommy to train, and why he had shown so little hesitation about killing his coworkers in Delia's office. Hughes gave orders to have Jeff transferred to his own organization.

The search for Christine took slightly longer. His people tracked her down in Vancouver, where she was working as an instructor in a fitness club. Hughes shook his head at the idea of such a place and at a woman doing the instructing. He thought, as he had before, that he'd never get used to the future no matter how long he lived in it.

Her background was normal, non-violent, unlike Jeff's. Hughes wondered why she had been so ready to kill people she knew—even Tommy, her lover.

The reasons didn't really matter, he supposed. He knew she would play her role because he had already seen her play it. His duty now was to keep himself from feeling anything.

She's a ghost, he reminded himself, even though you slept with her. You killed her, so you know she's a ghost.

He told Jeff and Christine that a complete, innocuous background would be created for them and they would be inserted into the organization of Delia Garrison, one of their new boss's most dangerous rivals. They would play the role of office workers. A man named Tommy Stillwell, Garrison's guardian, would ask for volunteers to be bodyguards to Garrison. They were both to volunteer. At a prearranged signal, the two of them would kill those around them in the outer office, and then Jeff would assassinate Garrison. They would both be appropriately rewarded.

Jeff accepted his new assignment happily. He didn't question any of it. He was eager to start and seemed disappointed when Hughes told him that he would have to wait for Christine to be trained.

"Awada," Hughes said to Christine, "I want you to focus on

Stillwell. He's dangerous, but you'll know how to disarm him."

Christine grinned. "I know how to do that." Her expression changed. "I don't know about the other stuff, though. I've never killed anyone. I've never even seriously hurt anyone before."

"Stillwell is your assignment. You'll have to kill him."

She shivered. "Maybe Jeff could do all the shooting, and I could just watch. In case he needs help, I mean."

Jeff laughed at her. "If you can watch it, you can do it. If you can't do it, you won't be able to watch it. Anyway, it's really easy."

Too true, Hughes thought. "Holtzman's right. Anyway, I know you can do it."

"How can you know that, Mr. Hughes?"

"I know more about you than you realize."

"Just like you know what this Stillwell guy is going to do?"

"In a way. Holtzman, you don't need any of this training. I think you should work on your office skills instead. Your skills don't match the background we've invented for you."

"If you say so, sir," Jeff said reluctantly. "Would it be okay if I spent some time on the target range first? I feel like I'm getting rusty."

"Go ahead."

"Thanks!" He walked away whistling.

"He really likes shooting," Christine said.

"He likes killing. He's very good with the Heckler. You need to work with it a lot more."

"I hate the noise. I hate the way it feels. Does it really matter all that much?"

Remembering, Hughes realized that he wasn't sure. He hadn't seen the slaughter in the outer office, only the aftermath.

Knowing what he now did about Jeff, he thought it likely that Jeff had killed all of those workers by himself, without any help from Christine. "Maybe not. Maybe we can depend on Jeff. Let's try some other training. Maybe I should show you a couple of ways to kill people with your bare hands."

"Hey, that's something I could use back in my regular life!"

Hughes forced a smile. "Yes. Back in your regular life."

When one of their hand-to-hand training sessions moved from the gym to his bedroom, it seemed to Hughes like a strange combination of déjà vu and inevitability. When he touched Christine's astonishing body he was overcome as much with memory as with desire.

In the middle of the night, she said, "You *do* know me! Just like you said. It's amazing how much you know about me. You know just what I like and what I need. It's like you've made love to me before."

He kissed her so that he wouldn't have to reply.

In the morning, she said, "I love you. I've never felt this way about anyone so quickly before. I'll do anything for you."

"Ah." He touched her face. He didn't want to remember his last sight of that face a hundred years earlier.

She giggled. "The only thing I won't do is keep calling you Mr. Hughes. Not in private, anyway."

"Call me Lyman, then."

She shook her head. "That's still too formal. I'm going to call you Lye."

He lay on his back with his hands laced behind his head and stared at the ceiling. "Lie," he said.

"Is that all right?" She sounded anxious, worried that she

had gone too far.

He turned toward her and pulled her to him. "That's fine. It's okay. Whatever you like."

The old memories of what was to come flooded in against his will. It was her ease with the Heckler that would alert Tommy in time. "I am going to have train you to shoot, though. I'm sorry. I'm so sorry."

When Jeff and Christine moved over to Delia Garrison's organization—fresh recruits to InterAgency, according to the only records the Garrison people would be able to see—Hughes told them that it would be too risky for him to contact them directly. "I'll be watching you. Those offices are completely bugged. If anything goes wrong and you need help, I'll know about it. But I also know that nothing's going to go wrong."

"Thank you, Mr. Hughes," Jeff said a bit too loudly. "I'm very grateful to you for this opportunity. I won't let you down, sir."

"I know you'll do just what I expect of you, Holtzman."

Christine said, deliberately speaking in the same loud voice, "Thank you, sir. I won't let you down either, and that's no *lie.*" She winked.

He did watch them from time to time. He watched their first few days on their new job. He watched them being recruited by Tommy. He watched as Tommy thought he was training them. He watched Christine and Tommy go to bed together.

But when he sent them the signal to begin their attack, he was in his office with all the screens and sounds turned off. He sat in the silence, staring through the window at the vast, empty landscape, and remembering what was happening.

In 2045, Hughes watched Ellen Maxwell arrive and be met by a jovial passerby named Greg. This Greg was an IA agent, carefully trained by Tommy Stillwell, who had chosen the man's name and set of mannerisms as a tribute to the man named Greg who had given him a ride in 1995. Watching Tommy watching Ellen and the fake Greg, Hughes was amused that the younger man had gone to that much trouble.

Shows he still has emotions, Hughes thought.

In 2051, Hughes transmitted orders down through the hierarchy of a revolutionary organization. This was the descendant of the underground movement founded by Frank and Ellen at the end of World War Two. After their deaths, through layers of proxies, Hughes had gained control of it. Now it was finally about to fulfill its purpose.

He instructed the organization's leaders to gather at a spot in western Colorado to deal with the problem represented by one of its newer members.

After making sure that Tommy would see nothing but empty, rock-strewn ground, Hughes settled in front of a monitor that showed the small group and the young woman facing them. The sound was turned off. The scene was as bright and clear as though it were daylight.

He watched as another woman appeared suddenly and raced to the young woman being interrogated. The newcomer embraced her. How utterly alike they were, he marveled.

Around the two women, puffs of dirt erupted where bullets struck the ground. The revolutionaries were firing into the surrounding dark and falling. One of the women gripped the other tightly with one hand and fumbled at something with the other.

There was a brilliant flash of light, and the screen went blank for an instant. When the picture came back, he could see only a roiling cloud of dust.

"Back," he said.

The picture played backward. The dust disappeared. The screen went blank, then came alive with the flash of light again.

Hughes slowed the reverse play down to a crawl, until he reached the terrible instant when the blast erupted between the chests of the two women.

"Forward," he said. "Slowest speed."

He had to watch this. There was no choice.

One of the women vanished. The other blew apart in horrible slow motion.

He tapped the spot on the screen where part of her face began to separate from the rest of her and move away. "Follow that object," he said.

Switching between ground cameras and satellite images as necessary, the computer complied. It showed him the trajectory of a human eye and part of a human face as it arced across the open space and fell between two rocks in the dark, fifty feet away.

He opened a line to a member of the attacking force and told him where to look. "You'll find a human eye," he said. "Or most of it. Send it to me."

He would put together the package for Tommy. That would be his penance.

In the late 2080s, Hughes arranged for a new type of character to appear in various forms of popular entertainment:

retrospectors. The idea caught on quickly in that jaded, bored, pessimistic decade.

In 2095, Frank Anderson arrived and was met by yet another passerby named Greg. This one was a robot programmed and controlled by Tommy Stillwell—except that those controls could be overridden by Hughes.

Wheels within wheels, Hughes thought. Turning, driving each other, being driven. What controls what? I'm the most powerful man in the world, the first real worldwide dictator in human history, but I'm controlled by time, by what I know has happened and will happen. I'm not much different from that robot. Some day, I'll be free.

Oh, some day!

And then, at last, it was 2097.

Thirty–Eight

Lyman Hughes looked out over the landscape for a long time. He wasn't sure if he would ever use this office again.

"I'm not sure," he said aloud, savoring the words. "I don't know what's going to happen."

Beyond his window, to left and right, the view was framed by the dark walls of the crack in the sandstone cliff. Far away, the horizon was flat. Closer, a long, black train rushed by, west to east, across the plains. Still closer was flat, raised ground covered with dry prairie grass.

Hughes turned from the window at last.

He left his apex of power and traveled in stages, downward, through his headquarters complex toward his destination. He moved easily through the domains of power brokers whose teams of bodyguards would have been astonished had they known how easily and undetectably Hughes passed through their defenses.

He reached the bottom of the complex. He was now in an empty corridor far beneath the level of the prairie. He faced a blank wall and said, "Open."

A section of the wall vanished, and Hughes stepped

through into another, identical empty corridor.

"Close."

Behind him, the wall was solid again. The two IA complexes were once again isolated from each other. Hughes continued his long, unhurried voyage.

Finally he was walking down a corridor the walls and ceiling and floor of which were opaque from his side but, as he knew perfectly well, transparent from the other. But the heavily armed men and women above, below, and to either side of him saw an empty corridor and could not hear his footsteps.

He entered the elevator at the end of the tunnel and said, "Tempus level."

Sometimes, he was still amazed at how young and energetic he felt. That didn't happen often these days. He stepped out of the elevator and up to the entrance to the large room ahead, and then he stopped and waited, having to restrain himself, to wait patiently. Kid in a candy store, he thought. Trying to wait till it's time to start gorging himself.

From the doorway, he watched as Tommy was sent back to 1945, wanting to say something to his earlier self, wanting to go with him. He stood still and said nothing.

One of the team members said, "Eddie, I think we'd better get the hell out of this building while we still can."

"I'd like you to stay," Hughes said.

He walked into the room and spoke to them and put them at their ease.

"Sir," Eddie Iselin said, "what happens now?"

Tommy looked around at the wonderful machines that had launched him on his strange journey so long ago. Now, for him, that journey was over, and another and even more wonderful one was beginning.

The great river had left its rocky, constricting channel behind. It no longer rushed and roared madly. It flowed more slowly, quietly, spreading out unconfined onto a limitless plain. Its course was undetermined. Tommy could see neither banks nor channel, only the immense, slow, steady current—unstoppable, but unconfined at last. All paths were open to it. All he knew was that he would be carried forward on it, willingly without control. He would have no knowledge of what was coming.

After all those years, those lifetimes, he had fulfilled his duty. Now, every day, every moment, forever, he could act without worrying about the course of the timestream. At last, he was free.

He smiled. "Now the future begins."

About the Author

David Dvorkin was born in 1943 in Reading, England. His family moved to South Africa after World War II, and then to the United States when David was a teenager. After attending college in Indiana, he worked at NASA in Houston on the Apollo Project, then at Martin Marietta in Denver on the Viking Mars lander project. His aerospace career ended in 1974. Thereafter, until 2009, he worked as a software developer and technical writer. He and his wife, Leonore, and their son, Daniel, have lived in Denver since 1971.

In addition to non-fiction, David has published many science fiction, horror, and mystery novels. For details, as well as quite a bit of nonfiction reading material, please see David's website: http://www.dvorkin.com/

David is on Facebook at
http://www.facebook.com/DavidDvorkin
and on Twitter at http://twitter.com/David_Dvorkin
His blog is http://eyeblister.blogspot.com/

For information about the self–publishing service that David operates with his wife, please see https://www.dldbooks.com/

David in 2019

Lightning Source UK Ltd.
Milton Keynes UK
UKHW050058031220
374378UK00032B/1642/J